freedom

A COMMEMORATIVE
ANTHOLOGY TO
CELEBRATE THE
125TH BIRTHDAY
OF THE BRITISH
RED CROSS

A COMMEMORATIVE
ANTHOLOGY TO
CELEBRATE THE
125TH BIRTHDAY
OF THE BRITISH
RED CROSS

with a foreword by
HRH
THE PRINCESS
OF WALES

*f*reedom

and contributions by
OVER THIRTY
BRITISH AUTHORS
& ARTISTS

compiled by
BELINDA SOMERLEYTON
& SARA LOW

in aid of
THE BRITISH
RED CROSS

LITTLE, BROWN
AND COMPANY

A *Little, Brown* Book

First published in Great Britain in 1995 by
LITTLE, BROWN AND COMPANY

Collection copyright ©
SUFFOLK BRANCH OF THE BRITISH RED CROSS 1995

The contributions are copyright respectively:

Copyright © Blake Morrison 1995
Copyright © Anthony Shaffer 1995
Copyright © Anthony Loyd 1995
Copyright © Helen Fielding 1994
Copyright © Candia McWilliam 1990
Copyright © Ted Hughes 1995
Copyright © Eric Ambler 1972, 1990
Copyright © Maeve Binchy 1995
Copyright © Julia Blackburn 1991
Copyright © Ronald Blythe 1995
Copyright © Andrew Motion 1995
Copyright © Byronic Investments 1994
Copyright © Frederick Forsyth 1982
   (Reproduced by permission of Curtis Brown Ltd,
   London)
Copyright © Jilly Cooper 1981
   'Kate's Wedding' by Jilly Cooper, first
   published in *Lisa & Co.*

Copyright © Henrietta Miers 1995
Copyright © Jeffrey Archer 1988
Copyright © P.D. James 1995
Copyright © Herbert Lomas 1995
Copyright © Tim Heald 1995
Copyright © Pauline Cutting 1988
Copyright © Rachel Billington 1995
Copyright © Deborah Moggach 1995
Copyright © Rachel Cusk 1995
Copyright © Anthony Thwaite 1995
Copyright © Nick Danziger 1990
Copyright © Linda Kitson 1983
Copyright © Tim Fargher 1993
Copyright © Howard Morgan 1992
   (From a private collection)
Copyright © Peter Brookes 1995
Copyright © Susan Ryder 1993
Copyright © Jason Gathorne-Hardy 1994

The moral right of the authors has been asserted.

A CIP catalogue record for this book is available from the British Library.

ISBN 0 316 91167 4

Typeset by M Rules
Illustration reproduced and printed by George Over
Jacket printed at the White Quill Press
Printed and bound in Great Britain by Clays Ltd, St Ives plc.
Paper made at the Silverton Mill, supplied by Grampian Paper Ltd

LITTLE, BROWN AND COMPANY (UK)
BRETTENHAM HOUSE
LANCASTER PLACE
LONDON WC2E 7EN

acknowledgements

We could not have compiled this book without the invaluable assistance of a great many people. First we must thank all our generous contributors for donating their time and talent so willingly. Then our thanks must go to Jeffrey Archer for putting us on the right track. Without our friend and agent Merric Davidson we would have stumbled to a halt. His unfailing enthusiasm and encouragement kept us going through some difficult times. We must also thank Michael Peters and the design team at Identica, the late William Loyd, Blake Morrison, Mark Fiennes, and, of course, our editor at Little, Brown, Hilary Hale.

B.S.
S.L.
May 1995

HRH The Princess of Wales
Patron, 125th Birthday Appeal
Vice President, British Red Cross
and Patron, Red Cross Youth

KENSINGTON PALACE

In over 10 years of close
association with the British
Red Cross, I have been
deeply moved & impressed
by the sheer dedication of
Red Cross workers both with
vulnerable populations overseas
& in every community here
at home.

They work in a fine
tradition - this year the
British Red Cross celebrates
125 years of caring in crisis.

This anthology also follows
a fine tradition: in 1939,
Her Majesty Queen Elizabeth
The Queen Mother wrote the

preface to a book similar to
this. Its aim was to raise
funds to help the British
Red Cross to continue its
work during the horrors of
World War two.

Today, the challenges
facing the society at home
& overseas are no less
daunting & the need to raise
funds is no less vital.

That is why I am
enormously grateful to all
those who have generously
contributed to this book &
to all who, by buying it,
have supported the British
Red Cross .... Thank You.

Diana.

February 1994.

the contributors

Nick Danziger on the border

Linda Kitson khao-I-dang: thailand

Tim Fargher garden dancing faun

Howard Morgan zagreb

Peter Brookes freedom

Susan Ryder door to the terrace – escallerilla

Jason Gathorne-Hardy freedom series

*f*reedom

Blake Morrison

pick your own

Blake Morrison was born in Skipton, Yorkshire. He is the author of two books of poems, *Dark Glasses* and *The Ballad of the Yorkshire Ripper*, two critical studies of 'the Movement' and Seamus Heaney; a children's book, *The Yellow House*, and the prizewinning memoir *And When Did You Last See Your Father?* Formerly literary editor of the *Observer* and *Independent on Sunday*, he lives with his wife and three children in London.

Love among the loganberries,
the womby pods
and dangly genitalia
drawing us down the grass
with cartons and colanders,
baskets and cake-tins,
to the canes in rows
stiffened by fencing wire,
their bright notes
pitched against the green
of leaves like steak-knives
and palisades of thorn.

Blackberries, blueberries,
whiskery gooseberries,
raspberries, tayberries,
florets of calabrese,
pippins, plum-bums,
rush-matted sweetcorn,
broad beans in ermine,
swan-necked courgettes,
straw-bedded strawberries,
squashed-on-the-floor berries,

beans pegged out like washing,
bottom-heavy pears:

here we go
down the lush corridors
of the PYO farm,
plucking and plundering,
pulling out the stops,
as an east wind
smelling of rape
rustles over lakes
of lapping polythene,
our children in warpaint
with giveaway stains
round their mouths.

And these long aisles
we walk for a season
are what freedom is,
or privilege,
under our own steam
driving here,
under our own yoke

bending to harvest,
the gates open,
the crops unguarded,
the earth not cracked by drought
or red with blood.

In the dead months
I open the freezer
and take from its clouds
a bag of bilberries,
holding it like a compress
at my brow,
shaking off the crystals,
undoing the tie,
then spilling out the gems
to weigh for dinner,
the fruits of history
tipping the scales.

Anthony Shaffer

it's a free country, innit?

Anthony Shaffer was educated at St Paul's, and Cambridge University. From 1951 to 1955 he practised law as a barrister, and subsequently, until 1969, he was a partner in a successful film production company, scripting, directing and producing many television commercials.

In 1969 he resigned to take up writing full time and in 1970 *Sleuth* appeared. It was one of the greatest theatrical hits of all time in London, New York and throughout the world, winning the Tony Award as the Best Play of the Year.

His other stage plays include *This Savage Parade* (1963 revived and revised 1987), *Murderer* (1975), *Widow's Weeds* (1977) and *The Case of the Oily Levantine* (1979) which was presented in New York in 1982 under the title *Whodunnit.*

In 1972 he wrote the screenplay for *Forbush and the Penguins* which starred John Hurt and Hayley Mills and in 1974 he turned *Sleuth* into a film which starred Laurence Olivier and Michael Caine. That same year he wrote the screenplay for the Alfred Hitchcock film *Frenzy.* Other screenplays include *The Wicker Man*, which won the Grand Prix for Filmes Fantastique in Paris, and *Absolution*, which starred Richard Burton, and three Agatha Christie adaptations: *Death on the Nile, Evil under the Sun* and *Appointment with Death* with Peter Ustinov as Hercule Poirot.

Tony recently developed the storyline for the film *Sommersby* starring Jodie Foster and Richard Gere, and is currently writing a screenplay, *Ataturk*, based on the life of Kemal Ataturk for Olivier Consultants Overseas Ltd.

When I was first asked to write this piece on Freedom, I was tempted to decline – and not only because the piece was free!

In fact, that should have been sufficient reason in itself to do it. A free act – that is to say an act tendered without the thought or actuality of reward is believed to be in many Eastern religious philosophies a substantial enabling factor in the journey towards transformation, in that, like the quality of mercy in *The Merchant of Venice*, it liberates and blesses the giver as well as the receiver.

That the Red Cross is fully cognisant of this, and that its basic *raison d'être* is the free act, is indisputable. One only has to see on television the thankful eyes of a starving African child, or indeed the innumerable, grateful outcasts of war ministered to by them, to know that they are blessed. I can only hope that this small, free act of my own will attract the same benison.

The other reason for my initial reluctance was simply ignorance. What, I asked myself, did I know about the subject? Absolutely nothing. Like many people I had taken it for granted all my life in England – at least the four basic freedoms of speech, of conscience, and from want, and fear, that Franklin Roosevelt talked about in his 1944 address to the nation, *The Four Freedoms.*

It's all very well for Jean Jacques Rousseau to say 'Man is born free, yet is everywhere in chains', but in England those chains are scarcely visible, or audible – at least they don't clank very loudly. From time to time we hear of, or experience, official oppressions – the monstrous tyranny of clamping, for example, or verballing by the police, or imbecilities by our fiscal pundits, or the judiciary, but mostly what we suffer from are the trivial restraining influences of archaic manners, ingrained snobberies, and tiresome obeisances to middle-class aesthetic, and sexual timidities, and that's about the size of it.

Recently many traditional inhibitions have been eroded. For example on Sundays, not to speak of weekdays, the pubs can now open more or less when they like, and Pakistani corner shops can sell us primitive provender without fear of incurring the hypocritical religious wrath of people who for the most part don't spend their weekends in cities, and therefore have no need of open shops on the Sabbath. The Lord Chamberlain has ceased to butcher fine plays in the terrified interests of a moribund morality, and Lady Chatterley's ecstasies between the moleskinned thighs of Mellors can safely be read by all – even 'our wives and servants'.

'It's a free country, innit?' is one of the most repeated shibboleths you will hear, spoken as if Freedom were an end in itself, to be enjoyed unexamined and not earned.

In Kafka's *Report To An Academy*, the captured and newly caged ape says to the Academy members, 'Had I known it then, my cage was no more confining than the one you live in, the cage men have built for themselves so elaborately. But if men have built this cage, you ask me, then *who* is the keeper? Who gives you the illusion of freedom?' No one replies to him, and he continues, 'That is why I say to you that men are constantly betrayed by the word "Freedom".'

In other words what is being said is that if one is not free interiorially, Freedom is just an emotive word. And to be free within oneself, one must divorce oneself from the fettering attachments of reactive energy, from likes and dislikes, from our very animal nature itself, and all the elaborate and relentless conditioning we have undergone, and accepted – most of it without question, since the day we were born, and indeed before it!

We must consciously learn that Freedom is a means to be used for further aims, not as a licence for ignorant opinion. Its value lies in the extent to which it can assist the development of life. To possess and proselytise Freedom with no real passionate life for which to use it is the bitterest farce. Life never means complete freedom. Every action and relation is an added bond. Life is to be attained, not through a non-moral, mindless freedom of caprice, but through a glad welcoming and loyal fulfilment of every bond and obligation which comes in the daily path of life. So that paradoxically, the willing acceptance of fetters is what guarantees Freedom.

It is not a right, and saving Rousseau's presence, we are not born with it, as we are not born with any rights at all. They are either accorded by common agreement, or they do not exist. 'I know my rights' is the second most meaningless statement mouthed by the masses.

You will listen in vain for the phrase 'I know my duties'. As

Thomas Paine tells us, 'those who expect to reap the blessings of Freedom, must, like men, undergo the fatigue of supporting it'.

This burdensome ingredient of Freedom is of course a constantly recurring theme in literature. Wordsworth in his *Ode to Duty* writes:

> 'Me this unchartered freedom tires.
> I feel the weight of chance desires.'

'This will remain the land of the free,' writes Elmer Davis in his essay *But We Were Born Free*, 'only as long as it is the home of the brave' – by which he meant the vigilant.

And in *The Fall*, Camus tells us 'Freedom is not a reward or a decoration that is celebrated with champagne. Nor yet a gift, a box of dainties designed to make you lick your chops. Oh no! On the contrary it's a chore, and a long distance race, quite solitary and very exhausting'.

But is it all worth it? In fact do we really want Freedom at all? Isn't it more comforting to be given the taboos, and tablets of stone, to have the no-go areas clearly marked out for us, to accept without question the concept of the vengeful, white-bearded schoolmaster in the sky whose every objurgation is a withdrawal of free will, and who continuously shouts at us in terms of commandment? Isn't it a lot easier to ignore the whole beastly thing? Don't we really agree with Eric Hoffer in *The True Believer*, that 'unless a man has the talents to make something of himself, freedom is an irksome border'?

And Ralph Waldo Emerson takes the detestation of

Freedom much further. 'It is awful to look into the mind of man,' he muses in his Journal, 'and see how free we are, to what frightful excesses our vices may run under the whited wall of a respectable reputation. Outside among your fellows, among strangers, you must preserve appearances, a hundred things you cannot do; but inside the terrible Freedom!'

Or more gloomily, there is the inevitable reflection – is it even possible for mankind to be free in any full sense of the word? Men and women cannot be free if they don't exist; they can't exist if they don't eat; and they can't eat if they don't work. But to have to work at definite tasks, hours and places is not freedom. It is compulsion, and living willy-nilly in a pre-determined groove. 'Roll on the end of the shift, or the weekend, or the next public holiday' was the constant cry of the miners I once worked with. The oft referred to dignity of labour is largely an illusion in much industrial toil, and though the technology may well exist to free large sections of the community from routine drudgery, the long implanted, largely unexamined, puritan tradition of the work ethic binds us to the tyranny of the pick, the shovel, and further afield, the desk. No, the suspicion grows that we don't really want Freedom.

In the last few centuries it has received more tributes than virtually any other concept. There has been public debate on every sort of freedom, economic, political, religious. Yet there has not been a corresponding increase in independence of mind, and very few of us would actually like to have what E.B. White described as his 'first and greatest love affair with this thing we call freedom, this lady of infinite allure, this dangerous and beautiful and sublime being who restores and supplies us all'.

He was specifically talking about the vitally important pact which man has with himself – 'to be all things to himself, and to be identified with all things; – to stand self-reliant, taking advantage of his haphazard connection with a planet, riding his luck, and following his bent with the tenacity of a hound.'

It is of course the daunting nature of the endless panegyrics to Freedom or Liberty which curiously enough tend to erode one's ability to stand self-reliant. It is the same with all the objects of tacitly granted adulation.

'Give me Liberty or give me death!' 'Liberty, Equality, Fraternity!' 'Eternal vigilance is the price of Liberty!' 'The tree of Liberty must be refreshed from time to time by the blood of patriots and tyrants! It is its natural manure!' And of course there is the inscription on the Statue of Liberty itself: 'Give me your tired, your poor, your huddled masses yearning to breathe free'. Etc, etc, etc . . .

It is the fear of pompous abstraction that invites our contempt, and helps to keep us 'everywhere in chains'. Freedom as an abstraction by itself obviously does not exist, for us. It has to be more concrete. You have to be free from something. Free from a bullying boss, or tyrannical teacher, or an aggravating ailment, or an idiosyncratic idea – or, more grandly, from oppression or persecution, or from bigotry. But none the less 'eternal vigilance' is still necessary to preserve it.

Many of us in the West feel so rich in our opportunities for free expression that we often no longer know what we are free from. Neither do we know where we are not free; we do not recognise our native autocrats when we see them. We must always remember that the dagger plunged in the name of Freedom is plunged into the breast of Freedom. This virtually defines Political Correctness. This insidious new strangler vine operates mostly as an abysmal conformity imposed by the lately liberated to betray the essence of the liberty they have just achieved!

Conformity as we know, is the jailer of Freedom, and one of the saddest things about it is the ghastly sort of non-conformity it breeds: the routine protesting, the endless, dullard demos, the unreflective umbrage, the rigid counter-fetishism.

It all only endorses the late nineteenth century reflection that if you speak with the speech of the world, you must think with the thoughts of the few. And above all you must keep a low profile. As Ibsen tells us in *An Enemy of the People*, never put on your best trousers to go out to battle for Freedom and Truth!

Anthony Loyd

asylum

Anthony Loyd was born in 1966. After being educated at Eton, he worked in Australia for a year, before going to Sandhurst from where he was commissioned into the Royal Greenjackets. He served with them in Northern Ireland, but in 1990 he transferred to the Royal Highland Fusiliers in order to go to the Gulf War.

On leaving the army in 1991 he enrolled for a year's course at the London College of Printing and Journalism, and in 1993 he left England for Bosnia as a freelance reporter. He was lucky enough to have a few articles accepted by the *Telegraph*, and was then taken on by *The Times*. In 1994 he was nominated Stringer of the Year, and at the time of writing he is reporting for *The Times* from Grozny.

The staff were nervous. The gunfire had been creeping closer for several days now. It made them twitchy and temperamental with their charges. Dr Hassanovic, the hospital director, no longer returned the vacuous morning salute of patient Topic who had over the years become a fixture by the main entrance, waiting to greet the doctor's arrival dressed in a ceremonial military jacket, his attempted formality offset by his unshaven countenance and dribbling leer. Nor did the doctor continue to compliment Dina on the garish make-up she applied each day in clashing smudges across her plump features. This upset her at first and she wept a little. He became grey and worn-looking, his immaculately combed hair greasy and unkempt.

These were foreboding signals, though wasted on most of the patients. But the new noises began to affect them at night; the rattling detonations and tremorous thumping, not so far now, producing a subliminal fear that made them shout and weep more than usual. By Wednesday the fighting was very near. The patients were confined to their rooms, less for Joey the servile trustee, who followed the director everywhere that day, concern furrowing his simple face. Soldiers trudged past the complex of buildings in small groups, sullen and downcast, else mean and angry. One fired a machine gun over the roof of the main ward, whooping in amusement at the cries it produced from inside. From my room I could see Hassanovic arguing with a group of them beside his car. There was a scuffle and the vehicle pulled away slowly, rifle barrels protruding from its windows. Hassanovic walked back to the hospital doors in silence. His nose was bleeding. It was a bad day for him – not even half of the fifteen staff had come to work.

Separate and alone, I continued to be treated by him with a familiar and frank courtesy that for my part I reciprocated with docility. This was something I had little choice in at that time. For over two years his medicaments had dulled my consciousness and mood, lessening each day to little more than a warm void of unrippled simplicity. Yet now somewhere within me a glimmer of cognitive hope glowed. I was aware of the significance of these events; if the doctor was considering flight then I did not wish to be obtrusive amongst his thoughts.

He came to me that night with two of his orderlies. I was not altogether surprised. They padlocked a length of chain from my ankle to one of the window bars, an action that I made no effort to resist. Though he could not look me in the eye there was no apology in the doctor's words. Fear afforded him a simple strength of purpose and he spoke quickly, his voice hollow of conviction, stating simply that he had to leave but would return as soon as he could. It appeared that Joey would be responsible for our lives, and Hassanovic expressed his wish that I would co-operate with him as fully and passively as was required until the staff could return. I nodded submissively, but my jaw muscles were tight in their efforts to repress a smile – the first for a very long time.

Silence followed his departure, broken occasionally by sporadic giggles from the main building. The first snows of winter illuminated the courtyard outside, and with the temporary absence of gunfire, their light somehow alleviated the brooding atmosphere of uncertainty. I lay on the bed, sometimes clinking the chain with my foot, pulled my greatcoat around me, and stared intently at the plumes of breath that reached towards the ceiling.

For three days Joey coped. He took to his new responsibility as a cockerel recently released from life in a pen; hesitant, speculative caution quickly replaced by a fragile arrogance that gradually smoothed his knit brow. He recruited those of more able mind to assist him in the hospital's daily routine, and the patients responded with the Pavlovian complicity of long-term incarceration; forming broken, awe-addled queues twice a day for their meals, collected each morning by Joey and his stooges from the larder stocks and cooked on a ramshackle wooden stove in the forecourt. A portable generator was refuelled in the afternoon under his auspices and the light it provided, though restricted to the corridors, assuaged the harshness of the early darkness and the fears it brought.

If it had not been for his prurient, if relatively innocuous, interest in young girls then Joey could probably have lived freely the life of a smalltown simpleton. He had spent some years in Canada, during which time he affected his nickname, before being deported for a trivial sexual offence, and on his return had ended up working as an odd-job man for a factory boss, a party member of considerable influence. The discovery by the boss of several pairs of his young daughter's knickers in Joey's tool shed, together with a not inconsiderable mass of pornographic literature, ended this lifestyle and after a short prison term (the judge had known the boss personally), Joey had come to the hospital. He was neither dangerous nor curable, and as the years had progressed he had become more a part of the hospital than a patient. He talked to me more than any other, though he kept his distance from my window bars. Beyond a mild embarrassment he bore no great awareness of his misdeeds and revealed his history to me with shuffling directness.

As the patients' mood now changed from one of stupefied incomprehension at the novelty of their predicament to a suspicious joy, they motivated one another with actions of well-intentioned naïvety. Dina and a geriatric woman, whose gross obesity appeared to lend her a strength beyond her toothless years, carried food up to those too infirm to make the journey down, and organised teams to strip soiled bed linen, washing it in one of the out-houses.

There were mishaps of course. A fight broke out in the food queue on the second morning for no apparent reason and in a mêlée of blundered punches and shouted grunts somebody crowned Kavic with a saucepan of scalding beans. Kavic was mute, and stood pathetically for several stunned seconds, saucepan lopsided over his head, beans dripping in steaming globs down his face and shoulder, before Joey took control of the situation, wheedling and imploring, self-doubt naked in his tones for all their chance effectiveness.

He lacked even more certainty in dealing with Dina's

uninhibited rampancy. Minutes after word spread that the staff had gone she had been found copulating frantically in the kitchen with Draganovic and Lendo midst a crowd of enthralled onlookers; subsequent and no less public liaisons with Topic had left him goggle-eyed and exhausted. Joey took to berating her partners, a move which did not make him popular, while trying to encourage Dina to be more discreet. It worked for a time and between washing the linen she established a makeshift boudoir in Hassanovic's office.

The hospital had been built with an opulence indicative of our former nation's Sixties confidence, then incompetently filled in the manner of its lumbering reality. The very old, who had no one or nowhere, lived in the uppermost ward. Two of the floors below contained a variety of the state's designated mental detritus, whose psyches varied from noticeable eccentricity to those requiring permanent supervision. The old system had been especially keen to deem any alternative from the society's norm as deviant and somehow sick. Some hundred in all, the patients here were malleable enough, providing they had the right care.

The complement of administrative and staff quarters lay on the ground floor. Across the courtyard lay my isolated and impromptu cell. A transit passenger caught by the war's chance eighteen months before en route between 'secure' units that now no longer existed, blown asunder by the unleashed energies of the conflict, I had been held here since, as the war ripped away the fabric of any structure that could decide my fate otherwise. I was not mad, but my offences were manifold and serious.

And on the second night, in the absence of Hassanovic's drugs, dreams returned to me. I had not dreamed for two years. Casting aside the blankets of narcosis came crystal visions and shooting lights that imploded into my chest, pumping in racing coloured streams through stagnant blood, sending strobes of brilliantine light through my dimmed eyes once more; I raced weightless over landscapes and cities of another age, through clouds flashing in electric schisms of blue that ripped and rewrapped the people below in glowing perfection; on a barren smoking hilltop I stretched my aching and sodden wings in sunlight and breeze, strong again, and hateful.

Awake I remained captive. Joey came to feed me as he did each day, and empty my slop bucket, but always with company, and always afeared. Sure that he knew the whereabouts of the key, I had asked him directly to unlock my chain and release me. He had hung his head and mumbled apologetically that he could not do that, that Dr Hassanovic, who would be back soon, had been most specific. I mused for a time on how best to persuade the little man otherwise. Then on the fourth day the men with guns arrived and everything changed.

They swaggered confidently through the snow to the main doors, eight of them, weapons slung casually across their shoulders or crooked in their elbows, pausing only to stare at the handful of patients preparing the stove for the morning's cooking. Joey met them on the steps and smiled ingratiatingly. Pushing past him they went inside, their silence following them through the building, emptying it of voices. They left shortly, and behind them fear sat heavily in their wake. Joey conducted the usual schedule, but more raw-nerved and jumpy than ever, his wards more prone to fight and cry amongst themselves.

The soldiers returned before dusk. There were more of them than before, perhaps twenty. This time they were loud, laughter and shouts heralding their arrival, and this time they stayed. Their noise continued for most of the night, carrying to me clearly across the yard, punctuated twice by shooting, and again, in the early hours of morning, by Dina's screams that probed for long and unabated minutes into the cold night air.

As the sun rose a group of them searched the outhouses. Vulpine and clumsy they crashed hurriedly through various rooms, though seeming to find little of value. I kept at a distance from the window and though at one point I heard heavy footfalls in the passage they ignored my cell. Other of the men began to appear from the main building, piling their booty together in the courtyard. It included the generator, boxed food stocks, sacks of vegetables, and jerrycans of fuel. They must also have found Hassanovic's pharmacy, for medical supplies were stacked high on the food. I could see none of the patients. A crudely painted green truck appeared. The soldiers loaded it, and in three short trips emptied the courtyard of everything. Then they left us, and did not return.

It was some time before Joey appeared. Glancing furtively from left to right he stepped into the yard and stirred the tyre-crunched snow with one foot, shoulders jerking with his sobs as heavy flakes began to drift down from the sky's gun-metal grey, settling thickly around him. I called out weakly, holding my chain up to the bars in an open palm. He looked up, and walked slowly forward, weak and broken and resigned.

Hassanovic patted his hair self-consciously as the road dipped out of the town and began its winding descent to the hospital. The buildings on each side grew fewer and stopped suddenly at the foot of the snow-covered woodland. Civilians had not yet begun their weary trickle back to their homes and less for the occasional band of troops the area appeared deserted and forlorn. A cold draught raced through the holes in the windscreen, and the clutch squealed painfully as the driver, a young soldier, slowed for an ice-covered bend. In the back seat his two escorts murmured amongst themselves. They stank of sweat and tobacco.

The doctor's thoughts were mixed with sensations of guilt and anxiety. He had had no choice, he told himself; no means to evacuate the patients, no place to take them to. But he had abandoned them nevertheless. To his relief a government army offensive had retaken a strategic hilltop above the town only a week afterwards. He hoped that little could have happened to the patients in this time. The enemy forces had melted back into the forests and resumed their original lines to the east. An officer had imparted this news less than an hour earlier after arriving at the farmhouse in which the municipality's authorities and principal figures, among them Hassanovic, had sheltered. His troops had cleared the hills around the hospital, he said, suggesting Hassanovic return immediately with a military escort. The man had no knowledge of what condition the patients were in.

A feeling of dread knotted the doctor's stomach as the car neared the gates, which was immediately assuaged by the sight of Topic. Someone had taught him a new salute and he stood to lopsided attention, right arm stretched stiffly toward the sky, his fingers locked straight, palm down. He looked more haggard than usual, but the leering grin was the same. The escorts frowned. Hassanovic waved and shook his head to himself.

Yet the yard was empty. Snow coated the wooden stove, and washing hung in pathetic white rows on lines around it, rock-iced and white. There was no sign of Joey. Casting a glance at the darkness behind the barred window across the yard, Hassanovic hurried into the hospital. Pools of water lay in the empty corridor, which smelled of urine and excrement. Kavic's face peered at him from a doorway, drawn and afraid, before he lurched forward to greet the doctor. Other patients emerged slowly, cowed and silent. They did not know where Joey was, and shrugged sadly at Hassanovic's questions. In his office he found Dina. She appeared to be in some sort of catatonic trance. Her face was bruised, one side covered in dried blood, and she stared at the wall without acknowledging the doctor's presence. Upstairs two of his geriatric patients had died of the cold. Their bodies lay wrapped in sheets in the corridor. Others stared at him listlessly from their beds. Some began to cry when they saw him. A fire had been lit at one end of the ward which had blackened the walls with smoke. Hassanovic strode down the stairs and ran to the captive's cell. He found Joey there, bent backwards over the bed. The chain was wrapped tightly around his neck and his face was swollen and black. Of the captive there was no sign.

Linda Kitson

khao-I-dang: thailand

I visited this camp in 1983, and shall never be able to forget that day. It was precariously placed on the Thai–Kampuchian borders, on the route path for the perennial attempts to invade Thailand. A high net surrounds it, with watch towers overlooking the terrain. Imagine a fifty-mile radius holding 65,000 people. It seemed so harrowing, but the reality was that this camp represented the maximum potential for safety, re-habilitation, and for FREEDOM. (The word Thai means free.)

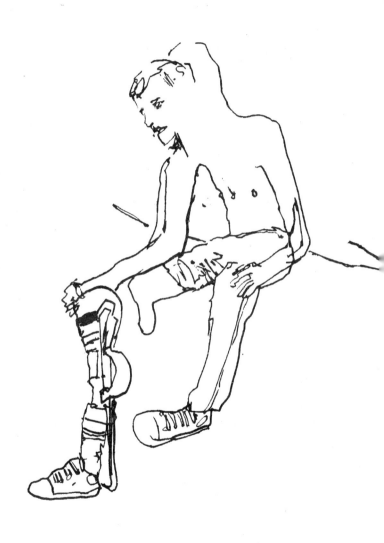

Khao-I-Dang: THAILAND

Red Cross Refugee Camp
August 3rd. 1983

Linda Kitson

Linda Kitson studied at the Ecole des Beaux Arts in Lyons, St Martin's School of Art, and the Royal College of Art where she took her Master's degree in 1970. She has been a regular visiting lecturer at the Royal College of Art, Camberwell School of Art and other London art schools.

In 1982 she was commissioned by the Imperial War Museum as Official War Artist in the Falklands campaign. She was awarded the South Atlantic Medal; the museum holds sixty of her drawings in its permanent collection. Other projects which have resulted in exhibitions have included Cambridge college life; the châteaux and vineyards of Bordeaux; the newspaper world of Fleet Street; and a visual record of the making of David Puttnam's film *The Killing Fields*. She has also been the subject of two BBC documentaries.

Linda Kitson has illustrated Claudia Roden's cookery book *Picnic* with landscape drawings, as well as, for the Folio Society, Albert Camus' *The Plague* and Antoine de St Exupéry's *Wind, Sand and Stars*. In addition to her one-person shows, Linda Kitson has been for over twenty years a regular contributor to the Royal Academy Summer Exhibition.

Helen Fielding

cause celeb

Helen Fielding was born in Yorkshire and now lives in London. She works in television and in newspaper journalism, and has produced documentaries for Comic Relief in Ethiopia, the Sudan and Mozambique. She writes regularly for the *Independent on Sunday*.

The impossible divide between the wealth of the Western world and poverty of the Third stands as a great barrier to freedom on both sides: freedom to live without guilt or shame on the one; freedom simply to live on the other.

Cause Celeb *tells the story of well-meaning but fumbling attempts by modern day celebrities to overcome the barrier.*

Rosie Richardson, a London PR girl, escapes the confines of life with a famous but oppressive boyfriend, Oliver, and his celebrity social life, to the wide open spaces and sense of purpose of relief work in Africa.

Four years later a massive new influx of starving refugees threatens Safila camp, where Rosie works. Frustrated by the cautious response of the aid organisations she returns to London, breaks into the celebrity circuit and brings Oliver and a member of the TV production staff back out to Africa for a live emergency appeal.

In these final chapters the comedian Julian Alman, the actress Kate Fortune, TV presenter Corinna Borghese, together with Rosie's fellow relief workers – Betty, O'Rourke, Henry and refugee leader Muhammad – travel to the Dowit mountains where tens of thousands of malnourished refugees are gathered, hoping for help.

IT WAS cloudy again, and out in the open desert the wind was getting up, carrying a lot of dust with it. Kate and Corinna were side by side in the front of the Landcruiser. O'Rourke was driving. I was in the back with Oliver. The rest of the convoy were behind.

'Shit,' said O'Rourke, braking. A small goat trotted away ahead of us. 'Where did that come from?' It was getting increasingly difficult to see anything – it was like looking through a yellow fog.

'This weather isn't doing us any favours, is it?' said Oliver.

'That depends. Sometimes it looks rather striking when the sun shines through this stuff,' said O'Rourke. He and Oliver seemed to get on quite well at times. Maybe it was sleeping together that did it. 'I'm not happy about rolling up straight away with these food lorries,' he went on.

'Neither am I,' I said.

'Why not?' said Corinna. 'What's the matter with you now? You can't turn up to a famine without bringing something to eat.'

'Frightfully bad form,' murmured O'Rourke.

'It depends how many Keftians there are,' I said. 'We don't want to start a settlement there.'

'Isn't that better than them coming to Safila?' said Oliver.

O'Rourke let out a tsking noise.

'No,' I said. 'The water supply's not up to it, and it's too close to the border.'

'But you can give them some food to keep them going?' said Oliver.

'Yeah, but we have to do it right. We don't want a riot,' said O'Rourke.

'Anyway, let's wait and see what we find,' I said. 'There might only be a couple of dozen. It might be a false alarm.'

'Jesus, it had better not be,' said Oliver.

'What's that?' said O'Rourke, starting to slow down.

'Oh, my God,' said Kate Fortune, straightening up and looking ahead. 'Oh, my God.'

What she was looking at was a group of corpses, lying at the side of the track.

There wasn't anything we could do except cover them up. They were young men who had starved to death, which suggested that they might have been sent ahead to warn us that the refugees were coming. The place was about a quarter of an hour's drive from Dowit. We left the two food trucks there. We knew now we were going to find a very bad situation and we needed to assess it first, and make a plan for the food. As we drove away, I glanced back and winced at the sight of trucks of food from England parked beside the people who had already died of hunger.

The red shapes of the Dowit mountains loomed ahead. I wondered whether, if I had just been driving past them as usual, I would have been able to tell that something terrible was happening there, or if they only seemed so forbidding now because of what I knew. The dust was growing heavier in the air, as if there would be a sandstorm soon. The sun was trying to break through, but it was with a weak, watery light.

A track led off the road to the left towards the mountains, and passed by means of a short corridor through the rock into the plain in the centre. The convoy stopped where the track met the road. The sound of a drum was coming from the mountains. It was a slow, single, hollow beat. Clive said that he thought they should keep the satellite dish and equipment here as they would not be able to get a signal inside the mountains. Then I saw figures appearing through the dust. They looked as though they were moving in slow motion because they were trying to run towards us but their legs, which were as thin as the bones beneath the skin, were not strong enough to carry the weight of their bodies.

Muhammad was already hurrying towards them. The skin on their faces was pulled back tight as though they were grinning, but they were not grinning. O'Rourke and I started walking towards them too. The expression in their eyes was terrible, because it was so human, in bodies made unhuman by starvation.

A boy who looked about seventeen had reached Muhammad now and was talking to him. The boy was talking slowly, trying to concentrate, as if he was dizzy. His teeth looked very big in his mouth and the top of his head was unnaturally large because there was no hair on his scalp, and no fat or muscle on his face, only skin. He had a piece of brown cloth like sacking wrapped around him and you could see the sockets of his shoulder above it.

'He is coming from my region,' said Muhammad. 'He is saying that there are many thousand refugee inside the mountain.'

The boy started to speak again, touching slowly between his eyes with his thumb and first two fingers as if he was trying to clear his head.

'He is saying they have no food now for many day. He ask if we are having food for him.'

Muhammad was not speaking in perfect English as he usually did. O'Rourke and I looked at each other, registering the line of decisions which lay ahead.

'We go and look, and then go back for the trucks?' O'Rourke said.

'Yes. I think so, yes.'

We gave the people who had come out to meet us some high-energy biscuits which we had put in the back of the Landcruiser.

Oliver was speaking to the crew of the satellite dish, and he told us they were going to park between the road and the mountains and try to set up the link.

As we drove along the track which led into the mountains, we passed more and more people but we kept driving now. Some of them turned round and followed the truck when they saw that we would not stop. Others stood still, looking bewildered.

Kate Fortune had started hyperventilating and making noises. She put her hand on O'Rourke's arm as he was driving, and told him that she felt ill, and he said, 'Look, shut up.'

As we drove into the narrow opening in the mountains it was very eerie because the dust was swirling around the rocks and the people were still coming towards us, jabbing at their mouths with their fingers. We drove through a very short corridor, like a fissure, with the rock rising sheer on either side, then the track turned a corner and opened onto the plain in the centre of the mountains. It was about three-quarters of a mile across and not flat, but dipping down and uneven and surrounded by the high walls of the mountains. Smoke was hanging above the ground from all the fires, and below it the whole of the plain was covered in people, sitting on the ground, thousands and thousands and thousands of people. There was very little movement but the sound was immense: it was the sound of a great number of people crying. I remember looking out of the window of the jeep and seeing the face of a young girl. I remember being shocked that her tears were so full and wet because the rest of her body looked so withered, dried up and finished that you could not imagine where the moisture had come from for the tears.

Everyone started to climb out of the vehicles. Muhammad was talking to a group of men who had come forward to meet him. They looked as though they were village headmen although they might have been RESOK. I was looking over to my left where the sound of the drum was coming from, and I started walking very slowly through the people towards it.

In a clear area to the left, which rose in a slope towards the base of the mountains, they were laying out the dead. There was a line of about twenty or thirty bodies, with people mourning all around them and, behind, a group of men were using a pole to dig a grave. And people were coming from different directions, carrying bodies in their arms. When I got to where the corpses lay a man was placing the body of a child in the line. The child was in a sack and the body was so frail that the man seemed only to be laying down the weight of a rolled-up towel. Some of the bodies were on stretchers and they were all covered with something. One was wrapped in paper sacks, on which was printed, 'A Gift from the People of Minnesota'. Further down was a blue blanket with a woman's feet sticking out of the bottom and between them two tiny feet.

At the end of the row a woman was squatting next to the body of her son. She had taken the cover from him and she was clapping her hands above his head as if she were trying to wake him. She looked as though she was trying to do everything she could think of to stop her pain. She was shaking her hands as if she was trying to get water off them, then covering her eyes, then holding the sides of her head, then holding her son's head and talking to him, then trying to bring him to life again by clapping above his head, but nothing could alter anything. When I looked at the body of the boy lying in front of her, useless and dead, I can remember thinking that it was stupid that he had died of starvation. It seemed stupid that all that grief had happened, not because of some sudden accident or unavoidable illness, but because the boy had no food, when there was so much food in the world.

Most of the people were just sitting or lying on the ground in groups. They were so weak and dazed that they were not responding to our presence or to anything. I had never seen people so malnourished and still alive. I made my way back slowly through them to where Muhammad was still talking to the headmen. I realised that I was crying and made myself stop.

As I walked past the Landcruiser I paused because Corinna was leaning against the back of it. Both her fists were clenched very tightly and her shoulders were hunched. She was crying in a way that forced her face into dreadful shapes beneath her sunglasses and wrenched her body. I saw her crying and did not try to comfort her. I watched her groaning and racked and I was glad, because she was not made of concrete, or lycra, or perspex as I had thought. She saw me looking and pressed her forehead against the back window of the Landcruiser. Then she said, 'Could I have a cigarette?'

I gave her a cigarette and lit it. Kate was sitting in the Landcruiser with her head in her hands. Julian and Oliver were both standing alone looking dazed. I could not see Henry or Betty or Sharon. O'Rourke was crouched over a child. He was not making any sound, and looked exactly the same as he always did when he was treating the children except that there were tears streaming down his face.

I did not know what to do. I stood dazed like the others and stared at it all. It was such a monumental horror that it felt as though nothing should be the same any more, and nothing should continue: none of us should speak or do anything, the sun should not be moving across the sky, and the wind should not blow. It did not seem possible that such a thing as this could be taking place without the world having to shudder to a halt and think again.

* * *

THE ONLY way of dealing with it was not to think too hard but simply to do one task after another: to do one thing and then to do the next thing.

O'Rourke, Henry, Muhammad, Betty and I gathered by the vehicles. There were somewhere between ten and twenty thousand people on the plain. The sun was breaking through the dust now and there were thick shafts of light, like girders, lighting up great areas of the people.

'This place is just asking for an epidemic,' said O'Rourke.

We decided that, while Muhammad and I started on the rehydration and feeding, Henry would check that the water supplies were clean, and set up defecation zones. Betty would organise measles immunisation. O'Rourke and Sharon would start a clinic for the worst cases.

'What about the broadcast?' said Betty. It was one thirty. We were due on air at four o'clock.

'Those forty tonnes of food are not going to last long here,' said O'Rourke. Oliver and Julian were still standing staring at the crowd. I made my way over to Oliver. 'Come on,' I said. 'Come on. You have to go and organise the broadcast. You have got to make it work. Take the Landcruiser back to the satellite dish and tell them what you've seen.'

He looked at me blankly.

'Go on, Oliver,' I said.

Corinna was walking towards us. She was wiping her eyes and looked as though she was pulling herself together.

I looked at Oliver. He was still staring around helplessly.

Muhammad came and joined us. He placed a hand on Oliver's shoulder and took him a little way away, talking to him.

'I'll help,' said Corinna. 'Tell me what I can do.'

I asked her to drive back to where we had left the food lorries and bring them back here.

'Ask them to wait outside the mountains till we're ready. Will you be all right with the four-wheel drive?'

I'll be fine,' she said.

'I could ask Henry to go instead.'

'No, I'll be fine. You need him here.'

'Wait, look, I'll come with you,' said Julian.

'You stay here,' she said. 'It doesn't need two of us.'

'Tell me what I can do,' said Julian.

'We need to organise the food next,' I said.

After a while Oliver and Muhammad came back. Oliver looked better and said he would drive back to the satellite dish and start working out what we should do.

The village headmen were gathering around Muhammad.

'Will these men organise the distribution?' I asked Muhammad.

'Yes, of course.'

I looked around, trying to work out where we could start. 'Are the people in any sort of grouping?'

'Yes. They have tried to stay in their villages.'

'How many villages are represented here?' I asked.

He spoke to the men again.

'Perhaps five hundred villages.'

'We'll start with the under fives. And the most serious cases. And we'll set up a feeding centre here and rehydrate them at the same time. Then maybe we can start getting food out to the rest later.'

'We must feed the mothers too,' said Muhammad.

'Yes, we'll feed the person who comes with the child.'

'I will talk to the headmen,' said Muhammad. 'They will organise it.'

I was trying not to imagine anything except what was before

us, and not to imagine it getting worse so as not to let dread come out or panic. I looked around for Julian, and said that we needed to build three enclosures out of stones.

'Yes, right, good,' said Julian, bending down to pick up a large stone. 'Here?' He looked as though he was ready to do it himself, single-handed.

'We have to get some people together to help '

I started to ask the people around us, the ones who were strong enough, but it was hard to explain what we wanted to do.

'What are the enclosures for?' said Julian. And I told him we needed separate areas for the immunisation, for giving out the high-energy biscuits and for feeding the really bad cases with a wet ration.

'We need walls round them so everything stays under control,' I said, but I didn't know if that were possible, since there were so many desperate people. Then Julian started miming out what was to be done, which made the people laugh in spite of what was happening but they understood and started gathering the stones. A man came up who spoke some English and that helped us, because then the Keftians could take over the organisation. We were working on the area which was immediately to the right when you entered the mountains, so it would be easy to unload the trucks. Soon about three hundred people were collecting stones and starting to build the walls.

I kept looking over to where all the vehicles were parked at the end of the rocky corridor. The television crew were milling around agitatedly. A thick cable was lying along the track, and they were frantically attaching more to the end of it. Oliver kept driving up and down the corridor, going back to the satellite dish. They were like wasps going in and out of a nest.

At three forty-five the enclosures were built, and each one was crammed with children and sick people, sitting or lying on the earth, waiting in lines. The village leaders were arriving all the time with new cases, supporting them or carrying them. Every so often a group of people would suddenly run in one direction, because some of the food had been spilled and everyone would scrabble on the ground, picking up whatever they could find, and eating it. Outside the walls there were crowds of people, pressing forward, looking in. There was the sound of high, agitated voices above the wailing. It was difficult to keep calm because outside the walls people were crowded a dozen deep, holding out their children to us to show us that they were dying and begging us to let them in. Fights were breaking out, because it was so unfair to be on the wrong side of the wall.

I kept looking at my watch then down at the camera crew but the situation still seemed the same. People kept driving off down the corridor and coming back again. I couldn't understand what was going on. I thought Corinna and Julian should be down there rehearsing by now, but they were in the next enclosure, helping with the distribution of the biscuits.

'I think I'd better go down and find out what's happening,' I said to Muhammad.

As I walked across the slope towards the vehicles, Oliver was coming up to meet me. 'It's not working,' he said, as soon as he was close enough. His face was screwed up in a scowl, self-pitying.

'Why not?' I said, swallowing hard.

'There's a problem with the dish.'

'What?'

'It's got dented.'

'Dented?' I was blinking very quickly. 'What happened?'

'I don't know. They reckon a stone must have hit it when they were driving.'

'Is there anything they can do?'

'They're trying to hammer it out but it's a delicate job. It has to be absolutely smooth.'

'Will they do it, do you think?'

'To be honest, Rosie, we're stymied.'

I rubbed my forehead frantically. We didn't have enough food. There was another Circle Line plane waiting at Stansted. It could be loaded and here in twenty-four hours. We could have airlifts every other day till the crisis was over, but not if there was no broadcast. The lives of all these many thousands of people actually depended on a piece of television equipment which was dented. It seemed a stupid way for the world to be but there we had it. And now there was only half an hour to go.

'Do you know what you're going to do in the programme, if they can get it working?' I said.

'Yes. I've worked that out at least,' he said.

'Don't you need Corinna and Julian here? Where's Kate?'

'She's in the Landcruiser. There's no point bothering with her.'

I looked over. She was sitting sobbing, pulling at her hair.

'Yes, you might as well send Corinna and Julian down. But

you carry on with the feeding. I think that's going to be more use, to be honest. We'll call you if we have any joy.'

I tried to carry on but it was very hard to concentrate. I knew that we had just one hour between five and six to blast this horror out to the world and it was our only chance. But there was nothing I could do.

At ten minutes to four, a shout went up from the camera crew. I saw the cameraman starting to point the camera at Julian and Corinna. Corinna was looking towards me, giving a thumbs-up. I stuck my fist in the air, made my way out of the enclosure and started running towards them. As I drew close, panting and stumbling over the stones, Oliver roared out of the corridor in the Landcruiser.

'We can't get the fucking signal,' he was shouting as he strode across the sand. 'The dish is working but we can't get the signal. We're in the shadow of the fucking mountain. Fuck. Fuck. Fuck. Fucking Vernon. We should have stayed where we were.' He was banging one fist against the other, striding around, uselessly. It was five past four now. The show would be on the air in England, with no link from Nambula.

'Muhammad,' Oliver said suddenly, 'is there any way of getting a vehicle higher up?'

'Yes, there is a track but it is very steep. If you go out and follow the edge of the mountain to your left, you will find it after two hundred yards.'

'Where does the track lead to?' said Oliver. 'Is there anywhere we can drop the cable down?'

Muhammad pointed to the mountains above the enclosures, squinting into the sun. They were almost sheer: great curves of red rock. 'The road is climbing up there on the out-side behind the ridge, but you will find there is a place where you can look over the plain. Perhaps you can throw the cable down there, above where they have built the enclosures.'

'OK,' said Oliver, already striding towards the vehicles. 'I'll go up there with some of the lads. Get the camera over there in the feeding centre and we'll drop the cable down to you.'

At twenty past four, with forty minutes to go before the broadcast ended, Julian and Henry were waiting at the foot of the mountains, holding the end of the cable, looking up, hopefully, surrounded by crowds of Keftians. The rest of us were a hundred yards away on the other side of the wall, inside the wet rations enclosure. We were working out where the camera should be, and what we should do. I kept looking around the plain at all the people and thinking how much we had wanted this not to happen. We had brought the cameras to it too late, and still we couldn't make the programme work. A man came up and spoke to Muhammad, and he looked as though he was going to collapse.

'Huda is here,' he said. 'Will you come with me?'

It was Huda Letay, the woman he had asked me to find up in Kefti. Muhammad was kneeling beside her, holding her hand, moving the blanket higher over her chest to where the bones of her shoulders stuck out through the skin. Her hair was reddening and frizzy, only clumps of it remaining because of the marasmus. At the other side, Huda's mother was hold-ing her twin babies. They were screaming and the skin was wrinkling on their legs because there was no muscle under-neath. They were about a year old, two little boys, with big eyes. When they stopped crying they had grumpy expressions, which were very appealing. Huda was lying with her head back, her bulging eyes staring up at the sky, moving her head from side to side. I think she knew who Muhammad was because as he spoke to her she made a little noise.

I turned back to see what was happening on the mountain. Julian and Henry were clambering up the boulders which lay at the bottom holding their end of the cable, and looking up all the time. The rock rose in a clear, smooth sweep above them. Then the mountain fell back through another area of boulders and loose rocks, before rising up in a perfectly smooth shoulder to the summit. High above us, standing at the top of the loose rocks, were Oliver and one of the crew boys. Two more of the boys appeared round the side of the rock carrying a large coil of cable on a metal frame.

It was going to be difficult to get the cable down to the sheer drop unless they carried it over the area of loose rocks, but that was steep and looked as though it would shift if they walked on it. Oliver joined the men bending over the cable and I watched as they started lifting something. They brought it a few feet off the ground and started swinging it. They swung, once, twice, three times, and then they threw it. It was a boulder in a net. It bounced down over the loose rocks, dragging the cable behind it, towards the sheer drop. As it bounced it loosened the rocks below which were falling with it. Six feet from the edge it stuck behind a pinnacle of rock. An avalanche of stones began to roar over the precipice, crashing down onto the rocks below, making the people scatter.

Oliver started to make his way, gingerly, down over the

loose rocks and boulders towards where the cable was stuck. Suddenly a whole section began to move underneath him. He was sliding with it towards the sheer drop. Corinna screamed. More stones were falling over the edge now, Oliver was grabbing with his hands, trying to get a hold, then he flung himself sidewards and caught hold of the pinnacle, kicking at its base. He clung on, as the rocks rushed beneath him over the edge, and as they fell, among them was the boulder attached to the cable, which was snaking down the drop now.

Oliver was still clinging to the pinnacle. I couldn't see what was happening at the bottom of the mountain, because the refugees were all crowding around. Suddenly there was a commotion behind us. I turned and saw the cameraman blundering towards us, pointing the camera. Corinna was following. 'Go go go,' said the cameraman to no one in particular. 'Go. We've got the link. Go go go. Go go go. Twenty seconds. Stand by.'

The soundman was holding out an electronic box and an earpiece. I grabbed the electronic box, shoved it in Muhammad's hand, and the earpiece in his ear. The cameraman pointed the camera at Muhammad and the soundman picked up the boom and held it over Muhammad. 'You are on a wide shot, yes?' Muhammad said to the cameraman coolly. 'If you raise your hand when you are ready for me to speak I will speak.'

I glanced at my watch. Ten to five.

'Ten seconds till they come to us,' said the cameraman. 'A really wide shot first,' ordered Muhammad, 'so that the viewers can see the whole plain.'

I could hear angry voices coming out of his earpiece.

'But I am the man on the spot,' said Muhammad indignantly. 'You must play music over the wide shot then fade it when you come to me. You have music there?'

There was more angry shouting from his earpiece.

'They want one of the celebrities,' said the cameraman. 'Corinna, come on love where are you?'

'Let Muhammad do it,' Corinna said.

The cameraman looked at her.

'Let Muhammad do it,' she said again.

'Yes, let him do it,' said Julian.

I looked up at the mountain. Oliver was slowly hauling himself back up towards the crew on the end of a rope.

Muhammad was speaking to Huda and her mother, and watching the camera out of the corner of his eye. The camera was panning round the feeding centre as Muhammad had ordered. Huda was weak, but listening to what he was saying, nodding slowly. The cameraman started to raise his hand and Muhammad looked at Huda for a count of two then slowly turned to stare straight into the lens.

'Nearly twenty years ago,' he began, 'Dr Henry Kissinger made a proclamation to the World Food Programme in Rome. "We must," he said, "proclaim a bold objective: that within a decade, no child will go to bed hungry. That no family will fear for its next day's bread. And that no human being's future and capacity will be stunted by malnutrition."'

He paused, and helped Huda to sit up higher.

'For six weeks now, the United Nations, the EC, the aid agencies and the Western governments have known that tens of thousands of people in the highlands of Kefti had no more food. They knew that they were travelling here to seek help, walking day and night with empty stomachs, watching their children and old folk die on the way. The Keftian people were starving to death as they walked but still travelling in hope that they would find sustenance here on the borders of Nambula. And what have the UN done in that time? What have the Western governments sent? What is waiting for these people here? Nothing.'

He gestured out towards the plain and the cameraman followed his arm.

'Year after year you have seen – and you will see – pictures like these on your screens. Year after year your governments, your organisations, with their grain mountains and colossal budgets, fail to help us in time. Year after year, you, the ordinary people like us, are asked to reach into your pockets to save us when it is too late. And now we are asking you to save us again. Why?'

He turned to Huda.

'This is Doctor Huda Letay, who was my college friend when we studied economics together at the University of Esareb.'

He waited for the camera to find her. Huda's head was rolling on the earth. Her mouth was open as if in a scream.

'She is twenty-seven.'

Muhammad reached round and put his arm behind her shoulders. He beckoned the microphone to come closer. Huda's mother laid the twins beside her. And Huda raised her head to speak. 'These are my children,' she said, in a voice that was scarcely a whisper. 'One week ago their sister has died of hunger. Four days ago their brother the same.'

The soundman was looking at the cameraman, trying to get the boom lower, closer to her head. 'Yesterday their father too.'

She was leaning closer to the camera now, staring straight into the lens. A movement caught my eye. Kate Fortune was standing behind the camera, gesticulating, wearing her peach turban.

'Half the world is rich and half the world is poor,' Huda continued. 'I am not resentful of you, who live in that rich half, only I wish that I and my children live there too.'

She paused to cough. The babies had begun to cry, and the soundman was still trying to get the boom closer. 'I was born in the wrong half of the world,' she said. Her voice was hoarse now. 'I do not wish to die. And if I must die I do not want to die like this, without dignity, lying in the dirt like a beast.' She started to cough, and closed her eyes, leaning back against Muhammad's arm. He eased her up a little whispering to her.

She opened her eyes again and lifted her head. 'I was born on one side of the line and you on the other. I will die here. My children and my people need food and so I must abase myself and beg.' The coughing overcame her again. 'We need help from everywhere and every place. *Really* we need that help. Not for to dance or to feel ... comfortable, only to live.'

And then her eyes closed and she sank back against Muhammad's arm again, coughing, then lying still as he stroked her head.

* * *

'ABSOLUTELY DEFINITIVE.' The director's voice, two thousand miles away in London, was still beaming down to us from the skies. 'Seriously moving to have a live death.'

It was beyond sunset now, and the desert was red. Oliver and I were in the control van, which was parked outside the mountains at the foot of the track leading up to the satellite dish. The broadcast had been over for an hour and a half. Credit card donations were flooding in, and so were the accolades. The back of Oliver's shirt was torn and his forearms were covered in cuts from the rocks.

'Oliver, I think you should tell him that Huda's in a coma. She's not actually dead,' I whispered.

'. . . Vernon with you?' crackled the voice of the director over the sound system.

Oliver pressed a button and spoke into the microphone. 'Not at this precise moment,' he said. 'Vernon is a little unwell.'

'Tell him we've had a call from the Independent Television Commission congratulating CDT. Looking good. Looking good.'

There was a pause while the line crackled.

'Just had a phone call from Stansted. Circle Line plane took off five minutes ago. Should be with you . . . twelve hours' time. Oh-oh. Hang on. New total, two million three hundred and ninety-seven thousand pounds aaaaaaand counting . . .'

There was the sound of a champagne cork popping. 'Oh-oh. Hang on. Wait a moment. Wait a . . .'

Oliver broke into a smile. 'Two million three hundred and ninety-seven thousand pounds,' he said to the group which was gathered outside the door.

'Hey! I've got the *News* on the phone,' said the director's voice.

'. . . want to airlift out the twins. The dead woman's twins.' More crackling.

I grabbed the microphone, and pressed the switch.

'Can you confirm that they want to evacuate two infants out of twenty thousand people?'

There was more crackling.

'Affirmative,' said the director.

'And does it have to be those two?'

'Affirmative. The dead woman's kids.'

'What if they've died already?' I said. 'Will they take a different two?'

'Confirming that it must be the kids of the woman who died on the programme . . . twins . . .' More crackling.

'But she isn't dead yet.'

'OK . . . *Daily News* guy here in the studio wanting to talk to his photographer . . . got the photographer with you?'

Outside there was the cry of an animal, somewhere far away over the sand. The photographer appeared in the doorway and came up the stairs. Oliver pressed the microphone button for him.

'Steve Mortimer here,' said the photographer, turning round with a flourish and hitting Oliver in the face with his camera bag. There was a pause for the time lag.

'Steve, hi, Rob here,' said a different voice over the talkback. 'How yer doing, mate? Listen. We want the kids. You got the pictures? You got the live death?'

'Sure,' he said.

'But—' Oliver began.

'OK, that's enough. We lose the line in five. Big thank yous to everyone. Absolutely fantastic. Out of this world. Oh-oh. Hang on. One last thing. The guy that spoke at the end, the one holding the dead woman. They want him brought over . . .' The line was lost in crackle. 'Natural . . .' crackle, crackle . . . 'Want him as regular on CDT before the franchises. Get him brought back with you or send him with the kids. OK. This is it, Nambula, we're losing you. Well done again, everybo—'

And then there was nothing more: just the hollow note of the drum and the loud, ringing silence of the desert.

The mountains were dark shoulders against crimson. A jeep was drawing up. Doors opened and slammed shut, voices rang out through the dusk. Julian, Muhammad, Betty and Henry were all emerging.

'Rosie!' Julian was making his way towards me, his face furrowed with concern. 'Rosie,' he said. 'I know what I want to do.'

'What's that?'

'Well, first of all I want to give all the money I can. And I'm going to really work when I get back to keep the campaign going. But I want to do something more. I'm going to adopt those babies,' he said. 'The little twins, you know, the orphans. You know the mother's dead now?'

I looked for Muhammad. He was limping away from the vehicles, on his own.

'I want to help the family,' Julian went on. 'I'm going to

bring them back to live with Janey and Irony and me.'

'I'm having those babies,' snapped Kate Fortune.

'But you've already got a Romanian baby,' said Julian indignantly.

'Sorry, loves, the *News* has got 'em,' said the photographer.

'Er. Don't want to point out the Orville Obvious,' said Henry, 'but surely there's enough babies to go round? I mean, even if it's orphans you're after, probably a good few more up there. No reason why everyone has to have the same ones, is there? Or am I being a total thicko?'

Corinna was leaning against the caravan, smoking a cigarette. She saw me looking at her and gave me a sympathetic smile. She had been a different woman all afternoon, warm, sisterly, supportive. She walked over towards me now, leaned forward, brushed something away from under my eye and said 'Tired?' I hoped the famine hadn't turned her into a lesbian.

Betty was trying to get all the jeeps parked in a cosy circle.

'Come along,' she was saying. 'We must eat. Nobody's eaten a thing since breakfast. An army can't march on empty stomachs. No use to the refugees if we can't get on with the job. I made sure Kamal put some bread and corned beef in before we set off. Should be enough to go round, I think. I've even got a tub of mustard. Mind you, it's English. I prefer a milder mustard myself.'

'What a woman. Thank goodness we've got Betty to look after us,' said Roy the soundman, reverently.

A hundred yards away, in the gathering darkness, Muhammad was leaning on his stick, staring towards Kefti, where the clouds were like coals against the red glow. I picked my way across the scrub towards him.

'I'm sorry,' I said, when I was beside him.

After a while, he said, 'It is very hard to bear.' And then, 'But she was wonderful, was she not?'

'Yes, she was.'

'And if there's a time when it is true to say a person did not die in vain . . .'

'. . . then this was it.'

'But still, it is very hard.'

We were standing in complete darkness now, but it was the warm, enfolding darkness of those nights. There had been headlights approaching for some time from the direction of Safila, and now the vehicle was drawing up. Inside Betty's circle of vehicles, the faces were lit by torches and firelight. All the group were together except O'Rourke, who was still with the refugees. The doors of the jeep opened and the troll-like figure of Vernon emerged, fulsome bottom first. We could hear the tone of his voice but not the words. He sounded defensively blustery.

'Do you know what I fear?' said Muhammad.

'Tell me.'

'That even after all this, very quickly, for everyone else, it will be as if it never happened.'

'I know.'

We stood in silence for a while.

'They want you to go back with them, the television people, did you hear?' I said.

'No.'

'Would you want to?'

'And collude in that corrupt sickness?'

'Corrupt sickness is not confined to the West,' I said, 'as we both know.'

'I mean the sickness of the chosen few,' he said. 'If I despise the unfair division of this world, the uneven granting of gifts, then when I have my chance to be plucked from the anonymity of the disadvantaged and placed within the enclosure of the privileged, when the gifts are about to shower down on me, do I say yes, or do I say no?'

'What will you achieve by saying no?'

He thought for a while, and then said, 'Spiritual treasures.'

'Well, I think that might be the length and breadth of it.'

He shook his head.

After a while I said, 'If you go to London now you might be able to do something. You're being invited to join the Famous Club. You'll get lionised by the media, and you'll have a measure of power. If you get the mass of ordinary people behind you, then sometimes you can change things a bit.'

'Do you really believe so?' he said. 'Do you? This is the third famine which has smitten and destroyed us in my lifetime, and it is always the same. Afterwards the cameras and the journalists come, and then the officials make plans, and they promise it will never happen again. Then all is well for a while, they grow bored, and then it happens again.'

'Maybe we have to keep trying. Maybe it gets a little less bad each time, there's a bit more development each time, it makes you a bit less vulnerable. Maybe you have to go to London and push to speed it up.'

'And sacrifice myself?'

'It's not much of a sacrifice. You'll be pretty comfortable. You'd get a bit rich. You'd know you'd never risk dying of hunger again.'

'But of thirst,' he said, 'spiritual thirst. I would be accepting the inequity of the system. I would be Britain's tame, one-legged African refugee, a novelty, a token. No longer myself.'

Someone was making their way from the group towards us. It was impossible to see who it was, but we could hear them stumbling over the scrub. It was an uneven patch of ground.

'Hi.' Oliver emerged from the blackness. He looked very thin now.

'Well done, my friend,' said Muhammad. 'You were a hero.'

'They're all going now,' said Oliver. 'Back to El Daman.'

'Now?' I said.

'Yes. They want to drive through the night and get back there tonight.'

'I will leave you,' said Muhammad.

Oliver and I stood looking at each other in the darkness.

'You did a very great thing,' I said.

'I made an heroic gesture. Anyone can do that once. Doesn't last long, everyone sees, makes you feel fantastic.'

'You could have been killed.'

'Well, I wasn't. It's the O'Rourkes of this world who are the heroes, slogging away unsung, surrounded by diarrhoea. He's still up there, isn't he?'

'This wouldn't have happened without you. All the work in the world would have made no difference without any food.'

'Don't be ridiculous.'

Then, after a moment's thought, he said, 'But actually it wouldn't, would it?'

'No. You made it happen at every stage.'

'I feel . . . very . . . oh, I don't know. Thanks anyway. Thanks for . . . I mean, God, I sound like Julian. I think—'

'What?'

'I think. I dunno. I'm sorry I've been . . . This has been great for me. I feel . . . Jesus, what do I feel? I feel . . . good. I feel more . . . good than I've ever felt. Maybe I'll be different now. Maybe everything will be different.'

And there was a moment of real closeness between us. I thought how much we had both learned.

'Rosie, I want to ask you something.'

'Yes?'

'I want to ask you to come back with me.'

I glanced across at him nervously. 'Er. You know I can't do that.'

'I am asking you to come back with me.'

'I can't. I have to stay here.'

'Rosie.' He was beginning to raise his voice. Footsteps were starting towards us across the scrub. 'I am ASKING you to come back with me.'

'You don't really want that. You don't really want me. You know you don't.'

'It's O'Rourke, isn't it?'

'I've got a job to do.'

'Rosie, I am asking you to come back with me.'

'No.'

'I've done this thing, and we've saved the situation and now I AM ASKING YOU . . .'

'Of course I'm not sodding coming back with you,' I burst out. 'You've seen what's going on up there.'

'You love O'Rourke,' he said, 'don't you?'

'Oh, puh-*lease*, Oliver.' Corinna appeared out of the darkness. 'Can't you see the girl's got more on her mind than bloody men? Here you are, little one, I've brought you a sandwich.'

'I'm going back to the fire,' said Oliver.

'Oliver,' I said, catching his arm, 'thank you.'

'Do you know,' said Corinna when he had gone, 'I think we have all gained more than we've given, here. I think we will all be profoundly altered by this.'

I said nothing.

'Don't you think so? Weren't you completely altered when you first came out here?'

'In some ways,' I said. 'But in some ways I think people always stay the same.'

We could see the tail-lights of the departing convoy, long after we had ceased to hear the sound. Betty, Henry, Sharon and I stood watching them, not knowing quite what to do now. I was trying to imagine what life was going to be like in Safila without Muhammad. He had decided to go with them.

'Dears, I must tell you the most marvellous news,' said Betty.

There was a pause while we tried to lift ourselves out of our thoughts.

'What's that, Bets old thing?' said Henry, after slightly too long. 'Don't tell me, you're going to adopt the twins as well?'

'No, silly,' said Betty coyly. 'Well. Roy. You know Roy the sound engineer?'

'What, the one you were talking with behind the caravan before he left?' said Sharon.

'Charming fellow,' said Henry. 'Bit of a Crispin Crashingbore at times, but by and large, absolute charmer.'

'He's asked me to marry him.'

'That's wonderful,' I said.

'Don't like to throw a dampener on the proceedings,' said Henry. 'Bloody marvellous, couldn't be more delighted. But aren't you already married, old sock?'

'Oh, yes, of course I know. But when all this trouble with the famine's sorted out here, and Dr O'Rourke takes over, I'm going to go back to England and start divorce proceedings, and start again with Roy.'

'What's that?' said Henry. Ahead of us a white djellaba was just visible, approaching with a limp.

'Is that you, Muhammad?' I called.

'No, it is an apparition,' came his voice.

'I thought you were going to London to speak for your people.'

He swung towards us on the stick. 'I decided it was better to stay with my people here,' he said, breathing heavily. 'We must fight from within, we must insist that we may cultivate, we must demand that food be kept in storage in our highlands, so that when disaster strikes again we need not leave our homes.'

'Bloody hell, Muhammad,' said Henry. 'Turned into a bloody saint-style person. Throw up your chance of fame and fortune to insist on the right to grow tomatoes.'

'The shallow and flippant nature of your character never ceases to appal me,' said Muhammad, joining us where we stood and leaning an arm on Henry's shoulder.

The others set off back to the camp, and I drove back to pick up O'Rourke. As I reached the end of the rocky corridor and emerged onto the plain, the moon was coming up over the mountains, throwing a white light onto the scene. On the rising ground to my left, the dead were still being carried to the burial ground, the bodies were still being laid out and the graves still being dug. I could see the lamp still lit, over in O'Rourke's clinic, where he was working. I walked over to him.

'Have you nearly finished?'

'Finished?' He could hardly keep his eyes open.

'Come on. You'd better get some sleep. You've got to start again tomorrow.'

I left him to finish off, and walked over to check on the feeding centres. When I came back he was packing up his equipment into boxes. I helped him load them into the jeep.

As we drove out of the rocky corridor and down to the main road, the lights of the convoy were just visible in the distance heading for El Daman.

'I feel like five kinds of shit driving away and leaving this,' said O'Rourke.

'At least you're coming back in the morning.'

'It worked then, did it, your broadcast?' he said, with the quick smile.

'Yes,' I said. 'Bit late, but it worked.'

After the broadcast there were three months of hard labour for us. The population of the camp doubled and there were journalists and cameras constantly at large. There were frequent rumours that Fergie was coming out on a mercy dash to bring royal jelly and ginseng, that Elizabeth Taylor was coming with Michael Jackson and a mini-funfair, or that Ronnie and Nancy Reagan were planning to spend Christmas with us. Most of them proved to be false alarms, but still it was unsettling and nerve-racking for staff and refugees alike.

All the publicity, time-consuming as it was, meant that questions were asked publicly. The European and American governments and the UN came in for a lot of stick. Even we had completely underestimated the sheer magnitude of the disaster in the highlands: for two months people continued to pour down in unimaginable numbers. The scene we had witnessed at Dowit was re-enacted time and time again along the length of the border.

Safila was better off than most of the camps because of the food from Charitable Acts and because we had raised our profile right from the start. The journalists always came to us first. We were in the centre of the media spotlight and the big shots could not afford to let the situation get too bad for us. Elsewhere it was appalling.

Safila played host to all sorts of political dignitaries and discussions about how to stop disaster happening again. The latest plan I heard before I left was that there are to be grain stores positioned and kept stocked all the way along the border, and an agreement with Abouti that the aid agencies can take food into Kefti if ever the harvest is threatened again. As Muhammad put it, 'If ever that comes to pass then I will both marry Kate Fortune and become her hairdresser.' Stranger things have been known, of course.

Betty stayed on for a couple of months to see us through the worst of it, then departed for a desk job in London and Roy the soundman. Parcels of candied peel and decomposing date and walnut loaf have started arriving with touching regularity. Linda asked to be sent back to Chad and left about six weeks ago. Henry became very serious and adult for about a month but is now once again preoccupied with the contents of Fenella Fridge and Sian's Boris Bra.

And O'Rourke: he's asleep now, actually, in my bed under the mosquito net. I keep glancing up from the desk, watching him, in the glow from the hurricane lamp. He snores a bit, but I'm getting used to it.

Candia McWilliam

strawberries

Candia McWilliam was born in Edinburgh. She has three children. Her novels are *A Case of Knives*, *A Little Stranger* and *Debatable Land*.

'Church or chapel?' would ask my nurse, and my parents would set their mouths. My nurse was asking if my high-church father or atheist mother would care for an arched piece of bread from the top of the loaf or a squared-off piece from the bottom. Whichever either chose, it would be buttered to the edge and smeared with fish paste. We were having tea in the white day-nursery, which always smelt slightly of singeing. My parents did not care for each other, and they detested Nurse, but could not agree as to her disposal. I loved her.

As though massively exhausted, my father began, 'Nan,' (this was to convince himself that he had come from genera-tions of people who had employed servants) 'Nan, no more can you impute the Romanesque line of that particular crust solely to churches than you can suggest that our friends the Welsh worship in boxes; or, if, by "chapel", you mean some-thing more Romish, while the Gesu in Rome could conceivably be considered squat, I cannot myself be sure that it might be seen as a square.' Did he talk like this? If not in fact, certainly in flavour. He never stopped, never definitely asserted, incessantly and infinitesimally qualified. He was an architect but however did he draw his straight lines? How, once he had begun it, did he stop drawing a line? He might continue, 'The fish paste, Nan dear, is, I must acknowledge, an apt touch for the believer when one brings to mind the ichthic idiogram for the name of Our Lord scrawled on the lintels of Byzantium or in the sands of Palestine; this reduction, indeed, of fish, this distillate of the deep, this patum of piety.'

Did he speak in his intolerable manner out of hatred for our unadventurous nursery world, the humiliating occasional necessity of spending time with the son he had somehow got on the stony woman sitting low in the nursing chair? I am certain he did not speak from love of words, for all his polylalia; he issued his words as though they strained the sphincter of his mouth, and sank, drained, whenever he at last completed a sentence. To ensure freedom from interruptions, he moaned at not quite regular intervals, as though his speaking mechanism were running down. He also breathed energetically and gobbled at his cheeks.

My mother in contrast was so quiet as to suggest illness. When she spoke, the remark would be of the sort that made me pleased I had no brothers or sisters. The thought of anyone having to hear the things my mother said made me embarrassed. Today she said, 'Did you know, my pigeon, the firescreen is worked in silk from worms which have eaten nothing but the white mulberry's leaf?' It was her overworked absence of banality which made me uncomfortable. I do not now think she was affected, rather, I think she may have escaped into willed eccentricity, which combined with an already eccentric nature. I have inherited her warmth towards esoterica; she had none for people, but she loved her dreadful facts.

Unlike my mother, I have always felt inhibited by the idea of displaying curious information in daily converse. I find it hard to imagine dropping into a free, swiftly moving conversation, odd bits of factual knowledge; they seem to choke the progress and clarity of the thing. I loathe those men who just happen to know about monorchitism in dictators or the curative properties of the toxic members of the potato family. I like best knowledge which comes from comprehension. I do not care for ornamental knowledge, as worn by my mother. Expository or even revelatory knowledge are what I like. Since I became an adult, the mathematics of space and time have been my particular weakness.

But then, on the rug of knotted grey and green cotton rag, concentrating on the knotting's soft randomness to drive time off, I was years from my final resting place, the study of finite-dimensional vector space. I have mentioned that I was an only child. I had no friends. If you have bundled and divided the genetic fibres I have offered you, you will not be surprised. But I did have, on my father's side, some cousins, and I liked them.

We were to see them the next day, for the funeral of a great-aunt of mine and of theirs. She had died alone in her flat by the river. On my last visit before her death, accompanied by my mother and by Nurse, my great-aunt had been alert in her freezing flat. She was as sane as a horse and my mother behaved normally for at least an hour. Nurse was scandalised by the cold, and told my mother so. My mother replied, 'Cold is so very good for keeping the more highly-strung tropical blooms fresh.' There was a very small posy of flowers at my great-aunt's flat, and it was made out of wire and buttons. It lived in a vase with a blurry view of a castle painted on one side, strangely out of register, as though the transfer had been done by someone trembling badly. Beside this vase lived a photograph of my four cousins and me. This photograph pleased me in two ways, once warmly, for love, and once in a hot mean way. We were richer – in money – than they, and my coat, even in a photograph, was clearly better fitting, better cut, and of better cloth. I would be wearing this coat to the funeral.

Tea over, Nurse bathed me and read a story to me, a story too young for my age in order to foil nightmares. We also conspired to keep me a baby, so my parents needed her and she could hold my own helplessness against her dismissal, when it came.

My parents overcame their fraught lassitude for long enough to give me a goodnight talk on the warping of furniture ferrules in comparative latitudes (my father) and the lost-wax art of a man (am I tidying the past unmercifully?) called Gloss O'Chrysostom (my mother). If he had listened, and she had momentarily emerged from her hypochondriacal trance, they might have found one another quite interesting. As it was, he worked at home, there was not yet a war to take and glorify him, and she simply had too little to do. I, as a child, was not sickened by all that rich leisure, since that is a child's state, to judge its own circumstances the norm. And children have not learnt to measure time. Nevertheless, through observing my parents observe time and its passage (clocks, watches, timers, tolling, chiming, sounding, and the terrible mealtime gong), I was fast losing that innocence.

I said prayers to Nurse, having rescinded to my mother the elaborate pieties she knew I had enunciated to my father. My private prayers were simple, 'God bless me and God bless Nurse and God bless the Morton cousins.' Their Christian names were easier than mine, John, Bobby, Mary and Josephine. Noel Coverley was my name. I have two middle names which I will tell no one. They attest the intimate spitefulness of my father, who has ensured that I recollect his coldness and his pretensions every time I fill in an official form. Thus he has slung my adult self about with the unhappy overdainty child I was. My grandfather had been the brother of their grandmother. It was the sister of these two who had died in the cold flat by the river. Another thing I love about mathematics of the sort I live among is the way that they blunt the points of time's callipers, by stretching them so far apart, into other sorts of time. Families do the opposite, all the relationships marking time so clearly on that short wooden ruler.

She lay in her coffin and the flowers held out in the steady cool for the whole service, which was long, and presided over by Anglican nuns. My parents and Nurse and I (in the coat) were driven in our grey Morris. The cemetery was beyond Chiswick. The cousins and their parents had come in a car they had hired for the day. Our driver sat in our car. Theirs went for a walk and bought a paper and a bag of pears. Nurse, who was a thorough Presbyterian and averse to what she called 'smells and lace', shared the pears with him. She was partial to a little fruit.

It was my first funeral. Several things about it were unbearable yet intensely pleasurable. The only completely awful thing was the thought of a person in a box. The words of the service went to my head, so my tears were delicious. The 23rd psalm seemed to paint a nursery Arcady where a nurse and not a parent was in charge. We would all be good and fear would be cast out. For the duration of the funeral, I ceased fretting. I did not once look at my mother's defiant white cerements, her alarmingly druidical hat.

The mother of the cousins wore a woolly mulberry thing and she gave me a nice smile when the sermon was threatening to break the richly religious mood. Each of my cousins wore a navy blue felt hat. I had almost chewed through the elastic on my own hat. I could feel its petersham ribbons on the back of my neck. I was a skinny boy with blue knees and pale red nostrils. I had the strength of ten. I was always hungry, though I did not eat in front of my parents if I could help it.

We crossed the road that divided the church from the graveyard where my great-aunt was to be buried. I was prepared for this burying to be the most shocking thing I had seen, worse than my father battering on my mother's door, worse even than seeing a dog shot. So I was better off than Mary and Josephine whose faces crumpled as they saw the spadeful of earth land on that box containing a person. Perhaps they had suddenly realised that they might not live for ever. There was a wind, and while there were fewer motor cars in those days, the dirt from the Great West Road was worse. Our eyes filled with grit and our noses with the smell of cinders. John and Bobby did like men; they screwed up their faces so that no tear could possibly find its way out. I, being 'delicate', was expected to cry, and did so with unmixed pleasure.

The only thing which shook me was the presence of another, unknown, child at the funeral. She was standing with two adult people. She made them look ridiculously large. She might have been my sister, she was so thin. She had a smirk behind her becoming tears. Her mother and father looked sleek and almost impolitely well-groomed. The small girl was dressed in a blue velvet cape with white fur like a frosty Eskimo doll. From the blue velvet bag she carried she extracted, still crying with her face, a peppermint disc the size of a florin. I smelt it amid the wool and naphtha. I looked reverent and stared hard at her from under my lowered lids.

It was not only the mint of which I was jealous. Would this child come back to the cousins' house? Would she offer them more highly-flavoured snippets than I let them have from our different way of life? Was she related to me? Or to them, and not to me? I sent up a prayer which mentioned my great-aunt only incidentally. Its main petition was that my cousins did not, or would not, excessively care for this child.

My mother took my hand in her gloved one. The kid felt like the lids of mushrooms. I knew what she was going to say and had a pretty good idea what she was going to do. Piously, for health reasons, against burial, she was about to break a glass capsule of eucalyptus beneath her nose, and blow it loudly. It was only since I had become seven that she had ceased doing the same for me in any exposed place. She then said, 'While we have a moment of peace' (what a moment, our family at prayer in a windswept graveyard) 'my dove, just take heed of your mother when she reminds you simply to rise above the dirt and devastation at the house of your cousins, who are by no means as fortunate as you. Naturally, for reasons of politeness, we cannot fail to attend the proceedings, but I know I can trust you not to have any needs or to give in to any temptations you may encounter.' She meant don't go to the lavatory and don't eat.

One of the two lessons of that day was that death makes me hungry. It is as though food, the staff of life, were a spell against falling into dust.

The burial done, my parents and I joined Nurse. She had the sweetly acid smell of pears on her. Her grouse-claw brooch had already that day achieved much in the way of irking my mother. We all got into the grey car. It slunk through the small streets near the Morton house. The driver could not park in their street; he would have blocked it. We had passed on the way a vehicle as long as a lifeboat and red as a fire engine. Its chauffeur was upholstered in cherry red, with cavalryman's boots. A whip would have been unsurprising. My parents, who until now had exchanged no sentence, only my father's accustomed latent speech and my mother's dammed silence, looked at each other. That in itself was unusual. They spoke together, 'Victor and Stella.' My father continued, my mother no doubt wrung out by the effort of speech. 'And the odious child, a vision in coneyfur. I wonder they did not drown it. Of what possible use is it to them?' My father was in this way approaching one of his favourite topics, the child-rearing customs of the Spartans. He did that turn especially for Nurse, who could not control her outrage, even when she knew she was being riled on purpose. My mother remained silent, thinking no doubt of the struggle awaiting her in the Mortons' house.

Their father I called Uncle Galway. He taught history, cricket and Latin at a nearby school. Aunt Fan taught part time at the school, when she was not busy with her children. Her subjects were botany and maths. She occasionally taught dressmaking, though even the pancloths she knitted were out of shape.

Their house was attached to its neighbour. It gave the impression of being a big cupboard, perhaps because nothing inside it was put away. In the sitting room, the temperament and pastimes of the Mortons were apparent. The room was stuffed with books, rags, wools, jigsaws, a tricycle, a tank of tarnishing but sprightly goldfish, a cat on a heap of mending, jars of poster paint, a shrimping net and some wooden laundry tongs lying on top of a crystal garden in its square battery-jar of waterglass.

Upstairs, I knew, there would be clothes everywhere, in optimistic ironing baskets, over bedheads, stuffed into ottomans. Everywhere were clothbound books, yellow, maroon, tired blue. In the bedrooms there was a good chance of hearing mice; the Mortons were allowed food wherever and whenever they wanted it. They kept apples and sweets in their chests of drawers, where socks might have been in another house. They were a family which shared it secrets.

The sitting room went straight into the kitchen. Today both rooms were occupied by those who had come on after the funeral. Why were my family, with so much larger a house, not entertaining the party? Their sallow social tone might have been suitable to the decorous gloom conventionally required by a funeral. But they had not offered. It seemed better, at the end of a long life, that there should be not my parents' mean, ordered luxury, but what I saw spread out almost indecently in the kitchen, soft cheeses, deep pies, steaming fruit tarts, jugs of custard and of cream. Aunt Fan was dispensing the food with a battery of unsuitable implements, pie with an eggslice, trifle with a silver masonry tool, cheese with a palette knife, cream from an Argyll. It was a bright mess of colour and juice, squashiness and superfluity. Nurse and my mother stiffened, the one as she saw good food in quantity, the other as she perceived the prowling spectre of uncontrol with its attendant bacteria, spillage and decay.

My cousins fell on me, wagging like pups. Each of them held a thick slice of well-buttered black cake, so by the time they had greeted me I was an object of horror to my mother. She took a long look at me, winced, drew herself up, ruffled and settled her shoulders, and bent, in movement like a riverbird, to unbutton and remove my now Mortonfied coat.

Nurse fetched a plate for herself. My unspoken arrangement with the cousins was, as usual, to get myself upstairs unobserved. I think now that their parents colluded in this against my mother. The house's muddle was a considerable help. I now, too, surmise that my mother's desire to be free of me was even stronger than her dedication to germ warfare. And on this occasion it was clear that she could hardly remove her glare from the pair of grown-ups who must be Victor and Stella. They were tall and, separated from their curiously superior child, clothed in blatancy and confidence. My itch for vulgarity responded to those glittering froggings and facings.

But what concerned me was their daughter, now free of her velvet cape and revealed in a white cotton dress smocked in unfunereal red. The collar was embroidered with very small red strawberries, natty *fraises du bois*. The buttonholes down her back were sutured in the same bright red. Her hair was long, thin and white. She had no front teeth, just two gum spaces. This gave her a lisp. Bobby introduced us. She was Coverley too, her grandfather my grandfather's brother. How had my father overlooked, in his passion for overinformation, especially where it touched upon himself, a whole knot of family? My cousins obviously liked this girl. So I hated her.

'Hello,' she said. 'Is that woman your nurse?' I saw Nurse, for an instant, without love. She was piling a large plate high with food, all mixed up. Her skirt was wide as a fender.

'Yes, she is. And where's yours?'

'Left, they always have; can't bear it.' So she was one of those bad children who rushed through nurses and showed off about it.

'What do you do to them?' I asked, not in admiration as she might have hoped, but prissily.

'It's not me, it's my father, and I can't possibly say. I don't know exactly but shall soon enough my mother says. The last one broke his ivory hair brushes and tore up some of his clothes. My mama says it is something I shall learn all too soon. Men have a rolling eye, she says.' All this with the tooth-less lisp. In spite of her chilling self-command, something gave me a hint of fellow feeling.

'Is your mother mad?' I asked. From observing Aunt Fan, I knew that my own mother was not typical.

'Is yours?' asked the child. 'She looks it.'

'Come on, you two.' It was Mary. She stood between me and the other cousin, whose name was apparently Lucy, taking her left hand and my right. Mary was shorter and sturdier than we were. Nurse came over and blocked our way to the stairs. She did not mean to; she was just that fat. I looked up and saw she had two plates, spilling with good things, leaking over the edge. I read the names of the china in her shiny hands, 'Spod' and 'Crown Derb'. Her fingers covered any remaining letters. Each of the plates had been broken, at least once. Now they were riveted, and should not have been used for food. Where the cracks were, a deep purple was beginning to appear, the juice of black fruits.

Nurse was a small eater, but she heaped her plate at the Mortons' house.

'Just go and fetch a cup of black tea, dear,' she told me. She was not smiling.

'And would you,' she spoke to Lucy, 'get a slice of lightly buttered bread?'

Equipped with this thin meal, we returned to Nurse. She wore her bowler-style hat indoors. She peered out from under it. The coast was clear.

She filled the narrow stairway as she led us up its druggeted steepness to the bedroom where our cousins had made a table of Josephine's bed.

'Pass me the tea, dear,' she said. 'And before either of

you' – she spoke to me and to Lucy – 'starts on your meal, it's bread and butter. Sit down.'

We sat at opposite sides of the child's bed and she placed in front of each of us a gleaming incoherent feast on broken china. She looked at Lucy, who appeared less menacing up here. She smiled at her and the little girl smiled back, showing side teeth like buds.

Taking a white cloth from the holdall whose cane hoops lived at her elbow, Nurse said to Lucy, 'Lift up your hair, love, and Nurse will tie this round your neck. You don't want fruit juice on those smart strawberries. Eat the bread and butter, the both of you, then you can say you had bread and butter when you're asked. Church, Lucy. Chapel, Noel.'

I explained to Lucy what it was that Nurse meant. All those nurses, and she didn't know a single thing. Eating opposite me and bibbed up in the white cloth, Lucy became at once an ordinary little girl, hungry, skinny, released for an afternoon from the obligation to be odd. By the time we had finished our tea on the bed her untoothed gums were purple and I loved her.

Already equipped with the deviousness and instinct to flirt of a grown woman, she had been dissembling ignorance, she told me years later, when she pretended not to know what Nurse meant by 'Church and Chapel'. 'I was putting you at your ease,' she said. By then we were smokers, and, as I held up a light for her, we looked through the pale flame to the bright red burning tip of the cigarette, bright in the dark like a wild strawberry on dark moss.

Nick Danziger

An Essay
on the border

The US – Mexican frontier at Tijuana

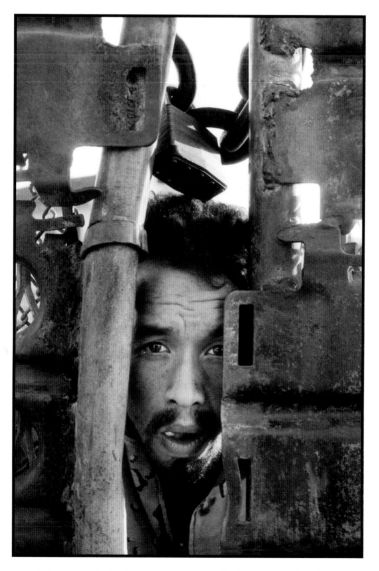

A Mexican on the border fence separating Mexico from the American Dream.

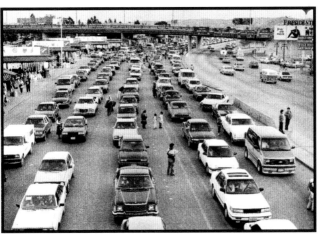

Over 50 million people are checked across the US-Mexico border at Tijuana each year.

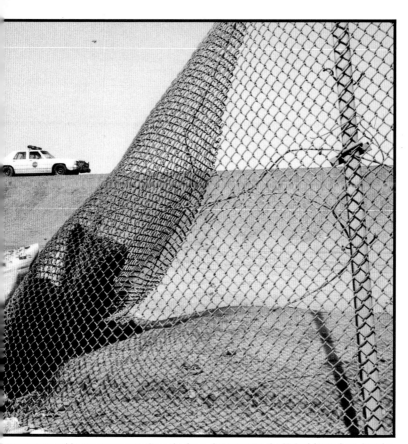

Between two worlds: two young men sit on the fence that separates the United States from America

Piggy banks for sale in Tijuana.

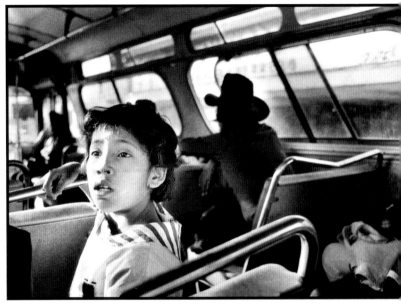

A young boy dreaming of El Dorado.

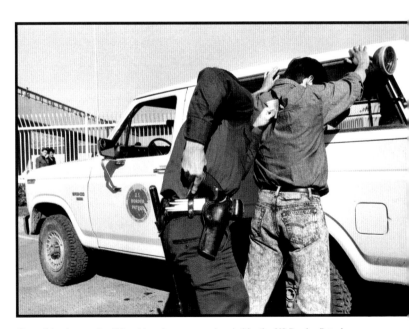

One of the thousands of illegal immigrants apprehended by the US Border Patrol.

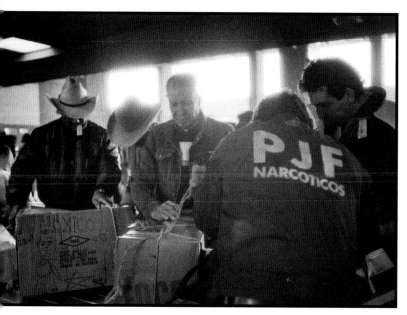

Nothing can stop the tidal wave of undocumented migrants.

First world meets Third World as American youngsters pass local beggars on their way into the US immigration hall.

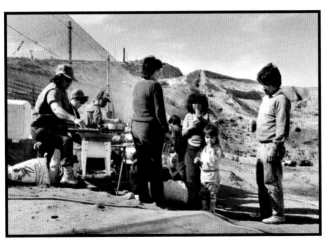

On the US side of the border Mexican hot dog stands sell tamales and tacos to would-be migrants

On one hill just on the US side of the border dozens of undocumented migrants wait for nightfall

One empty-handed couple with only the clothes they wear are among tens of thousands of Mexicans congregate along the border.

Every day a new hill is colonised and makeshift houses built.

In one evening s
from three to el
p.m. the Border
Patrol apprehen
1,300 illegal
immigrants in th
San Diego sector

Nick Danziger trained at Chelsea School of Art, but his passion for travel, which took hold at the a
thirteen, has seen him move into the fields of photography, journalism, writing and television. His
BBC *Video Diary War Lies and Videotape*, a graphic account of the plight of orphans confined in a m
asylum in war-torn Afghanistan - which featured the work of the International Red Cross hospital in
- won the prestigious Prix Italia for Best Television Documentary. Nick is currently Fellow of Photog
at Bradford's National Museum of Photography, Film and Television and is writing a book and p
together a photographic exhibition about Britain and its changing cultural landscape. He is author o
bestselling travel books, *Danziger's Travels* and *Danziger's Adventures*.

Ted Hughes

the freedom fighter

Ted Hughes was born in 1930. He is the author of numerous collections of poetry and books for children. In 1984 he was appointed Poet Laureate.

Holiday squeals, as if all were scrambling for their lives,
Panting aboard the 'Cornish Riviera'.
Then overflow of relief and luggage and children,
Then ducking to smile out as the station moves.

Out there on the platform, under the rain,
Under his rain-cape, helmet and full pack,
Somebody, still bowed over something,
Doesn't know he's missing his train.

He's completely buried in that book.
He's forgotten utterly where he is.
He's forgotten Paddington, forgotten
Timetables, forgotten the long rocking

Cradle of a journey into the golden West,
The coach's soft wingbeat – as light
And straight as a dove's flight.
Like a graveyard statue sentry cast

In blackened old bronze. He's reading a letter –
Or is it the burial service? The raindrops
Beaded along his helmet rim are bronze.
The words on his page are bronze. Their meanings bronze.

In his black bronze world he stands, enchanted.
His bronze mind is deep among the dead.
Sunk so deep among the dead that, much
As he would like to think of us all, he cannot.

Just beside 'Lost Property', I notice.

Eric Ambler

exquisitely
gowned

Eric Ambler was born in London in 1909 and now, after many years in Hollywood and Switzerland, lives in London again.

Eric Ambler's first novel, The Dark Frontier, *published in the UK in 1936, was not published in America until 1989. For the belated American edition he was asked to write an introduction. Here it is.*

The ageing thriller writer who makes prefatorial apologies for the shortcomings of his early work also makes a fool of himself. The fact that, although once young and inexperienced, he has learned much about his craft over the years is of no interest to new readers. They are looking for entertainment, not excuses.

They may, however, be entitled to explanations, especially of what may appear to be gross anachronisms. *The Dark Frontier* was my first published novel and I wrote it in 1935. What, it may be asked fifty years later, was I doing in those far-off early thirties, using the term 'atomic bomb' so familiarly and describing the effects of an atomic explosion as if the hideous thing already existed?

I lay no claim to special prescience. Having had a scientific education and through it gained access to academic journals, I had read about the early work of Rutherford, Cockcroft and Chadwick in the field, and understood some of its implications. How superficial that understanding was will be apparent now to any 'A' level student. The atomic bomb that I deduced was the work of a small team directed by one exceptional man of talent with a chip on his shoulder and grudges to bear. The difficulties of producing substances like enriched uranium, and the enormous resources, economic and industrial, that would be needed to overcome them, were factors I was able to ignore because I was only dimly aware of their existence.

My estimate of the critical mass likely to bring the bombmaker to the threshold of a fission chain reaction was more cagily vague. 'A little larger than a Mills grenade' was my 1935 guess and I allowed its explosive force to shift a thousand tons of rock. In 1935 I knew theoretically, that E probably equalled Mc^2, but could not quite accept the numerically awesome consequences of the equation. I mean, c^2 was such a huge and weird multiplier. And in some ways I was handicapped by my own experience of explosives. I knew what it felt like to throw a Mills grenade thirty yards and the way the burst clouted your ears if you threw short or were slow getting your head down. I knew because while a college student I had been in the Territorial Army. Multiplying the violence of an infantry weapon out of all proportion to its size and normal destructive power seemed a dramatically acceptable device. With TNT I felt that I was on even surer ground. One evening in January 1917, when I was nearly eight and living in London not far from Greenwich, there had been an accident at a munitions plant two miles away across the river. They were processing TNT there; something went wrong and over fifty tons of the stuff blew up. Not even on the Western Front had there been

such an explosion. It killed and wounded hundreds and flattened an entire factory area. The blast wave hit our street with
great force and broke a lot of windows. I remembered the feel
and sound of it. The idea of using a kiloton of TNT as a measure of explosive violence, even for a fictional nightmare
bomb, seemed far-fetched and possibly absurd. In the welter
of impulses, literary, political and commercial, that drove me
to start writing *The Dark Frontier*, the wish to parody was, at
first, central. I intended to make fun of the old secret service
adventure thriller written by E. Phillips Oppenheim, John
Buchan, Dornford Yates and their cruder imitators; and I
meant to do it by placing some of their antique fantasies in
the context of a contemporary reality. For plot purposes, the
reality I thought I needed was one of those unexpected
threats to world peace, one of those dark conspiracies of evil
men, that will succeed unless our hero can brave all dangers
and arrive in the nick of time to foil the wicked in their devil-
ish moment of near triumph. The development of an atomic
bomb in a small Balkan state ruled by a corrupt Fascist-style
oligarchy was likely, I thought, to yield an interesting crop of
villains. The real, though maybe not immediately present,
danger of the atomic bomb was surely a convincing threat to
world peace. After all, it had convinced me. But this was
parody. Were there not unities to be observed? Don Quixote
should not be expected to tilt at windmills defended by
machine guns. I should have threatened the world with something more obviously far-fetched – a secret army of robots, say,
or a polar submarine base sited over a volcanic thermal
spring. Or, if I were going to fool with matters that should be

taken seriously, perhaps I should think again and discard the idea of parody. But I was halfway through the book by then and reluctant to admit to myself the size of the mistake I was making. Besides, I felt committed to my folly. For the young, for new writers, parody can seem like a safety precaution, a form of insurance against adverse criticism.

It brings with it other handicaps and illusions. The matter of size and scale must be understood. Max Beerbohm, perhaps the century's master parodist, was always brief. With Max's help Henry James, G.K. Chesterton and Rudyard Kipling are each brought to judgement and petrified, temporarily at least, in a few short pages. Max's four acts of 'Savonarola' Brown's great poetic tragedy may be read aloud with stage directions, and to hilarious effect if well read, in less than thirty minutes. But Max was wise not to find the missing fifth act himself. The joke is over at the end of the fourth. Satire can be sustained by a single comedic idea and the wit to pursue it. Parody requires an established root system of critical insight and the constant nourishment of humour. Max could not have written *The Battle of the Books* and Jonathan Swift could not have trifled so engagingly with Joseph Conrad's heart of darkness. Parody can be the expression of literary dandyism.

Why then, it may be asked, if I were so alive to the difficulties of parody, especially those of sustaining it at length, did I take the risk? It is a fair question, so I will skip the nonsense about youth being a time for risk-taking, rule-breaking and experiment. Instead, I will try to give what I believe to be the answer.

When the English novelist Mary Webb died in 1927 not much notice was taken of the event. Her five or six novels, though of the earthy primitive, regional romantic school then in vogue, had not been popular. The circulating library public, while not averse to purple prose, tended to prefer the less fervid tone of others working in the genre, of healthier ladies like Sheila Kaye-Smith. The *Oxford Companion's* summing up of Webb as 'passionate, morbid and frequently naïve' still holds good. Perhaps she had been too close to the rustic quiddities and bucolic squalor about which she wrote. She was a country schoolteacher who married another teacher, worked in the country as a market gardener and died wretchedly, after a long struggle with exophthalmic goitre, at the age of forty-five. A year later she was made famous and two of her novels, *Precious Bane* and *Gone to Earth*, hastily retrieved from oblivion, had become bestsellers. It could have happened only in England, but even there it was remarkable. British politicians have often declared their love of literature and even quoted the Latin poets in their speeches, but few have been prepared to praise the work of a particular novelist. One sees the difficulty, of course; the kind of fiction a politician enjoys, or pretends to enjoy, will tell the voters more about the man's true disposition than may be good for his political health. Prime Minister Disraeli, himself a novelist, had a short, impudent answer for those who sought to probe his literary taste buds – 'When I want to read a novel I write one.' In 1928 Prime Minister Stanley Baldwin, the trusty pipe-smoking, true blue Tory statesman who had seen England safely through the General Strike and whose safe hands were later to accept the abdication of King Edward VIII, threw caution to the winds. He praised a novelist publicly. True, she was a woman and dead; there would be no political mileage in it for anyone except her publishers; but the event was still extraordinary. The occasion Baldwin chose for the delivery of his eulogy was the annual dinner of the Royal Literary Fund, an old and honourable charity. He praised her lyrical intensity and evocation of the Shropshire landscape. The speech was widely reported in the better newspapers and the Mary Webb bandwagon began to roll. Mr Baldwin gave it a final shove by writing an introduction for a new edition of *Precious Bane* and the other novels soon began to appear in a collected edition. As Britain sank deeper into the Great Depression, Mary Webb's purple prose, 'blending human passion with the fields and skies', according to Baldwin, penetrated the circulating libraries and lingered about the shelves like the after-smell of a cheap air freshener. This was true artistry. Mr Baldwin had said so.

At the time my literary tastes were those of any other guilt-ridden young man who had rejected all orthodox religious texts in favour of the teachings of C.G. Jung, G.I. Gurdjieff and Oswald Spengler. The novels of Dostoevsky and the plays of Ibsen were my bedside books. I wallowed in the nether worlds of George Gissing and Knut Hamsun and mooned with George Moore over the fate of *Esther Waters*. For me in those days misery and madness were the stuff of dreams, even when the dreamer was as troubled as Strindberg or as haunted as Kafka. Why, then, did I find *Precious Bane* so insufferable?

Mainly, I think, because of its pretentious breast-beating.

All that blending of human passion with the fields and skies that Mr Baldwin so admired was for me no more than an untimely and artless revival of the Victorian poets' pathetic fallacy by an author writing beyond her means. The incidence of psychoneuroses and violent crime among Shropshire yokels may have been exceptional at the time, but the attempt to render it as high tragedy was a mistake. Mrs Webb's adolescent insights stimulated by overdoses of schoolroom Wordsworth could produce nothing more tragic than high-sounding gush. I hated it, and in doing so failed to appreciate the rich splendour of its absurdity.

Cold Comfort Farm was published in 1932 and was an immediate success. The author, Stella Gibbons, was thirty at the time, and although she had published a book of poetry and worked as a magazine journalist, this was her first novel. As parody it was and remains unique. Who could resist her brisk way of explaining primal scene trauma as 'saw something nasty in the wood shed' or the aura of dignity with which she invested Big Business, the bull, and the herd of wayward cows he served so faithfully? Their very names – Graceless, Pointless, Feckless, Aimless – brought a gust of fresh air to the milking shed. *Cold Comfort Farm* followed the narrative pattern of the genre it was to destroy by describing in rather too much detail the history of a family. Mary Webb's hare-lipped heroine had been Prudence Sarn. The Cold Comfort family are Seth, Elfine and Aunt Ada Doom. But the book has long ceased to depend on its elements of parody. In 1933 France took the unusual step of awarding Stella Gibbons, an Englishwoman, the important Fémina Vie Heureuse Prize for literature. *Cold Comfort Farm* is a wittily conceived and beautifully written comic novel. The French were recognising it as a work of art.

Stella Gibbons seems never to have quite recovered from this early success. None of the good novels she wrote later was nearly as good as the first, and her only sequels to it were short stories. She had always thought of herself as a poet, and more interested in the nature of God than in human beings. Well, it must be an eerie moment when one finds oneself in one's eighties and still the only novel-length parodist to be published in the twentieth century. Mine cannot have been the only prentice hand to have been tempted by the brilliance of her achievement.

A revised edition, then, presents the failed parodist with a chance to tidy up. What came out of the defective parody was a thriller with a difference. True, it invited some suspension of disbelief, but it did not expect the reader to swallow nonsense or to tolerate really bad writing. However, one of the hidden dangers of parody is that one may find oneself actually enjoying the process of writing 'in the manner of' some excruciatingly awful stylists. I recall, in particular, E. Phillips Oppenheim. The Prince of Storytellers his publishers used to call him. He made a fortune which ran to a yacht on the French Riviera. Some of his novels had such good stories to tell that for his teenage readers, of whom I was one, the rococo style seemed part of the entertainment. I was a teenage smoker too. These bad juvenile habits catch up with the sinner later in life. Thirty years or more after *The Dark Frontier* was published, a respected and, at that time, greatly feared critic named Clive James made my work the subject of an essay in a literary magazine. He had his reputation as a killer to sustain, of course, but I escaped with only a few bruises and one bad cut. The cut was deep. In his piece he used a sentence from my first novel to demonstrate that I had improved slightly as a writer over the years. The middle-aged Ambler, he assures us with a smirk, would never think of describing a well-dressed woman as 'exquisitely gowned'. The young Ambler hadn't even hesitated.

I was appalled. How was I to explain that it had been the young Ambler parodying the euphuistic Oppenheim who was to blame? He was supposed to be a critic. Why hadn't he seen that the phrase 'exquisitely gowned' was pure Oppenheim? It ought not to have been there, of course. The fault was mine. Back in those days young authors, and old, were expected, rightly in my opinion, to be their own editors. There were house styles in punctuation and in euphemism for the coarse or blasphemous – 'beggar' for 'bugger', 'crikey' for 'Christ' and so on – which one accepted uncomplainingly because one was told that irritating or giving offence to book-buying librarians and strait-laced readers was not the best way to sell books. In those days readers were more touchy and often wrote pedantic letters of complaint to publishing houses or, worse, to the big book wholesalers who could refuse to stock a book and distribute it. They had copy-editors who read books in proof for them. That was to protect themselves against the absurd libel laws of England, as well as to report on dirty words. None of them would have bothered with 'exquisitely gowned'. That was left to me, and I had missed it. I worked on those revisions at night. I must have nodded.

Well, the blot has gone at last. However, there are, I find, limits to what may legitimately be done by way of revision. For instance, quite early in the story our amnesiac hero finds himself in Paris and committed to a dangerous Balkan adventure. Feeling that he may be called upon to defend himself, he goes into a gunsmith's in the boulevard St Michel and buys a Browning automatic and ammunition for it.

When I first reread this I laughed aloud. A gunsmith in the old Boule' Miche'? I ask you. As every old Paris hand will recall, the lower end runs through the heart of the Latin Quarter and along one side of the Sorbonne. In the early thirties it was the cheap and noisy section of an *arrondissement* which included the Luxembourg Gardens, the boulevard St Germain, much of the University of Paris and most of the attractions of what was then understood by the phrase Left Bank. The river end of the Boule' Miche', however, had big, impersonal cafés and their patrons did not include Sartre and Picasso. Their customers were mostly office workers who lived in the suburbs and students, students of all ages and levels of poverty. The goods in the stores were shoddy and those who sold them spry. There was a ready-to-wear men's tailor who exploited the fad for jackets without lapels – '*très chic, très sport, presque cad.*' *Prix CHOC 280ff.* – and a milliner who pirated scarf designs from the Right Bank couturiers and sold reproductions printed on art silk with dyes that ran. In the narrow side streets there were dismal apartment buildings, *prix-fixe* restaurants and small hotels where, on at least one floor, bedrooms were available by the hour. It was a quarter in which one might find a place to pawn a revolver but would not expect to buy one.

In my time as a writer I have committed a few solecisms and made some silly mistakes, but I have not, on the whole, been careless. When unsure of facts and unable to verify guesses, I have gone warily. I was especially careful with what used to be called 'local colour'. I could not really believe that I would have placed a gunsmith in the boulevard St Michel unless I had known for certain that there was one there. Memory had to be assisted. I thought myself back into one of those small hotels behind the Sorbonne – in the rue Victor Cousin, since we are recalling the irrelevant – where one could live so cheaply when the French franc was eighty to the pound sterling. How did one get there? One walked from the métro station, Luxembourg. Ah, yes. That was it.

In the early thirties it became a habit with me to go as often as I could to France. I had to travel cheaply: never first class and second only when there was no third available. This was usually on international trains or on fast night services between cities. My fellow travellers on these second-class journeys were mostly French of the middle bourgeoisie of small business, travelling salesmen and the like. Unaccompanied women would most likely have sleeping car reservations. The characters I studied most attentively were the travelling salesmen. I knew something of the ways of their English counterparts, and the mere fact of one of these prosperous knights of the road denying himself the comfort of a *couchette* in a sleeping car meant to me that he was almost certainly fiddling his expense account. Of course, those were the golden days before credit card billing made false expenses less easy to claim.

Preparations for dozing the night away tended to have a ritual quality. First, there would be the stroll along the corridor to check that the sample cases were safe in the baggage racks, then a visit to the WC. Outside in the corridor again a cigarette would be smoked. Back in the compartment there would be the loosening of the collar stud, the unlacing, or unbuttoning, of ankle boots and, finally, the application of scent. This was eau-de-Cologne or a similar lavender water, and it was sprinkled liberally on a handkerchief which was then used to wipe the face and hands. The whole compartment benefited, of course. Ventilation was poor and we were a smelly lot in those days. Middle-class townsmen might change their underwear twice a week if they were single or if they had married money, but for most once a week was customary. A daily change was for the rich or the depraved. A sprinkling of cologne was evidence of a respectable upbringing, as was the possession of a clean white handkerchief. For those allergic to lavender, the alternative defence against the smells of confined humanity was tobacco, and there were always plenty of compartments for smokers on the trains. Nights spent in them, however, invariably seemed much longer. In the small hours there would be noisy disputes about window-opening and *courants d'air*. The *non-fumeurs* were more restful.

And probably still are. The intention behind this thick slice of European social history was not to encourage non-smokers or to sell deodorants but to explain how I came to know that in France in those days a great many travelling men used to carry guns. They carried them in their overnight bags along with the bottle of cologne, the flask of rum or brandy and yesterday's newspaper. The bag was of the satchel, briefcase type – the French called it a *serviette* – and when it was open, the contents were clearly visible. Not that there was ever any attempt at concealing them. The first time I saw one of these guns was when its owner put it on the seat beside him while he rummaged in the bag for a box of toothpicks. It was a .25 single-action revolver, made in Belgium and, I found later, popular because cheap.

How cheap I never discovered. The French friends whose views I sought thought strongly about guns. The husband said that in town only jewellers needed guns. The wife said that women of a certain age should have pistols to protect their honour or to take their revenge on faithless men. I asked if it were true about *crimes passionelles* going unpunished in France. 'The little guns women keep in their purses never do much harm,' she said with a shrug. 'If the man is unlucky the law is reasonable.'

But that was in the towns. What about the country? Ah, said the man, there one needed a heavier weapon. Every peasant and all his kids had shotguns and would mistake a man for a rabbit if given half a chance. In the Dordogne and parts of Provence it was still bandit country, as bad as Corsica. Here in France those at greatest risk were the *automobilistes*. In bandit country the possession of a private car was sufficient evidence of personal wealth, and highway robbery was all too easy. All drivers with any sense went armed. When driving, he kept his gun, an excellent Czech automatic, wrapped in grease-proof paper, in the door cavity pocket on the driver's side. At other times he kept it locked in the toolbox with the spare inner tube and first aid kit. It was no trouble; border police and customs men expected drivers to be armed; the *gendarmerie* in some parts of the country counted on it.

I could not quite believe all this, I did not want to believe it. That French travelling salesmen should find it necessary to carry guns I was prepared to accept. French thieves went armed – *Paris Soir* said so – and it wasn't only jewellers who carried valuable samples. In the movies nervous householders kept revolvers in the drawers of bedside tables. Perhaps some French householders did so too. But in car-door pockets? Surely not. Door pockets were for maps and driving gauntlets and slim boxes of Balkan Sobranie cigarettes.

The girl with whom I had been sharing a bed had left me and gone off with rich Greek friends to Cannes. The following day I had to go back to London and my job in advertising. The idea of moping in a café did not appeal to me so I went in search of a puppet theatre I had heard about. It was in the Luxembourg Gardens. That was how I came to know that there was a gunsmith's in the boulevard St Michel. It was at the upper end near the Luxembourg, away from the Latin Quarter I now loathed, and was located in the ground-floor arcade of an office block. The display window was *très sport* – shotguns in blued steel and walnut, decoy birds and suede ammunition waistcoats – but in the showcases at the back of the store there were plenty of handguns.

I had decided to put the whole subject out of my mind; but

on the cross-Channel steamer from Dieppe to Newhaven I got talking to a Frenchman in the bar. He was going to London for the first time and asked the barman how to get from Victoria to Belsize Park. The barman, a Brighton man, did not know for sure. I did. The Frenchman was going to work in an Oxford Street language school for six months to see if he liked the work. My guess was that he would not, but instead of saying so I asked if he drove a car. He did; at home he drove his father's. When he drove did he carry a revolver?

The gun, he explained somewhat sheepishly, was his father's. Old-fashioned men, men of a certain age, liked to carry a gun when they were driving.

This was Freudian country. I preferred to read Jung. Again I put the subject out of my mind, until, a couple of years later, I needed an approximate location for a gunsmith in Paris. I see no reason to revise it. Nowadays, I read neither Freud nor Jung.

I rest my case. However, for the ill-natured who like to poke at old scar tissue to see if wounds have really healed, the sentence, 'She was exquisitely gowned,' was part of a descriptive paragraph placed just before the electric power failure in the Zovgorod Opera House – the very page before.

Maeve Binchy

liberty green

Maeve Binchy was born in Co Dublin and went to school at the Holy Child Convent in Killiney. She took a history degree at UCD and taught in various girls' schools, writing travel articles in the long summer holidays. In 1969 she joined the *Irish Times*. For some ten years she was based in London writing humorous columns from all over the world; today, she divides her time between London and Co Dublin, where she also has a home.

The Peacock Theatre in Dublin was the scene of her two stage plays, *End of Term* and *Half Promised Land*; her television play, *Deeply Regretted By* won two Jacobs Awards and the Best Script prize at the Prague Film Festival.

She is the author of several volumes of short stories: among them *London Transports* and *Dublin 4; The Lilac Bus*, which has been filmed for television and *Silver Wedding*. Her novels include *Light a Penny Candle, Echoes* (the TV film of which has been shown throughout the world), *Firefly Summer, Circle of Friends*, now being filmed in Co Kilkenny, and *The Copper Beech*. Her latest novel, *The Glass Lake*, was published in September 1994 in the UK, and is due in the Spring of '95 in the United States.

She is married to the writer and broadcaster Gordon Snell.

Everyone assumed that Libby Green had been born and christened Elizabeth. What else could Libby be short for? And when she was growing up everyone read the Crawfie diaries, about the little princesses who were called Lillibet and Margaret Rose. Princess Margaret had not been able to pronounce her elder sister's name. It was very endearing, and people thought it must be the same with Libby. Couldn't get her tongue around a big word like Elizabeth. Wasn't it sweet.

After a while Libby never bothered trying to explain. It was too complicated to say that she had been called Liberty. It sounded like the name of a shop, or one of those funny little bodices you wore to keep your chest warm and flatten it at the same time. Or the Liberty Bell in Philadelphia. All in all it was much easier to say it was short for Elizabeth.

And it was not a matter of being unfaithful to her parents' dreams for her; they talked about little else but freedom and liberty in their house when Libby was growing up. The American Declaration of Independence was framed in the dining room, the words of the French national anthem had been stuck on a piece of cardboard on the back of Libby's door as long as she could remember. All over the house the walls were hung with Paine's Declaration of the Rights of Man and an extract from the Magna Carta.

In other families during the war children remembered talking about the Blitz, the blackout, the Morrison shelters, digging for victory and careless talk costing lives. In Libby's house they talked about equality and freedom and the Spanish Civil War, and the conscientious objector.

One of her grannies said that the most important thing in the world was having an aired vest and never sleeping in a damp bed. The other granny said that having clean socks and being regular were life's two priorities. Libby knew that this couldn't be right, because Mother and Father thought it was all to do with meetings and posters and standing up for people's rights.

There were always refugees staying during the war, and even after it. People were coming from different lands where they weren't free. Libby knew that this must be the most important thing. Specially since the bathroom was always full of non-free people, and sometimes she had to share her bedroom with girls or women who came from far away places where things weren't run properly.

Libby was very bright and hard-working. Miss Jenkins told Mother and Father that she would certainly get a place at the grammar school. They were pleased for her but worried because it was rather far away; it would mean two bus trips each way each day.

'Lots of people do that,' Libby said, afraid that she might be going to lose an education because they were afraid to let her take two buses.

'It is her key to a whole new world,' Miss Jenkins said, astounded that so many parents raised objections when their children were offered the chance of a lifetime. There was always something, like the cost of school uniform or the fear of their moving into a different class system. She was surprised at the Greens, they were usually such forward-looking people. How strange that they should feel so mother-hennish about letting their daughter travel what was not a great distance. Surely they, of all people, would realise the freedom that a child would get from a good education. And they should be able to give a bright twelve-year-old the freedom to take a bus, for heaven's sake.

But then Miss Jenkins didn't know what Libby's life was like at home and, out of loyalty to Mother and Father, Libby didn't tell her.

It would be hard to explain that she didn't go out to her friends' houses after school because Mother and Father were so uneasy until she got back. It was often simpler to stay home. She could invite people in, but then it always seemed odd that she couldn't accept their hospitality so she didn't encourage friendship; it gave her more time to study, of course, but it was all a bit lonely. Not so much fun getting high marks if you didn't have a great friend to giggle with in between, and to rejoice or sympathise with over all the adventures of the world.

But when she got to grammar school it was different, and Libby met another marvellous teacher, as nice as Miss Jenkins this time; it was a Mrs Wilson. She watched out for Libby, ensured that she became part of the debating team, that she was allowed to go to sports events.

'What do they think will happen to you?' Mrs Wilson

snapped once in exasperation. 'It's 1950, for heaven's sake; you are fifteen.'

Libby hung her head.

'It's their way of showing me how fond of me they are, I think,' she said in a low voice.

'The greatest way to show people how fond you are of them is to give them some freedom,' said Mrs Wilson.

Libby said nothing; the teacher was immediately ashamed.

'Don't mind me; maybe I'm jealous, no one cared enough for me to watch out on the road until I came home,' she said.

But Libby knew that wasn't true: Mrs Wilson thought her parents were jailers, and foolishly repressive. At times Libby thought that too, but she hated other people thinking that about them. They were her parents, she could see how much they loved her, and worried about her. She knew all the things they did for her. How her father painted her grazed knee with iodine, how her mother brought her cocoa in bed, how they listened when she told them tales about school. How her father worked long hours as a clerk in a solicitor's office, how her mother took in typing and book-keeping work to help with the expenses. And she, Libby, caused a lot of the expenses; shoes were always wearing out, and there were school trips to places, and pocket money. She was as protective of them as they were of her, and she loved them.

There was a half-term camp. All the other sixteen-year-olds were going; but Libby's parents said no, truly, they couldn't spend a whole weekend wondering was she all right, had she fallen into a swirling river, had one of the rough boys forced himself on her, had their bus driver got drunk, had their teachers been careless.

Libby gave in, without very much of a struggle, and that night as she was looking sadly out of the garden shed towards the west where the others had all gone, singing on their bus tour, only a few tears of self-pity came down her face. As she wiped them away she saw a struggling pigeon trying unsuccessfully to launch itself. It had a broken wing, and its round eyes looked anxious, its cooing sound had no confidence. Libby put it in her cardigan and took it indoors. She watched the scene almost as if she were outside. The three of them calmed the pigeon and put it in a box of shavings. Her father made a delicate splint for the wing and her mother helped him so that she supported the broken wing. They got bread and milk for the bird, and a few cornflakes. They put a lid on the box and cut holes in it. Its muffled rhythmic cooing sounded much less agitated, Libby thought, and she saw her mother reach for her purse.

'Go and get it some bird-seed Libby, we know it would like that.'

How could you not love people so good and generous as this just because they wouldn't let you go on the school outing?

For days she stroked the pigeon's head and admired its feathers. She had never really looked at a pigeon close up before. A wonderful white line on the bend of each wing, a bill that was nearly orange; its big chest, which trembled less as the days went on, was purple brown with underparts of creamy grey.

'Lovely little Columba,' she said to it over and over.

'Why do you call it that?' her father wanted to know.

'It's Latin for a dove or a pigeon too . . . I think,' she said.

He looked at her with undisguised admiration. 'To think a daughter of mine would know the Latin for things,' he said, delighted. 'But it's nearly time to let Columba go, I'd say.'

'Go?' Libby didn't believe it. This murmuring, cooing bird had got her over the disappointment of half term, it had brought her back to school without any hard feelings about the parents who had deprived her of a great trip. And now they were going to send it away.

'You can't talk about freedom, Libby, and then not let a wild animal fly away free,' her father said.

'There's no use in preaching one thing and practising another,' said her mother.

They went out to the little back garden and stood near the shed where they had found Columba and watched the bird soar away.

As she looked up into the sky Libby felt that she grew up. She joined the people who understood things rather than those who just learned things and accepted them.

She knew that her parents would never let her go free because they had no idea she was a prisoner. She watched them shading their eyes in the evening sun and looking on, delighted that their work had restored a bird to the wild.

Just as they had been happy to look after displaced Europeans immediately after the war; as they had brought tea to old tramps under bridges when neighbours said that the tramps should be taken into care, washed and tidied and

minded for their own good; and as her parents had been
unpopular with a lot of people for opposing fox hunting; and
had written letters to the Royal Family about shooting-parties
on their estates, and to film stars about fur coats. Libby's parents had looked happy when they had come back, cold and
tired, from their protest marches with their banners, from
their committee meetings, from their fund-raising for causes.
All of these had been good things. They were just blind to her
need to be free.

So in that moment of growing up, Libby decided she would
look after her own freedom. She linked arms with them back
to the house.

'I wonder what Columba will have for his tea?' she said
cheerfully. 'Nobody to hand a plate of bird-seed tonight.'

They looked pleased, as if they had feared she would make
more fuss.

'Come on, I'll make your tea for you anyway, I'll do beans
on toast,' said Libby. '*And* I'll cut off the crusts.'

'Nobody had such a good daughter,' her mother said,
squeezing Libby's arm.

Libby felt a pang of guilt. Her mother did not know that
she had grown up about twenty seconds ago and that nothing
would ever be the same again.

At school, she changed. She joined the others after class, she
got to know them, to talk to them. She came home on a later
bus. She steeled herself to walk in cheerfully and face the
reproach and anguish and concern. She was always calm and
regretful that they felt such anxiety on her behalf, but this new
adult Libby never suggested altering her behaviour. She was so

non-confrontational, so willing and eager to help and be part of the family when she was at home that she eventually broke down a great deal of their resistance. She arranged that she apply for University places far far from home, and lived her life on campus, writing a long newsy letter once a week, and making three-minute phone calls and coming home every vacation for a while. Sometimes she invited friends home to stay.

In her last year at University she brought Martin to meet them. 'Is he the one?' her mother asked her.

'I very much hope so,' Libby said.

'You won't do anything . . . I mean you will be very . . .'

'Oh, I won't and I will,' Libby laughed, as she helped her mother dry the dishes. Martin was politely talking to her father about his garden shed.

'But what I mean is you're not . . .?' her mother couldn't finish the question.

'The answer is yes.' Libby tortured her mother for a moment. 'Yes, I am most certainly thinking of marrying him.'

Her mother was both relieved and startled at the same time. She seemed glad that Libby wasn't saying yes to an open sexual relationship, but amazed that her child was about to marry and start a home of her own.

'Well, you have always been free to make your own decisions,' Libby's mother said, sincerely believing this to be true. She hugged her daughter and wished her all the happiness in the world.

Libby and Martin got jobs in nearby schools in London, and a small flat with a garden. Martin came from a big family: he

Born in 1952, Tim Fargher studied at St Martin's School of Art. He has exhibited regularly in London, and in Suffolk where he lives with his wife Elizabeth and their four children. He has worked extensively abroad, most notably to commission in the Sultanate of Oman, as well as in Italy and most recently in Portugal, and the Isle of Jura, Scotland.

Tim Fargher's range of work includes portraiture, landscape, and allegorical figure paintings. He has exhibited etchings and photographs. In the last two years he has taken up sculpture, mainly using the lost-wax process of casting figures in bronze. Those relating to themes of Opera were exhibited at Glyndebourne, and at the Portland Gallery, in 1994.

His work is significantly represented in private collections in the United States, Hong Kong, Italy, Germany, Switzerland, Oman, and in the UK. Corporate collections include Prudential Assurance, Ransome's Dock Ltd, and Bartle Bogle Hegarty.

had three brothers and two sisters. Nobody ever had any privacy, any time to themselves.

From the start their married life was happy. They didn't crowd each other out. Libby, so glad not to be questioned about what took her so long on the way home from work, fell into the habit of calling in on the library and bookshops. Martin stayed on and played football with the boys; sometimes he had a pint with the sports master. They shopped together on Saturdays, and took a bag of washing to the launderette. They did twenty minutes serious house-cleaning every morning and kept their place looking fine. They often asked each other why people made such heavy weather out of being married and running a home.

Every second Sunday they visited each other's families.

Libby's parents still had causes, petitions and crusades. Martin's parents still lived a crowded communal lifestyle.

'No babies for us to play with on a Sunday?' Martin's mother would say, disappointed, looking at Libby's flat stomach every fortnight as if it might have swelled since the last visit.

'It's your decision, fertility is a matter for people themselves, but will we ever be grandparents?' Libby's mother would enquire.

There was plenty of time. So much to do, so many children to teach, so many projects to set up in the library, and children's corners in the bookshop, and like-minded friends to call round for Sixties-type meals and conversations.

Libby was almost thirty before she began to think of the future, of someone who might be part her and part Martin –

who would, therefore, be a wonderful child. So she stopped taking the contraceptive pill. She remembered the day that she got the result of her test; it was the day she discovered that Martin was having an affair.

A great deal had been written about personal freedom in the Sixties. People had to have their own space, make their own choices. We were not the jailers of other people, even those to whom we might be bound by marriage vows. Perhaps it wasn't an affair, more a whirl, a fling, a *thing* even. People talked of having a *thing* with other people, nothing to break up a home over.

She waited for a couple of weeks before she told him that they were to be parents.

'Oh shit,' Martin said.

So Libby knew it was more than a whirl or a thing, it was an affair: a love affair.

They hadn't wanted it to happen, Martin explained. He and Janet had not set out looking for something like this. But it just had. There was no denying it, pretending it didn't exist, the huge attraction between them. There was only one life, this was it, it wasn't a rehearsal. He and Janet had to take their happiness.

Libby nodded glumly.

'It's early days still. The pregnancy thing, I mean, it's not too late – for an abortion?' Martin asked.

'I have no idea,' Libby said, and left the house.

She went to the bookshop; they were stock-taking. She helped them until ten o'clock. When she got home there was a note from Martin.

'I've gone to Janet's, I assumed you would not want me here when you got back.'

She sat and looked out at the stars in the sky for a long time. It was the weekend to visit her parents, so Libby went alone. She told her parents about the baby and they seemed very pleased. She didn't tell them about Martin. It didn't seem right to dim the pleasure.

In the weeks that followed she told them little by little. Always in a matter-of-fact voice. She never let them know of the nights of despair, the plans to kill Janet, the dream sequences where he would come back and she would forgive him the affair, defining it only as a fling. She never told them at school, nor in the library, nor in the bookshop where she thought that Mr Jennings knew something was amiss, but he was too much of a gentleman to mention it.

The medical examination showed that the baby was, in fact, going to be two babies. The baby-minding for twins would be more serious. She would not survive on a school salary alone, and if Martin were to leave the flat as he promised she could not ask him to support two children he didn't want. She asked for a paid job in the library, and one in the shop. She told them why.

'I thought you and your husband had the perfect marriage,' said the librarian, as she got Libby a few hours. Mr Jennings said nothing, but wrote to head office and got Libby a very good part-time job.

The babies were a boy and a girl. There were flowers from Martin with a note saying he wished her every happiness and he didn't know the etiquette in matters like this, but she

would have his eternal admiration and gratitude for giving
him his freedom.

She hadn't known it was possible to love as much. Their little faces, their tiny fists, their sheer innocence and the way
they depended on her for everything. Her life was fuller and
happier than she could have believed possible. At school,
where she worked a half day, people said Libby must be made
of stone; she had shown no sense of loss when her husband
went off, she was able to leave those babies to a minder. Some
women were as tough as nails. In the library they said she was
a tragic figure but brave, brave like Joan of Arc. Mr Jennings
said nothing about her, but often brought the catalogues
around to Libby's house so that she could read and make her
choices of what to order from her own fireside.

Libby's parents came to call. They loved their grandchildren and as the children grew they were full of
encouragement for them.

'Go ahead, climb that tree!'

'Surely you'll let them ride bicycles on the main road,
Libby. What harm could come to them? You must let them go
out with their friends on their own.'

It was as if their own restrictions of twenty-five years ago had
never existed. And as she listened to them speak, Libby knew
that she must listen. She must grow up again as she had grown
up the evening her pigeon had flown away.

You couldn't love something and keep it a prisoner. No
matter how much her heart would break she had to give her
children the wings that they already wanted. So she lived by
this principle. Even though she must have inherited her own

parents' anxieties she showed no trace of them. She lay sleepless waiting for her sixteen-year-old twins to come back from a party in someone's car. Or, when they were eighteen, for her son to wheel his motorbike into the back garden. Or, when they were nineteen, for her daughter to come home later and later from dates with a leather-jacketed, low-browed man who looked at worst as if he were a serial killer and at best a professional heart-breaker.

She spent longer hours in the bookshop. Mr Jennings suggested she leave the school and work there full-time. It was a big decision but she was surprised how few people cared. Her son and daughter were too busy being twenty, her parents too tied up in their own concerns, her ex-husband too concerned with serious litigation. Janet apparently had not understood how he and Harriet had become involved, not wishing to hurt anyone but we only had one life, this was not a rehearsal and they had to take their chances at happiness.

When the twins were twenty-one they told her that they were going to Australia, one with a good job, the other with a *de facto* relationship which would guarantee a visa.

Australia wasn't far, they said. It wasn't forever. They'd come back; she'd come out to visit.

Her heart was like lead, her face was a frozen mask, as she presided over their departure. Sometimes she overheard them on the phone talking to friends: 'No, she doesn't mind at all, glad to get rid of us I'd say.'

Could they really think that? These children whom she'd loved for twenty-one years? Always on her own; Martin had taken no part in their lives. They had never sought him out.

Now they would be gone, and on the other side of the earth. They would think that she didn't care, that their leaving was something that probably suited her.

She went like a robot to the airport to see them off. She waved until their plane must have been well over France and maybe further south over Italy. Her eyes were unseeing as she turned away to go back to her empty flat. She walked towards the exit without seeing the man sitting waiting for her. Ken Jennings, his eyes full of hope.

'Oh, what are you doing here?' Libby cried, embarrassed to have been seen so nakedly vulnerable, standing mourning her children who had flown away.

'Waiting,' he said simply.

'But what were you waiting for?' She looked at him with gratitude. It was so good to have him here to take away the empty feeling.

'For freedom, I suppose,' Mr Jennings said thoughtfully. 'The freedom for me to ask you and tell you things I have wanted to ask and tell for years, and for you to listen without too much else taking up your heart.'

This time Libby Green didn't feel she was growing up. She had grown up long ago, there was no further growing to do. But she did feel she understood more about this freedom thing. By giving it you got it. She wondered did everyone else know this, or was she the only person in the world who understood?

Julia Blackburn

the emperor's last island

Julia Blackburn was born in London in 1948. She is married with two children and lives in Suffolk. She is author of *The White Men* (1979), *Charles Waterton* (1989), *The Emperor's Last Island* (1992) and *Daisy Bates in the Desert* (1994).

The Emperor's Last Island *tells the story of Napoleon's final years on St Helena. Here was a man who had once seemed capable of conquering the whole world, suddenly trapped on a tiny volcanic island in the middle of the South Atlantic Ocean and held there, helpless and impassive, until his death. He was guarded by battalions of soldiers, by a fleet of armed naval vessels and by a bustling hierarchy of officials, all busy with the task of watching him. But he was not only captured physically, he was also hemmed in on all sides by his own memories of past greatness and defeat, and by the myths and legends that had grown up around him, turning him into a being with unreal and superhuman powers.*

The more I discovered about the history of St Helena, the more it seemed to me as if the island itself was as much of a prisoner as the Emperor and in a curious way the two of them were equally obsessed by images of a lost past. When it was first discovered by the Portuguese in 1502, St Helena was described as a green oasis, with trees covering even the most steep-sided rocks and only land snails, beetles and a single species of bird to disturb the quiet. The Portuguese released a few goats which soon increased in size and number, then came rats, spiders, dogs and cats, people and more people, and bit by bit the land was stripped of its trees, the rains washed away the topsoil and whole areas were made desolate. For some reason, perhaps because of its remoteness, the place also became riddled with bureaucracy, so that every aspect of people's lives was controlled by laws and regulations.

But before St Helena's 'captivity' it did have a period of strange glory and fame when it was inhabited by a single man called Fernando Lopez. He lived there from 1512 until his death in 1546 in a state of extreme and extraordinary isolation, and during that time he worked on the island, turning it into a paradise garden that was cultivated and yet wild, isolated and yet inhabited. He created an image of perfection and human freedom which fixed itself in the imagination of travellers for centuries afterwards.

> Be not afeard. The isle is full of noises,
> Sounds, and sweet airs, that give
> delight, and hurt not.
> Shakespeare, *The Tempest*

A place can be haunted by the people who knew it long ago and who stared at the stones under their feet, the leaves on the trees, and out at the far distances and horizons that encircled them. Something about St Helena's isolation seems to concentrate this sense of the land being haunted, soaked to the bone with the lives of people who were once here, and are now long since dead. It is as if the island's own loneliness creates a feeling of kinship that stretches back to everyone who has ever stood on this little platform which seems to be balanced on the very edge of the world.

I have been told that when the children of St Helena are asked who they consider to be central to their island's history, they do not think of mentioning Napoleon – he has become the property of historians and curious foreign visitors – but turn instead to the story of a Portuguese nobleman called Fernando Lopez. More than anyone else who has become embedded in this place, he stands out as the most vivid personality for them. Napoleon would have been told about Lopez as well; he was always glad to listen to the talk of slaves or children, people of no consequence who did not feel the need to be afraid of him, who would come and sit with him, and answer his questions. So he would have learnt all that there was to know about this strange exiled man, the island's first inhabitant, who seems to have been as lonely as the place he lived in. And since the two men had certain things in common, perhaps there were times later when their ghosts sat down together and discussed their thoughts about the life that they had led on the island.

After it had been discovered in 1502 St Helena remained uninhabited for several years. The wirebirds, snails and insects continued with their quiet existence, and the goats spread out across their new territory. Maybe the Portuguese stopped here occasionally to replenish their supplies of water and food as they made their slow journey back from the Indian sub-continent, but if they did, they never bothered to mention the fact in any of their surviving records, and no other nation as yet knew anything about the island's existence.

Fernando Lopez arrived here in 1515. Because of a crime he had committed he had no right hand, no left thumb, no nose and no ears, and the hair of his head, his eyebrows and his beard had been plucked out – a practice that was known as 'scaling the fish'. According to one account the fingers of his left hand had also been removed.

Lopez spent thirty years on the island. For most of that time he was entirely on his own, and for stretches of uninterrupted years he spoke to no one and was seen by no one, and went and hid in the greenness of the forest whenever a ship approached the harbour. On one occasion he did make a brief visit to Portugal, but then his only wish was to be allowed to return to his solitary home.

The story of this man with his grotesquely wounded face and his maimed hands is told by three early writers on Portuguese history. One of them saw him on the island, although it seems that he only caught sight of him from a distance and never managed to speak with him, and the other two wrote about him not long after his death. These accounts were written very simply, without comment of emotion, but just the idea of how this man must have looked serves to give him a complex personality, and it is easy to understand how the last years of his life were absorbed into the heart of the island, until man and place were in some ways indistinguishable.

Lopez was a Portuguese nobleman who left his home and his family and went with a group of soldiers under the leadership of General D'Alboquerque in search of new lands to conquer and claim for the Portuguese Empire. In 1510 they crossed the Indian Ocean from Arabia, and arrived in Goa on the southwest coast of India. After a brief battle they captured the ancient fortress town and claimed the ownership of the land that they stood on, and the vast unknown continent that lay beyond it. Because they had not got enough military strength to push their claim, D'Alboquerque set sail for Portugal to fetch more warships and more fighting men while Lopez and some of the soldiers were left behind to guard the fortress and to wait for the return of their general. D'Alboquerque was away for two years, and when he finally came back, bristling with reinforcements, he found that the men he had left behind had betrayed his trust in them, and had adopted the Muslim faith and the way of life of the local people. The traitors were rounded up without any resistance and brought before him, and since he had promised to be lenient they were not killed, although more than half of their number died during the three days that they were punished 'by black torturers and young men'. Lopez received the heaviest punishment because he was of noble birth and had been made responsible for the whole group. When it was all over, he and the others who had survived were released from the ropes and chains that bound them, and were set free to go wherever they chose. They all went and hid themselves somewhere in the countryside, so that neither their terrible wounds nor their shame could be seen.

Three years later D'Alboquerque was dead, and Lopez emerged out of hiding and took a passage on a ship bound for Portugal. He was planning to return to the wife and children he had not seen for so long, and to return to his house, his people, his language and his homeland. After many days at sea the ship stopped at the island of St Helena to replenish its supplies of water, and it was then that he realised he could not bring himself to complete his journey. He went ashore and hid himself deep in the forest. When the boat was ready to leave the sailors searched for him but could not find him, so they left some provisions on the shore and went on their way.

Lopez dug himself a hole in the ground in which to sleep. He had been provided with a barrel of biscuits and a few strips of dried meat, a tinder box and a saucepan. There were many edible herbs and fruits to be found, and it would not have been difficult for him to catch fish or nesting birds, or even one of the goats. The island was extremely benevolent; there were no wild animals here to harm him, no insects or reptiles to bite him, no diseases to sap his strength. In spite of the wind and the rain, the weather was always mild, and the trees were thick with sheltering leaves. A year went by before another ship appeared and dropped anchor in the bay that is now the port of Jamestown.

> The crew was amazed when they saw the grotto and a straw bed on which he slept . . . and when they saw the clothing they agreed it must be a Portuguese man.
>
> So they took in their water and did not meddle with anything, but left biscuits and cheeses and things to eat, and a letter telling him not to hide himself next time a ship came to the island, for no one would harm him.
>
> Then the ship set off, and as she was spreading her sails a cockerel fell overboard, and the waves carried it to the shore and Fernando Lopez caught it and fed it with some rice which they had left behind for him. (Hakluyt Society, No. 62)

The cockerel was the first living creature to share the man's solitude. At night it roosted above his head and during the day

Julia Blackburn

it pattered after him and came to him when he called it. Time
went on and Lopez learnt to be less afraid; slowly he grew
into the habit of appearing when a ship was at anchor, coming
to talk to the men who came ashore. Everyone who met him
must have been moved by a sense of pity and of horror, and
since Lopez refused to be separated from the island, the
sailors treated him as if he was a sort of saint, a man carrying
on his shoulders a huge weight of human suffering and
estrangement. And since they could not take him with them
and give him the freedom of their own way of life, they offered
him gifts; they inundated him with anything they could find
which they thought might please him. They gave him the
seeds of vegetables and flowers; they gave him young palm
trees and banana trees, pomegranates and lemons, oranges
and limes. They also gave him living creatures: ducks and
hens, pheasants and partridges, guinea fowl with their shrill
warning shouts, peacocks with their harsh screams, turkeys,
bullocks and cows, pigs, dogs and cats, even more goats, and,
accidentally. a certain number of rats which came ashore
when no one was looking. And so Lopez became a gardener
and a keeper of livestock. With his single hand he worked
tirelessly and relentlessly, planting and clearing, digging and
tending, until under his care whole stretches of the landscape
were utterly transformed. Among the ebony, the redwood and
the gumwood trees he created gardens, vineyards and
orchards, and because of the rain, the wind and the fertility of
the soil, the seeds of many of the plants took root and flourished in parts of the island where he was not tending them,
and because it was impossible to keep such a quantity of birds

and animals in captivity, they also learnt to roam freely across the steep green landscape.

And this is how the island of St Helena became fused in people's minds with the idea of a rich garden growing on a rock in a distant ocean, a place of natural and yet unnatural perfection, fruitful throughout the year, cultivated and yet wild and without any human disturbances. It was hardly surprising that everyone who came here talked about this place that they had seen and the man who ruled over it like a king without subjects. In time the story was told to the king and queen of Portugal, and they summoned Lopez to appear before them at their royal palace in Lisbon. He came, unwillingly but obediently, and when he was offered anything he might desire, he asked simply to be taken to see the Pope in Rome so that he could confess his sins, and when he had seen the Pope, he begged permission to be taken back to the island he had come from. After this brief incursion into the world of men, Lopez was again visited by his old fears, and he stayed in hiding in the forest whenever he saw a ship approaching, and agreed to show himself only once it was promised in the king's name that no one would try a second time to carry him away.

And Fernando Lopez felt assured, so that he no longer used to hide himself, and spoke with those who came here, and gave them the produce of the island, which yielded in great abundance. And in the island he died, after living there a long time, which was in the year 1546. (Hakluyt Society, No. 62)

The extraordinary oasis that one man had created survived relatively unchanged for some years after his death. Portuguese sailors and soldiers who were too ill to continue on their journey would be left here to convalesce and gather their strength. A wooden chapel was built near the harbour, along with a few simple houses, but there were never more than a few men here at any one time, and there was no permanent settlement. The groves of citrus trees, the date palms and banana trees, the pineapples and pomegranates, all flourished, especially in the sheltered valley that rose up steeply from the harbour, and in a valley further to the east that came to be known as Lemon Valley. The wild domestic animals, the wild domestic birds and the rats ranged over the entire surface of the island, eating what they needed and multiplying. It was said that no matter what the season there was always enough fruit to fill the holds of six ships and there were wonderful herbs that could cure the scurvy within eight days. A man armed with a stick need not go far or exert himself much before he had secured the carcass of some plump bird or a large, well-fed and familiar animal.

On all sides the ancient forests stood as silent witnesses to the changes that were being brought about. The pigs, dogs, goats, cats and cattle were moving across the landscape like heavy earthbound locusts, but it would be a while before the effects of their presence were felt. The goats could eat the low branches and the young saplings of the trees, but they could not damage the bark of the old ebonies and gumwoods. The pigs could dig up the roots from the rich but shallow soil, but as long as the trees remained standing, that soil would be held fast, and no amount of rain or wind could sweep it away. So, in spite of the newly imported inhabitants, the island still had its strange and fertile beauty, with the old world and the new flourishing in apparent harmony.

The first book that attempted to provide a thorough and accurate account of St Helena was called the *General Description of Africa*. It was published in 1573, although the text seems to have been based on reports from travellers who visited the island during the 1550s. It explains that St Helena is an earthly paradise, a place where a man can refresh his soul as well as his body, where the climate is always mild, and the food is plentiful, there is no sickness and not a single wild creature that could cause any harm. But by the time that the book was published, the island was already beginning to change character and its gentle benevolence was being shaken. Huge poisonous spiders, as big as a clenched fist, had arrived from Africa and settled in the banana trees, and there was a species of stinging fly the size of a grasshopper whose origins were unknown. Vicious battles were being fought between the colonies of dogs, cats and rats, and the rats were in the ascendancy and had taken to nesting in the high trees where they disrupted the roosting peacocks and other birds.

In 1581 the battle for mastery and power moved from the animal into the human realm. An English pirate captain called James Fenton came across St Helena accidentally, and determined to chase out the Portuguese so that he might possess the island and 'there be proclaimed Kyng'. This scheme came to nothing but in the following year another Englishman, Captain Cavendish, discovered the island while returning from a voyage round the world. He stayed there for twelve days, and he explored it, mapped it, wrote about it, and charted its position very exactly in the middle of the Atlantic Ocean. From then onwards the secret was broken, and a succession of ships from various countries arrived to examine the land and fight over its ownership. They developed the habit of collecting fruit by cutting down whole lemon trees and taking the trunk with its richly decorated branches on board ship with them when they were ready to leave. Sometimes they would uproot or trample on the produce of the wild gardens and orchards when they had no use for it themselves; it was a simple way of denying it to anyone who happened to arrive after them.

By 1610 only a few lemon trees were left and they were hard to find. There were none remaining on the hills close to the harbour, but there was still a grove big enough to provide 14,000 lemons at one picking at Lemon Valley, further along the coast. By 1634 it was said that there were less than forty lemon trees on the whole island: twenty in Lemon Valley and the rest scattered all over the place. However, the native trees were still growing thickly across most of the island's surface, and there was 'an abundance of Hoggs, store of little speckled guinea Henns, partridges and Pigeons, also doggs, and Catts (runne away) of whome the Companie killed divers'. (Gosse, pp. 29-30).

Maybe because it was so very far away and although many people had heard of it few had actually seen it, or maybe because human beings cannot bear very much reality and often prefer to see what they imagine rather than what lies before their eyes, whatever the reason, the written descriptions of St Helena were hardly altered in spite of the passage of time and the changes that time was bringing with it. By the late eighteenth century, when the island was almost naked, stripped of its covering of earth, plants and trees everywhere except in the higher regions and in cultivated gardens, the *Portable Geographer's Gazetteer*, a standard reference work which was available in a number of editions in French and in English, was able to explain confidently:

> The hills are for the most part covered with verdure and large species of tree such as ebony etc. The valleys are very fertile in all kinds of excellent fruits, vegetables, etc. The fruit trees there bear at the same time flowers, green fruit and ripe fruit. The forests are full of orange, lemon and citrus trees. There are game birds in quantity, poultry and wild cattle. No savage or hurtful animal is found there, and the sea is full of fish. (Quoted in Masson, P. 98)

Napoleon had occasionally held St Helena in his mind, long before he made the slow sea crossing that brought him there from France. When he was a young man studying at the military academy at Auxonne he had filled a notebook with information about the lands that were at that time under British rule, and on the top line of an otherwise empty page he had written in his restless handwriting, 'St Helena, a small island'. In 1804 he even considered capturing this small island that could be so useful as a military base in the middle of the

South Atlantic: '1,200 to 1,500 men will be required . . . The English are in no wise expecting this expedition and it will be a simple matter to surprise them' (Masson, p. 97). The expedition never materialised, but he did prepare himself by finding out all he could about the nature of St Helena. He was bound to have read the *Portable Geographer's Gazetteer* in its French edition, as well as the other descriptive books that were available at the time; they all echoed each other in their accounts of this green oasis where fruits were ripe all the year round. And so, when Napoleon was approaching the place that was to hold him captive for the final stage of his life, he had strong preconceptions about what it would be like.

Ronald Blythe

walking away
from hitler

Ronald Blythe was born in Suffolk and much of his work reflects his East Anglian background. His books include *The Age of Illusion, Akenfield, The View in Winter, Divine Landscapes* and *From the Headlands.* His collected short stories were published in 1985. His work has been translated and been given a number of literary awards, including the Royal Society of Literature Award and the Society of Authors' Travel Scholarship. He lives in the Stour Valley. His most recent book is *Private Words* – a study of the personal writings of the Second World War.

Returning from the shops, Frau Moser made her way to the town hall, there to take her ritual gaze at its statuary. Great men and women from the borough's history gesticulated with swords and crosses from a high Portland stone arcade; bishops, soldiers, a Romano-British princess, each figure fixed in a riot of carved foliage. There were *putti* and mottoes and all the orders of architecture twining about each other. Frau Moser loved this wildly civic building. It was the only thing in the otherwise intensely architecturally controlled little town which could remind her of Vienna. Which was odd because during all the years she and Arnulf had lived in that city they had never given its florid sculpture a second thought.

Thinking of Vienna – when did she not? – Frau Moser wondered for the thousandth time what it was which had kept them from escaping until the eleventh hour? The Freuds and all their other friends had discreetly slipped abroad long since, quietly emptying the Berggasse. But she and Arnulf had waited until the waiting grew to be a grown-up version of the dangerous childhood game of last-across. Had they been brave or idiot? She tossed the question around in her head as she strode home, dodging phlegmatic women cowled in headscarfs, groups of gunners from the barracks, sailors from the harbour and hordes of yelling boys and girls. It was Saturday morning. The Sabbath. These English, they were stolidly calm, just as the Germans were stolidly something else. How calm would they be when the latter arrived – as they must? What could stop them now that France had fallen? It was all a house of cards. Flattened; the Nazis would walk in. In which case, why had they – she and Arnulf – escaped? She could not be calm. Often she shook with terror. Certain 'incidents', as the newspapers called them, were starting to add up as they had done in Vienna less than a decade ago. Would they put off fleeing to America until the penultimate hour? What *were* they to do? Where were they to go, she and Arnulf? She looked into passing faces as if for answers. None was tremulous.

She could remember being quite amazingly calm in Vienna, even when she heard of the round-ups. Like the posturing town hall, she and Arnulf had let the strong and ornamental façade of their house on the Berggasse put on a brave front for them, and somehow it worked. Now and then from an upper window she had caught debating faces looking up. One grim day they discovered a well-drawn rat chalked on the fine front door, but there was never a brick through the glass, never entrance. It was uncanny. Yet she never shook and Arnulf most certainly did not. So why in England did she so shake into tears that passers-by would look away? And how, should they enquire, which they never did, could she explain? That she wept because they had escaped, yes, but into shabbiness. Shabbiness! They should think themselves lucky! Four young officers, swinging along in brand new uniforms, all shoulders-back and snowy grins, parted to let her through with elaborate good manners, and again she was back in the

Berggasse house where thick curtains failed to block out
bursts of marching feet. Once more she heard orders, laughter and a neighbour's cries. She and Arnulf had sat mute.

One day, just as they had finished breakfast, he had said,
'Listen to this,' and had read from an English poem:

> 'To throw away the key and walk away,
> Not abrupt exile, the neighbours asking why,
> But following a line with left and right,
> An altered gradient at another rate.'

She had listened obediently, rather than attentively; he was
working on his English.

'Well?'

Arnulf repeated the verse and would have done so yet
again when the penny dropped.

'Oh, Arnulf – when?'

'Now. At once. Tomorrow.'

He then went to his consulting-room as usual. Emerging
after what seemed to her like a lifetime for dinner, he saw the
modest case in which she had packed a few treasures, opened
it and replaced them where they normally belonged.

'Not mother's silver clock!'

They ate their last dinner in the family house in silence,
hoping and praying that it would indeed be a Passover meal.
Next day they left, Arnulf in his open-necked Aertex shirt and
herself in a Shantung dress and white cardigan – picnic gar-
ments. They did not, of course, throw away the key but placed
it where anyone searching them would expect to find it, in the

Frau Doktor's handbag, along with just enough money for an excursion and her housekeeping cheque-book. In every other respect they obeyed the English poem to the letter, walking away from the Berggasse to the Westbahn, and then along the everlasting Mariahilferstrasse to the railway station. This was uproarious with singing troops, banners, kit and girls. The small middle-aged woman smiled at them as she manoeuvred herself through their joyful confusion to the ticket-office, whilst her tall thin husband hung on to the picnic basket. This contained, as well as cakes, sausage, coffee in a thermos flask and two novels, a Brownie camera and a towel, their passports and tickets to Berne. The tickets had arrived, miraculously, via New York, and the passports had but one more month's validity. Tickets, passports, Frau Moser had afterwards recalled, to seventeen, Totman's Yard, their present 'temporary' yet inescapable address. It could have been Buchenwald, and she never forgot it. She asked God to make her thankful but for some reason He had not.

Totman's Yard was one of those packed Victorian courts reached by alleys which housed the labour force of dull towns. It was a tumble of blackened brick dwellings, shared lavatories and stand-pipes, and surprisingly private lives. A ghetto, thought Frau Moser the moment the Jewish Refugees' Association guided them to it.

'Not for long. Just for the time being. And such good sorts, such rough diamonds next door.'

Linen lines were hooked from a central mast to each cottage like a maypole. Dogs, cats and innumerable children perched on doorsteps. Seventeen contained four narrow rooms, a steep staircase, a porcelain sink, a copper, a gas-stove and, from behind, a view of a sluggish creek in which more boys and girls, and some gulls, shrieked. Across the Yard was a pub called The Volunteer, and a minute shop which sold sweets, paraffin, groceries, cigarettes, firewood and newspapers.

'Now, darling, remember what we agreed,' said Arnulf.

This was to make the best of things. Soon, any day now, he would be appointed chief consultant at one of the large mental institutions which were such a feature of this part of England. How could the untemperamental English go so mad? Psychoanalysis would let out their insanity. And he, Dr Arnulf Moser from the Berggasse, the student of Sigmund Freud himself, would be offered the house which went with the appointment, a fine ugly red house with a huge garden in the grounds of the asylum. True, it would be a long way from Vienna, but it would also be far from Totman's Yard. Life, as he was beginning to see it, was a business of regulated escapes. One day, after the war, who knows, he might end where he began. Great cities, even when trammelled into slime and rubble by armies, like damaged woods greened again. His people would escape from their camps to cultivate them. History was, among many other things, a record of picking up the pieces.

Frau Moser's response to this cheeriness was a fleeting smile as her husband spoke, and a howl when he left her alone. He took evening walks by the harbour and she drew the black-out curtains and let herself go. She wept not for those losses which Arnulf never ceased to mourn – their paintings, books, jewels, clothes, the poor deserted cat Maxi – but for themselves in limbo. She was once weeping in what she knew to be a disgustingly uncontrolled way when accordion music broke in. Peeping through the net of an unlit bedroom, she saw a curious ballet-like scene. A young man was playing a glittering instrument, all filigree, pleats and mother-of-pearl, whilst women in pinafores and lads in braces waltzed. The scene was moonlit but aided by searchlights. For the first time Frau Moser wondered what would happen to such people when Hitler came. When Arnulf next left her alone her despair had vanished. She quite missed it, this long-permitted hollow into which she could void her unhappiness. The next-door woman noticed a difference in her.

'You're looking better, dear – more yourself.'

These crying fits over, Frau Moser took to observing her neighbours and accepting that they spied on her. The Yard was a bricked-in universe, mean yet vital, with its own pulse racing away day and night. Most of its inhabitants worked in the tent factory whose galvanised roof shone over it, although soon it would be camouflaged. Not that it mattered now, any-more than the dragging of old farm vehicles across the country lanes to create barricades could matter. The Wehrmacht must flood through – what – who – could stop it? And immediately after that the processing camps would be set up, and through the mill she and Arnulf must go, whilst this working-class into whose crevice they had crept, pro tem, would be worked, worked, worked until they collapsed. Trained in such matters, she noted a lack of hysteria. Perhaps this foolish calm was epidemic, for Arnulf was behaving as though nothing worse than penury could happen, and spying out the land, as he called it. He made a list of all the hospitals, mental or otherwise, in the vicinity and chugged around in buses to see them. They were enormous, some an insane distance from their entrance gates and lost in foliage, all with chimney stacks which emitted a sickly plasma-like smoke which never quite got away, but hung around until the air absorbed it. Arnulf became his own inspectorate and jotted in his notebook, '500 beds (?), staff quarters, some kind of new recreational wing, therapy centre, close control; 100 beds (surely not, though probable), run-down; small, with patients in the garden; a workhouse,' and so on. The asylum at Hanger's Green could be progressive. Would Esther mind the Superintendent's Lodge? It was both heavy and poky. They could make a start here and then move on to London. One of these recces brought him to St Barbara's, a magnificent Victorian madhouse masquerading as an aristocratic country seat – coats of arms, heraldic flag and all. He looked up St Barbara in the public library; she was the patron saint of gunpowder. It was there that he wrote a brief letter requesting an interview, careful to add after his name just one of his several qualifications. Psychology was still a small world. One either knew everyone in it, or none.

This was the first of many such letters. Their courteously negative replies made Arnulf imperious, then touchy, then furious, then bewildered. These fellow professionals were masters of dismissal. One or two did welcome a chat over a cup of tea or a glass of sherry 'when you are passing', but they knew how to show him out. What they could not say was that, for them, the glut of brilliantly qualified specialists from Germany and Austria was one of the problems of the war.

Thus two years passed. The Jewish Refugee Association paid the rent of ten shillings a week. Indeed, paid for everything. His inability to earn demoralised Arnulf. Nothing came in except the Association's monthly bare-bones cheque. Once the Association forwarded a document on which he was to make a full inventory of all they had left behind – house, furniture, bank deposits, works of art, 'for future claims'. When he did so the figure became enormous. Who could take it seriously? Why oh why had they not sent money abroad – in 1935, say? People they knew had. Perhaps all those Streicher cartoons of the Jews as looters had had their effect. Why had they so carefully escaped – with nothing? Physician heal thyself, thought Arnulf, looking at the person he was then but finding no logic in what he did. Listing these lost possessions made Esther weep. During the last two years she had managed to stow them away at the back of her mind, where they had started to become unmissed. Now here they were fully evaluated and in full view – the watercolours, her mother's gilded bed, all the books and the beloved house itself with its stately run of steps up from the pavement and loud door-knocker.

'I know, I know, my darling.'

Arnulf cradled her head in his big hands.

'I have been trying to forget.'

'That is not a good thing to do. It is the Herr Doktor speaking.'

'You needn't worry; the town hall refuses to let me.'

'The *town hall?*'

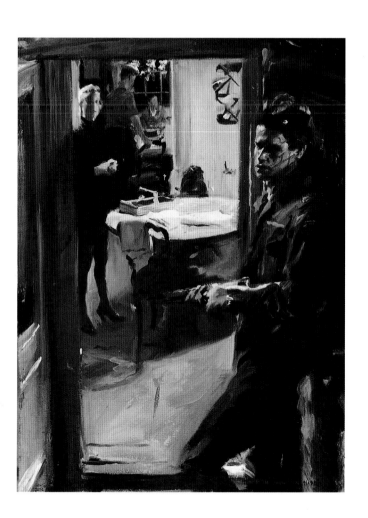

Howard Morgan

Howard Morgan was born in 1949. His numerous Royal and private commissions include HM the Queen, HM the Queen of the Netherlands (Unilever Tricentennial celebrations), HRH Prince Michael of Kent (for Mark Masons), TRH the Prince and Princess of Hanover, Antoinette Sibley, and Mr and Mrs Neil McConnell. He has a permanent display of work at the National Portrait Gallery and his exhibitions include Anthony Mould 1983, Claridges 1984, the Richmond Gallery 1986/87, 1988, 1989 and 1990, Agnews 1986, Cadogan Contemporary watercolours 1988, 1989, 1990 and 1991, and the Lithography Park Walk Gallery 1990. He is a member of the Royal Society of Portrait Painters.

'Yes, it reminds me of the Pestsäule.'

This was the famous Viennese plague pillar around which writhed carvings of everything from the Blessed Trinity down, and which was a kind of stone totem-pole of the Christian imagination.

Arnulf said that he had scarcely glanced at the Pestsäule and had never noticed the town hall.

'Oh, come!'

His loftiness took her right back to their courting days when he was the highbrow student who affected never to have heard of some popular cult or other. The inventory posted back to the Jewish Refugee Association, a line seemed to be drawn under the Berggasse, making it possible to take the narrowness of their present life more naturally, more for granted. The war went on and on, engulfingly so. It swallowed up the accordion player, who was never seen again. It left the Yard with old men and children, and young women running wild with Americans. They gave Esther the time of day, but nothing more. 'Mornin', Mrs Moser.' Arnulf they regarded suspiciously. At night they lay in bed listening to the crump and cough of anti-aircraft batteries, and staring up at the bumpy whitewashed ceiling, expecting it to fall. With little talk of Vienna and none of Jerusalem, they became like those animals which, during a hard winter, reduce all activity to the minimum. This inertia began to tell on Esther, this plus the Craven-A cigarettes which she endlessly smoked. For she acquired a sallow, pared-down look and an occasionally hectic eye. Arnulf began to look old.

This torpor evaporated quite suddenly. The woman who

ran the Literary Institute called. There were several such clubs and societies in the town. They met in shabby none-too-warm rooms and fought each other for guest speakers. Some were political, others artistic. The Mosers had taken to sampling them, sitting at the back, often wanting to join in but aware of creating a tiny commotion when they did. Theirs was not so much an out of place accent as an out of place intelligence. They also sounded German. For the British this was a comical sound. Hitler, orating, brought the wrong kind of tears to their eyes. Thus, mouse-like at the rear of the monthly Literary Institute talks, it never crossed their minds that the chairman, this large woman with the 1920s shingle, knew exactly who Arnulf was. She advanced into the hallway with outstretched arms. She had never lost a speaker yet.

'Dr Moser! I have been meaning to call for ages. Mrs Moser!'

She had not; Ursula Bloom had let her down. Frantic, she had pawed through the membership file and there under 'interests' Dr Moser had written 'Goethe'. Would he, could he, speak on Goethe? The Institute had always *longed* to hear about Goethe.

Arnulf smiled. 'I will tell you about Hölderlin – how about that?'

'Hölderlin . . .?'

'A great favourite of mine. I will talk about him. Translate some of him.'

At first Esther was delighted with this unexpected development, this coming back to life, but when Arnulf began to call his talk 'the Lecture', and had copies of his translations cyclostyled at the stationers so they could be handed out, and put all his honours and degrees on the poster, she became apprehensive. He was overreaching.

'Just talk, Liebling, then read a few of the poems. That is all they expect.'

On the night, with the silver-black mop of hair greased to shine and wearing a nice blue serge suit which cost fifteen shillings second-hand, and with his gold spectacles glittering, Arnulf was introduced as 'a most distinguished guest among us'. It was four years since he had last lectured. There was a full turn-out and he told the listening rows about the poet who had walked away, and about Hölderlin's madness which wasn't madness, and he should know, being a friend of Sigmund Freud. And he read from the *Diotima* verses so beautifully that Esther heard once more the dark boy sprawling on the Stadtpark grass, his head in her lap. He was right, she corrected herself, to turn this evening into a statement of who he was and what he was, and she felt proud of him.

Afterwards, there was the usual crowd around the tea-urn. A lot of elderly men and women who lived in library books, youthful soldiers and sailors with Penguins jutting from their gasmask packs, grammar-schoolboys, aged clergymen, would-be writers, maidenly creatures with Proust in their handbags. And Mrs Seabrook. She was an occasional attendee but a notable one, with her piled yellow hair, fresh cotton dresses and diamond regimental brooch, her low rich voice and her breeding. For what else could one call it? Arnulf had seen her before, but she was seeing him for the first time. She was in her way a seer, shifting from vision to vision, discarding the last to take up the next. At this moment by the tea-urn her sights were not on Hölderlin but psychoanalysis. The medical qualifications after Arnulf's name on the programme, and his references to Freud and Jung, spread infinite prospects before her. As well as a seer, Pauline Seabrook was a disciple, a born follower to date of Mrs Baker Eddy, Krishnamurti, Major Douglas, Prunella Stack, Emile Coué ('Every day, in every way, I'm getting better and better') and Oswald Mosley. Her feeling for poetry was less peripatetic. She had listened with tears to Arnulf reading Hölderlin. It was a virtue in her to give herself utterly to language. But when Hölderlin ended and reminiscences of Freudian Vienna began, Mrs Seabrook was once more on her way to a new master. (A new craze, her husband Colonel Seabrook called it.)

And so it was, a week later, and a heatwave at its height, that Arnulf once more caught a village bus from the town, one which bounced and rocked past St Barbara's Asylum into the deep and, for him, still unexplored countryside. This had little appeal for either him or Esther. They liked streets and parks. Beyond these they were both lost. Mrs Seabrook had sent him a pencilled map and the conductress assured him that he would be put down at the right spot. The summer hedges grew richer, denser, the tar bubbled under the tyres. There was a smell like hot sweet socks. Wearing the blue serge suit – it was a consultation – Arnulf felt faintly sick. The bus was like an oven. The conductress sang, 'I'll be seeing you'. So did the driver.

'In the ordinary way, dear Dr Moser, we would of course have fetched you, but the petrol ration, you know. However, there are compensations. You will adore the walk from the windmill where the bus will drop you. A fair old way, as they say in our part of the world, but a lovely, lovely way. I can't tell you how I envy those who walk that footpath for the first time! And then, at the end of it, a good English luncheon. I hope you have a good appetite to match.'

He refolded the letter. Before sending him these instructions she had encountered both Arnulf and Esther in the local Food Office with 'the need to talk' written all over her. They scanned her face and in their emotional un-English way showed open solicitude. Esther laid a hand on Mrs Seabrook's brown arm.

'Oh, not me – my husband. But this is neither the place nor the time to bother you with my troubles. So unethical, please forgive me.'

Arnulf took the bull by the horns.

'You wish to consult me professionally?'

'My husband, the Colonel, should – must.'

'Do you understand what it would entail?'

Thinking he meant the fee, she said, 'Yes, yes, of course.'

Arnulf paused. She looked anxious. Then he agreed. A consultation. Esther drew back to study a poster about ration-books. Mrs Seabrook was giving an address, ominously adding, 'And give yourself plenty of time.' Arnulf was contrasting the muted contralto of her voice with her fingers, which looked as if they did nothing but dig in the earth. She curled them up protectively when she noticed him staring. There was a wedding, an engagement and a signet ring, locked together on one finger.

On the way home Esther said, 'It is she who needs analysis.'

'Now, now, Liebchen!'

The windmill stop proved to be ten miles from the town and the footpath to the farm a mile and a half of sagging, tangling undergrowth. No one had walked it for months. Bean scent made him sneeze. Arnulf was not made for this kind of opulence and plunged along like a swimmer in uncongenial waters, pressing his way through, looking ahead for land. The Seabrooks' farm came into view only when he was on top of it. There it lay, as it had done for centuries, in all its determined obscurity. He saw Mrs Seabrook waving and calling 'Cooeee . . .' He stumbled through the last of the corn and weeds to an untended lawn, sticky, spattered with pollen, clasping his cheap new briefcase and thunderingly angry. Put out. She stopped laughing and said, quietly in the low-register voice, 'Dear Dr Moser, you found us.'

She wore the blue cotton dress of the Hölderlin lecture but minus the regimental brooch. Her feet and legs were bare and scratched, her marvellous hair heaped high on a comb.

'What a scorcher! Real summer at last!'

She took him to a corner of the stackyard where a huge tablecloth was spread on the ground. Such piles of plates, cutlery, glasses – who else could be coming? Arnulf felt sweat trickling down his back and from under the tight trouser-band round his belly. He also felt disgusting. The tablecloth was spread in the full sun. Dogs had to be shooed away from it. There were far cries from a tennis court, maybe. Every now and then Spitfires and other planes took off from an airfield which could not be more than a few yards away, or so it felt.

They made surprisingly little noise but cast black crosses on the burnt landscape. There was an uproar of larks.

Mrs Seabrook took Arnulf's case and put it out of the sun, smoothing it as though it was of great value.

'First you deserve a drink. Second, we're going to have a lovely, lovely afternoon.'

She brought him beer in a tankard.

'Our own brew.'

No longer nauseous from the journey but foolishly uncomfortable in the suit, Arnulf's lips touched the chilly pewter with relief. He ached to sit but there were no chairs. Most of all he longed to be in a big cool room with shuttered windows, a room like his consulting-room on the Berggasse, with its marble Persephone and glass-fronted bookcases and parquet floor. Its serenity surged through him. 'To throw away the key and walk away . . .'

'And what happened to the Mosers?' the prisoners at Auschwitz would ask in a whisper. 'They *escaped*.'

A fragment of a psalm which had lodged, forgotten, amidst the lumber which he called the subconscious, rushed to the forefront of his mind, poignant, ravishing.

> 'Let the sighing of the prisoner come
> before thee, according to the greatness
> of thy power preserve thou those that
> are appointed to die . . .'

'Make yourself comfortable, Dr Moser,' Mrs Seabrook was calling from the kitchen window. 'No standing on ceremony here!' She laughed, revealing well-shaped discoloured teeth. But when she saw him dabbing his forehead, she ran out to hurry him to a cloakroom. He washed and felt better. Now he must confront her with the purpose of his visit. The consultation. After they had eaten, naturally. When he mentioned it, he was surprised to see her momentarily irritated. She brushed goosegrass from her skirt with slow considering movements to gain time.

'Now let me see . . . your bus goes at five. Hurrah! that means we have the whole afternoon. Goody, goody. And we'll certainly find a way to run you back to the windmill stop. We should be able to manage that! The war, what a damned nuisance.'

She carried food out, food such as Arnulf had not seen for years – fruit, salad, chicken, rice, home-made bread, masses of vegetables, all piled in old china and scrubbed wooden bowls. Seeing Arnulf's expression, she said, 'We're not going to let that Mr Schicklgrüber get us down, are we!' She rang a big brass handbell and instantly three children raced from the orchard, two boys and a girl. He guessed them to be somewhere between twelve and sixteen. They were naked.

'Put something on for lunch, darlings.'

They returned in khaki shorts.

'Edward, Eric, Pamela, say how do you do to Dr Moser.' Their flawless naturist bodies spoke to him, not only of their mother's sun-worship phase, but of the singing phalanxes of Hitler Youth winding through the Austrian hills. Now that the layers of Mrs Seabrook's enthusiasms were coming into view, Arnulf's analyst's mind began to tick. But his haunches protested. He rolled from one to the other, sitting on the ground as long as he could. Then he stood – 'I'm afraid I'm not built for this!' Edward rushed to fetch a chair and returned with his father.

'My husband Colonel Seabrook. Geoffrey, this is Dr Moser.'

Arnulf gripped the hand of a dying man of eighty or more, a man of great height and reduced flesh. He wore cricket whites and plimsolls. Where the shirt gaped, tufts of hair fluttered on the parchment skin like thistledown. A lifetime's engaging grin had set into its final rictus. All three children were strikingly like him and not at all like their mother. Each was his young self, Pamela too in a sense. He tucked into the food with appetite. It was 'Pass this and pass that' and, when the girl rose to wind her arms round his neck and rock him to and fro, 'Am I to suffer indigestion as well as —'

'Shush, Geoffrey.'

'It can hardly be a secret,' grinned the Colonel.

A month, thought Arnulf. A month, no more. So, married to someone very nearly twice her age, a progressive thinker – a charitable assessment – still very handsome, an artist, a sucker for false prophets, a good mother, a poor farmer, and currently, like half the females who sought 'help' on the Berggasse, entranced by Sigmund and his heirs. Arnulf recognised all the symptoms, and he remembered the old advice, which, boiled down, was 'Get yourself a job'. However, there might well be a need for some medical help after the funeral. He found himself grieving for the lovely children who were about as deathless a group as could be imagined, and who were so untouched by corruption. Corruption, elegant in flannels, was holding out his glass for wine, more wine. Something else occurred to Arnulf. Had a new widow in her new grief come to him in Vienna, would he not have listened? Of course he would. So why feel this guilt about accepting Mrs Seabrook as a patient? Hölderlin had brought her to him. Others would follow. He and Esther were at last taking the first steps away from the route which led to Totman's Yard. The war itself would end.

Luncheon over, he was shown the farmhouse. There were pots of wild flowers, oil-lamps, billowing curtains, sleeping cats, fat chintzy chairs and scattered books. Mrs Seabrook was as good as her word. Guiding Arnulf to a nook with wing-chairs and port, she said, 'Now to business,' and disappeared. Her husband emerged from the shadows, held up the decanter and looked pleased.

'We are honoured. We don't get this every day.'

When Arnulf suggested that it might be rather chilly sitting inside after the garden – he meant for his host – Colonel Seabrook replied, 'Not nearly as cold as I am going to be before the summer is out.'

There was a vast silence. Arnulf became professional.

'What kind of treatment are you having?'

'Quinine and the Sacraments.'

Tennis shrieks and some lowing as milking-time drew near. 'I am a very old-fashioned sort of chap, Dr – Moser, was it?' – and he told Arnulf all about his cancer, which didn't hurt, or hurt much, and how, because there was so little of him left, there was little left to die. 'But my wife is taking it badly.'

'Forgive me, but I sense that she is taking it very well. She is strong and she has the family.'

It was the hour for platitudes.

The Colonel was greatly amused. His jaw-crack of a smile widened wickedly.

'You don't know her – how could you? I will tell you something. It is my wife who is fighting off my death, not me. That is why you are here, to make me put up a fight. She tells me you are a famous chap in your way, knew Freud and all that kind of thing. But dear, dear old chap, what *can* you do? I am eighty-seven. Married late, had the children at the last minute – good-looking bunch, don't you think? – and I am still being adored. My wife is a very enthusiastic girl – you'll find out. Enthusiastic about everything. Taking this up, that up. Never a dull moment. Never ill herself. Had those babies – well you can see there couldn't have been many complications. Runs this farm. Even does some of the ploughing. I'm not much help these days. Very gone on me still. Lucky old Geoff, that's me. *And* very lucky at the end. You can't wait, you know. When you get this far, you can't wait. You will see when your time comes. She'll have this place, my reduced pension, and the children. There's nothing in the bank. What else can I tell you?'

Mrs Seabrook was sitting in full sun picking over some soft fruit when Arnulf rejoined her. She thought he had returned to bring her into the consultation and looked disconcerted when he told her that her husband was asleep. Also, that there was no consultation. Just a talk.

'But you've *got* to help him. I brought you here especially to get all this death stuff out of his head. You saw him. He eats well. He's full of life. It's the rector, putting ideas into his head.'

Arnulf crouched by her side and took her hand, forcing

her eyes to hold his. 'It is cancer of the liver, the quickest kind – you know it is, don't you? Did you think that analysis would divert it for a year or so? Well, it might – until the winter. And then at the same time it is not "cancer" but perfectly natural death, which he welcomes. He has told you that soon you can only possess him in your children. In that boy who is him all over again. That's what he said. That's what he said I have to tell you.'

Mrs Seabrook was neither comforted nor made reasonable by Arnulf's language because it was so antiquated. To have a distinguished psychologist in the house and to have to listen to the kind of things which old Dr Bull down the road would have said had she let him! Nor did she like the perspiring Dr Moser touching her. She stood up, towering over him, and reminded him that she had *engaged* him to attend her husband in his capacity as a psychologist and that he had agreed to do so. She could how him his letter.

They quarrelled on in the hot afternoon. The young people played invisibly, their shouts flying over the hedge. Arnulf's long-disappeared professional interest had leaped back to protect him from what this powerful woman was saying, which at times was pretty dreadful. The adrenaline which had made him such a consummate listener in Vienna coursed through him. The more Mrs Seabrook abused him – rather as though he was a grocer who had delivered the wrong order, he thought – the more he heard. Trained and attuned, correctly readjusted by her revealing tirade, his ear picked up the good and the bad in her. The anti-semitism and parlour-fascism, the longing in her to re-create an earthly paradise in

which the body became spirit. He heard with this restored
ear for such unsaid revelations how she had had to marry a
military hero and at the same time turn her back on the war.
Her inconsistencies and her restless search all the time for
something 'different' and 'better' would have in other circumstances made him like her, but liking or hating could
have no role to play now. He was Sigmund's heir and an unre-
stricted channel for behaviour and outpourings. To put it in
a nutshell, as these English said, it was Mrs Seabrook, of all
people, who had unblocked the vacuous silence which had
settled on him as part of the price for being a refugee, and
who alone was responsible for letting the old fascination with
everything 'human' race through him. A woman like her! A
common casebook type! A woman who, once the first protective veil of manners fell in the first rage, had no further veils
to hide her. What was making her so angry with him? It was his
refusal to talk her husband back into the sun, if only for a year
or two. To persuade him to postpone his heaven. Well, no one
did this in the consulting-rooms of the Berggasse. He eventually soothed her down by not putting up a fight. She
apologised, wept. The young people reappeared, saw that this
was no place for them, and slipped from sight. Arnulf saw the
future – a start!

She went to make tea. He discovered a Housman among
her telltale books – *Mein Kampf,* Mrs Baker Eddy, *Pelmanism,
Moral Rearmament, Naturism, Married Love* – and read:

> From the wash the laundress sends
> My collars home with ravelled ends;

I must fit, now these are frayed,
My neck with new ones London-made.

Homespun collars, homespun hearts,
Wear to rags in foreign parts.

She did not run him to the bus-stop as she promised.
Instead she walked with him all the way, talking wildly but no
longer accusingly. Now and then she would hold back briars
with her brown grubby hands to let him pass. Waiting by the
windmill, she said, 'I have talked too much. I haven't let you
say a word. How did you escape?'

'I won't know until I've written up my notes,' he told her.

Andrew Motion

on the run

Andrew Motion was born in 1952. He has published six collections of poetry – the most recent being *Love In a Life* (1991) and *The Price of Everything* (1994) – and two biographies – *The Lamberts* (1987) and *Philip Larkin: A Writer's Life* (1993). He has won the Dylan Thomas Award, the Somerset Maugham Award, and the Whitbread Prize for Biography.

Pity the sprinter
born to endure
a maybug life
where seconds are not
just hours but days
scraps of his shell
red orange and blue
glued to his thighs
the shield of his chest
still wet still wet
when it's time to die

rewind again
not a maybug no
a man in pain
his feet alight
on blistering earth
although his brain
thinks nothing of fire
only of water
a rolling wave
he can't outrun
and can't run through

Freedom

rewind again
no not in pain
look at the close-up
a terrified man
whose face sinks in
the way flesh does
one moment between
a bomb-blast crash
and whining steel
which shreds thin air
into delicate strips

rewind again
no none of these things
take one more look
the flaring eyes
in the steady head
straightened rooms
where a lifetime ago
miles from home
a whiplash cracked
on a back already
gorged with blood

rewind again
where ash-grey streets
were a boring maze
of bolted doors
and cut-off phones
where a measured track
with its feeble tape
was the stroke of luck
which might just lead
to a shot like this
and freedom come

rewind again
with arms held out
and a shout gone up
which just for now
is the only sound
the world allows
nothing to do
with straightened rooms
behind the eyes
or a lifetime's fear
or the time to die.

Frederic Raphael

freedom's
fame

Frederic Raphael was born in Chicago in 1931. He was educated at Charterhouse and St John's College, Cambridge, where he was a major scholar in Classics.

His first novel, *Obbligato*, was published in 1956 and was followed by *The Earlsdon Way* (1958), *The Limits of Love* (1960), *A Wild Surmise* (1961), *The Graduate Wife* (1962), *The Trouble with England* (1962), *Lindmann* (1963), *Orchestra and Beginners* (1967), *Like Men Betrayed* (1970), *Who Were You With Last Night?* (1971), *April, June and November* (1972), *Richard's Things* (1973), *California Time* (1975), *The Glittering Prizes* (1976), *Heaven and Earth* (1985), *After the War* (1988), *The Hidden I* (1990) and *A Double Life* (1993). His collections of short stories include *Sleeps Six* (1979), *Oxbridge Blues* (1980), *Think of England* (1986) and *The Latin Lover* (1994).

He has also written two biographies, *Somerset Maugham and His World* (1976) and *Byron* (1982), translations (with Kenneth McLeish) of *The Poems of Catullus* (1976) and of *The Oresteia* (1978, televised as *The Serpent's Son*). He adapted several classical myths in *Of Gods and Men* (1992).

Frederic Raphael is married with three children and divides his time between France and England. He is a Fellow of the Royal Society of Literature.

'Eternal spirit of the chainless Mind!
Brightest in dungeons, Liberty! thou art
For there thy habitation is the heart –
The heart which Love of thee alone can bind;
And when thy sons to fetters are consign'd –
To fetters and the damp vault's dayless gloom,
Their country conquers with their martyrdom,
And Freedom's fame finds wings on every wind.'

Byron, *Sonnet on Chillon*

The Swiss, of whom Byron's hero Bonnivard – celebrated in his avowedly glib sonnet – was a brave fellow-citizen, are obliged to follow the French in being unable to make any verbal distinction between freedom and liberty: '*liberté*' must cover both terms. It could be argued, with a touch of malice, that the difficulty which the French have always had in finding common ground with each other within their regularly dichotomised society may not be *caused*, but is certainly *symbolised* by the linguistic poverty which corners them in the use of a single term to designate individual, metaphysical and political freedom.

Is it entirely by chance that the French, often aping the Germans, relish philosophical systems purporting to supply intellectual underpinnings to social doctrines, whether of freedom or of its curtailment? The English, by eminent contrast, have felt no pressing need to authorise individual liberty by flourishing metaphysical warrants; John Locke, however influentially misguided his notion of the new-born mind as a *tabula rasa*, based his ideas on what he took to be an empirical assessment of human possibilities. Only on the mainland of the old continent does the desire for an all-inclusive, *a priori* machinery of public and private morals dominate philosophy. European pundits may have reacted against the moral *imperium* of the Catholic Church, but they often turn out to supply a substitute orthodoxy for that of Rome.

European Socialism, in its more optimistic phases, was almost as much a religion as a political movement and the French Left was pleased to describe itself as a family, with all the kissing cousinage and Oedipal affiliations which that institution, so hated by André Gide, could be expected to offer. Even in England, there was some justice in T.S. Eliot's Jesuitical assertion that Bertrand Russell's essay *Why I am Not a Christian* was, in some sense, born of Christian apologetics; it could not have been conceived in an unChristian climate. How can we ever walk away from the shadow of a language which, in the cant vocabulary of structuralism (yet another congeries of heretical clerks), is said to speak *through* us quite as much as we speak it?

Nostalgia for a single metaphysical currency has had much less claim in Anglo-Saxon countries than it has within the ancient constituency of Catholicism. In Britain and the USA, at least until recently, the play between public Liberty and private Freedom has been more elastic; continentals hanker after an overall system in which liberty itself might become an entailed (or disgraced) element of their *Weltanschauung*, but few Englishmen have felt the need for that kind of imported luxury. Immunity from regimenting creeds is not the least of their liberties.

Only in war-time do the British accept conscription, whether literal or spiritual. Generally, they prefer to digress on common ground rather than to have their society determined by ideological shibboleths or rendered uniform by systematic tailoring. In this they have more in common with the Athenian creators of democracy than with the interpreters, inheritors and impersonators of Holy Writ.

What do, and should, we mean by common ground? In unstrident practice, need it come to more than the possession of a common vocabulary? Those who share a common sense of social possibilities do not need to re-invent the wheel, or the language, every time they want to reach agreement (if only to differ). The speaking of another language, more recherché or perhaps more refined, or of street argots and clannish codes, is not ruled out by giving fundamental importance to a common language. Without it, the useful commerce of ideas, and even of polemics, becomes questionable; when people can no longer disagree fruitfully, a society disintegrates. To maintain that people should mean *roughly* the same things if they are to achieve coherence in diversity, which is the defining characteristic of the civilised state, is by no means to deny the likelihood of disagreement, both semantic and practical, within the context of shared assumptions about the limits of the tolerable.

What we elect to have in common enables us to mediate quarrels in such a way that they can avoid being murderous and, with luck, become productive of liberating harmonies. Free speech is not an accorded privilege but the defining condition of a free society; the supposed weaknesses of democracy, its nattering divisions, are precisely what render it articulate, and hence resilient. I remember being in an unusually silent Athens during the rule of the Colonels – ignobly, if surreptitiously, underwritten by Washington and London – and telling a Greek friend how England was loud with the diatribes of opposing parties and how the country was frustrated with strikes and incompetence. 'It sounds wonderful,' he said.

The notion of civility, in which the idea of the City (of men and, in St Augustine's image, of God) has its radical place, is as much spatial as social. The evolution of democracy demanded an open place where men could meet and vote *and see each other do so.* Such an unwalled meeting place contrasted with the locked and gated palace, in which kings and tyrants conspired – breathed together – in an exclusive air of privilege. In a society of free men, argument replaced *fiat*; only the verdict of the majority could translate dissent into decision. A palace might be plain outside, as in archaic Asia Minor, but it was sumptuous within; that of Gyges, who invented money, was notoriously jaundiced with the gold he secreted from the common people: his subjects were shut out both from the profits of his rich state and from its councils.

It is a pretty coincidence, at least for admirers of Friedrich von Hayek and Milton Friedman, that when the Athenian populace came to have a meeting place, they used the *agora*,

which means 'market', for their gatherings. The topography
of the Open Society – to use Karl Popper's ringingly happy
phrase – demands an open space to which, for citizens, there
is no limited access. It is tempting to see the auditorium of the
theatre of Dionysos, a second civic space where entertaining
(and alarming) debate – ritualised in the formality of tragic
dialogue – took place under critical surveillance by the citizens, as a further vital element in the topography of freedom.
The use of the *agora* as the fulcrum of the democratic state
chimes with a society in which there is a free circulation of
wealth, if not necessarily the 'market economy' so dear to
those who would seek, still in the name of freedom, to make
ruthlessness the motor and money the lubricant of morals.

The common ground need not be as level as a parade
square nor its definition precise; the ability to march in step is
not a paramount civil virtue. Despite Plato's penchant for
geometry, rigid rectilinearity is not a city's most admirable
attribute (we need not even believe that the Platonic polity –
a model of unfreedom, like so many Utopias – was much
more than a *satirical* conceit). In mundane terms, the common ground is an area where loutish or lordly ambushes do
not threaten and where the free, perhaps loud, play of opinions and ideas can take place without intimidation. It is, above
all, no one's property.

What could ever guarantee absolutely the civility on which
freedom is posited? The belief that it is natural to be a demo-
crat and to respect the views of others is an ardent fiction,
more noble than Plato's 'noble lie', but hardly less synthetic.
Might one not argue that our personal freedom, and the 'free

will' which typifies it is also an ardent construct rather than a natural phenomenon?

The possession of a common vocabulary does not imply that we should all say the same things (arguably, it implies the opposite), still less that what we say should be without nuance or provocation. Community implies that, as in a court of law, we may argue about meanings (and re-define terms), but that no one can claim privileged knowledge of what a word means, or 'should' mean, in such a way that others are *forced* to use it in a tendentious sense: a common language must be the vessel of clarity, but – unlike 'basic English', for instance – it must not be hostile to nuance. It announces itself not only in its general intelligibility but also in its capacity to express disagreements in such a way that its grammar, in the widest sense, becomes an impersonal corrective, capable of jibbing at nonsense, like a cough from a tactful judge, and innately disposed to favour coherent answers to social and moral questions. Through a civilised language, even the dead retain the vote and add their wisdom to our arguments. It is in this sense that great writers and wise citizens can hope for immortality in the literature and speech of an unabased society.

The fantasy of a private language, in which more nuances, more subtleties can be codified than in vulgar speech, is not only self-contradictory, in philosophical terms (Wittgenstein pointed out that the speaker of a private language would not even be able to understand himself), it is also the habitual recourse of the autocrat who insists that words must mean what he says they mean, neither more nor less. Such a tyrant is refuted, if (alas) not always dethroned, by his words having no meaning unless they are rendered in the common language he seeks to subvert or supplant. Free speech entails public examination and evaluation; it is conducive to criticism as well as to all those uncontrollable laxities which tyrants so regularly denounce. In banning humour (Plato deplored loud laughter), they seek, always in vain, to abort the unpredictability which is instinct in all freedom of speech.

Vladimir Nabokov forecast the collapse of the Soviet Union on linguistic grounds alone, and was the only man to do so: he claimed, improbably but rightly, that the great Russian language itself would eventually evict those who crushed its subtleties. How typical that he, as an entomologist, should nominate as the fundamental rule of nature 'the survival of the frailest'! Russia, he always insisted, would free itself from the power which the dictatorship of the Party, and its crooked leaders, sought to exercise over it. The language of Pushkin could not tolerate the tenancy of sloganeers. Only a dandy and self-conscious artist such as Nabokov could have dared, in this way, to concede no distinction between aesthetic and ethical revulsion: he regarded the cruelty and the prose style of the Soviets with the same implacable disgust. A régime whose vocabulary debarred both grace and common sense could not but degenerate into brutal and ridiculous chaos.

All totalitarianism falls into ruinous contradiction the moment it tries to deny that freedom of choice which the existence of negation – the ability to say 'no' – itself guarantees. This freedom is not a fortunate grace; it derives logically from the fact that whatever can be asserted can also be denied. This 'irresponsibility' in language is loudly shivered at by George Steiner, in *Language and Silence* and elsewhere, but he confuses the fancied stimulus of censorship with the dividends of reticence: it is precisely because language has, as he might say, no morals (which grammar somewhat denies) that it can *always* respond.

As Antigone's defiance of Creon reminds us, the right to say 'no' is ineradicably, perhaps duplicitously, embedded in any viable language; it may be repressed, it may even be punished by death, as in Antigone's and in Mandelstam's case, but no enduring language, and hence no society, is conceivable without the possibility of denial. This assurance provides frail comfort under the tyrannies whose first weapon is the appropriation of a monopoly of the negative, but its permanent loss is a logico-empirical impossibility. Freedom of speech is – to use a Lévi-Straussian term in a sense which the structuralist approach to myth would hardly sanction – *embedded* in the notion of language itself; almost as soon as man can say anything, he is armed to say 'yes' or 'no'. In view of this, no deep psychological analysis of man is essential to establish the existence of free will. Whether or not we are programmed by the double helix (Shakespeare's mortal coil), the uncontrollable ambivalences of language promise that man can always demand freedom, even if the consequence is that he literally negates himself; he is certainly at liberty to do so. Whether we like it or not, the contrariness of speech will invariably rupture every monolithic programme and interdict every interdiction. Duplicity (which sex and the reproductive process mirror and perhaps sponsor) exerts the same slow, green pressure as a blade of grass when it threads the weak spots in a slab of

Portland stone and finally finds its piercing way to the light.

Who can say, or needs to discover, to what degree Nabokov's *méchanceté* ('wickedness' does not quite convey the French word's combination of sly perversity and contrary egotism) was motivated by snobbish disdain for the vulgarity of the Soviet rulers and for the mundane conformity in which they sought to mould human activity? The libertine and the apostle of liberty have close, if unreliable, affinities. Byron, to whom Nabokov's *Ada* pays skittishly outrageous tribute, is the great European example of the insider-outsider, a Janus whose ambivalence in sexual and social matters rendered him both scandal and totem (in this regard, lame Byron limped after lame Oedipus, his senior in mythology). If his lordship was taken a little too seriously on the continent, where the translators usually missed his teasing ironies, and too lightly in England, where it was convenient to take his political radicalism as a way of disguising his moral indignity, Byron remains the advocate of a kind of liberty which, without any large system, glories in commonness and common sense, though George Gordon would not, I suspect, ever choose to renounce his peerage.

Unsurprisingly, Byron was anathema to the Victorians. The presumptuous destruction of his journals, by his own publisher, John Murray, and his intimate friends Hobhouse and Tom Moore, was an act of iniquitous devotion by men who sought to protect the poet's reputation in the eyes of posterity by a prophylactic auto-da-fé. Byron has, nonetheless, become a by-word for outrageousness. He expressed his craving for liberty by wanting to have, and do, things both ways. Kingsley

Amis' latest novel is called *You Can't Do Both* (I yield to no one as a prompt reader of his titles), but Byron refutes him and remains, for selective persons, the rampant example of the I-dealism to which 'permissiveness' can lead, assuming that you have the talent, the profile and the money.

The term 'permissiveness' belongs, of course, squarely to the rhetoric of repression, it suggests that free behaviour is the result only of whatever licences are accorded by central authority. In the rhetoric of liberty, on the other hand, freedom derives not from a *relaxation* of rules but from the conscious capacity to set, and then to honour, them. Free people, the libertarian argues, do not speak or act freely as the result of a ukase; the smiles of those who make a *show* of being free, or happy, as peasants did in Soviet propaganda films, demonstrate precisely what it is *not* to be happy. Nabokov regarded the 'art' which framed and procured these false images as the very instance of aesthetic treason. In our own comfortably untragic, merely sad and comic world, we are less often bullied into acquiescence with the prevailing 'ideology' than tickled into it by the media to which circulation and viewing figures are the measure of what is worthwhile. In the perverted Benthamite reckonings of the networks, the applause of the mass audience is equated with what is good for it. When freedom of choice becomes a matter of economics, to dissent from the majority taste can be conveniently stigmatised as undemocratic; 'élitism' is now a denunciatory term applied to all suspected of not clapping with due enthusiasm to the majority's beat. Freedom *from* choice is the luxury offered by all extremists.

It is no part of democratic loyalty to endorse, or share, the tastes or opinions of the majority. In a free society, the rule of the majority is an arbitrary way of selecting a line of action, not of determining its virtues. Even if 99.9% of the population agreed that something should be done, it would do nothing to prove that it was *right* to do it; ethical and aesthetic issues cannot be resolved by a show of hands. Furthermore, whatever it may imply in stone on every *mairie* in France, equality is not a function of liberty nor liberty its synonym. It is impossible, as Jonathan Sumption and Keith Joseph once argued, on Hayekian principles, for a society to enjoy liberty and yet ordain equality. This does not entail that it is wrong, still less that it is unfeasible, to legislate piecemeal against unjust inequalities, especially in the field of opportunity (though here the right of the talented to prevail cannot be read, without disastrous results, as a symptom of injustice). Equality before the law has nothing to do with status and everything to do with procedural honesty. When Margaret Drabble argues, apparently sincerely, for everyone to have the same salary, she reveals the limitations of sincerity: such equality would bring human intercourse to a halt.

The apparently self-evident justice of one-man/one-vote does not, as it might be convenient to claim, argue for the equal value of everyone's opinion; it is because it is a practical impossibility to evaluate the correct quotient of influence to give to the wise man's view as against the fool's or the charlatan's that a free society *postulates* an equality which no evidence can prove to be a fact of nature. The intelligent and the knowledgeable may, in practice, have only one vote but, luckily for society, they have other means of making their influence count. It was not for nothing that the Greeks postulated a Goddess *Peitho*, who was the patron of persuasion.

To give equal weight to every citizen's vote does not in any way confer the force of *truth* on, for instance, the referendum (it is nearly always those with peremptory temperaments, like Mrs Thatcher, who – if only when baulked – find sudden virtue in the corporate yell). If what the majority voted for thereby became *true* or even, supposedly, right (rather than current policy or law), the rule of majorities would be as prejudicial to freedom as it would be dangerous to art, science and honour. There is neither paradox nor puzzle here, though confusions can be engendered by a false account of what democracy means or by demagogic appeals to 'the people' and its *volkisch* infallibility. 'The people' do not come into their liberated own if their orchestrated yes or no is declared to be the last word; they are more often led into bondage in the trappings of freedom. The referendum has signed away more liberties than it ever procured; its use in Switzerland appears benign, but even there it is a device, however pragmatic, which confers a wished-for unity on a trinity of disparate communities.

In general, we may depend upon it that those who clamour for freedom from the inadequacies of politicians by advocating constant reference to 'all the people' are the barkers of the arbitrary. Given influence or office, they soon become the willing sycophants of the powerful: Montaigne's friend, Etienne de la Boëtie drew their stinging portraits, with precocious accuracy, more than four and a half centuries ago, in his essay on '*la servitude volontaire*'.

The origins of liberty and of the burden of freedom are both historical and mythical. The fundamental myth which haunts the Western imagination is that of Eden. Before the Fall, Adam and Eve were allegedly at one with God and in a state of innocence; they neither did evil nor were they acquainted with even the possibility of doing it. They could supposedly 'speak' to animals and knew the true names of everything in nature. Wittgenstein may have maintained that if lions could talk, we could not understand them, but he came after the Fall. Were Adam and Eve free when in their paradisi-acal state? They were free *of* freedom, one might say. As God's creatures, they were not His slaves, but their happiness was conditional on honouring His ordinance that they should *not* do something: the Tree of Knowledge was expressly forbidden them, just as the locked room in the castle was out of bounds to Bluebeard's bride. In each case, the avoidance of undue curiosity entailed both happiness and – dare one say? – immaturity. At the root of our notion of freedom there lies an uneasy relationship with knowledge; God might be accused of having given an unfairly alluring flavour to the fruit he advised against tasting. By decreeing what should not be done, He instigated that long fascination with the forbidden which Nabokov underlined, with delicate crudeness, when he pointed out that incest and nicest were anagrams of each other.

Eve's seduction by the snake gave her an appetite for the forbidden which was synonymous with 'knowledge'. Some feminists see a distorted version of the mother goddess, Cybele, in the wicked snake. In their view, the male-oriented myth of Genesis was designed to disparage female power; it is not implausible to see the snake's solicitation of Eve as a gesture of liberation from male dominance. On this account, Eve was being recruited to the female side in order to *recover* lost powers; the knowledge which was forbidden her was, one might say, *already* hers, although she did not know it. Her 'innocence' was a form of repression from which the snake sought to deliver her.

According to the more conventional reading, it was not Eve's desire to retrieve intellectual insights which disposed her to bite the apple. Milton's 'first disobedience' denoted an end to the unthinking bliss which Eden continues to symbolise. Whatever the charms of feminist revision, it is difficult now not to see Eve's *acte gratuit* as the source of her (and our) inexorable 'freedom', of which exile from blissful innocence is an inevitable ingredient.

If one pursued the counter-reading of the Eden myth, it could be said falsely to portray the woman as the *cause* of our unhappy state in which, in fact, she has been unjustly enslaved by the male. More commonly, though less wittily or provocatively, Eve's deviance, or defiance, has been seen as an original sin from whose yoke humanity can never be free until it is redeemed by a Second Coming. Only then will those who merit salvation, or by Grace are granted it, return to a condition of timeless Edenic innocence in which, I daresay, they can all enjoy Ms Drabble's minimum/maximum wage, since time will have a stop.

Presumably the Millennium will put an end not only to wage differentials but also to the pursuit of knowledge, which the Fall began. Man's appetite for knowledge is a function of his ejection from that seamless continuity with Reality which his unfallen state accorded him. It is tempting to ask whether the freedom which enabled Eve to 'sin' was superfluous to the needs of the first couple. Had God not granted them the possibility of diverging from His commands, what defect would it have entailed in their blissful state, other than the opportunity to ruin it? It is pious to argue that generosity impelled God to give man the freedom to choose to be obedient, without which good behaviour would have lacked merit. A less genial view might be that the giving of free will to Adam and Eve was an act of divine *méchanceté*, of Nabokovian ingenuity, on the part of a deity who, given His omniscience, must have known (since He knew everything) that Eve would never resist the blandishments of the serpent.

The theological cruxes which have for so long filled the Garden of Eden with their brambled skeins cannot, of course, be straightened out by playful recension; their wrangling complexity denotes the problem which man has had in deciding both what he is and what he wants to be. The notion of the natural law, enacted by St Thomas and implicit – in secular form – in the idea of Universal Human Rights, is sustained by the hope, the dream or the fantasy of a recovered Eden. By conscious virtue or responsible planning, it is hoped that humanity can recoup its innocence without losing its knowledge. The return to such a state of natural balance and righteous respect depends on the belief that a condition of more or less Edenic stability will necessarily follow from the elimination of *abuses*. The assumption is that worldwide harmony can be restored. Universal Rights, on this reckoning, have a sort of *republican* divinity: they constitute the unfortunately lapsed blueprint of what was, or could be, the fundamental code for human freedom.

Unfortunately, it does not demand the cynicism of Talleyrand, or of his modern disciple Henry Kissinger, to see that the unity of the world – in which we are all incited to see ourselves as the crew of a single small space ship – and the notion of its harmonic redemption amount to a sentimental fiction. The increasing evidence of the earth's junior status in the immense universe may chasten or thrill us; it may liberate the happy few from antique delusions, just as Galileo's telescope definitively dislodged mankind from its central vanity, but the diversity of human beings is as certain as their superficial fraternity.

The good and the bad news are delivered, as so often, in the same package. It is practically inconceivable that mankind can arrive at universally observed standards in public or private affairs or that, if it did, it would still be capable of civilised progress. The recognition of humanity's petty standing and fragile prospects of survival may be salutary, but it cannot make life worth living nor provide a brave prospectus. Resignation and modesty may, at times, be seemly but the lure of the unknown, to which we accede in the exercise of freedom, must always trump them. The myth of Prometheus and his rejection of submission even to the will of Zeus promises that the heretic has his long place in the grammar of European motives. We cannot agree to be obedient to any authority, whether forceful or benign, without betraying what, in a deep sense, Wittgenstein called our language.

The horrid example of the Romantics, with their Herderian penchant for the innate wisdom of the *Volk*, threatens to foul any discussion of the naturalness of defining a people by its language, but it is, I think, possible to find a way of both ennobling and extending the limits of community without embracing the flabby vacuousness of the global village. In fact, the myth which Aeschylus revised, renovated and, to a degree, invented in *The Oresteia* lies deeply embedded in the European language, that nexus of metaphors and forms which, transcending particular national languages, supplies our fractured community with its abiding hopes and fears. It is this conjunction of what we dread with what we must learn to treasure which Aeschylus so unforgettably contrived in the resolution of the conflict between the old chthonic forces, the so-called Furies, and the new divinities on Mount Olympus. The genius of Aeschylus lay in seeing that unless the darkness can be recruited to harmony with the light, unless what we fear becomes incorporated and useful in what we hope, there is no chance of achieving what Wittgenstein meant when he spoke of saying 'the new thing in the old language'. The single currency of a mint language could create only a false Eden, in which some snake will always be found to cozen some man or some woman into reverting to the bloody ways which bland formulae have sought to occlude.

What political system has ever been more insolent with supposition or more freely *fabricated* than Athenian democracy? Its procedures were in no way a *natural* development; it derived, in the first instance, from sly contrivance by Kleisthenes, who used the tradition of tribal voting in order to break the power of the old aristocrats and, by the wilful creation of an intelligently confusing arrangement of new tribes and procedures, gave Athens a new cohesion. He resolved contradictions which might have led to civil rupture and used their energy to compound Athenian strength.

Aeschylus celebrates the synthetic unity of the old and the new Gods, and of the citizens who look to them for guidance. In his myth too, feminists can find sources of indignation. The evil which blighted Greece derived, men claimed, from Helen the destroyer and her twin sister, born of the same egg, Klytemnestra, who killed the returning Agamemnon and began the trail of blood which ended on the Areopagus in Orestes' amnesty. However, even in the course of liberating Athens from the automatic pollution which the old laws decreed, Aeschylus recognises, though finally he does not honour, Klytemnestra's rage at the sacrifice of Iphigeneia. We cannot ever arrive at a new and clean beginning, immaculately free of the dark gods whom Aeschylus and Athens were wise enough to incorporate (and tactfully re-name) rather than to repress. The imprisoned liberty which Byron saluted in his sonnet on Chillon may well have uglier cell-mates who, crushed by bland edicts, can also find dangerous wings unless their force is recruited to the common knowledge and freely acknowledged, even savoured, by those who find it alien. The process of ennobling the savage and of reconciling the incompatible is not a matter of extending rights or of posed hand-shakes; it requires the kind of imaginative harnessing of old hatreds into energetic common purposes and in the excavation of common ground of which Aeschylus furnished abiding paradigms both in *The Oresteia* and in his Prometheus. In each case, compromise is revealed as an agonising and dangerous choice, not a bland business of communiqués; freedom from the old demons requires their conscious co-optation in fresh enterprise and, as Spinoza first said, and the Communist party mischievously parroted, the recognition of a certain kind of necessity. Freedom is both indivisible and the fruit of division; duplicity – yes *and* no – is our nature and our fate. Why else do we so often see the masks of comedy and tragedy depending from the same nail?

Frederick Forsyth

there are no snakes in ireland

After education at Tonbridge, Frederick Forsyth, who had qualified for a pilot's licence a few days after his seventeenth birthday, signed on in the RAF and gained his wings at nineteen, becoming the youngest pilot in the Air Force. Then he went into journalism and it was in the Reuter bureau in Paris that he amassed the detailed information about the OAS which was to become the basis of *The Day of the Jackal*.

He later transferred to Berlin and that enabled him to compile the dossier about Nazis still in high-ranking positions in Germany which was the controversial feature of *The Odessa File*.

Next, he covered the Biafra war both for the BBC and as a freelance. This not only gave him the material for his only non-fiction work, *The Biafra Story*, but also brought him into direct contact with the world of the mercenary soldiers: hence *The Dogs of War*.

These international bestsellers and his more recent novels *The Devil's Alternative*, *The Fourth Protocol*, *The Negotiator*, *The Deceived* and *The Fist of God* have confirmed Mr Forsyth's unparalleled reputation as a writer of thrillers based on the chilling realities of today's world.

His other works include *The Biafra Story* (non-fiction), *The Shepherd* and an acclaimed collection of short fiction, *No Comebacks*.

McQueen looked across his desk at the new applicant for a job with some scepticism. He had never employed such a one before. But he was not an unkind man, and if the job-seeker needed the money and was prepared to work, McQueen was not averse to giving him a chance.

'You know it's damn hard work?' he said in his broad Belfast accent.

'Yes, sir,' said the applicant.

'It's a quick in-and-out job, ye know. No questions, no pack drill. You'll be working on the lump. Do you know what that means?'

'No, Mr McQueen.'

'Well, it means you'll be paid well but you'll be paid in cash. No red tape. Geddit?'

What he meant was there would be no income tax paid, no National Health contributions deducted at source. He might also have added that there would be no National Insurance cover and that the Health and Safety standards would be completely ignored. Quick profits for all were the order of the day, with a fat slice off the top for himself as the contractor. The job-seeker nodded his head to indicate he had 'goddit' though in fact he had not. McQueen looked at him speculatively.

'You say you're a medical student, in your last year at the

Royal Victoria?' Another nod. 'On the summer vacation?'

Another nod. The applicant was evidently one of those students who needed money over and above his grant to put himself through medical school. McQueen, sitting in his dingy Bangor office running a hole-and-corner business as a demolition contractor with assets consisting of a battered truck and a ton of second-hand sledgehammers, considered himself a self-made man and heartily approved of the Ulster Protestant work ethic. He was not one to put down another such thinker, whatever he looked like.

'All right,' he said, 'you'd better take lodgings here in Bangor. You'll never get from Belfast and back in time each day. We work from seven in the morning until sundown. It's work by the hour, hard but well paid. Mention one word to the authorities and you'll lose the job like shit off a shovel. OK?'

'Yes, sir. Please, when do I start and where?'

'The truck picks the gang up at the main station yard every morning at six-thirty. Be there Monday morning. The gang foreman is Big Billie Cameron. I'll tell him you'll be there.'

'Yes, Mr McQueen.' The applicant turned to go.

'One last thing,' said McQueen, pencil poised. 'What's your name?'

'Harkishan Ram Lal,' said the student. McQueen looked at his pencil, the list of names in front of him and the student.

'We'll call you Ram,' he said, and that was the name he wrote down on the list.

The student walked out into the bright July sunshine of Bangor, on the north coast of County Down, Northern Ireland.

By that Saturday evening he had found himself cheap lodgings in a dingy boarding house halfway up Railway View Street, the heart of Bangor's bed-and-breakfast land. At least it was convenient to the main station from which the works truck would depart every morning just after sun-up. From the grimy window of his room he could look straight at the side of the shored embankment that carried the trains from Belfast into the station.

It had taken him several tries to get a room. Most of those houses with a B-and-B notice in the window seemed to be fully booked when he presented himself on the doorstep. But then it was true that a lot of casual labour drifted into the town in the height of summer. True also that Mrs McGurk was a Catholic and she still had rooms left.

He spent Sunday morning bringing his belongings over from Belfast, most of them medical textbooks. In the afternoon he lay on his bed and thought of the bright hard light on the brown hills of his native Punjab. In one more year he would be a qualified physician, and after another year of intern work he would return home to cope with the sicknesses of his own people. Such was his dream. He calculated he could make enough money this summer to tide himself through to his finals and after that he would have a salary of his own.

On the Monday morning he rose at a quarter to six at the bidding of his alarm clock, washed in cold water and was in the station yard just after six. There was time to spare. He found an early-opening café and took two cups of black tea. It was his only sustenance. The battered truck, driven by one of the demolition gang, was there at a quarter past six and a dozen men assembled near it. Harkishan Ram Lal did not know whether to approach them and introduce himself, or wait at a distance. He waited.

At twenty-five past the hour the foreman arrived in his own car, parked it down a side road and strode up to the truck. He had McQueen's list in his hand. He glanced at the dozen men, recognised them all and nodded. The Indian approached. The foreman glared at him.

'Is youse the darkie McQueen has put on the job?' he demanded.

Ram Lal stopped in his tracks. 'Harkishan Ram Lal,' he said. 'Yes.'

There was no need to ask how Big Billie Cameron had earned his name. He stood six feet and three inches in his stockings but was wearing enormous nail-studded, steel-toed boots. Arms like tree trunks hung from huge shoulders and his head was surmounted by a shock of ginger hair. Two small, pale-lashed eyes stared down balefully at the slight and wiry Indian. It was plain he was not best pleased. He spat on the ground.

'Well get in the fecking truck,' he said.

On the journey out to the work site Cameron sat up in the cab which had no partition dividing it from the back of the lorry, where the dozen labourers sat on two wooden benches down the sides. Ram Lal was near the tailboard next to a small, nut-hard man with bright blue eyes, whose name turned out to be Tommy Burns. He seemed friendly.

'Where are youse from?' he asked with genuine curiosity.

'India,' said Ram Lal. 'The Punjab.'

'Well, which?' said Tommy Burns.

Ram Lal smiled. 'The Punjab is a part of India,' he said.

Burns thought about this for a while. 'You Protestant or Catholic?' he asked at length.

'Neither,' said Ram Lal patiently. 'I am a Hindu.'

'You mean you're not a Christian?' asked Burns in amazement.

'No. Mine is the Hindu religion.'

'Hey,' said Burns to the others, 'your man's not a Christian at all.' He was not outraged, just curious, like a small child who has come across a new and intriguing toy.

Cameron turned from the cab up front. 'Aye,' he snarled, 'a heathen.'

The smile dropped off Ram Lal's face. He stared at the opposite canvas wall of the truck. By now they were well south of Bangor, clattering down the motorway towards Newtownards. After a while Burns began to introduce him to the others. There was a Craig, a Munroe, a Patterson, a Boyd and two Browns. Ram Lal had been long enough in Belfast to recognise the names as being originally Scottish, the sign of the hard Presbyterians who make up the backbone of the Protestant majority of the Six Counties. The men seemed amiable and nodded back at him.

'Have you not got a lunch box, laddie?' asked the elderly man called Patterson.

'No,' said Ram Lal, 'it was too early to ask my landlady to make one up.'

'You'll need lunch,' said Burns, 'aye, and breakfast. We'll be making tay ourselves on a fire.'

'I will make sure to buy a box and bring some food tomorrow,' said Ram Lal.

Burns looked at the Indian's rubber-soled soft boots. 'Have you not done this kind of work before?' he asked.

Ram Lal shook his head.

'You'll need a pair of heavy boots. To save your feet, you see.'

Ram Lal promised he would also buy a pair of heavy ammunition boots from a store if he could find one open late at night. They were through Newtownards and still heading south on the A21 towards the small town of Comber. Craig looked across at him.

'What's your real job?' he asked.

'I'm a medical student at the Royal Victoria in Belfast,' said Ram Lal. 'I hope to qualify next year.'

Tommy Burns was delighted. 'That's near to being a real doctor,' he said. 'Hey, Big Billie, if one of us gets a knock young Ram could take care of it.'

Big Billie grunted. 'He's not putting a finger on me,' he said.

That killed further conversation until they arrived at the work site. The driver had pulled northwest out of Comber and two miles up the Dundonald road he bumped down a track to the right until they came to a stop where the trees ended and saw the building to be demolished.

It was a huge old whiskey distillery, sheer-sided, long derelict. It had been one of two in these parts that had once turned out good Irish whiskey but had gone out of business years before. It stood beside the River Comber, which had once powered its great waterwheel as it flowed down from Dundonald to Comber and on to empty itself in Strangford Lough. The malt had arrived by horse-drawn cart down the track and the barrels of whiskey had left the same way. The sweet water that had powered the machines had also been used in the vats. But the distillery had stood alone, abandoned and empty for years.

Of course the local children had broken in and found it an ideal place to play. Until one had slipped and broken a leg. Then the county council had surveyed it, declared it a hazard and the owner found himself with a compulsory demolition order.

He, scion of an old family of squires who had known better days, wanted the job done as cheaply as possible. That was where McQueen came in. It could be done faster but more expensively with heavy machinery; Big Billie and his team would do it with sledges and crowbars. McQueen had even lined up a deal to sell the best timbers and the hundreds of tons of mature bricks to a jobbing builder. After all, the wealthy nowadays wanted their new houses to have 'style' and that meant looking old. So there was a premium on antique sun-bleached old bricks and genuine ancient timber beams to adorn the new-look-old 'manor' houses of the top executives. McQueen would do all right.

'Right lads,' said Big Billie as the truck rumbled away back to Bangor. 'There it is. We'll start with the roof tiles. You know what to do.'

The group of men stood beside their pile of equipment. There were great sledgehammers with seven-pound heads;

crowbars six feet long and over an inch thick; nailbars a yard long with curved split tips for extracting nails; short-handled, heavy-headed lump hammers and a variety of timber saws. The only concessions to human safety were a number of webbing belts with dogclips and hundreds of feet of rope. Ram Lal looked up at the building and swallowed. It was four storeys high and he hated heights. But scaffolding is expensive

One of the men, unbidden, went to the building, prised off a plank door, tore it up like a playing card and started a fire. Soon a billycan of water from the river was boiling away and tea was made. They all had their enamel mugs except Ram Lal. He made a mental note to buy that also. It was going to be thirsty, dusty work. Tommy Burns finished his own mug and offered it, refilled, to Ram Lal.

'Do they have tea in India?' he asked.

Ram Lal took the proffered mug. The tea was ready-mixed, sweet and off-white. He hated it.

They worked through the first morning perched high on the roof. The tiles were not to be salvaged, so they tore them off manually and hurled them to the ground away from the river. There was an instruction not to block the river with falling rubble. So it all had to land on the other side of the building, in the long grass, weeds, broom and gorse which covered the area round the distillery. The men were roped together so that if one lost his grip and began to slither down the roof, the next man would take the strain. As the tiles disappeared, great yawning holes appeared between the rafters. Down below them was the floor of the top storey, the malt store.

At ten they came down the rickety internal stairs for

breakfast on the grass, with another billycan of tea. Ram Lal ate no breakfast. At two they broke for lunch. The gang tucked into their piles of thick sandwiches. Ram Lal looked at his hands. They were nicked in several places and bleeding. His muscles ached and he was very hungry. He made another mental note about buying some heavy work gloves.

Tommy Burns held up a sandwich from his own box. 'Are you not hungry, Ram?' he asked. 'Sure, I have enough here.'

'What do you think you're doing?' asked Big Billie from where he sat across the circle round the fire.

Burns looked defensive. 'Just offering the lad a sandwich,' he said.

'Let the darkie bring his own fecking sandwiches,' said Cameron. 'You look after yourself.'

The men looked down at their lunch boxes and ate in silence. It was obvious no one argued the toss with Big Billie.

'Thank you, I am not hungry,' said Ram Lal to Burns. He walked away and sat by the river where he bathed his burning hands.

By sundown when the truck came to collect them half the tiles on the great roof were gone. One more day and they would start on the rafters, work for saw and nailbar.

Throughout the week the work went on, and the once proud building was stripped of its rafters, planks and beams until it stood hollow and open, its gaping windows like open eyes staring at the prospect of its imminent death. Ram Lal was unaccustomed to the arduousness of this kind of labour. His muscles ached endlessly, his hands were blistered, but he toiled on for the money he needed so badly.

He had acquired a tin lunch box, enamel mug, hard boots and a pair of heavy gloves, which no one else wore. Their hands were hard enough from years of manual work. Throughout the week Big Billie Cameron needled him without let-up, giving him the hardest work and positioning him on the highest points once he had learned Ram Lal hated heights. The Punjabi bit on his anger because he needed the money. The crunch came on the Saturday.

The timbers were gone and they were working on the masonry. The simplest way to bring the edifice down away from the river would have been to plant explosive charges in the corners of the side wall facing the open clearing. But dynamite was out of the question. It would have required special licences in Northern Ireland of all places, and that would have alerted the tax man. McQueen and all his gang would have been required to pay substantial sums in income tax, and McQueen in National Insurance contributions. So they were chipping the walls down in square-yard chunks, standing hazardously on sagging floors as the supporting walls splintered and cracked under the hammers.

During lunch Cameron walked round the building a couple of times and came back to the circle round the fire. He began to describe how they were going to bring down a sizeable chunk of one outer wall at third-floor level. He turned to Ram Lal.

'I want you up on the top there,' he said. 'When it starts to go, kick it outwards.'

Ram Lal looked up at the section of wall in question. A great crack ran along the bottom of it.

'That brickwork is going to fall at any moment,' he said

evenly. 'Anyone sitting on top there is going to come down with it.'

Cameron stared at him, his face suffusing, his eyes pink with rage where they should have been white. 'Don't you tell me my job; you do as you're told, you stupid fecking nigger.' He turned and stalked away.

Ram Lal rose to his feet. When his voice came, it was in hard-edged shout. '*Mister Cameron . . .*'

Cameron turned in amazement. The men sat open-mouthed. Ram Lal walked slowly up to the big ganger.

'Let us get one thing plain,' said Ram Lal, and his voice carried clearly to everyone else in the clearing. 'I am from the Punjab in northern India. I am also a Kshatria, member of the warrior caste. I may not have enough money to pay for my medical studies, but my ancestors were soldiers and princes, rulers and scholars, two thousand years ago when yours were crawling on all fours dressed in skins. Please do not insult me any further.'

Big Billie Cameron stared down at the Indian student. The whites of his eyes had turned a bright red. The other labourers sat in stunned amazement.

'Is that so?' said Cameron quietly. 'Is that so, now? Well, things are a bit different now, you black bastard. So what are you going to do about that?'

On the last word he swung his arm, open-palmed, and his hand crashed into the side of Ram Lal's face. The youth was thrown bodily to the ground several feet away. His head sang. He heard Tommy Burns call out, 'Stay down laddie. Big Billie will kill you if you get up.'

Ram Lal looked up into the sunlight. The giant stood over him, fists bunched. He realised he had not a chance in combat against the big Ulsterman. Feelings of shame and humiliation flooded over him. His ancestors had ridden, sword and lance in hand, across plains a hundred times bigger than these six counties, conquering all before them.

Ram Lal closed his eyes and lay still. After several seconds he heard the big man move away. A low conversation started among the others. He squeezed his eyes tighter shut to hold back the tears of shame. In the blackness he saw the baking plains of the Punjab and men riding over them; proud, fierce men, hook-nosed, bearded, turbaned, black-eyed, the warriors from the Land of Five Rivers.

Once, long ago in the world's morning, Iskander of Macedon had ridden over these plains with his hot and hungry eyes; Alexander, the young god, whom they called The Great, who at twenty-five had wept because there were no more worlds to conquer. These riders were the descendants of his captains, and the ancestors of Harkishan Ram Lal.

He was lying in the dust as they rode by, and they looked down at him in passing. As they rode each of them mouthed one single word to him. Vengeance.

Ram Lal picked himself up in silence. It was done, and what still had to be done had to be done. That was the way of his people. He spent the rest of the day working in complete silence. He spoke to no one and no one spoke to him.

That evening in his room he began his preparations as night was about to fall. He cleared away the brush and comb from the battered dressing table and removed also the soiled doily and the mirror from its stand. He took his book of the Hindu religion and from it cut a page-sized portrait of the great goddess Shakti, she of power and justice. This he pinned to the wall above the dressing table to convert it into a shrine.

He had bought a bunch of flowers from a seller in front of the main station, and these had been woven into a garland. To one side of the portrait of the goddess he placed a shallow bowl half-filled with sand, and in the sand stuck a candle which he lit. From his suitcase he took a cloth roll and extracted half a dozen joss sticks. Taking a cheap, narrow-necked vase from the bookshelf, he placed them in it and lit the ends. The sweet, heady odour of the incense began to fill the room. Outside, big thunderheads rolled up from the sea.

When his shrine was ready he stood before it, head bowed, the garland in his fingers, and began to pray for guidance. The first rumble of thunder rolled over Bangor. He used not the modern Punjabi but the ancient Sanskrit, language of prayer. '*Devi Shakti . . . Maa . . .* Goddess Shakti . . . great mother . . .'

The thunder crashed again and the first raindrops fell. He plucked the first flower and placed it in front of the portrait of Shakti.

'I have been grievously wronged. I ask vengeance upon the wrongdoer . . .' He plucked the second flower and put it beside the first.

He prayed for an hour while the rain came down. It drummed on the tiles above his head, streamed past the window behind him. He finished praying as the storm subsided. He needed to know what form the retribution should take. He needed the goddess to send him a sign.

When he had finished, the joss sticks had burned themselves out and the room was thick with their scent. The candle guttered low. The flowers all lay on the lacquered surface of the dressing table in front of the portrait. Shakti stared back at him unmoved.

He turned and walked to the window to look out. The rain had stopped but everything beyond the panes dripped water. As he watched, a dribble of rain sprang from the guttering above the window and a trickle ran down the dusty glass, cutting a path through the grime. Because of the dirt it did not run straight but meandered sideways, drawing his eye farther and farther to the corner of the window as he followed its path. When it stopped he was staring at the corner of his room, where his dressing gown hung on a nail.

He noticed that during the storm the dressing-gown cord had slipped and fallen to the floor. It lay coiled upon itself, one knotted end hidden from view, the other lying visible on the carpet. Of the dozen tassels only two were exposed, like a forked tongue. The coiled dressing-gown cord resembled nothing so much as a snake in the corner. Ram Lal understood. The next day he took the train to Belfast to see the Sikh.

Ranjit Singh was also a medical student, but he was more fortunate. His parents were rich and sent him a handsome allowance. He received Ram Lal in his well-furnished room at the hostel.

'I have received word from home,' said Ram Lal. 'My father is dying.'

'I am sorry,' said Ranjit Singh, 'you have my sympathies.'

'He asks to see me. I am his first born. I should return.'

'Of course,' said Singh. 'The first-born son should always be by his father when he dies.' 'It is a matter of the air fare,' said Ram Lal. 'I am working and making good money. But I do not have enough. If you will lend me the balance I will continue working when I return and repay you.'

Sikhs are no strangers to money lending if the interest is right and repayment secure. Ranjit Singh promised to withdraw the money from the bank on Monday morning.

That Sunday evening Ram Lal visited Mr McQueen at his home at Groomsport. The contractor was in front of his television set with a can of beer at his elbow. It was his favourite way to spend a Sunday evening. But he turned the sound down as Ram Lal was shown in by his wife.

'It is about my father,' said Ram Lal. 'He is dying.'

'Oh, I'm sorry to hear that, laddie,' said McQueen.

'I should go to him. The first-born should be with his father at this time. It is the custom of our people.'

McQueen had a son in Canada whom he had not seen for seven years.

'Aye,' he said, 'that seems right and proper.'

'I have borrowed the money for the air fare,' said Ram Lal. 'If I went tomorrow I could be back by the end of the week. The point is, Mr McQueen, I need the job more than ever now; to repay the loan and for my studies next term. If I am back by the weekend, will you keep the job open for me?'

'All right,' said the contractor. 'I can't pay you for the time you're away. Nor keep the job open for a further week. But if you're back by the weekend, you can go back to work. Same terms, mind.'

'Thank you,' said Ram, 'you are very kind.'

He retained his room in Railway View Street but spent the night at his hostel in Belfast. On the Monday morning he accompanied Ranjit Singh to the bank where the Sikh withdrew the necessary money and gave it to the Hindu. Ram took a taxi to Aldergrove airport and the shuttle to London where he bought an economy-class ticket on the next flight to India. Twenty-four hours later he touched down in the blistering heat of Bombay.

On the Wednesday he found what he sought in the teeming bazaar at Grant Road Bridge. Mr Chatterjee's Tropical Fish and Reptile Emporium was almost deserted when the young student, with his textbook on reptiles under his arm, wandered in. He found the old proprietor sitting near the back of his shop in half-darkness, surrounded by his tanks of fish and glass-fronted cases in which his snakes and lizards dozed through the hot day.

Mr Chatterjee was no stranger to the academic world. He supplied several medical centres with samples for study and dissection, and occasionally filled a lucrative order from abroad. He nodded his white-bearded head knowledgeably as the student explained what he sought.

'Ah yes,' said the old Bengali merchant, 'I know the snake. You are in luck. I have one, but a few days arrived from Rajputana.'

He led Ram Lal into his private sanctum and the two men stared silently through the glass of the snake's new home.

Echis carinatus, said the textbook, but of course the book had been written by an Englishman, who had used the Latin nomenclature. In English, the saw-scaled viper, smallest and deadliest of all his lethal breed.

Wide distribution, said the textbook, being found from West Africa eastwards and northwards to Iran, and on to India and Pakistan. Very adaptable, able to acclimatise to almost any environment, from the moist bush of western Africa to the cold hills of Iran in winter to the baking hills of India.

Something stirred beneath the leaves in the box.

In size, said the textbook, between nine and thirteen inches long and very slim. Olive brown in colour with a few paler spots, sometimes hardly distinguishable, and a faint undulating darker line down the side of the body. Nocturnal in dry, hot weather, seeking cover during the heat of the day.

The leaves in the box rustled again and a tiny head appeared.

Exceptionally dangerous to handle, said the textbook, causing more deaths than even the more famous cobra, largely because of its size which makes it so easy to touch unwittingly with hand or foot. The author of the book had added a footnote to the effect that the small but lethal snake mentioned by Kipling in his marvellous story '*Rikki-Tikki-Tavy*' was almost certainly not the krait, which is about two feet long, but more probably the saw-scaled viper. The author was obviously pleased to have caught out the great Kipling in a matter of accuracy.

In the box, a little black forked tongue flickered towards the two Indians beyond the glass.

Very alert and irritable, the long-gone English naturalist had concluded his chapter on *Echis carinatus*. Strikes quickly without warning. The fangs are so small they make a virtually unnoticeable puncture, like two tiny thorns. There is no pain, but death is almost inevitable, usually taking between two and four hours, depending on the bodyweight of the victim and the level of his physical exertions at the time and afterwards. Cause of death is invariably a brain haemorrhage.

'How much do you want for him?' whispered Ram Lal.

The old Gujerati spread his hands helplessly. 'Such a prime specimen,' he said regretfully, 'and so hard to come by. Five hundred rupees.'

Ram Lal clinched the deal at 350 rupees and took the snake away in a jar.

For his journey back to London Ram Lal purchased a box of cigars, which he emptied of their contents and in whose lid he punctured twenty small holes for air. The tiny viper, he knew, would need no food for a week and no water for two or three days. It could breathe on an infinitesimal supply of air, so he wrapped the cigar box, resealed and with the viper inside it among his leaves, in several towels whose thick sponginess would contain enough air even inside a suitcase.

He had arrived with a handgrip, but he bought a cheap fibre suitcase and packed it with clothes from market stalls, the cigar box going in the centre. It was only minutes before he left his hotel for Bombay airport that he closed and locked the case. For the flight back to London he checked the suitcase into the hold of the Boeing airliner. His hand baggage was searched, but it contained nothing of interest.

The Air India jet landed at London Heathrow on Friday morning and Ram Lal joined the long queue of Indians trying to get into Britain. He was able to prove he was a medical student and not an immigrant, and was allowed through quite quickly. He even reached the luggage carousel as the first suitcases were tumbling onto it, and saw his own in the first two dozen. He took it to the toilet, where he extracted the cigar box and put it in his handgrip.

In the Nothing-to-Declare channel he was stopped all the same, but it was his suitcase that was ransacked. The customs officer glanced in his shoulder bag and let him pass. Ram Lal crossed Heathrow by courtesy bus to Number One Building and caught the midday shuttle to Belfast. He was in Bangor by teatime and able at last to examine his import.

He took a sheet of glass from the bedside table and slipped it carefully between the lid of the cigar box and its deadly contents before opening wide. Through the glass he saw the viper going round and round inside. It paused and stared with angry black eyes back at him. He pulled the lid shut, withdrawing the pane of glass quickly as the box top came down.

'Sleep, little friend,' he said, 'if your breed ever sleep. In the morning you will do Shakti's bidding for her.'

Before dark he bought a small screw-top jar of coffee and poured the contents into a china pot in his room. In the morning, using his heavy gloves, he transferred the viper from the box to the jar. The enraged snake bit his glove once, but he did not mind. It would have recovered its venom by midday. For a moment he studied the snake, coiled and cramped inside the glass coffee jar, before giving the top a last, hard twist and placing it in his lunch box. Then he went to catch the works truck.

Big Billie Cameron had a habit of taking off his jacket the moment he arrived at the work site, and hanging it on a convenient nail or twig. During the lunch break, as Ram Lal had observed, the giant foreman never failed to go to his jacket after eating, and from the right-hand pocket extract his pipe and tobacco pouch. The routine did not vary. After a satisfying pipe, he would knock out the dottle, rise and say, 'Right, lads, back to work,' as he dropped his pipe back into the pocket of his jacket. By the time he turned round everyone had to be on their feet.

Ram Lal's plan was simple but foolproof. During the morning he would slip the snake into the right-hand pocket of the hanging jacket. After his sandwiches the bullying Cameron would rise from the fire, go to his jacket and plunge his hand into the pocket. The snake would do what great Shakti had ordered that he be brought halfway across the world to do. It would be he, the viper, not Ram Lal, who would be the Ulsterman's executioner.

Cameron would withdraw his hand with an oath from the pocket, the viper hanging from his finger, its fangs deep in the flesh. Ram Lal would leap up, tear the snake away, throw it to the ground and stamp upon its head. It would by then be harmless, its venom expended. Finally, with a gesture of disgust he, Ram Lal, would hurl the dead viper far into the River Comber, which would carry all evidence away to the sea. There might be suspicion, but that was all there would ever be.

Shortly after eleven o'clock, on the excuse of fetching a fresh sledgehammer, Harkishan Ram Lal opened his lunch box, took out the coffee jar, unscrewed the lid and shook the contents into the right-hand pocket of the hanging jacket. Within sixty seconds he was back at his work, his act unnoticed.

During lunch he found it hard to eat. The men sat as usual in a circle round the fire; the dry old timber baulks crackled and spat, the billycan bubbled above them. The men joshed and joked as ever, while Big Billie munched his way through the pile of doorstep sandwiches his wife had prepared for him. Ram Lal had made a point of choosing a place in the circle near to the jacket. He forced himself to eat. In his chest his heart was pounding and the tension in him rose steadily.

Finally Big Billie crumpled the paper of his eaten sandwiches, threw it in the fire and belched. He rose with a grunt and walked towards his jacket. Ram Lal turned his head to watch. The other men took no notice. Billie Cameron reached his jacket and plunged his hand into the right-hand pocket. Ram Lal held his breath. Cameron's hand rummaged for several seconds and then withdrew his pipe and pouch. He bean to fill the bowl with fresh tobacco. As he did so he caught Ram Lal staring at him.

'What are youse looking at?' he demanded belligerently.

'Nothing,' said Ram Lal, and turned to face the fire. But he could not stay still. He rose and stretched, contriving to half turn as he did so. From the corner of his eye he saw Cameron replace the pouch in the pocket and again withdraw his hand with a box of matches in it. The foreman lit his pipe and pulled contentedly. He strolled back to the fire.

Ram Lal resumed his seat and stared at the flames in

disbelief. Why, he asked himself, why had great Shakti done this to him? The snake had been her tool, her instrument brought at her command. But she had held it back, refused to use her own implement of retribution. He turned and sneaked another glance at the jacket. Deep down in the lining at the very hem, on the extreme left-hand side, something stirred and was still. Ram Lal closed his eyes in shock. A hole, a tiny hole in the lining, had undone all his planning. He worked the rest of the afternoon in a daze of indecision and worry.

On the truck ride back to Bangor, Big Billie Cameron sat up front as usual, but in view of the heat folded his jacket and put it on his knees. In front of the station Ram Lal saw him throw the still-folded jacket onto the back seat of his car and drive away. Ram Lal caught up with Tommy Burns as the little man waited for his bus.

'Tell me,' he asked,' does Mr Cameron have a family?'

'Sure,' said the little labourer innocently, 'a wife and two children.'

'Does he live far from here?' said Ram Lal. 'I mean, he drives a car.'

'Not far,' said Burns, 'up on the Kilcooley estate. Ganaway Gardens, I think. Going visiting are you?'

'No, no,' said Ram Lal, 'see you Monday.'

Back in his room Ram Lal stared at the impassive image of the goddess of justice. 'I did not mean to bring death to his wife and children,' he told her. 'They have done nothing to me.'

The goddess from far away stared back and gave no reply.

Harkishan Ram Lal spent the rest of the weekend in an agony of anxiety. That evening he walked to the Kilcooley housing estate on the ring road and found Ganaway Gardens. It lay just off Owenroe Garden and opposite Woburn Walk. At the corner of Woburn Walk there was a telephone kiosk, and here he waited for an hour, pretending to make a call, while he watched the short street across the road. He thought he spotted Big Billie Cameron at one of the windows and noted the house.

He saw a teenage girl come out of it and walk away to join some friends. For a moment he was tempted to accost her and tell her what demon slept inside her father's jacket, but he dared not.

Shortly before dusk a woman came out of the house carrying a shopping basket. He followed her down to the Clandeboye shopping centre, which was open late for those who took their wage packets on a Saturday. The woman he thought to be Mrs Cameron entered Stewarts supermarket and the Indian student trailed round the shelves behind her, trying to pluck up the courage to approach her and reveal the danger in her house. Again his nerve failed him. He might, after all, have the wrong woman, even be mistaken about the house. In that case they would take him away as a madman.

He slept ill that night, his mind racked by visions of the saw-scaled viper coming out of its hiding place in the jacket lining to slither, silent and deadly, through the sleeping council house.

On the Sunday he again haunted the Kilcooley estate, and firmly identified the house of the Cameron family. He saw Big

Billie clearly in the back garden. By mid-afternoon he was attracting attention locally and knew he must either walk boldly up to the front door and admit what he had done, or depart and leave all in the hands of the goddess. The thought of facing the terrible Cameron with the news of what deadly danger had been brought so close to his children was too much. He walked back to Railway View Street.

On Monday morning the Cameron family rose at a quarter to six, a bright and sunny August morning. By six the four of them were at breakfast in the tiny kitchen at the back of the house, the son, daughter and wife in their dressing gowns, Big Billie dressed for work. His jacket was where it had spent the weekend, in a closet in the hallway.

Just after six his daughter Jenny rose, stuffing a piece of marmaladed toast into her mouth. 'I'm away to wash,' she said.

'Before ye go, girl, get my jacket from the press,' said her father, working his way through a plate of cereal. The girl reappeared a few seconds later with the jacket, held by the collar. She proffered it to her father. He hardly looked up.

'Hang it behind the door,' he said. The girl did as she was bid, but the jacket had no hanging tab and the hook was no rusty nail but a smooth chrome affair. The jacket hung for a moment, then fell to the kitchen floor. Her father looked up as she left the room.

'Jenny,' he shouted, 'pick the damn thing up.'

No one in the Cameron household argued with the head of the family. Jenny came back, picked up the jacket and hung it more firmly. As she did, something thin and dark slipped from its folds and slithered into the corner with a dry rustle across the linoleum. She stared at it in horror.

'Dad, what's that in your jacket?'

Big Billie Cameron paused, a spoonful of cereal halfway to his mouth. Mrs Cameron turned from the cooker. Fourteen-year-old Bobby ceased buttering a piece of toast and stared. The small creature lay curled in the corner by the row of cabinets, tight-bunched, defensive, glaring back at the world, tiny tongue flickering fast.

'Lord save us, it's a snake,' said Mrs Cameron.

'Don't be a bloody fool, woman. Don't you know there are no snakes in Ireland? Everyone knows that,' said her husband. He put down the spoon. 'What is it, Bobby?'

Though a tyrant inside and outside his house, Big Billie had a grudging respect for the knowledge of his young son, who was good at school and was being taught many strange things. The boy stared at the snake through his owlish glasses.

'It must be a slowworm, Dad,' he said. 'They had some at school last term for the biology class. Brought them in for dissection. From across the water.'

'It doesn't look like a worm to me,' said his father.

'It isn't really a worm,' said Bobby. 'It's a lizard with no legs.'

'Then why do they call it a worm?' asked his truculent father.

'I don't know,' said Bobby.

'Then what the hell are you going to school for?'

'Will it bite?' asked Mrs Cameron fearfully.

'Not at all,' said Bobby. 'It's harmless.'

'Kill it,' said Cameron senior, 'and throw it in the dustbin.'

His son rose from the table and removed one of his slippers, which he held like a flyswat in one hand. He was advancing, bare-ankled, towards the corner, when his father changed his mind. Big Billie looked up from his plate with a gleeful smile.

'Hold on a minute, just hold on there, Bobby,' he said, 'I have an idea. Woman, get me a jar.'

'What kind of a jar?' asked Mrs Cameron.

'How should I know what kind of a jar? A jar with a lid on it.'

Mrs Cameron sighed, skirted the snake and opened a cupboard. She examined her store of jars.

'There's a jamjar, with dried peas in it,' she said.

'Put the peas somewhere else and give me the jar,' commanded Cameron. She passed him the jar.

'What are you going to do, Dad?' asked Bobby.

'There's a darkie we have at work. A heathen man. He comes from a land with a lot of snakes in it. I have in mind to have some fun with him. A wee joke, like. Pass me that oven glove Jenny.'

'You'll not need a glove,' said Bobby. 'He can't bite you.'

'I'm not touching the dirty thing,' said Cameron.

'He's not dirty,' said Bobby. 'They're very clean creatures.'

'You're a fool, boy, for all your school learning. Does the Good Book not say: "On thy belly shalt thou go, and dust shalt thou eat . . ."? Aye, and more than dust, no doubt. I'll not touch him with me hand.'

Jenny passed her father the oven glove. Open jamjar in his

left hand, right hand protected by the glove, Big Billie
Cameron stood over the viper. Slowly his right hand
descended. When it dropped, it was fast; but the small snake
was faster. Its tiny fangs went harmlessly into the padding of
the glove at the centre of the palm. Cameron did not notice,
for the act was masked from his view by his own hands. In a
trice the snake was inside the jamjar and the lid was on.
Through the glass they watched it wriggle furiously.

'I hate them, harmless or not,' said Mrs Cameron. 'I'll
thank you to get it out of the house.'

'I'll be doing that right now,' said her husband, 'for I'm
late as it is.'

He slipped the jamjar into his shoulder bag, already containing his lunch box, stuffed his pipe and pouch into the
right-hand pocket of his jacket and took both out to the car.
He arrived at the station yard five minutes late and was surprised to find the Indian student staring at him fixedly.

'I suppose he wouldn't have the second sight,' thought Big
Billie as they trundled south to Newtownards and Comber.

By mid-morning all the gang had been let into Big Billie's
secret joke on pain of a thumping if they let on to 'the darkie'.
There was no chance of that; assured that the slowworm was
perfectly harmless, they too thought it a good leg-pull. Only
Ram Lal worked on in ignorance, consumed by his private
thoughts and worries.

At the lunch break he should have suspected something.
The tension was palpable. The men sat in a circle around the
fire as usual, but the conversation was stilted and had he not
been so preoccupied he would have noticed the half-

concealed grins and the looks darted in his direction. He did not notice. He placed his own lunch box between his knees and opened it. Coiled between the sandwiches and the apple, head back to strike, was the viper.

The Indian's scream echoed across the clearing, just ahead of the roar of laughter from the labourers. Simultaneously with the scream, the lunch box flew high in the air as he threw it away from himself with all his strength. All the contents of the box flew in a score of directions, landing in the long grass, the broom and gorse all around them.

Ram Lal was on his feet, shouting. The gangers rolled helplessly in their mirth, Big Billie most of all. He had not had such a laugh in months.

'It's a snake,' screamed Ram Lal, 'a poisonous snake. Get out of here, all of you. It's deadly.'

The laughter redoubled; the men could not contain themselves. The reaction of the joke's victim surpassed all their expectations.

'Please, believe me. It's a snake, a deadly snake.'

Big Billie's face was suffused. He wiped tears from his eyes, seated across the clearing from Ram Lal, who was standing looking wildly round.

'You ignorant darkie,' he gasped, 'don't you know? There are no snakes in Ireland. Understand? There aren't any.'

His sides ached with laughing and he leaned back in the grass, his hands behind him to support him. He failed to notice the two pricks, like tiny thorns, that went into the vein on the inside of the right wrist.

The joke was over and the hungry men tucked into their

lunches. Harkishan Ram Lal reluctantly took his seat, constantly glancing round him, a mug of steaming tea held ready, eating only with his left hand, staying clear of the long grass. After lunch they returned to work. The old distillery was almost down, the mountains of rubble and savable timbers lying dusty under the August sun.

At half past three Big Billie Cameron stood up from his work, rested on his pick and passed a hand across his forehead. He licked at a slight swelling on the inside of his wrist, then started work again. Five minutes later he straightened up again.

'I'm not feeling so good,' he told Patterson, who was next to him. 'I'm going to take a spell in the shade.'

He sat under a tree for a while and then held his head in his hands. At a quarter past four, still clutching his splitting head, he gave one convulsion and toppled sideways. It was several minutes before Tommy Burns noticed him. He walked across and called to Patterson.

'Big Billie's sick,' he called. 'He won't answer me.'

The gang broke and came over to the tree in whose shade the foreman lay. His sightless eyes were staring at the grass a few inches from his face. Patterson bent over him. He had been long enough in the labouring business to have seen a few dead ones.

'Ram,' he said, 'you have medical training. What do you think?'

Ram Lal did not need to make an examination, but he did. When he straightened up he said nothing, but Patterson understood.

'Stay here all of you,' he said, taking command. 'I'm going to phone an ambulance and call McQueen.' He set off down the track to the main road.

The ambulance got there first, half an hour later. It reversed down the track and two men heaved Cameron onto a stretcher. They took him away to Newtownards General Hospital, which had the nearest casualty unit, and there the foreman was logged in as DOA – dead on arrival. An extremely worried McQueen arrived thirty minutes after that.

Because of the unknown circumstance of the death an autopsy had to be performed and it was, by the North Down area pathologist, in the Newtownards municipal mortuary to which the body had been transferred. That was on the Tuesday. By that evening the pathologist's report was on its way to the office of the coroner for North Down, in Belfast.

The report said nothing extraordinary. The deceased had been a man of forty-one years, big-built and immensely strong. There were upon the body various minor cuts and abrasions, mainly on the hands and wrists, quite consistent with the job of navvy, and none of these were in any way associated with the cause of death. The latter, beyond a doubt, had been a massive brain haemorrhage, itself probably caused by extreme exertion in conditions of great heat.

Possessed of this report, the coroner would normally not hold an inquest, being able to issue a certificate of death by natural causes to the registrar at Bangor. But there was something Harkishan Ram Lal did not know.

Big Billie Cameron had been a leading member of the Bangor council of the outlawed Ulster Volunteer Force, the hard-line Protestant paramilitary organisation. The computer at Lurgan, into which all deaths in the province of Ulster, however innocent, are programmed, threw this out and someone in Lurgan picked up the phone to call the Royal Ulster Constabulary at Castlereagh.

Someone there called the coroner's office in Belfast, and a formal inquest was ordered. In Ulster death must not only be accidental; it must be seen to be accidental. For certain people, at least. The inquest was in the Town Hall at Bangor on Wednesday. It meant a lot of trouble for McQueen, for the Inland Revenue attended. So did two quiet men of extreme Loyalist persuasion from the UVF council. They sat at the back. Most of the dead man's workmates sat near the front, a few feet from Mrs Cameron.

Only Patterson was called to give evidence. He related the events of the Monday, prompted by the coroner, and as there was no dispute none of the other labourers was called, not even Ram Lal. The coroner read the pathologist's report aloud and it was clear enough. When he had finished, he summed up before giving his verdict.

'The pathologist's report is quite unequivocal. We have heard from Mr Patterson of the events of that lunch break, of the perhaps rather foolish prank played by the deceased upon the Indian student. It would seem that Mr Cameron was so amused that he laughed himself almost to the verge of apoplexy. The subsequent heavy labour with pick and shovel in the blazing sun did the rest, provoking the rupture of a large blood vessel in the brain or, as the pathologist put it in more medical language, a cerebral haemorrhage. This court extends its sympathy to the widow and her children, and finds that Mr William Cameron died of accidental causes.'

Outside on the lawns that spread before Bangor Town Hall McQueen talked to his navvies.

'I'll stand fair by you, lads,' he said. 'The job's still on, but I can't afford not to deduct tax and all the rest, not with the Revenue breathing down my neck. The funeral's tomorrow, you can take the day off. Those who want to go on can report on Friday.'

Harkishan Ram Lal did not attend the funeral. While it was in progress at the Bangor cemetery he took a taxi back to Comber and asked the driver to wait on the road while he walked down the track. The driver was a Bangor man and had heard about the death of Cameron.

'Going to pay your respects on the spot, are you?' he asked.

'In a way,' said Ram Lal.

'That the manner of your people?' asked the driver.

'You could say so,' said Ram Lal.

'Aye, well, I'll not say it's any better or worse than our way, by the graveside,' said the driver, and prepared to read his paper while he waited.

Harkishan Ram Lal walked down the track to the clearing and stood where the camp fire had been. He looked around at the long grass, the broom and the gorse in its sandy soil.

'*Visha serp*,' he called out to the hidden viper. 'O venomous snake, can you hear me? You have done what I brought you so far from the hills of Rajputana to achieve. But you were supposed to die. I should have killed you myself, had it all gone as I planned, and thrown your foul carcass in the river.

'Are you listening, deadly one? Then hear this. You may live a little longer but then you will die, as all things die. And you will die alone, without a female with which to mate, because there are no snakes in Ireland.'

The saw-scaled viper did not hear him, or if it did, gave no hint of understanding. Deep in its hole in the warm sand beneath him, it was busy, totally absorbed in doing what nature commanded it must do.

At the base of a snake's tail are two overlapping plate-scales which obscure the cloaca. The viper's tail was erect, the body throbbed in ancient rhythm. The plates were parted, and from the cloaca, one by one, each an inch long in its transparent sac, each as deadly at birth as its parent, she was bringing her dozen babies into the world.

Jilly Cooper

kate's wedding

Jilly Cooper comes from Yorkshire but now lives in Gloucestershire with her family and an assortment of dogs and cats. Her journalism was a feature for many years of the *Sunday Times*, and more recently of the *Mail on Sunday*, and she has made many television appearances, including *What's My Line?* Her recent novels, *Riders, Rivals, Polo, The Man Who Made Husbands Jealous*, were all number one bestsellers. Her latest book is *Araminta's Wedding* – a country house extravaganza, with illustrations by Sue Macartney-Snape. She is currently working on a novel about an orchestra, called *Appassionata.*

As soon as they reached the motorway, Hugh gave the dark blue BMW its head. 'Good thing we waited until after the rush hour,' he said. 'Who are you writing to?'

'Some people called Lacey,' said Kate.

'The Talbot-Laceys? They've sent us a present even though they can't make the wedding? That's interesting. What did they give us?'

'Wine glasses – twelve of them, not awfully pretty.'

'Vera Talbot-Lacey has exquisite taste,' said Hugh rather coldly. 'You should see their house in the country.'

'Who are they anyway?' asked Kate.

'He's the senior partner at Burns and Marlowe,' said Hugh, lighting his pipe. 'I've defended one or two of his clients – not unsuccessfully, I may say. It wouldn't be a bad idea to add something at the end of the letter about asking them to dinner as soon as we've settled in.'

Kate sighed. All Hugh's friends appeared to be extremely successful, and also had to be asked to dine after they were married to further Hugh's legal career. At this rate she might as well open a restaurant. Half the guests at the wedding would be influential solicitors, barristers and even judges. The reception was going to be like something out of Gilbert and Sullivan. Hugh was destined for great things in life. Her parents were delighted she was going to marry him.

She glanced at his regular-featured, handsome profile: dark hair, just beginning to go grey at the temples, brushed into smooth wings over very clean ears; dark-brown eyes, shrewd behind heavy horn-rimmed spectacles. At thirty-seven, he had been considered a confirmed bachelor by his friends. Oh definitely not queer, my dear, he'd had loads of suitable, even glamorous girlfriends, but just cautious about making a mistake. He had handled too many seamy divorce cases, seen the appalling underside of so much domestic life, to enter into marriage lightly.

Kate went back to her letter. The next moment, Hugh swerved to avoid a car that had pulled out in front, and Kate's pen shot across the page. She clenched her fists so hard that even her nails, bitten down to the quick, dug deeply into her palms. She counted very slowly to ten – then tore off the page and crumpled it up. She mustn't snap at Hugh, not after yesterday's appalling demonstration.

She had gone straight from work to the house they had bought in Canonbury in order to be near the Law Courts. When Hugh arrived, she was up a ladder painting the kitchen ceiling. He had poured himself a drink, and was just telling her about the case he'd won against all odds that morning, when suddenly her hand had slipped, and the tin she was holding crashed to the floor splashing white gloss all over the newly laid cork tiles.

Hugh had then pointed out that it would have been advisable to have covered the floor with newspaper first, and Kate had thrown a complete fit of hysterics. Hugh had done nothing, just sat watching her helplessly until the screams and shouts subsided into choking sobs. Then he'd poured her a large slug of whisky into a white mug.

'I'm desperately sorry,' she gasped.

'It's just pre-wedding nerves,' he said patting her shoulder briskly. 'It's been far too much for you, keeping on your job to the last moment, master-minding the wedding from London, and painting the house every evening. I'm going to take you away for the weekend.'

'But I can't possibly,' she had shrieked. 'I've got *hundreds* of letters to write, and Vanessa's coming over for a bridesmaid's dress fitting, and I've got to finalise things with the caterers and the florist, and finish off the painting here . . .'

'Everything can wait,' interrupted Hugh firmly. 'It's still a fortnight to the wedding. You're stopping work at the end of the week, so you'll have a clear seven days after that to sort everything out. I'll get Eddie from the office to come and finish off the painting here. I'm going to ring the Hillingdons and see if we can spend the weekend on their boat.'

Oh not the Hillingdons, Kate was about to scream. They were a very role-reversed couple. Jonty Hillingdon ran the house, wrote cookery books, and did cookery programmes on television; Muriel, his wife, was a very successful architect who had gentlemen friends and travelled abroad a lot. They both drank too much, and gave wild parties where famous people got off with other famous people. Kate doubted whether Hugh would have liked them quite so much if they hadn't been *so* successful. They were the last people on earth with whom she felt she could relax.

But Hugh had already dialled the number. She could hear his request to stay the weekend greeted by shrieks of joy down the other end of the telephone.

'Muriel is absolutely delighted,' he said, as he put down the receiver. 'There's another couple going down to the boat tomorrow morning, but it sleeps six, so there's loads of room for us. Jonty will do all the cooking, so it'll be a nice rest.'

'I can't rest when there's so much to do,' said Kate, knowing she was being ungracious as she sulkily mopped up the paint on the floor with a cloth soaked in turpentine.

'I was actually thinking of myself,' Hugh had said evenly, pouring himself another drink. 'I've had a lot of pressure at work over the last few weeks, and you haven't been very bearable in the evenings recently, my darling. I'd quite like a break from all these scenes.'

Contrition had swept over her. 'Oh God, I'm sorry,' she muttered, scrambling to her feet. 'I'm being so selfish.'

She threw the rag on the draining board, and put her arms round him, leaning against the broad, solid back, feeling the dark blue cashmere of his jersey soft against her face. 'I've become so self-obsessed,' she moaned, 'I'll be fine after the wedding, I promise.'

Hugh had turned round and pulled her into his arms. 'I know you will,' he said, his hands feeling for her breasts. 'But you really mustn't lose any more weight, darling, or there won't be anything of you. Come on,' he whispered, his breath quickening, 'they put the spare room bed in this morning, why don't we go upstairs and Christen it?'

Before she could stop herself, Kate had stiffened. 'I've got a bit of a headache,' she said truthfully, then could have bitten her tongue off at the appalling lameness of the excuse.

Hugh had shrugged his shoulders and let her go. 'You've been having far too many headaches lately,' he snapped, 'you ought to get your eyes tested.'

And now they were driving down to the Hillingdons' floating sin palace for a weekend of relaxation. As they turned off the motorway Hugh stopped for petrol. Collecting the bill, he put it neatly folded into his wallet, beside a rather awful photograph of Kate taken at their engagement party. Hugh got bills for everything. Even when he took her out to dinner, she was passed off as one of his clients.

'What did you get for Muriel and Jonty?' he said, as he started the car up again.

'Taramasalata, smoked oysters, pâté, a melon, some asparagus, strawberries, and yes, three bottles of champagne,' said Kate, peering into the carrier bag on the back seat.

'It wasn't necessary to go that far,' said Hugh frowning, 'I've already bought them half a dozen bottles of Sancerre, and some very good claret.'

'I wanted to, they've been so kind to me,' said Kate.

Jonty and Muriel *had* been very friendly towards her, probably to compensate for the fact that they resented her annexing their most eligible spare man ('He's the only straight bachelor we know, darling,' Muriel had said when they first met), and because Kate hadn't turned out to be quite the mettlesome sport they had hoped she might be. All these presents were an attempt to hide the fact that she didn't much like Jonty and Muriel either. She must try to get on with Hugh's friends, they were going to be her future.

It was too dark to write letters now, the sun had set leaving a pinky apricot glow on the horizon ahead, and the rest of the sky a drained sapphire blue. One very bright star, followed by a little star, had just appeared on the left. They were driving along country lanes now, the headlamps lighting up signposts buried deep in cow-parsley. Summer had just taken over from the spring, wild roses were closing along the hedgerow. The hawthorn blossom, although turned rusty brown, was still giving off its disturbingly sweet, soapy smell. The country always unsettled Kate, it was as though by cooping herself up in her tiny London flat she had cut herself off from all primitive instincts of the outside world.

'Half-past nine,' said Hugh, glancing at the car clock. 'We've made very good time. I could certainly use a drink.'

Kate got out her mirror, and tucked the loose strands of hair into her chignon. Hugh liked her hair up – he had a thing, he said, about the napes of women's necks – but recently she had lost so much weight, that the style only emphasised the pinched, drawn pallor of her face. She wished she'd had time to wash her hair, but she'd worked late at the office that evening, trying to get everything straight before she left at the end of the week. She dreaded giving up work and leaving all her friends there.

Kate's boss had taken her out to lunch that day in a last ditch attempt to persuade her to stay on. 'You're far too intelligent,' he had told her over the second bottle, 'to spend the rest of your life making casseroles and polishing the silver spoon in Hugh's mouth. Time to brood, Kate, is the great enemy of the married state. I can keep your job open for a month, but no longer.'

But Kate had shaken her head and refused his offer. She was so tired, all she wanted to do after she was married, between cooking dinners for Hugh's smart friends, was to sleep for six months. She was still dressed in the foxglove pink suit and black high-heeled shoes that she had worn to work, and intended to change into old clothes the moment she got on the boat.

'Here we are,' said Hugh, swinging off down a side road: a dark tunnel heavily overgrown with trees. Goosegrass and this-tles scratched the paint of the car. Through the open window Kate could hear a duck quacking and the muted piping of sleepy birds. She breathed in the rank feline smell of wet net-tles and damp undergrowth. Ahead gleamed the river, and there flanked by willows, her brass work gleaming in the head-lights, was moored the Hillingdons' boat. She was painted dark blue, a flag with a skull and crossbones was mounted on her bows. Red curtains glowed behind the saloon windows. Her name – the subject of much ribaldry – was painted along her bows in gold letters: *M.V. Virgin Queen.*

Muriel came rushing out of the galley. 'Darlings, you've made it!' she shouted. 'Jonty's just putting on the spuds so you've got time for several huge drinks.'

Teetering across the gangplank in her high heels, Kate stumbled into Muriel's arms, and the two women were forced to embrace each other more fondly than either of them would have wished. As Kate extracted herself from the large scented bosom and the jangling braceletted arms, she realised that Muriel was far more tarted up than she would normally have been for Hugh. Her streaked blonde hair was newly washed, and she was wearing a white, heavily-frilled shirt, hanging outside a pair of tight, black velvet trousers, which cleverly disguised a thickening waistline. The all-too-knowing Cambridge blue eyes had been carefully made up, and suntan, aided by a thick layer of tawny brown make-up, hid the network of red veins on her cheeks. She had reached an age when she tended to look better under artificial light, but she was still an extremely glamorous woman. Kate wondered who the other couple were for her to have gone to so much trouble.

In the galley, Kate found Jonty whisking about in a plastic joke apron of a naked woman's body with stripper's tassels hanging from the nipples. Above it, his whisky-soaked, tea-planter's face with its carefully brushed-forward greying hair, looked ridiculously incongruous. He was dropping mint into the boiling new potatoes.

'Isn't it the most erotic smell of the summer?' he said. 'Hello, Kate dear, you look as though you need a stiff one.'

'That could have been better put,' said Muriel roaring with laughter. She always saw *double entendres* in the most innocent of remarks. She reminded Kate of a hyena, outwardly cackling with mirth, but inwardly watchful and predatory.

'I've brought you both some goodies,' said Kate, hastily handing Jonty the carrier bag.

'Oh how lovely,' said Muriel, grabbing it and looking inside. 'But you shouldn't have, darling, you ought to be saving every penny for getting married. We must get the Bollinger on ice instantly for tomorrow's lunch, and isn't that a lovely suit you're wearing, I love pink. Why don't I look like that at the office, Jonty darling?'

'You don't get up early enough,' said Jonty.

'I've got better things to do in the morning,' said Muriel, winking at Kate.

'The best thing you can do now is to get Hugh and Kate some ice, and stop gassing,' said Jonty, handing Kate a large gin and tonic. 'If you all stay in here any longer playing bumpsey daisy, you won't get any dinner.'

'I must go and change,' said Kate, as Muriel dropped an ice ball and a piece of lime into her glass.

'Go next door and introduce yourself first,' said Muriel.

Leaving Hugh to give Jonty a blow by blow account of the longevity and quality of the bottles of wine he had brought down, Kate took a slug of her drink and went next door. The saloon with its shiny wood pannelling, polished tables, and old-fashioned lamps, had been so subtly and seductively lit by Muriel, that it was a few seconds before Kate could make out the beautiful girl stretched out on one of the red leather banquettes. Her golden hair hung down her back like laburnum, and her long limbs, in the skimpy orange dress, were so smoothly and uniformly brown that they looked as though they had been dipped in a vat of milk chocolate.

'Hi,' she said, with a dazzling toothpaste-commercial smile. 'I'm Georgina Arlington.'

Why the hell didn't I spend the last twenty-nine years of my life in a beauty parlour, thought Kate.

'Hello,' she said shyly.

The beautiful girl looked her over slowly, and suddenly seemed terribly pleased about something. 'I believe you know Tod already,' she said.

The man who'd been sitting in the shadows in the corner rose to his feet. 'Hello, Katie,' he said drily.

For a second, Kate gazed into the lean brown face with its clear, all-too familiar, grey eyes. Then the smile was wiped off her face like a power cut. Her glass crashed to the floor. She clutched onto the edge of the door. She thought she was going to faint.

'Tod,' she gasped, 'is it really you?'

'Really me,' he said evenly. 'It looks as though you need a refill. Jonty! Can we have another quadruple gin and tonic.'

A couple of seconds later when Hugh entered the saloon, he found Kate on her knees, frantically rubbing gin and tonic into the rush matting with a paper handkerchief.

'Dar-ling,' he said irritably, 'I do wish you'd stop dropping things. Paint yesterday, drink today.'

'Hope it isn't you tomorrow,' said Georgina with a giggle.

Hugh looked up, took in her beauty at a glance, promptly whipped off his spectacles, and removed his pipe from his mouth.

'Good evening to you,' he said in that warm, enthusiastic voice he reserved for rich clients and important members of the legal profession. 'I'm Hugh Lancaster.' He shook hands with both Tod and Georgina.

'Did someone say Kate wanted another drink?' said Muriel popping her head round the door.

'I'm desperately sorry, Muriel, I dropped the first one,' muttered Kate, still mopping frantically to hide her confusion.

'Doesn't matter a scrap, sweetie. Jonty and I always have plastic glasses on the boat, so we can chuck them at each other with impunity. Good thing it wasn't a Bloody Mary or you'd have wrecked that beautiful suit. Are you feeling all right?' she went on as Kate scrambled to her feet. 'You look as white as a sheet.'

'I think she's just seen a guest,' said Tod, and picking up the bottle of white wine on the table, he filled up his and Georgina's glasses with a hand, Kate noticed wryly, that was perfectly steady.

'Here you are, Kate,' said Jonty, coming in and handing her a brimming glass. 'One G and T.'

'Thanks,' mumbled Kate, grabbing it. 'I'm just going to change into something more comfortable.' She fled into the next door cabin.

Muriel followed, carrying her small suitcase. 'Lucky Hugh, if this is all the luggage you've brought,' she said. 'I can't go down to the shops without a pantechnicon, I drive Jonty crackers.'

She straightened the tartan rug on the upper bunk, and replaced a wild rose that had fallen out of the vase by the window.

'How pretty the flowers are, how kind of you,' said Kate, finding every word an effort.

'But they fade so quickly, like us, darling,' said Muriel, admiring her glowing face in an ancient, speckled mirror. 'Doesn't that girl, Georgie, make one feel a hundred, and isn't *he* absolute bliss. I met him at the Royal Academy press preview last year, and have been trying to persuade him to come down here for a weekend ever since. I'd hoped we might be able to cultivate him as our new spare man – now we've lost dear Hugh to you – but he seems suddenly to have become very involved with Georgie. Sorry not to give you and Hugh the double bunk next door,' she said once more letting out her cackle of hyena laughter, 'but as Tod and Georgie got down here this morning, it was a question of first come, first serviced so to speak. Poor Jonty and I have to shack up in the saloon after everyone's gone to bed, so we never get much kip on these trips.

'Darling,' she went on, suddenly concerned, 'you really do look washed out, are you sure you're all right? Mind you, engagements are an absolute swine. Jonty and I got so uptight, we never stopped rowing the month before our wedding, but we've managed to notch up seventeen years together fairly amicably, so don't worry too much. Change quickly and come and join the party.'

The moment Muriel had gone Kate collapsed onto the bottom bunk, covering her sweating face with her hands, trying to control the frantic thumping of her heart. Gradually, the shock of seeing Tod again gave way to horror that, after all these years, he should catch her looking so awful: with lanky, week-old hair scraped back, make-up worn off after a day's work, and dark circles beneath her eyes.

Her hands were shaking so much she could hardly undo the buttons of her suit. She hadn't even brought anything pretty to change into, just a pair of baggy old cords that had never fitted her properly, a couple of shirts in colours that didn't particularly suit her. In her frenzy to get everything straight, all her good clothes were neatly washed and ironed at home, waiting to be transferred to the fitted cupboards of the new house.

She took down her hair, but it kinked unbecomingly where it had been drawn back into the chignon, so she put it up again. Lipstick and blusher only seemed to offset her corpse-like pallor, while eyeliner only emphasised eyes that were small and red-rimmed from too many sleepless nights.

'Oh God,' she said with a sob, 'I can't face him yet.'

She heard howls of mirth coming from the saloon and jumped in a frenzy of paranoia. Scrabbling round in her bag, she found a bottle of tranquillisers, swallowed one with a great slug of gin, and collapsed back onto the bunk.

It was nine years since she and Tod had first met and fallen in love. She'd been in her second year reading Law at Bristol University, and when she'd first taken Tod to stay with her parents in Bath they had been horrified. Tod not only had long hair and a beard, never wore a tie, and was no respecter of middle class values, but he had also chucked in a very good job in advertising to try and make the grade as a painter, and never having any money seemed always to be bumming off Kate. Kate hadn't minded the bumming at all, her parents gave her a generous allowance, and what was hers was Tod's as well. She knew he was the most generous person in the world when he was in funds, and she was convinced that one day he'd be a great painter. She didn't even mind that sometimes when he was painting he'd lose all sense of time, and turn up three hours late for a date, with only a few roses pinched from the Principal's precious garden as a peace offering.

What did finish her, however, once when she'd gone home alone for the weekend and returned a day early because she was missing him so desperately, was to have his studio door opened by a wanton-looking redhead wrapped in a green towel, and to find the redhead's clothes strewn all over the bed and the floor.

Kate had run sobbing from the flat. Tod had caught up with her in the park, wearing only a pair of jeans, his bare feet turning blue with cold on the frozen grass, and she remembered thinking how thin and underfed he looked without his shirt. Ashen-faced and trembling, they had faced each other.

'Stop it, Katie, stop crying,' he had pleaded with her. 'She doesn't mean a thing, I picked her up at a party last night, it's you that I love.'

'You can't love me,' she had screamed back, 'if the moment my back's turned, you go to bed with that . . .' She couldn't even get the words out.

'Look,' said Tod, grabbing her arms to prevent her bolting, 'I respect the fact that you don't want to sleep with anyone until you marry. I've never abused that, have I, *have I*,' he added, his fingers biting into her flesh so sharply that she winced. 'But I'm a very physical man, and I've got physical needs. I can't live like a monk. I love you, I'd do anything in the world to keep you, I'd marry you tomorrow, but we can't just live off your parents' allowance. Please try and understand.'

But she'd pulled away from him, racing through the

starched leaves, out of the park. She had gone back home to Bath and, with the all-too-eager connivance of her parents, had refused ever to see him again, to speak to him on the telephone, or to answer any of his letters. Her parents, in fact, were so overjoyed that she'd finished with Tod, they didn't even mind when she completely ploughed her finals – they'd never thought a career was important for a girl – and had packed her off to South Africa for a year to recover.

For that year, she had moved through life like a sleep walker. Not a day passed without her dreaming about Tod, and longing for him. But she'd convinced herself, again heavily encouraged by her parents, that any kind of relationship with him would only bring unhappiness, because he was incapable of being faithful. Yet any man who pursued her – and there were plenty – seemed like waxworks when compared with Tod's blazing vitality,.

Finally she gave up the struggle and came back to England, aware that she could no longer live without him, only to find he'd gone to live in America. Her parents made very sure that they never handed on his address out there, which he'd left behind for her.

Very carefully, she had put her heart in the deep freeze and concentrated on her career. She didn't have the will to work for her degree again, but she took a job, as a secretary to a firm of solicitors, where, with her legal knowledge and obvious intelligence, she soon made herself indispensable.

'The wonderful thing about Kate,' her boss was fond of saying smugly to the other partners, whose secretaries always took two-hour lunches and rushed off to the ladies' loo clutching their floral sponge bags on the dot of five-fifteen, 'is that she never minds working late.'

Such was Kate's industry, that as the years passed her boss grew more and more successful, and was frequently able to employ Hugh Lancaster to defend his more well-heeled clients. A good-looking barrister, accustomed to success with women, Hugh had first been impressed by Kate's fragile, Snow Queen beauty, and then piqued by her complete indifference. He had laid siege: bombarding her with flowers, presents, and requests for dates, until she'd finally agreed to go out with him. After a few months, he had proposed, and she'd accepted, and he'd finally taken her to bed, and she had managed to conceal from him the fact that she had felt nothing.

Love will come, she told herself. I like and respect Hugh, my parents absolutely dote on him. I must just be patient. So she had thrown herself into plans for the wedding, filling the days and most of the nights with frenzied activity. But as the day approached, she was appalled to find herself thinking obsessively about Tod, wracked by erotic dreams of him by night and, by day, remembering the turmoil he had once reduced her to, merely by kissing her. Now to crown it she was stuck on the boat with him for the whole weekend. She felt blind panic as though she were in a lift, trapped between floors in the middle of a bomb scare.

A knock on the door made her jump so hard, she banged her head on the bunk above. It was Hugh.

'Come on, darling, we're all ravenous. Jonty has raised the Chicken Supreme to such a point of perfection, he'll sulk if you keep him waiting any longer.'

'So sorry, I was dreaming,' said Kate.

'Only got fifteen days to go,' said Hugh smugly, 'and you won't need to dream anymore, you'll have the reality.'

'I'll be out in a sec,' said Kate.

As she stood up, she felt dizzy again. Without realising it, she'd finished her drink. She knew perfectly well one shouldn't mix gin and tranquillisers.

They were all sitting down at the table when she went into the saloon.

'Go on Jonty's right, next to Tod,' said Muriel, ' and have some wine, you're light years behind the rest of us.'

Kate slid onto the bench, watching Jonty carve the chicken, the sharp knife sliding through the breast.

'Hungry?' he asked her, putting two slices on her plate.

'N-not wildly,' she stammered. 'My boss treated me to lunch, so I stuffed myself midday.'

'Give her more than that,' said Muriel, as Jonty spooned mushrooms and a thick cream sauce over the chicken slices, 'the poor sweet needs feeding up. At least you won't rupture yourself carrying her over the threshold, Hugh darling.'

Sitting beside Tod, Kate was aware of his hands, with their long sunburnt fingers, spreading butter on a piece of brown bread. She still couldn't bring herself to look at him. Instead she glanced across the table at Georgie, who was certainly gorgeous. Her slanting, thickly-lashed eyes were the speckled yellow-green of a William pear, and as she leant forward for the salt, the candlelight flickered on her warm, brown breasts and lovely, unlined throat. She was also gazing at Kate in fascination as if she was a priceless, centuries-old relic, unearthed on some archaeological dig. Could this faded, insipid creature really have been a girlfriend of Tod's? she seemed to be saying.

'We're all dying to hear how you and Tod know each other,' she asked. 'It must have been pretty traumatic for you to freak out like that. Did he interfere with you at Kindergarten or something? His story is you knew each other at Bristol.'

'We did,' said Kate, desperately trying to keep her voice steady. 'We went out for a bit.'

'Then she went off to South Africa,' said Tod lightly. 'And left me with a broken heart.'

'Must have been the only person who ever did,' said Muriel, shooting him a hot look.

'Was this the chap who made you fail your finals?' asked Hugh.

Kate blushed furiously. 'How did you know about that?'

'Your mother told me,' said Hugh. 'No potatoes, thanks Jonty.'

'He usually has that effect on women,' said Muriel. 'Girls committing suicide, or bolting into convents. I can never keep track of your sex life, Tod.'

'Makes two of us,' said Tod, helping himself to courgettes.

'Well, I don't intend to go into a convent, darling,' said Georgie, with a slight edge to her voice, 'I haven't got the right sort of cheekbones for a nun. This is absolutely marvellous chicken, Jonty.'

'Good,' said Jonty, filling up everyone's glasses. 'You're all being guinea pigs this weekend, I'm trying out all the recipes I'm doing for my next television series.'

'Can you cook?' said Georgie, sliding her speckled green eyes towards Hugh.

'Only basics,' said Hugh, 'I like to leave you girls to do kitchen things.'

'You're a male chauvinist guinea pig then,' said Georgie, giving him the full benefit of a smouldering glance, and deepening her cleavage by ramming her left arm against her left breast.

Hugh, for some reason, seemed to find this remark extremely funny. 'Don't tell me you're one of these feminists,' he said, smoothing his already smooth hair.

'Not at all,' replied Georgie, 'I just wish I could find a husband like Jonty, who realises the way to a woman's heart is through her stomach.'

'I've always thought it was a bit lower down,' said Muriel with a hyena cackle. 'Jonty's not very romantic, Georgie,' she went on, 'he's much more likely to quote Marika Hanbury Tennyson at one than Lord Alfred.'

'Lord who?' said Georgie, 'I don't like Lords. I had one once, and he kept wanting me to whip him. Now come on, Jonty, tell me how you make this. Then I can impress Tod's mother when she comes to London.'

'Well,' said Jonty, his blood-shot eyes sparkling, 'first you cook the salt pork and the bouquet garni in water for one hour . . .'

Hugh started talking to Muriel about mutual acquaintances who were coming to the wedding. 'Three Law Lords have definitely accepted,' he said, 'which is very gratifying.'

Tod turned to Kate. 'When are you getting married?'

'Tomorrow fortnight.'

'What time?'

'Three o'clock.'

'Hope you don't have an empty church – everyone'll be listening to the Oaks on their car radios.'

'Not my family,' said Kate. 'They're not very keen on racing.'

'Ah yes, I remember,' said Tod with a faint smile, 'Redwood Rover.'

Kate went crimson. Nine years ago Tod had been so convinced Redwood Rover was going to win the Cambridgeshire, he had persuaded Kate to pawn her pearls and lend him fifty pounds. Unfortunately, Redwood Rover had bucked his jockey off onto the rails just before the race. A few days later Kate's mother, nosing about in Kate's room, no doubt looking for incriminating evidence of her relationship with Tod, had discovered the pawn ticket in her diary, whereupon all hell had broken loose.

There was a long, agonising pause.

'Did you enjoy America?' Kate asked him. Oh, why did her voice sound as though she'd had injections for fillings on both sides of her face?

'Yeah, I did, it helped me commercially, too. Once I got established there, they started taking an interest in me over here.'

She still couldn't meet his eyes, but staring fixedly at the blond hairs on his arms, she had to fight an irresistible desire to touch them. Instead she said, 'What are you working on at the moment?'

'Well, I've just finished a mural in the new cathedral at Westmarton, and I'm getting together some pictures for an exhibition in Cork Street in September, then taking it over to Paris, and probably to New York in the spring.'

He spoke in his usual lazy, slightly husky drawl, but there was a steel tip to his voice. I've made it, he seemed to be saying, even though you and your family kicked me in the teeth.

'And Tod's going to do a bus too,' said Georgie, interrupting poor Jonty in mid-flow about how finely one must chop the fresh tarragon. 'Did you hear that, Muriel?' she went on, shouting down the table, interrupting Hugh in mid-flow about the vintage of the wine they were drinking, 'Tod's been commissioned by the Gas Board to paint a bus for their late summer advertising campaign.'

Muriel smiled warmly into Tod's eyes. But that's wonderful, darling what are you going to do?'

'Purring cats and rosy-cheeked brats warming themselves in front of roaring gas fires, I suppose,' said Tod, 'I can't imagine I'll be allowed to be very *outré.*'

'But lots of lovely lolly,' said Muriel.

Tod was drawn into conversation with her and Hugh now, and Jonty, undaunted, was back on course with the Chicken Supreme:

'You heat a small pan, put in the oil, and add the diced vegetables . . .'

For a minute, Kate was free to study Tod. Since they had last met he had shaved off his beard and moustache, so one could now appreciate the lean, suntanned planes of his face and the curves of the well shaped mouth. The straight, light-brown hair was shorter too, just curling over the collar of his grey denim shirt, which matched the stormy grey of those disturbingly direct eyes. He had also filled out – obviously no longer the starving artist. He looked in fact, as though he'd lived every day and most nights since he'd split up from Kate, to the full. He was no longer a beautiful, sensitive, romantic boy – the disciple whom Jesus loved – but a weathered, confident, overwhelmingly attractive man. As if aware of her scrutiny, he turned towards her. Immediately Kate dropped her eyes.

'How's the fishwife of Bath?' he asked. 'Frightfully excited about becoming the mother-in-law of an imminent Q.C. I should think.'

'Who's that?' said Hugh, putting his knife and fork together.

'I was just asking after your future mother-in-law,' said Tod.

'Oh, Elizabeth's a super person, isn't she,' said Hugh enthusiastically. 'And a very good bridge player too. I'm awfully fond of Henry as well, we get in a round of golf whenever possible. I couldn't be more fortunate in my in-laws,' he said, gallantly raising his glass to Kate.

'They must have changed,' said Tod flatly.

As he leaned over to fill up Georgie's glass, his arm brushed Kate, who jumped away as though she'd touched a live wire.

'You on the other hand haven't changed at all,' he said under his breath so only she could hear. 'Still the same eternally shrinking violet.'

Kate bit her lip.

'Anyone want a second helping?' said Jonty.

'Kate hasn't touched her first,' said Muriel accusingly.

Kate looked down at her plate with its congealing cream, shiny black mushrooms, and drying slices of chicken breast. She felt the sweat rising on her forehead and knew she'd be sick if she tried to eat anymore. 'I'm terribly sorry, Jonty, it was so delicious, I can't think why I'm not hungry.'

'I'll have it,' said Tod, forking up the two pieces of chicken, 'you've excelled yourself as usual, Jonty.'

Georgie cut a slice off one of the new potatoes she'd reluctantly shoved to the side of her plate. 'I can't think why you don't get fat, Tod, you never take any exercise.'

'He does,' said Muriel, looking at Kate.

'Sex doesn't count,' said Georgie, with a predatory smirk, 'I wish you'd come out jogging with me.'

'Jogging,' said Tod, 'is a totally barbaric pastime. If I'm out of doors, I like to look at things, not charge around giving heart attacks to all the local livestock.'

'I jog every morning,' said Hugh, as though that settled the matter.

'I can see you do,' said Georgie, admiringly. 'You look in really great shape. I'll come out with you tomorrow, if I wake up in time.'

'Splendid,' said Hugh, pulling in his stomach, 'I wish Kate would join us.'

'Give the poor girl a chance,' said Muriel, 'she looks shattered.'

'Perhaps you'll feel more like it, darling, once you've packed in your job,' said Hugh.

'Are you giving up work?' said Georgie enviously.

'Of course not,' said Hugh, briskly answering for Kate.

'She's going to have a full time job at home looking after me. I'm not keen on career wives, I'm sure it's the reason so many marriages break up.'

'What about Jonty and I, both slaving away?' said Muriel, indignantly.

'You two,' said Hugh, raising his glass to Muriel, 'are a delightful exception, but no one could deny, Muriel my dear, that you have an exceptionally well-trained husband.'

'Roll out the reversal,' said Jonty gathering up the plates. 'Who'd like some strawberries? I've marinated them in *Framboise.*'

'Me, please,' said Georgie, 'I can't resist them, such an aphrodisiac. Do you remember the dramatic effect they had on me in Paris, Tod?'

Kate suddenly thought she was going to faint again. She got to her feet, unsteadily clinging onto the table.

'I promise I'll rush round and cook, and wash up tomorrow, Jonty,' she said, 'but do you mind terribly if I go to bed?'

'Course not,' said Muriel. 'Are you feeling poorly?'

'Bit tired,' Kate muttered.

'Mind you sleep in in the morning,' said Jonty.

'I'll come and tuck you up in a minute,' said Hugh playfully, 'and no reading in bed.'

'We have to go through your cabin to get to bed,' said Georgie, 'so don't get panicky and think Tod's groping for you if he suddenly comes lurching through at two o'clock in the morning.'

Only for the second time that evening Kate looked straight into Tod's eyes.

'Don't worry,' he said, 'I'm far too ethical to try and gazump a house that's already been sold.'

He hates me, he absolutely hates me, was all Kate could think as she undressed. She was so distraught she took a couple of sleeping pills. She knew it was dangerous on top of drink and tranquillisers, but all she wanted now was oblivion. Then in total despair she fell on her knees, burying her face in the plaid rug which smelt of suntan oil, sobbing, 'Please, please help me God, I don't know what to do.'

When Hugh came to say goodnight ten minutes later, he found her fast asleep on the floor. She didn't even stir when he lifted her up and tucked her into bed.

Kate closed her eyes again and buried her face in the pillow, excluding the squawk of ducks from the river outside, and the sunlight seeping through the drawn curtains. Her head felt like a rugger ball after a Twickenham international. All she wanted to do was to go back to sleep for a month – and then, blissful thought, she'd miss the wedding. Stop it, she told herself furiously, how could she let poor Hugh down and her parents, and what about all the relations who were coming from all over the country in anticipation of two hundred bottles of Moët et Chandon and a family get-together, and the dressmaker who'd laboured so long and lovingly over her wedding dress, and worst of all her mother who trailed the length and breadth of Bond Street and Knightsbridge to find a pair of coral shoes to match exactly her David Schilling hat.

It was too late to stop the carnival. In order not to be 'an old maid' as her mother so charmingly put it, and miss the boat, Kate had burned all her boats. At this moment, Tod was probably lying fast asleep in Georgie's arms after a night of heavy passion. I hope she gets pins and needles, thought Kate, groaning and pulling the pillow over her head. Through a daze of misery and longing, she could hear the clatter of washing up and the whoosh of the shower. Gingerly she peered into the bunk above, and was shocked at the relief she felt that it was empty. Hugh must have gone out jogging.

She pulled back the curtain, and winced as the sunlight charged in. Outside she could see a tangle of emerald green weeds and a mane of yellow king-cups tossing above and below the dark level of the water. It was already very hot. She winced even more at her reflection in the mirror: deathly pale, eyelids puffy and red from enforced sleep, awful lank hair with a faint powdering of scurf on the middle parting. She must wash it at once.

In the galley she found Hugh, red faced and sleeked down from the shower after jogging, and exuding all the self-satisfaction of someone just returned from Early Service. He paused from reading the *Times* law reports to give her a perfunctory kiss on the cheek. Jonty was scraping new potatoes, and Muriel, looking splendidly mahogany, if slightly wrinkled round the stomach in a white bikini, was trimming the muddy ends off the asparagus. They all expressed such hearty pleasure that Kate had had such a long and wonderful night's sleep, that she started feeling guilty that they hadn't enjoyed a similar benefit.

'Let me do something,' she said.

'You are not going to lift a finger, darling,' said Muriel.

'We're all worried about you, I'm determined to send you back to London feeling really rested. Here's some coffee,' she handed one big olive green cup to Kate, and another to Hugh, who put down the *Times* with satisfaction.

'They've written three-quarters of a column on the case I defended yesterday,' he told Kate.

'Did they quote you?'

'Several times, which is gratifying.'

'How lovely, let me look.'

He handed her the paper. 'There: Burnham-Watts v The Inland Revenue.'

It was a very boring case, in which Hugh seemed to have routed the income tax people single-handed.

'I must stop at the next lock,' he said putting saccharine into his coffee, 'and see if I can get a *Telegraph*. They're bound to have reported it in more detail. When are we moving on, Jonty?'

'As soon as Tod's finished his picture. He got up at six to catch the light, says he'll be through by lunch-time.'

'Is he any good?' said Hugh.

'Oh very, I think,' said Muriel. 'In fact, if you've got a spare grand, it would be well worth buying one of his paintings now. They're bound to rocket in value over the next few years.'

'We bought four a year ago,' said Jonty, running water over the scraped potatoes. 'We reckon we're sitting on a gold mine.'

'That's worth knowing,' said Hugh. 'My rich uncle wanted to buy us a painting as a wedding present. If it's going to be a good investment, we must steer him in Tod's direction.'

Burnham-Watts v The Inland Revenue swum before Kate's
eyes. Stop discussing Tod like an issue of Unit Trusts, she
thought furiously. But all she said as she handed the paper
back to Hugh was, 'That's terrific, well done. You must be
thrilled. Can I possibly wash my hair, Muriel?'

'Well you could have done,' said Jonty, irritably turning
the sink tap which only yielded a couple of drips, 'but that
glamour pants girlfriend of Tod's seems to have used all the
water. What the hell am I going to cook lunch with?'

'We can take on more water at the next lock and have the
asparagus tonight,' said Muriel soothingly. 'And honestly,
Kate darling, don't worry about your hair, it looks fine. Dark
people are so lucky, dirty hair never shows on them.'

'Why don't you change into your bikini and get some sun?'
said Hugh.

Kate felt she would like to have taken Georgie's laburnum
yellow locks, like Porphyrio's lover, and wound them round
her throat and strangled her.

As there was no water to wash with, Kate had to make do
with cleansing cream and scraping a flannel over her body.
She had to go on shore, too, to go to the loo, and stung her
bottom on some nettles. When she finally got into her bikini,
she found the tiny deck at the back of the boat was a mass of
naked flesh. In fact, it was mostly Georgie, topless and virtually bottomless except for two tiny triangles of leopard skin.
She had plugged her hairdryer on an extra lead into a power
point in the saloon, and was drying her gleaming mane. Her
magnificent, heavily-oiled breasts quivered with each sweep
of the brush. My boobs were once as good as that, thought

Kate enviously. Hugh, in blue bathing trunks, binoculars round his neck for bird watching, lay a couple of feet away from Georgie doing the *Times* crossword and smoking his pipe. His solid English figure, slightly pear-shaped but kept in trim by exercise and rigorous self-control, was already turning red.

But not all the jogging in the world could ever have achieved the taut angular grace of Tod's body, with its broad brown shoulders, narrowing to lean hips, above long, long legs. He was wearing only a pair of faded blue jeans, sawn off above the knee and covered with paint. With a canvas perched on the bench seat and propped against the side of the boat, he was painting the hayfield on the opposite bank, catching the light, as the long grass turned in the warm breeze like an animal's fur. Only a dark line of beech trees on the brow of the hill divided the hay from a white hot sky above.

'It's beautiful,' breathed Kate.

Tod turned, nodded without smiling, and went back to work.

'You *do* look better. That sleep must have done you all the good in the world,' shouted Georgie above the whirr of the hairdryer.

Kate settled down between Hugh and the other side of the boat, as far away from Tod as possible, horribly aware of how unfavourably she must compare with Georgie. She hadn't seen the sun all summer. Her unpainted toe nails were slightly yellow, and she'd missed part of her leg while shaving it late on Thursday night, so black hairs sprouted above her left ankle like a little copse in the snow. At least my shoulders are so white, she thought gloomily, that any falling scurf won't show up. She settled down to her letters.

'*Dearest Vanessa,*' she wrote to one of her bridesmaids, '*so sorry you don't think the hyacinth blue suits you as well as it does Cressida.*'

Georgie was now reaching round to dry the hair at the back of the head which always stays wet longest. Her breasts rose dramatically. Hugh, Kate noticed with a wry, inward smile, was not making much progress with the *Times* crossword, he had only done two clues. Soon Muriel joined them, squashing them even more than ever. She, too, was writing a letter.

'Where's Jonty?' asked Georgie.

'Oh, getting Robert Carriered away in the galley,' said Muriel, then lowering her voice asked, 'How does one say "I'm missing you desperately" in Italian, Hugh?'

'*Ti amo stupidissimo,*' rattled off Hugh.

'How wonderful,' sighed Georgie, turning off her hairdryer, 'I wish I could speak languages like you.'

'*I'm sure if you wear a slightly pinkier lipstick, the blue will look marvellous,*' wrote Kate. God, what rubbish, she thought.

'Look, there's a bluetit,' said Hugh.

'Makes a nice change from brown,' muttered Kate under her breath.

'Where, where?' squeaked Georgie.

'Just above the meadow sweet,' said Hugh, handing Georgie his binoculars, which were still round his neck.

'I can't see,' wailed Georgie.

'To the right,' said Hugh. As she moved the binoculars, she pulled him towards her, until his shoulder was brushed against her left breast.

'Oh, there it is, the little darling!' she screamed, jumping up and down with excitement. 'Isn't it sweet.'

'You're going red, Hugh,' said Muriel pointedly.

'Let me oil you,' said Georgie.

'I'm fine,' said Hugh, lying down very hurriedly.

Looking up, Kate noticed his bathing trunks were standing up like a steeple. Involuntarily, she glanced at Tod, and saw he was staring in the same direction. Then he looked up, and caught her eye and laughed. For a second she felt her face flooded with crimson, then she buried herself in her letter. What appalled her most of all was that she wasn't more upset at Hugh lusting after Georgie.

Georgie kept plaguing her with questions about the wedding. 'Are you wearing white?' she asked.

'Yes,' Kate said.

'Symbol of virginity,' said Tod, adding indigo shadows to the dark green line of the beeches. 'I would have thought you were rather old at twenty-nine, Katie, to flaunt such lack of experience.'

Kate bit her lip. That was below the belt.

'You don't look twenty-nine,' said Georgie with more kindness than conviction, applying extra oil to her shoulders.

'Where are you going for your honeymoon?' asked Muriel.

'Greece,' said Kate.

'Why are they called honeymoons?' asked Georgie.

'Because they're usually extremely sticky,' said Tod.

'Ours won't be,' said Hugh heartily, joining in the general laughter.

'Anyone for drinks?' said Jonty, appearing red-faced in the doorway, with a drying-up cloth over his shoulder.

'I'd like some of that Bollinger,' said Muriel, automatically laying her arm over her letter.

'Me too,' said Georgie.

'That would suit us nicely too,' said Hugh, sounding like an American Express ad. He seemed to have regained his composure and his flat bathing trunks.

'What about you, Tod?' asked Jonty.

Tod, who was gazing abstractedly from the landscape to his painting, didn't answer.

'To-odd,' said Georgie, 'I've never known you refuse a drink.'

'Oh sorry, whisky and lots of water please, Jonty.'

'There *is* no water,' said Jonty petulantly. 'It's all been used up. You'll have to have soda, Tod, and you'll all have to make do with kipper pâté, quiche and salad for lunch.'

'That'll be lovely,' said Georgie, quite oblivious of the malevolent look Jonty was shooting in her direction.

'Who are you writing to?' he asked Muriel, who was putting her letter into an envelope.

'The GPO. They sent us a final reminder,' said Muriel blandly. She got to her feet. 'I'll come and help you with drinks.'

'I'm sure she wasn't writing to the GPO,' Georgie hissed to Hugh, the moment Muriel and Jonty were out of earshot. 'She wouldn't be missing them terribly.'

Peter Brookes

Peter Brookes got his BA at the RAF College Cranwell (London University) in 1965 and continued his studies at the Manchester College of Art (1965–66) and at the Central School of Art and Design (1966–69). Since then he has been working as a freelance illustrator. He regularly drew covers for *New Society*, *New Statesman*, *The Listener* and also works for *The Times*. Since 1982 Brookes has been a daily political illustrator and cartoonist for *The Times* and a cover artist of *The Spectator*. He often contributes caricatures to *The Times Literary Supplement*. Other work includes book jackets for Penguin Books, illustrations for the Glyndebourne Opera Festival (since 1991) and book illustrations for The Folio Society. He was a visiting lecturer in illustration at the Royal College of Art (1980–90). He held solo exhibitions at The Cartoon Gallery (1978/1991) and had his work shown at the Victoria & Albert Museum, the National Theatre, and other venues.

'She would if they'd cut her telephone off,' said Tod.

Georgie laughed. 'Perhaps she's having an affair with some gorgeous Italian count. How romantic. Do you know,' she added to Hugh, 'she told me she's taped Jonty's snoring, and she's going to play it back to him next time they have a row.'

'Suffering from seventeen-year itch, if you ask me,' said Tod, rummaging around for a tube of Cobalt. 'I wonder if Jonty has extra-Muriel affaires.'

'Shouldn't imagine so,' said Hugh knocking his pipe out briskly on the side of the boat, and obviously disapproving of the tenor of the conversation.

'It's so depressing, when you think of all the married couples who are two-timing each other,' sighed Georgie.

'Oh I don't know,' said Tod, unscrewing the tube of Cobalt, 'I've always thought that complete dishonesty between couples was the most important thing in marriage. Don't you agree, Katie?'

Kate looked up. Her heart sank. She saw nothing but contempt and hostility in his face.

The day steadily deteriorated. Lunch was a nightmare. Everyone drank too much. Kate sat opposite Tod, and every so often caught him looking at her incredulously, as though wondering what he'd ever seen in her. Hugh, to Muriel's delight, was plainly very taken with Georgie. He kept crinkling up his eyes, and didn't even put on his spectacles to eat the kipper pâté, which was most unusual as he was absolutely pathological about fishbones.

While Jonty was telling Kate in detail how to perfect Sole

Véronique, Kate overheard Hugh say in a low voice to Georgie, 'I couldn't possibly marry a glamour puss like you, I'd find you far too distracting. I'd never get to work in the morning.'

In between such leaden pleasantries, he was also extremely pompous about politics. Tod didn't bother to disagree with him, but Kate was aware of the two men disliking each other more and more.

After lunch, Tod put the finishing touches to his painting, Jonty and Hugh fiddled with the engine, and Georgie and Kate stacked up the washing-up in the kitchen, ready for more water at the next lock.

'It seems extraordinary,' said Georgie scraping crusts into the muck bucket, 'that both of us should have been girlfriends of Tod. I mean, we couldn't be more different. I expect he liked your mind, he said you used to be very clever.'

'Very kind of him,' snapped Kate. She didn't want to discuss Tod.

'I don't know how you could bear to give him up,' persisted Georgie.

'It was Lent, and the habit stuck,' said Kate.

'But I never met anyone who tired of Tod, before he tired of them. What makes him so irresistible, I suppose, is you know you'll never have the edge over him, because he's so much more hooked on painting than anything else. Some days he's so loving, others he hardly knows I exist. When he was painting that mural in Westmarton Cathedral, he didn't come home one night. I went bananas, I was sure he was with another girl. Then I went down to the cathedral, and found him still up a ladder slapping on paint at two o'clock in the morning, with the verger fast asleep in a pew. I'd have been petrified of ghosts.'

'That's lovely, darling,' said Muriel, coming into the galley followed by Hugh. 'Tod wants just a bit longer, so we'll start up the boat in three-quarters of an hour. Jonty and I are going for a walk.'

'I'm going to sunbathe,' said Georgie.

'Had too much sun this morning,' said Hugh, touching his shoulders gingerly, 'I'm going to have a kip. You better have one too, darling,' he added.

'I'm not tired,' said Kate quickly.

'Don't lie,' said Muriel. 'you've gone white as a sheet again.'

Hugh's fingers closed round her wrist like irons.

'Come on, time for bed.'

'That's right,' said Muriel, getting the usual *double entendre* into her voice. 'But *mind* it is a rest, we'll hang a do-not-disturb sign on your door handle.'

The moment Hugh closed the cabin door behind them, he was on her like a great octopus; breathing heavily, obviously turned on by Georgie. Kate couldn't bear it.

'Someone might come through,' she muttered.

'Don't be silly,' said Hugh, ripping off her bikini top. 'Everyone knows exactly what we're up to.'

'Not now,' she said, close to tears.

'I'm fed up with all this resistance,' he snarled, pushing her back onto the bottom bunk. 'What you need, my angel, is a good screw.'

In the end he forced her, the veins standing out on his forehead, the sickly smile of passion blurring the shrewd, distinguished lawyer's features, with Kate as dry and unyielding inside as the shell of a Scotch egg. The whole coupling was a disaster.

Afterwards she lay beside him, unable to speak with the horror of it, tears coursing into her lank hair.

'You'd better sort yourself out by Saturday week,' he had blustered furiously. 'I've had enough of this ridiculously uptight behaviour.' Then turning the knife for the prosecution, 'Why the hell don't you take a leaf out of Georgie's book.'

He had barged out of the cabin, and next minute she heard him plunge into the river to cool off. She would have given anything to get off the boat and run away through the hayfields, but she couldn't bear to drag herself away from Tod, before she'd had a few minutes to talk to him alone. She lay there listening to the boat starting up, and people clambering over the roof to avoid waking her. Soon they reached the lock, and the dark green slimy wall darkened the cabin window. As the water gushed in, and the *Virgin Queen* rose to the level of the next lock, she saw Muriel coming back, glowing with illicit excitement from posting her letter, and Georgie running round a green meadow, picking buttercups with shrieks of joy. At last they moved on. She knew she ought to drag herself up and help with the washing-up, but she couldn't face another heart to heart with Georgie.

The *Virgin Queen* sailed towards evening through clear khaki waters, low fields and occasional clumps of alders.

Kate went on deck to finish her letters. Everyone was up the other end. Georgie, at the wheel, egged on by Hugh, kept nearly driving the boat into the bank amid shrieks of laughter. They sailed into a series of oxbow bends, which seemed to turn the landscape about the boat like a kaleidoscope. A spire advanced and retreated, the water darkened with the changing sky. Along the banks, water rats, voles and insects were coming out for the night. A dragonfly shot by in a flash of peacock blue. A company of ducks in close formation paddled past. Midges hovered above the deck. Gradually the envelopes piled up beside Kate.

She was vaguely aware of more shouts of mirth from the galley. Then a shadow fell across her page. It was Tod. He handed her a gin and tonic and went over to the other side of the boat, standing with his back to her, absorbed for a minute in the rays of the setting sun, which were gilding the silver willows on the opposite bank. Then he came back and sat down beside her, picking up the envelopes and glancing at the addresses.

'Lord that, Sir Charles and Lady this, Lord Chief Justice that,' he said. 'Are these your friends?'

'Mostly Hugh's.'

'Hugh and non-Hugh.'

Her laugh came out too shrilly.

'Bloody midges,' she said, slapping a grey insect who was feasting on her right ankle.

'Let them eat Kate,' said Tod, lighting a cigarette.

There was a pause.

'You look well,' she said. 'And how's your mother, is she

265

still living in Somerset? I saw a photograph of your sister's wedding in *The Tatler* about two years ago, she looked awfully pretty. Is he a nice man she married, he looked super. I thought you might have come back for the wedding.' Her voice petered out miserably. There was another long silence. Her heart started to thump uncomfortably, she was having trouble breathing. 'Anyway,' she babbled on, frantically pleating the tails of her shirt, 'you seem to have got awfully famous since I last knew you. Have you got any exciting commissions coming up?'

'You asked me that last night,' said Tod curtly, 'and obviously didn't listen to the answer, and you're rattling like a burglar alarm.'

Because someone's just broken into me, Kate was tempted to say, and just stopped herself bursting into hysterical laughter. She took a gulp of her drink and choked. 'Goodness, you always made drinks too strong.'

The boat entered an avenue of weeping willows trailing their long green tresses in the water.

'They remind me of Georgie,' she said, looking at the bank. 'She's *so* beautiful, Tod.'

'I can't say the same for you,' said Tod bluntly. 'You look terrible. When did you go grey?'

'Grey! I haven't!'

'Look,' he picked up a strand of her hair.

'That's not grey, that's paint, I was painting the kitchen ceiling.' She started to laugh, and this time she couldn't stop.

Tod didn't laugh, he just stood looking down at her.

'You're in a mess, Katie.'

He leant over the side, and picked a white swan's feather out of the water. For a second, it lay in his palm, across the strongly marked heart and head lines. Then he gave it to her. 'That's for marrying Hugh.'

Kate gasped, and shrank away. The white feather, symbol of cowardice – it fluttered onto the deck.

'You're running away from life,' he said.

'I suppose you despise me for not marrying a sex maniac, like you.'

'I despise you for marrying someone you don't give a damn about because you're so terrified of being left on the shelf.'

'How d'you know I don't love him?' hissed Kate.

'You wouldn't have come down this weekend, looking like a road accident, not even bothering to wash your hair, slopping about in Oxfam rejects. You're all shrivelled up,' he went on brutally, 'like a plant that's dying from lack of water. Looking at you now, I wonder what the hell I ever saw in you.'

She drew back as though he'd hit her. 'Have you finished?' she said in a frozen voice.

'No I have not. You're selling out, Katie, to bridge parties, and committees and trivia, which won't mean a thing to you because you don't love him – and he doesn't love you either. He wouldn't be drooling over Georgie if he was getting his fun in the sack with you. But that was never your speciality, was it. I expect you're playing the same game as you did with me. What Katie did to Tod from a great height, and you didn't even provide a safety net.' He began to pace the deck.

Kate stood up, her trembling legs hardly holding her. 'I won't listen to another word.'

But Tod had seized her by the arms, and swung her round to face the bank. 'Do you know what building that is?'

Beyond a hayfield and quivering row of poplars were the russet ruins of an ancient church.

'That's Willingdon Priory,' said Tod. 'Nuns used to live there, but they were chucked out in the fourteenth century, for having men in and indulging in lewd behaviour. You can't suppress your sexual urges completely, Katie, you'll turn into a warped old bitch. And if you don't, he'll break you anyway – like a butterfly crushed in the waste disposal. Beneath all that bonhomie, he's an absolute shit. In a fortnight's time, you'll be married to him. The bride was dressed in a tissue of lies – my God!'

Kate tore herself away and fled to the cabin, throwing herself face down on the bed, shocked and moaning with horror. After a minute or two she scrambled to her feet, and looked in the mirror. Was she really as ugly as he said? The face that stared back, stricken and dry-eyed, seemed that of an old woman. She rushed to the loo. The smell of stale urine overwhelmed her, and she was violently sick, retching on and on, until it seemed her guts were being tugged inside out. A terrible headache took hold of her, her bones seemed to be slowly crushing her brain, and she clutched her temples in agony.

Someone banged on the door. 'Are you all right?' It was Hugh.

She couldn't bring herself to answer.

He rattled the door handle violently. 'Kate, say something.'

She opened the door, collapsing into his arms.

'What's the matter?' he said in concern.

'Migraine,' she said through gritted teeth.

He practically carried her into the cabin, and for the second night running put her to bed.

'Poor darling,' he said, obviously feeling guilty for forcing her to have sex earlier, 'You must have had too much sun. Shall I get you a doctor?' he went on, putting a sweating hand on her forehead.

She shook her head weakly. 'It'll go – if I keep still.'

She spent the rest of the evening dozing and being sick. Every so often Muriel or Hugh or Georgie put a conscience-stricken face round the door, and asked her if she needed anything. Occasionally there was a howl of mirth which was instantly hushed. Once Jonty started singing a rugger song, and was told to shut up. She knew they were relieved to be without her, and that she was casting a blight over their weekend, but felt too miserable, too ill, and too shattered to care.

Hours later, when it seemed that at last the pain in her head was beginning to recede, but not the pain in her heart, she heard them all coming to bed.

'Kate,' whispered Hugh. When she didn't answer, he pulled the sheet over her shoulders, kissed her on the forehead, and got into the creaking bunk above. Soon his breathing became a slight snore. She thought of Muriel with her tape-recorder, and wondered if that was all marriage was: an endless game of leaping to grasp the upper hand.

Soon the snoring was so loud, it seemed to rip the stuffy cabin apart. She got up and shakily crept through the saloon, where both Muriel and Jonty seemed to be snoring too, and out onto the deck. She felt dizzy and utterly exhausted.

The drained turquoise sky, full of stars, was already lightening on the horizon. Swathes of mist lay across the hayfields. The elders held up their white flowers, like lace mats, to the night. Kate sat down, breathing in their strange, acrid smell. Then remembering the sheer hopelessness of her situation, she put her face in her hands and wept. Suddenly she felt a hand on her shoulder, and nearly jumped out of her skin. A cigarette glowed in the half-light. It was Tod.

'I'm sorry, Katie,' he whispered. 'I shouldn't have given you that feather this afternoon. It was thoughtless and cruel, but I can't bear to see how much you've changed. You used to be so warm and tender and shining and beautiful.'

'And now I'm not,' sobbed Kate.

'No you're not,' he said gently. 'You remind me of a toy who's been overwound, and suddenly all the machinery gushes out, and it comes to a shuddering halt. You're on the verge of a complete crack-up. Now stop crying and listen to me.'

'I've listened to you quite enough,' said Kate with a gulp, but she stopped crying.

'You're keeping yourself busy,' he said, sitting down beside her and taking her hand, 'the way I kept myself busy after you dropped me.'

Kate caught her breath.

'Painting, painting, painting,' he went on, 'to fill up every minute of the day and night.'

'Did it affect you so much?' she whispered.

'You never considered that, did you,' he said, letting her

hands drop. 'Some of the suffering went into those paintings, they were the best things I've ever done. Through losing you I grew up. I suppose I should be grateful. But now you're doing the same thing: working, working and working so you don't have time to stop and think what it'll be like once you're married. You're going to have to share his bed every night, not just endure the occasional shuffle you can walk away from, and listen to him clearing his throat and sucking on his revolting pipe, and pontificating on and on with his stupid views, and giving endless dinner parties for his frightful friends.'

'You're back on form,' said Kate her voice rising. 'Sweeney Tod, character assassinator. Hugh is, I might tell you, regarded as a considerable catch.'

'Hush,' said Tod softly, 'don't wake the whole boat.'

He put a hand on her shoulder, and she had to fight an overwhelming temptation to turn her head and kiss it.

'Break it off,' he said. 'Please, you must.'

She took a deep breath. Tod must feel something to go on haranguing her like this. 'You don't think that you and I – could perhaps try again – I mean we used to . . .' her voice petered out miserably.

'No, I don't,' said Tod far too quickly to give her even a flicker of hope. 'You and I are caput. For ten years, I've carried this idealised picture of you round in my head. I've even still got a torn photograph of you in my wallet. It's been stuck together so often with sellotape, there's hardly any picture left. The only reason I came down this weekend was because Muriel said you and Hugh were coming. Any time up to yesterday evening, if someone had said Katie'll take you back, I'd have dropped everything. But now I realise, sadly, it's all over. Scratch the bark, and you won't find a trace of green underneath.'

She wanted to hurl herself into his arms, and tell him she could become beautiful, desirable, and happy once more, if only he would love her.

'But even if there's nothing between us,' he went on, lighting one cigarette from another, 'I still care for you. Christ, twenty-nine's nothing. Think of all the marriages that break up between people much older than you, and they find other people. You've years ahead in which to look for a man who'll really love you and look after you.'

'It would kill my parents.'

'Nothing but a direct hit from the nitrogen bomb would kill your mother. I suppose she's worried sick about being a grandchildless couple.'

'Well, that too,' admitted Kate. 'But they adore Hugh and I've given up my job and my flat.'

'Doesn't matter. I'll find you a job. I've got lots of mates in America, they'll fiddle you a work permit out there. If your parents chuck you out, you can come and stay with me until you get yourself together.'

'With you and Georgie?' she asked in a tight little voice.

'Sure – me and Georgie.'

'Will you marry her?'

'I might. She's decorative enough. I'd like some kids. But I seem to have lost the ability to feel very deeply about anyone anymore.'

Kate lost her temper. 'Practise what you preach,' she

howled at him. 'You shouldn't marry someone unless you are crazy about them either – and you shouldn't be so flaming smug. How dare you dictate my life to me. I'll marry Hugh, and I'll make a go of it, and I bet I'm a bloody sight happier than you are.'

She stumbled down the steps and into her cabin, and lay there shivering violently, as gradually fury gave way to utter despair. She would have liked to creep into bed with Hugh for some warmth and reassurance, but the fact that she knew he could give her none, only brought home the hopeless emptiness of their relationship. As dawn broke, and the river started waking up, her only thought was how to escape from the boat.

'Where are we?' Kate asked Muriel casually, as they, washed up after breakfast.

Muriel looked out of the window at the acid green bank of fading cowparsley.

'About a mile from Crickfold Lock,' she said. 'We're going to moor just the other side of it, and have a drink with some friends called Peplow at midday, then we'll turn round after lunch, and head back to the cars.'

'I seem to have lost all sense of direction,' said Kate, even more casually. 'Where's the nearest town?'

'Great Molesforth,' said Muriel. 'It's about six miles from Crickfold Lock. Nice little market town, with a lovely Norman church. I've got some very agreeable clients there. If it weren't so far from the river we could have taken a drink off them. Little forks go in there, darling.'

Kate suddenly felt bitterly ashamed for being such a lousy

guest. 'Thank you so much for having me to stay,' she said. 'You and Jonty have been so sweet.'

'Why don't the two of you stay on another day and enjoy the double bunk?' said Muriel. 'I tried to persuade Tod and Georgie, but he's got to get back to start work on his Gas Board bus.'

Hugh frowned when Kate said she didn't want to go to the Peplows. 'Have you given up altogether?' he snapped.

'I'm still a bit weak after yesterday.'

'I hope you don't mind if I go,' said Hugh, shoving tobacco down in the bowl of his pipe with a matchstick, 'Clarissa Peplow is Vera Talbot-Lacey's sister, and *he's* a judge.'

'And a good judge too,' said Kate. 'Of course you must go.'

'I do hope,' he added sucking at his pipe, 'that you'll behave in a more supportive fashion after we're married.'

Jonty wandered over to them, buttoning up a clean, pale blue shirt. 'I've just put the sea trout in the oven, Kate dear. Could you bear to take it out on the dot of half-past one. It's a new way of cooking it, which I think you'll all like. You just add chopped fennel, and very finely chopped garlic and then you . . .'

'That's enough, darling,' interrupted Muriel, coming out of the galley looking very nautical in a white sailor suit. 'If you take poor Kate through every fishbone we'll never get to the Peplows. And after last night I for one need a whole fur coat of the dog that bit me.'

At long last they went ashore. Kate, who was dying of impatience, could hear Georgie's shrieks as she nearly fell into the river. Gradually the voices and the laughter receded up the hill. She rushed down to the cabin, and started throwing things into her case. She was just getting out of her bikini, when she heard a step. Frantically tugging on her shirt, she kicked the half-packed suitcase under the bed – and only just in time. Tod stood in the doorway. Yesterday's sun had bleached and streaked his hair and darkened his skin to burnt Sienna. He looked like a Californian beach boy. They had not spoken since last night.

'Aren't you coming?' he said.

'No I'm not. I'm fed up with judges – and with flash, swollen-headed painters, too, for that matter,' she snapped. 'Why don't you run along like a bad boy and devastate Mrs Peplow?'

For a second, they glared at each other, then he grinned and said, 'All right, I will.'

Out of the cabin window, she watched him walking up the hill, with the graceful, loping athletic stride that she had always found so attractive in the old days. 'Don't go,' she wanted to call out to him. But she realised it was pure masochism to prolong the weekend. Quickly she threw the rest of her clothes and the great pile of letters into her case, and put on her pink suit. Even in her numb state of misery, she couldn't bring herself to travel by train in a split shirt and filthy trousers. She scribbled a quick note.

'Dearest Hugh, Terribly sorry for pushing off, but I need time to think things out. Forgive me for being so unutterably bloody this week-end. With love, Kate.'

She folded it over, wrote his name on top, and left it on the top bunk.

He won't understand, he'll be insane with rage, she thought, as she jumped onto the bank, ran along the tow path, and scuttled across the little wooden bridge onto the far side. Great Molesforth – six miles across the fields – and then she'd be free like Pigling Bland. She was in such a hurry to get out of eyeshot of the boat, that when she climbed over the first gate into a big field, she didn't bother to read the notice propped in the hawthorn hedge on the right side of the gate post. She tore across the cropped grass, feeling the thistles scratching her bare ankles. The sun blazed down relentlessly. Soon she was panting and sweating in her pink suit, but as she could still be seen from the river, she didn't let up. It was a pity she hadn't gone jogging with Hugh occasionally. The thought of him made her quicken her pace.

Two hundred yards from the river, she passed what she thought was a large black cow. Then she looked again, slowly taking in the cross little eyes, the matt of black curls on the forehead, the ring in the pinkish rubbery nose, the dangerously tossing head. She was reminded of Hugh. God, I can't get away from him was her last coherent thought. For a second she was frozen to the spot with terror, then turning on her heel, she ran for her life. The bull, suffering from the heat, maddened by flies and deprived of female company, let out an angry bellow and gave chase. Stumbling over the molehills, skidding on the cow pats, Kate raced towards the gate. She dropped her suitcase. One shoe fell off, then another. The bull was gaining on her, the thunder of his hoofs shook the ground. Her breath was coming in great sobs.

'Run for the river, for Christ's sake!' howled a voice from the bank.

With a moan of terror, twelve yards from the gate, she swung to the right. An eternity away, the stretch of water glinted in the sunshine. I'll never make it, she thought desperately. The bull was going so fast, he couldn't stop, and bucketed past her crashing into the hawthorn hedge. Surprisingly quickly, he extracted himself, and set off once more in maddened pursuit. She was only twenty-five yards from the river now, but he was gaining on her. She could feel his hot breath on her legs. Her throat was too dry even to scream. Ahead was a wall of nettles. For a second she faltered.

'Jump!' howled the voice in anguish.

Steeling herself she charged through the dense, agonising dark green wall, then she felt a sharp pain on her right side, and a leaden weight crashed into the small of her back, knocking all the breath out of her body, as it catapulted her into the river. I'm going to drown and it doesn't matter, she thought, as the oily filthy water closed over her head. She hadn't any energy left to swim. Next minute, someone had grabbed her and tugged her choking to the surface. It was a few seconds before she realised it was Tod. He towed her to the other side, and none too gently hoisted her up onto the bank.

'Where did he get you?' he said, as he scrambled up beside her, his hair, face and clothes plastered with black river mud.

'This side, I think,' she said weakly, putting a hand on her ribs.

Despite her protests, he ripped off her jacket to reveal a deep graze down her right side.

'Bloody little idiot,' he swore at her, mopping at the graze with the jacket sleeve. 'Another inch, and he'd have gone for your lungs.'

'I couldn't help it. I didn't know there was a bull in the field.'

'Where were you going anyway?'

'Home – to get away from you. Oh my god,' she put her hands in her skirt pocket.

'What's the matter?'

'I must have dropped my latch keys.'

Back on the boat, realising how near to death she had been, she started to tremble violently. Tod poured her a quadruple brandy.

'Get that inside you. Then have a shower, and wash the dirt away from that cut. I'll try and find the farmer and get him to move his bull, so we can retrieve some of your belongings.'

Her knees were still knocking together as she turned on the shower. To hell with Muriel's water supply she thought, as she washed first herself and then her hair. The joy of being clean again almost distracted her from the agonising nettle stings burning her legs. When she went back to the cabin, she found her note to Hugh lying on the bottom bunk. She was sure she'd left it on the top. As she tore it into little pieces, she wondered if Tod had read it.

When he came back, he found her in the saloon wrapped in a faded red towel, her long dark hair dripping down her back like a mermaid. For a second he stood in the doorway, his face completely expressionless. The mud had dried on his shoulders and hair, and had streaked down the side of his face. He looked like a miner just up from the pits. Then he walked into the room and put her bag, suitcase and keys down on the polished table.

'Sorry, I didn't find your shoes, but the bull was getting a bit restless.'

Kate was aghast. 'Didn't you get the farmer to move him? You could have been killed.'

Tod picked up her half empty glass of brandy, and drained it. Then he laughed. 'Bully boy wasn't half as interested in me as he was in you, actually. It must have been a nice change having a male pursuing you as single-mindedly as that. Why didn't you tell him you had a headache?'

Wham, with the hand that wasn't clutching the red towel, she slapped him across the cheek.

Enraged, they glared at each other, as the marks of her fingers slowly reddened on his mud-streaked face. Fists clenched, Tod took a step towards her.

'Whoo-oo.' said Muriel's voice, slightly tight, from the gang plank. 'Hello, angels,' she said, bursting into the saloon. 'Where *did* you get to, Tod. I'm *absolutely* starving, how about you both?'

Then she stopped, slowly taking in Kate dripping in her towel, Tod caked in mud, and the suitcase.

'What's going on?' she said, lighting up with excitement at the prospect of trouble.

Kate opened her mouth and shut it again.

'Nothing,' said Tod curtly, putting his hand up to hide the finger marks. 'Kate fell in, I pulled her out, and she had first shower.'

Suddenly Kate was aware of a terrible smell of burning

coming from the galley. 'Oh God,' she said, going green. 'I forgot to turn the oven off.'

Next minute Jonty bursts in, magenta in the face with fury. 'It's too bad,' he exploded. 'My sea trout is burnt to a cinder, and all the water's run out again.'

It's been a marvellous weekend,' said Hugh, as he kissed Muriel and got into his car.

'I'm desperately sorry about the sea trout,' said Kate for the thousandth time to Jonty.

Hugh wound down the window, to speak to Tod and Georgie. 'We'd love you both to come to the wedding. Shall we send you an invite?'

'Yes please,' said Georgie, turning a glowing brown face up to Tod. 'I love weddings.'

'I can't make it, I'm afraid,' said Tod. 'I've got to go to Paris as soon as I've finished painting the bus.'

'But I could go,' said Georgie, 'and join you on Sunday.'

'Of course, if you want to,' said Tod flatly.

He had gone round to Kate's side, and was standing drumming his fingers on the car roof. Then he bent down and kissed her on the cheek. 'I hope you'll be very happy,' he said softly. 'I'll give you the best divorce lawyer in town as a wedding present.'

'I hope Georgie can come,' said Hugh, moving into the fast lane on the motorway. 'The Law Lords would lap her up. Not very sorry Tod can't. Your parents were quite right, darling, he wouldn't have done for you.'

He's already done for *you*, thought Kate, and she got out her writing case.

'Still more thank-you letters,' said Hugh, getting out his pipe. 'You are a busy bee.'

'Just one more,' she said.

The sun at ten degrees was casting the tall shadows of moving cars onto the grass verge. Kate put her address and telephone number very clearly at the top of the page.

'*Dearest Tod,*' she wrote, '*I have decided not to marry Hugh after all. Thank you for making me realise it would have been a dreadful mistake for both of us. With all my love and God bless you, Katie.*'

Next morning at the office she typed his address on a brown envelope, so as not to upset Georgie, and posted it.

At first everyone was very understanding when she told them she couldn't marry Hugh. Hugh himself was kind but patronising. He immediately drove her down to her parents' house in Bath, explaining to them that Kate was in a highly over-emotional state and that Tod had been on the boat stirring it. Her mother and father told her to get a good night's sleep, she'd obviously been overdoing things. The doctor was called in to give her a sedative, and said she mustn't go back to the office for the last week.

Her boss understood perfectly, she had already left everything in apple pie order – he and all her friends from the office would see her at the wedding.

The next day when she showed no sign of changing her mind, the doctor was called back and spent an hour alone talking to Kate in the drawing-room. 'I'm terribly sorry, Elizabeth,' he said when he came out, 'but I don't find Kate the slightest bit deranged. She's bitterly sorry for upsetting everyone, but she's decided it would be wrong for her to marry Hugh, and that's that. Far better now – than in six months' or six years' time. Don't be too hard on her, it's taken a great deal of courage.'

It was Elizabeth Drayford who needed the sedatives after that. The scenes that followed were worse than Kate could ever have dreamed. Her father blustered and shouted, Hugh was bitter and vicious. He kept pointing out that he'd been made to look a complete idiot in front of his legal superiors, and what was to become of the new house and the speech proposing the toast of the bridesmaids, which he'd been perfecting for weeks.

Worst of all, her mother attacked her non-stop, one moment hysterical, the next vindictive. 'After all that work and planning,' she had screamed, 'you've let us all down. Throwing away the perfect husband just to become an old spinster. What I can't understand is *why*, when he's such a charmer, so brilliant, and such a good bridge player, and if you think you're going to spend the rest of your life mooning around here, you've got another think coming. Your father and I were going to turn your room into a second spare room. Lots of our married friends prefer not to sleep in the same room when they come and stay, you know.'

'Don't worry,' said Kate, trying to sound soothing, 'I'll go and live somewhere else, you don't have to bother with me anymore.'

'But why, why, WHY!'

'Hugh doesn't love me.'

'He would if you were nicer, you've been so awful to him lately.'

'And I don't love him.'

'That's the stupidest reason of all. You *like* him.'

'No I don't, I think he's a pompous prig and a bully, and he makes my flesh creep when he touches me and when he sucks on his revolting pipe.' Kate gave a sob as she echoed Tod's words.

'Do you think I loved your father in that alleycat way when I first married him?'

'You never loved him,' screamed Kate. 'That's why I'm such a mess. I never saw any love or affection between the two of you when I was a child. I was far too frightened of giving myself to Tod all those years ago, because you always drilled into my head that sex was wicked and horrible. Well, now I know it's only wicked and horrible with someone you don't love – like Hugh.'

'How dare you speak to me like that,' said her mother, turning an ugly blotchy red all down her neck. 'It's all Tod's fault, he's an absolute swine. You were quite happy to marry Hugh before you went on that boat. Anyway,' she went on with savage satisfaction, 'Hugh tells me Tod's got a beautiful young girlfriend of his own, and wasn't showing a scrap of interest in you. I bet he thought you'd let your looks go.'

And on and on, round and round went the torrents of abuse, continually re-cycling like a fountain, as for the next eleven days Kate steadily packed up all the three hundred wedding presents – cushioning the fragile ones with packing straw – and took them down to the post office to return them to all the judges and important lawyers who had so graciously sent them. At least I'll be able to get a job as a packer after this, she thought wryly.

But despite all the ranting, she found it rather like being in a submarine at the bottom of the ocean when a storm is raging above sea level. She was desperately aware that she had upset everyone and had behaved appallingly, but she could think only of Tod. She knew she had nothing to hope for. He had brutally spelt out on the boat that he no longer loved her. Yet she still sustained herself on the crumbs of hope that he might think better of her because she'd had the guts to break it off with Hugh, and perhaps acknowledge the letter she had written telling him.

As the days passed the telephone never stopped ringing, with relations and friends wanting to know if the wedding was really off. The doorbell also went continually, with neighbours dropping in on the pretext of offering sympathy to Elizabeth Drayford, but really avid to find out the grisly details of the break-up, because Elizabeth had been so smug about her daughter's dazzling match. And at each ring of the telephone or front doorbell, Kate's heart leapt that it might be Tod, but it never was. Nor was there any word from him amongst the pile of letters of commiseration which came in twice a day, and which she so feverishly scanned.

It was Friday night. The wedding would have been tomorrow and Tod must now have left for France. Kate had staked her all on a million to one chance that he might come back, and she had lost. She now had to face the fact that her world was in smithereens. She felt only relief that Hugh had gone, but how was she to drag herself through the rest of her life. Wasn't it A.E. Housman who had written: '*He who loves more than once, has never loved at all.*'

This weekend, too, she must find a room to live in, and then a job. After she'd paid, out of her own pocket, for the cake, the bridesmaids' dresses, the breaking-off announcement in the *Times*, the postage for returning the parcels, the deposit on the marquee, and a hundred and one other extras, she had only two hundred pounds left in the bank. It was enough perhaps for a plane ticket to Ethiopia or Katamoja, where she could work for people whose sufferings were so dreadful that hers would seem trivial by comparison.

She was thankful for the first time since returning from the boat weekend to be alone in the house. Her mother and father had gone to a drinks party on the other side of town. Her mother, who'd lost two pounds in weight as a result of all the stress, went off looking very pretty in the dress and the new coral shoes she had bought for Kate's wedding. This had triggered off yet another volley of abuse.

'I loathe and detest having to wear this,' was Elizabeth Drayford's parting shot. 'But after all the expense we've been put to, I shan't be able to afford anything else to wear for years.'

Left alone, Kate had a bath, washed all the packing straw dust out of her hair, and put on an old pair of pink denim trousers and a faded purple t-shirt. Then she went out into the garden. A thrush was singing, the air was full of the scent of honeysuckle and orange blossom, giant, dark blue delphiniums spiked the violet dusk. Pearly pink roses seemed to quiver in the stillness. Her father, she realised with a stab of remorse, had lovingly tended every plant to a pitch of perfection just in time for the wedding.

There was no time on the blank face of the sundial. Just like me, she thought miserably. I've reached the age of twenty-nine with nothing to show for it – except messing up other people's lives. She shivered and clutched her arms above the elbows for warmth. She must go in and do something about supper for her parents.

As she put the shepherd's pie into the oven, a key turned in the lock. Her heart sank, they were back already – her mother punchy and glittering-eyed from a surfeit of dry Martinis.

'Too humiliating,' she said, easing her feet out of the coral shoes. 'Everyone asked about the wedding. They all think you've been too awful, Kate. And Tom and Sue had their daughter and son-in-law there, with a heavenly baby in a carry cot. Sue took me upstairs to admire it. "Poor Elizabeth," she said, "I don't expect you'll ever have any little grandchildren now."'

Elizabeth Drayford got out her handkerchief and blew her nose loudly. 'Did you manage to get through to your Uncle Trubshaw and tell him the wedding was off?' she went on in a more bullying tone.

'I've been ringing all day, but haven't got an answer,' said Kate, 'so I've sent a telegram.'

'Well, I hope it gets through, I don't want Trubshaw turning up expecting a binge and having to entertain him all weekend.'

'Why don't you go and change out of that lovely dress, Elizabeth?' said Henry Drayford, who knew that if there was another scene he wouldn't get any dinner for ages.

'Everyone admired it,' said her mother resuming her martyred tone as she went upstairs, 'but all I could think of was that I should have been wearing it in happier circumstances.'

Kate sighed, nearer to breaking and despair than at any time in the last fortnight. She tipped the broad beans into a pan of boiling water.

'The garden's looking absolutely lovely, Daddy,' she said in a faltering voice, 'I've never seen it better, you must have worked so hard to make it look nice for tomorrow. I'm so sorry.'

Henry Drayford came over and patted her shoulder.

'Never mind, never mind, your mother'll get over it, everything'll seem better in a few days. Like a drink?'

She nodded, not trusting herself to speak, and watched him wander off towards the drinks tray in the drawing-room, cannoning off the kitchen door as he went.

She was just adding salt to the broad beans when she heard the roar of an engine, and a crunch on the gravel. Then she heard her mother scream.

'What's the matter?' she said, rushing into the hall in alarm.

'There's a bus coming up the drive!' screeched her mother, 'What on earth is it doing here? Henry! There's a bus outside, tell it to go away at once.'

'Think your mother's had a few too many,' muttered Henry Drayford, coming out of the drawing-room, carrying a large glass of whisky and a gin and tonic.

Kate ran to the hall window. Sure enough, a brilliant-coloured bus was coming up the drive, fantastically painted with hearts, roses, lilies, yellow irises and honeysuckle, all looped together with garlands of pale green ivy and pale pink ribbon. How beautiful was all she could think. Then she gave a gasp, and clung onto the window sill, for painted across the flowers in huge, scrawling, bright pink letters were the words. *I love Kate Drayford.*

A great lump came into her throat. She shut her eyes in disbelief, but the tears welled through them. Then she rushed to the front door, and read the words again. *I love Kate Drayford.*

Next minute the door of the driver's cabin opened, and a long, long pair of legs jumped out, with Tod at the top of them.

Kate tore across the gravel and crashed into him. 'Oh Tod, darling, darling. I thought you were in France.'

'And I thought you'd probably be out by now, on some pre-wedding stag night, whooping it up with all Hugh's relations. I didn't realise it was Friday, I got stuck in the weekend traffic.'

He put his arms round her and held her very tight. She could feel the frantic crash of his heart, and his blue shirt drenched with sweat. 'Katie darling, I know it's last ditch, but you can't marry Hugh, please don't. It'll break my heart.'

'But I'm not going to marry him,' she said half laughing, half crying, 'didn't you get my letter?'

'What letter?' he said in bewilderment.

'I posted you a letter about twelve days ago, saying I'd broken it off.'

'You didn't type the envelope?'

'Yes I did, it was a brown one. I thought Georgie might have opened it otherwise, and been upset.'

Tod gave a groan. 'Oh sweetheart. You ought to have remembered I never open bills. My God, I didn't realise. And all this time you've been waiting for me to get in touch, thinking I didn't care. I can't bear it.'

And there were tears in his eyes, as he bent his head to kiss her, holding her so tightly she thought her ribs would crack. She could feel the stubble grazing her cheek, and the thick hair under her fingers, and her stomach melted like hot wax in joy, and lust and amazement. Finally, she struggled for air, and he laid his cheek against her hair, stroking her face over and over with his hand, as if to prove she was really there.

'I was such a sod to you on the boat,' he said, 'but I was so hurt. I heard you were coming down with some marvellously suitable man. I was eaten up with jealousy, all I wanted to do was to pay you back for all the unhappiness you caused me, and show you there was absolutely no possibility of your ever hurting me again.

'I even kidded myself it was all over, until that bloody bull chased you, and I realised I was still hopelessly hooked on you, and I'd blown the whole thing. I would have come round earlier, but I psyched myself into thinking the only adequate peace offering was painting you a bus.'

'It's lovely,' said Kate in a choked voice. 'It's the loveliest thing I've ever seen, I can't really believe it. But what are the Gas Board going to say?'

'Well, they may kick up a bit of fuss about the caption,' said

Tod softly, 'but I know it's the right one. I *do* love Kate Drayford.'

Kate pulled away and looked at him – taking in the five-day-old beard, the black rings under the blood-shot eyes, the paint-stained shirt and jeans. She suppressed a gurgle of laughter.

'Really, Tod,' she said reprovingly, 'you look terrible. You've let yourself go in the last fortnight, you used to be *so* beautiful. If you really cared for me, you'd never let me see you like this. I don't believe you've washed your hair for days.'

Just for a second there was a flicker of doubt and anxiety in his face, then he saw she was laughing. 'Bitch,' he said, pulling her into his arms. 'My God, what fools we've been to waste ten years. Uh-uh,' he muttered, looking over her shoulder towards the house, 'Regan and Cornwall are approaching.'

Kate tried to turn round, but his arms tightened like a vice around her.

'Evening, Elizabeth. Hello, Henry. Sorry to intrude upon your hour of grief.'

'How dare you roll up here,' said Elizabeth Drayford in an outraged voice. 'I'm sure you were entirely responsible for Kate breaking off her engagement.'

'I hope so,' said Tod, 'I assure you she's much better off with me. I've come to ask for your daughter's hand in marriage, Henry.'

Kate jumped violently. 'Are you sure?' she said shakily.

'Quite sure,' he said, drawing her back to him, gently stroking her hair. 'I'm not monkeying about any longer.'

'Well, it's all very irregular,' muttered Henry Drayford.

'I have to confess,' said Tod, 'that if you withhold permission, I won't take a blind bit of notice.'

'Insufferable,' choked Elizabeth ducking as a bat came dive-bombing over. 'You haven't changed at all, Tod.'

'And you're wonderfully the same too,' said Tod amiably.

Suddenly they all jumped at the sound of frantic hooting, and a very old Morris just missed the gate post, and came up the drive in a succession of jerks.

'Good God, it's Trubshaw,' said Henry Drayford.

'I thought you told me you'd sent him a telegram,' said Elizabeth shrilly. 'You can't do anything right, Kate. Now we'll have to spend the whole weekend amusing him.'

'I got a special licence today,' said Tod, taking a stunned, ecstatic Kate by the hand and leading her towards the bus. 'Tell Trubshaw if he hangs on till Monday, he can come to Katie's wedding after all.'

Susan Ryder

Susan Ryder was born in 1944. She studied at the Byam Shaw School of Art from 1960–1964. In 1964 she was awarded the David Murray Travel Scholarship for Landscapes, and from 1964 to 1965 taught art at Claygate School, Esher.

Her first one-man show was held at the Haste Gallery, Ipswich in 1979 followed by a second in 1982. In 1990 she held a one-man show at W.H. Patterson, Albermarle Street, London, followed by three exhibitions at the same gallery each featuring six distinguished artists.

She is a regular exhibitor at the Royal Academy, the Royal Society of Portrait Painters (elected a member in 1992), and the New English Art Club (elected a member in 1982). Her work has also been included in numerous mixed exhibitions.

In 1982 she moved from Suffolk to London where, amongst her many portrait commissions, she was chosen to paint HRH The Princess of Wales, Miss Pears in 1984, Nicola Paget in 1991 and Lord Porter OM in 1994. She has recently completed a portrait of the Duchess of Grafton. Her prizes include the Barney Wilkins in 1990, the Alexon Portrait Competition in 1991, the New English Art Club Critics Award – second prize in 1991 and first prize in 1992.

Although a distinguished portrait painter, Susan Ryder is equally widely known for her paintings of interiors. She travels extensively, painting in France, Italy, India and Spain. She lives and works in London and Scotland.

Henrietta Miers

unveiled
freedom

Henrietta Miers read classics at St Anne's College, Oxford University, graduating in 1989. She then spent a year working as a researcher for the well-known French writer and anglophile, Philippe Daudy, before moving to Pakistan. There she lived in the North West Frontier Province in a remote valley bordering Afghanistan, first as a teacher in a local school and then as an intern working for the Women in Development section of the the Aga Khan Rural Support Programme. She returned to London and won a scholarship from The Aga Khan Foundation to do an MA in Development Studies at the School of Oriental and African Studies (University of London). She now plans to pursue a career in overseas development. She has also worked as a freelance journalist writing stories on development issues. At present she is working for Rwandan refugees in Goma.

This was the most inquisitive crowd I had ever managed to attract. I wanted to slip away unnoticed in the evening jostle of the small dusty town, but there I was, like a criminal caught on the run, awkwardly standing in a shop full of burqas while the entire street looked on. I stared at the rows of silk and cotton sacks hanging listlessly like ghosts in the airless room, each with hundreds of tiny neat pleats. The rich variety of colours on display – deep purples and blues and greens and mustard yellows – dispelled the uniformity of their shapes. Yet since whichever I chose would envelop me completely, it hardly mattered if the colour suited me or not. It would adopt a character of its own, reducing me inside to a prop – a tent pole – to hold it up and move it along, with a grille over my eyes through which to look out on to the outside world.

The murmur of the crowd grew louder, and Ali, my accomplice, nervously jingled his keys. My thoughts veered back to the task in hand, and I pointed decisively at a bundle of deep purple silk dangling in front of me. Ali was already thrusting some notes into the hand of the bemused shopkeeper, and negotiating a path for me through the crowded street. Then I was sitting in the silence of an air-conditioned Pajero, looking out at a sea of gawping men. 'Congratulations,' Ali shouted triumphantly, 'you have just purchased your ticket into Afghanistan.'

I was returning to Chitral, a town buried in the mountains of northern Pakistan where, for the last year, I had been teaching in a local school. It was early March and winter snows still blocked the Lowari Pass that links the Chitral valley with the rest of Pakistan. Three weeks had passed since the little plane had last been able to land. This left only one route open, a route which looped into a chunk of Afghanistan, following the Kunar river. The Pakistani government, for reasons I never understood, prohibited foreigners from entering Afghanistan, so I was to travel under the camouflage of a burqa, posing as Ali's wife. My disguise carried a dual purpose: it would allow me to slip past the border guards unnoticed, and it would lessen the danger of our jeep being ambushed by roaming Afghans who frequently hijacked passing Chitrali jeeps. If they heard a Western woman was on board, they would smell money and quite happily rob me of everything I owned.

We slept that night in a town called Timurgara, in a fort belonging to a fat and silent man introduced to me simply as Khan. After granting me a pious nod, he devoted the rest of the evening to ignoring my presence. (By way of explanation, Ali later divulged that Khan was deeply religious). Khan lived on the edge of the tribal territory that lay between us and Afghanistan. This, I was told, was more dangerous than Afghanistan itself, so we planned to cross it in the darkness of the early morning. I was to be driven by Ali and accompanied by his uncle Faisal, who made it his business to point out to me repeatedly the dangers of the venture we were undertaking.

At four in the morning we were on our way, and I, enmeshed in the folds of my burqa, looked out sleepily onto the fleeting shadows of the night through my trellised grille. The darkness slipped away and the shadows intensified. The jeep stopped and I awoke to find us surrounded by stationary vehicles and shadowy silhouettes milling around in the pre-dawn haze. Ali got out to consult a huddle of men, and returned grim faced. Tribal bandits were lurking ahead, ready to ambush a jeep rumoured to be carrying a Western woman, and we were waiting for a police escort to guide us through. Ali appeared suddenly nervous and ordered me to remain fully covered. The men outside had unanimously agreed that the British were to be blamed for our hold up, since while ruling India they had failed to subdue these lawless tribal territories. This they had announced to Ali as if they knew he was harbouring an English woman. I remembered the crowd outside the burqa shop. Faisal, delighting in his role as chief tormentor, compounded my fear by announcing that one of Khan's servants would have by now run ahead and alerted the bandits that a Western woman was at large hiding in a purple burqa. 'We're probably done for, we'll never reach Chitral,' he said gloomily, and pretended to pray.

The light grew stronger as we waited and the gesticulating figures transformed into fierce looking men. As the sun rose and the greys and pale blues of dawn took shape, the escort arrived, the convoy lined up and we began to snake along the road: 'Imagine that behind every tree is a bandit waiting to ambush,' said Faisal helpfully, waving at the tall eucylyptus trees that stretched ahead. The convoy slowed at a steep corner: 'You see, this is when the bandits attack, when the vehicles are forced to drive slowly.' Despite Faisal's words of doom my fear gradually diminished. I became acutely aware of my own invisibility. No one who harboured the slightest suspicion that my burqa was housing an impostor would dare to challenge Ali's honour. The threat of the bandits receded with the morning light and I felt strangely safe.

We zigzagged to the top of the Nawapass, the border between Pakistan and Afghanistan, where a sleepy guard waved us on. I threw back my disguise, wound down the window and breathed in gasps of cool air. Apart from the occasional melancholy donkey labouring under planks of timber, whipped on by solitary Afghans, there was no one in sight. Relaxing a little more I lit a cigarette. Seconds later Ali shouted 'burqa down', and amid a flurry of smoke and flaying purple silk I was back inside my burqa. Smoke filtered through my grille as we shot past a group of men by the roadside. Ali reprimanded me for my carelessness and Faisal reminded me of my fate if an Afghan discovered my true identity. I would be dragged from the jeep, robbed and probably raped. For several minutes I sat in silence, wondering how to pass the rest of the day cooped up inside what was becoming a furnace, with only a blinkered and criss-crossed vision of the empty land around me.

So long as I spied the figures on the road before they spied me, I pleaded with Ali, I could be back inside my disguise within seconds. He relented, and we all lapsed into contemplative silence, punctuated now and again by the 'burqa down' drill from the front seat. During one such drill I deftly re-covered myself only to see a donkey strolling casually across the road. Ali, I realised, was taking no chances.

Burqa down at Nawabad for a tea stop. Afghans loitered around the jeep, close enough for me to see their kohl-rimmed eyes. Ali brought me sweet milky tea, stewed, and I carefully manoeuvred the dirty saucer into my burqa. I longed to get out and stretch my legs, but still feeling guilty after the cigarette incident, decided not to push for further liberties. My prayers were answered when Ali noticed a puncture, and I was ushered out of the jeep and into a small black room while they changed the tyre. 'Careful how you walk,' taunted Faisal, 'They can tell you're a Westerner by your bad posture.' The sweaty interior of my burqa and the darkness and the rancid smell of the room depressed me. Ali brought me more tea, spicy pastries, and a freshly caught, half-cooked fish. He entered and closed the door furtively, like a nervous burglar, eager to prevent the outside light from exposing his guarded possession.

Back on the road, I was touched by the solitude and desolation of the land around me. Occasionally we passed clusters of deserted flat-rooved mud-brick houses, a solitary figure herding his flock of goats, a camel or two. The burnt out rusting shells of Russian tanks, one of which had been turned into a tea shop, and echoes of battles fought nearby between the Russians and the Mujahadeen. Only once did we pass through a small town, Chigha Sarai, the capital of the Kunar province. Here I spied the one woman I saw on the journey, just a shape in a floating black burqa being propelled along the roadside.

From within the darkness of my burqa, I tried to imagine a lifetime of seclusion from the world. Ali and Faisal came from Chitral, where women rarely meet men outside their immediate family and remain within the confines of their homes and villages. I asked them if they thought that this was a good thing. Ali saw Chitral as being stuck in the Dark Ages, in a time warp, held in the grip of the mullahs. 'Men have twisted the Prophet's words in order to oppress their women, and this has become tradition which none of us dare to defy. But the mullahs will lose their grip and women will one day be free.'

Faisal had other ideas. 'You women in the West,' he accused me, 'expose yourselves to all the dangers of the world.' Imagine, he said, pointing to a flashy gold watch on his wrist, that you have a beautiful and valuable possession like this, worth more to you than anything in the world. You don't want anyone to see it in case they try to steal it from you, so you hide it away and keep it for your own pleasure. This was why they concealed their women from the world, and Faisal doubted that things were going to change. Then I received a history lesson, the thread of which was that before the coming of Islam, women were treated as animals and buried alive when their husbands died. Islam has freed women and raised their status to equal man's. Purdah is merely a means of protecting them, not imprisoning them. 'Today, you are protected as a woman in purdah, but our women are protected for a lifetime. You women in the West may be free, but our women at least are safe.'

Safe from what, I wondered? Were all men potential adulterers, unable to restrain themselves in front of a woman?

Still, I told Faisal, I would rather be free, and we argued about the nature of freedom. How free is a Western woman, asked Faisal, who lives, as I did, in a conservative valley where the mullahs' power is strong? The events of my first night in Chitral, a year previously, came sharply to my mind. Surrounded by high walls, two outer courtyards and a heavy steel door onto the street, my new home had seemed safe enough to me. I was wrong. I had fallen asleep only to be rudely awakened a few hours later by a crashing door and heavy boots. In the darkness I could make out three figures moving around my room. Then I found myself lying, with the barrel of a kalashnikov pressed against my temple, breathing awkwardly into my pillow. My mind blanked and I waited for the shot. For several minutes after the pressure left my head and the crashing boots faded into the darkness, I lay still, wait-ing for the shot. This had not been what I was expecting at all.

The cook sent word to the Deputy Commissioner. 'It wouldn't be right for me to enter your house,' apologised the most superior bureaucrat of the valley. So I sat in his Pajero outside my front gate reporting the details of my intrusion while noticing that he was still in his pyjamas. He barked an order and returned home to bed leaving ten armed Chitrali police shyly grinning at me across my sitting room floor and another ten prowling my garden. I was being asked to write a statement and instructed to begin 'Respectfully, I beg to state . . .' I couldn't seem to go on from there, and someone had to coax me. 'What do you beg to state?'

The next day I received delegations of Chitralis, who came to apologise for my rude welcome to their valley, and to insist that my intruders were Afghans, some of the refugees who had settled in the valley and brought violence to a peaceful land. The Afghans denied it. An enquiry was launched, but no one was charged. Later I doubted the existence of the enquiry at all. Iron bars were hammered against my windows, huge locks attached to my doors, and from then on two armed guards snored loudly in my garden every night. No one attempted to explain to me the motive behind the intrusion. I was simply assured that I would never be disturbed again.

I had arrived in the middle of Ramazan, and the bazaar was gripped by a torpor that seemed to intensify the people's suspicious stares. For two weeks it rained relentlessly. The rain and the mist and the low heavy clouds shrouded the mountains that surrounded me. Roads in and out of the town flooded, and still it continued to rain, sometimes for days on end, dense, drenching and monotonous. It had never rained so hard in anyone's living memory. Some blamed it on the oil wells burning in Kuwait. In Kashmir skiers were reporting oily snow, and all around the Hindu Kush black rain was staining the mountains. It was raining all over Pakistan, all over Asia, all over the world. It was Allah's punishment for the folly of the Gulf War. Severed from the outside world, truth and fiction merged into one. I wrote in my diary, 'When will I ever get out of this valley?'

The end of Ramazan brought the end of the rains. The town celebrated Eid under a hot spring sun. Children dressed in brightly coloured outfits scuffled and smiled down the street, clutching pastries and boxes of sweets. Boys played with painted eggs and girls waved their orange hennaed hands in the air. The clouds disappeared leaving a crisp sky and my first sight of the mountain tops that had hemmed me in for so long. The bronchial wheeze of the little plane, soon to sound so familiar, brought letters and parcels from beyond the pass. The door to my prison was open, but I no longer wanted to escape.

Slowly I learnt the limits of my freedom. My every movement was monitored, my conversations limited, my friendships strained, my presence in the town condemned by the mullahs at Friday prayers. I made some mistakes, too. Early on I naïvely put my classics education to what I thought was good use and introduced my class to stories of the Greek gods. They listened, looking puzzled, and the next day the school rioted. Boys and girls streamed round the playground chanting 'There is only one God and he is Allah'. The children's fathers ignored me in the bazaar, fearing the accusation of intimacy with a Western woman.

There were a variety of measures I could take to alleviate the sometimes oppressive nature of my life. 'Use my runway for jogging,' the airport manager told me, and so in the cool of the evening I jogged. I could climb a mountain, drive up the valley in an open jeep, or phone home. I could visit an unmarried friend whose position forced her to observe strict purdah. She lived with her brother in a beautiful but dilapidated house perched above a sharp bend in the river. True purdah, she told me, is in your heart, not in your actions. Many women observe purdah to appease the mullahs and to maintain their family's honour, not because they believe in a system that imprisons them. Sitting in her garden drinking tea and listening to the roar of the grey river was my escape from the prying eyes of the bazaar. For her it was a prison. She was one of the few educated and secluded women who envied my freedom to roam around the world and resented the constraints that they suffered.

As I argued with Faisal that day from the interior of my burqa, it seemed so easy to condemn the patriarchal nature of a society that robs its women of the smallest grain of freedom. But many of the women appeared happy in their secluded lives. They pitied me for my freedom. These were the ones who saw the advantages of clinging to a purdah system that sheltered them. They looked upon their confinement and their veils with pride, content in the knowledge that they were upholding the honour of their families. How, they wondered, did I manage to earn a living, choose my husband *and* protect myself? With difficulty, I would sometimes want to reply. Yet I was convinced of the value of my freedom. Never would I wish to trade it, and all its dangers, for the protected seclusion of purdah and the shame of showing my face.

Jeffrey Archer

colonel
bullfrog

Jeffrey Archer was brought up in Somerset, the son of a printer. He was educated at Wellington School, Somerset and BNC, Oxford, where he gained an athletics blue, was President of the University Athletics Club, and went on to run the 100 yards in 9.6 seconds for Great Britain in 1966.

After leaving Oxford he was elected to the GLC as its youngest member and three years later at the age of twenty-nine, he became the youngest Member of Parliament. After five years he resigned from the House of Commons aged thirty-four, on the verge of bankruptcy, and wrote his first novel *Not A Penny More, Not A Penny Less*. Jeffrey Archer's latest book, *Twelve Red Herrings*, was published in July 1994.

Jeffrey Archer was made a Life Peer in the Queen's Birthday Honours List of 1992.

In 1991 he was co-ordinator for the Campaign for Kurdish Relief which raised over fifty seven million pounds for the Kurdish people.

He lives at the Old Vicarage in Grantchester with his wife, Mary, and their two sons, Will and James.

There is one cathedral in England that has never found it necessary to launch a national appeal.

When the Colonel woke he found himself tied to a stake where the ambush had taken place. He could feel a numb sensation in his leg. The last thing he could recall was the bayonet entering his thigh. All he was aware of now were ants crawling up the leg on an endless march towards the wound.

It would have been better to have remained unconscious, he decided.

Then someone undid the knots and he collapsed head first into the mud. It would be better still to be dead, he concluded. The Colonel somehow got to his knees and crawled over to the stake next to him. Tied to it was a corporal who must have been dead for several hours. Ants were crawling into his mouth. The Colonel tore off a strip from the man's shirt, washed it in a large puddle nearby and cleaned the wound in his leg as best he could before binding it tightly.

That was February 17th, 1943, a date that would be etched on the Colonel's memory for the rest of his life.

That same morning the Japanese received orders that the newly captured Allied prisoners were to be moved at dawn. Many were to die on the march and even more had perished before the trek began. Colonel Richard Moore was determined not to be counted among them.

Twenty-nine days later, one hundred and seventeen of the original seven hundred and thirty-two Allied troops reached Tonchan. Any man whose travels had previously not taken him beyond Rome could hardly have been prepared for such an experience as Tonchan. This heavily guarded prisoner-of-war camp, some three hundred miles north of Singapore and hidden in the deepest equatorial jungle, offered no possibility of freedom. Anyone who contemplated escape could not hope to survive in the jungle for more than a few days, while those who remained discovered the odds were not a lot shorter.

When the Colonel first arrived, Major Sakata, the camp commandant, informed him that he was the senior ranking officer and would therefore be held responsible for the welfare of all Allied troops.

Colonel Moore had stared down at the Japanese officer. Sakata must have been a foot shorter than himself but after that twenty-eight-day march the British soldier couldn't have weighed much more than the diminutive Major.

Moore's first act on leaving the commandant's office was to call together all the Allied officers. He discovered there was a good cross-section from Britain, Australia, New Zealand and America but few could have been described as fit. Men were dying daily from malaria, dysentery and malnutrition. He was suddenly aware what the expression 'dying like flies' meant.

The Colonel learned from his staff officers that for the previous two years of the camp's existence they had been ordered to build bamboo huts for the Japanese officers. These had had to be completed before they had been allowed to start on a hospital for their own men and only recently huts for themselves. Many prisoners had died during those two years, not from illness but from the atrocities some Japanese perpetrated on a daily basis. Major Sakata, known because of his skinny arms as 'Chopsticks', was, however, not considered to be the villain. His second-in-command, Lieutenant Takasaki (the Undertaker), and Sergeant Ayut (the Pig) were of a different mould and to be avoided at all cost, his men warned him.

It took the Colonel only a few days to discover why.

He decided his first task was to try to raise the battered morale of his troops. As there was no padre among those officers who had been captured he began each day by conducting a short service of prayer. Once the service was over the men would start work on the railway that ran alongside the camp. Each arduous day consisted of laying tracks to help Japanese soldiers get to the front more quickly so they could in turn kill and capture more Allied troops. Any prisoner suspected of undermining this work was found guilty of sabotage and put to death without trial. Lieutenant Takasaki considered taking an unscheduled five-minute break to be sabotage.

At lunch prisoners were allowed twenty minutes off to share a bowl of rice – usually with maggots – and, if they were lucky, a mug of water. Although the men returned to the camp each night exhausted, the Colonel still set about organising squads to be responsible for the cleanliness of their huts and the state of the latrines.

After only a few months, the Colonel was able to organise a

football match between the British and the Americans, and following its success even set up a camp league. But he was even more delighted when the men turned up for karate lessons under Sergeant Hawke, a thick-set Australian, who had a Black Belt and for good measure also played the mouth-organ. The tiny instrument had survived the march through the jungle but everyone assumed it would be discovered before long and confiscated.

Each day Moore renewed his determination not to allow the Japanese to believe for one moment that the Allies were beaten – despite the fact that while he was at Tonchan he lost another twenty pounds in weight, and at least one man under his command every day.

To the Colonel's surprise the camp commandant, despite the Japanese national belief that any soldier who allowed himself to be captured ought to be treated as a deserter, did not place too many unnecessary obstacles in his path.

'You are like the British Bullfrog,' Major Sakata suggested one evening as he watched the Colonel carving cricket bails out of bamboo. It was one of the rare occasions when the Colonel managed a smile.

His real problems continued to come from Lieutenant Takasaki and his henchmen, who considered captured Allied prisoners fit only to be considered as traitors. Takasaki was always careful how he treated the Colonel personally, but felt no such reservations when dealing with the other ranks, with the result that Allied soldiers often ended up with their mea-gre rations confiscated, a rifle butt in the stomach, or even left bound to a tree for days on end.

Whenever the Colonel made an official complaint to the commandant, Major Sakata listened sympathetically and even made an effort to weed out the main offenders. Moore's happiest moment at Tonchan was to witness the Undertaker and the Pig boarding the train for the front line. No one attempted to sabotage that journey. The commandant replaced them with Sergeant Akida and Corporal Sushi, known by the prisoners almost affectionately as 'Sweet and Sour Pork'. However, the Japanese High Command sent a new Number Two to the camp, a Lieutenant Osawa, who quickly became known as 'The Devil' since he perpetrated atrocities that made the Undertaker and the Pig look like church fête organisers.

As the months passed the Colonel and the commandant's mutual respect grew. Sakata even confided to his English prisoner that he had requested that he be sent to the front line and join the real war. 'And if,' the Major added, 'the High Command grants my request, there will be only two NCOs I would want to accompany me.'

Colonel Moore knew the Major had Sweet and Sour Pork in mind, and was fearful what might become of his men if the only three Japanese he could work with were posted back to active duties to leave Lieutenant Osawa in command of the camp.

Colonel Moore realised that something quite extraordinary must have taken place for Major Sakata to come to his hut, because he had never done so before. The Colonel put his bowl of rice back down on the table and asked the three Allied officers who were sharing breakfast with him to wait outside.

The Major stood to attention and saluted.

The Colonel pushed himself to his full six feet, returned the salute and stared down into Sakata's eyes.

'The war is over,' said the Japanese officer. For a brief moment Moore feared the worst. 'Japan has surrendered unconditionally. You, sir,' Sakata said quietly, 'are now in command of the camp.'

The Colonel immediately ordered all Japanese officers to be placed under arrest in the commandant's quarters. While his orders were being carried out he personally went in search of The Devil. Moore marched across the parade ground and headed towards the officers' quarters. He located the second-in-command's hut, walked up the steps and threw open Osawa's door. The sight that met the new commandant's eyes was one he would never forget. The Colonel had read of ceremonial hara-kiri without any real idea of what the final act consisted. Lieutenant Osawa must have cut himself a hundred times before he eventually died. The blood, the stench and the sight of the mutilated body would have caused a Gurkha to be sick. Only the head was there to confirm that the remains had once belonged to a human being.

The Colonel ordered Osawa to be buried outside the gates of the camp.

When the surrender of Japan was finally signed on board the US *Missouri* in Tokyo Bay, all at Tonchan PoW camp listened to the ceremony on the single camp radio. Colonel Moore then called a full parade on the camp square. For the first time in two and a half years he wore his dress uniform which made him look like a pierrot who had turned up at a formal party. He accepted the Japanese flag of surrender from Major Sakata on behalf of the Allies, then made the defeated enemy raise the American and British flags to the sound of both national anthems played in turn by Sergeant Hawke on his mouth-organ.

The Colonel then held a short service of thanksgiving which he conducted in the presence of all the Allied and Japanese soldiers.

Once command had changed hands Colonel Moore waited as week followed pointless week for news that he would be sent home. Many of his men had been given their orders to start the ten thousand-mile journey back to England via Bangkok and Calcutta, but no such orders came for the Colonel and he waited in vain to be sent his repatriation papers.

Then, in January 1946, a smartly dressed young Guards officer arrived at the camp with orders to see the Colonel. He was conducted to the commandant's office and saluted before shaking hands. Richard Moore stared at the young captain who, from his healthy complexion, had obviously arrived in the Far East long after the Japanese had surrendered. The captain handed over a letter to the Colonel.

'Home at last,' said the older man breezily, as he ripped open the envelope, only to discover that it would be years before he could hope to exchange the paddy fields of Tonchan for the green fields of Lincolnshire.

The letter requested that the Colonel travel to Tokyo and

represent Britain on the forthcoming war tribunal which was to be conducted in the Japanese capital. Captain Ross of the Coldstream Guards would take over his command at Tonchan.

The tribunal was to consist of twelve officers under the chairmanship of General Matthew Tomkins. Moore was to be the sole British representative and was to report directly to the General, 'as soon as you find it convenient'. Further details would be supplied to him on his arrival in Tokyo. The letter ended: 'If for any reason you should require my help in your deliberations, do not hesitate to contact me personally.' There followed the signature of Clement Attlee.

Staff officers are not in the habit of disobeying Prime Ministers, so the Colonel resigned himself to a prolonged stay in Japan.

It took several months to set up the tribunal and during that time Colonel Moore continued supervising the return of British troops to their homeland. The paperwork was endless and some of the men under his command were so frail that he found it necessary to build them up spiritually as well as physically before he could put them on boats to their various destinations. Some died long after the declaration of surrender had been ratified.

During this period of waiting, Colonel Moore used Major Sakata and the two NCOs in whom he had placed so much trust, Sergeant Akida and Corporal Sushi, as his liaison officers. This sudden change of command did not affect the relationship between the two senior officers, although Sakata admitted to the Colonel that he wished he had been killed in the defence of his country and not left to witness its humiliations. The Colonel found the Japanese remained well-disciplined while they waited to learn their fate, and most of them assumed death was the natural consequence of defeat.

The war tribunal held its first plenary session in Tokyo on April 19th, 1946. General Tomkins took over the fifth floor of the old Imperial Courthouse in the Ginza quarter of Tokyo – one of the few buildings that had survived the war intact. Tomkins, a squat, short-tempered man who was described by his own staff officer as a 'pen-pusher from the Pentagon', arrived in Tokyo only a week before he began his first deliberations. The only rat-a-tat-tat this General had ever heard, the staff officer freely admitted to Colonel Moore, had come from the typewriter in his secretary's office. However, when it came to those on trial the General was in no doubt as to where the guilt lay and how the guilty should be punished.

'Hang every one of the little slit-eyed, yellow bastards,' turned out to be one of Tomkins's favourite expressions.

Seated round a table in an old courtroom, the twelve-man tribunal conducted their deliberations. It was clear from the opening session that the General had no intention of considering 'extenuating circumstances', 'past record' or 'humanitarian grounds'. As the Colonel listened to Tomkins's views he began to fear for the lives of any innocent member of the armed forces who was brought in front of the General.

The Colonel quickly identified four Americans from the tribunal who, like himself, did not always concur with the

General's sweeping judgments. Two were lawyers and the other two had been fighting soldiers recently involved in combat duty. The five men began to work together to counteract the General's most prejudiced decisions. During the following weeks they were able to persuade one or two others around the table to commute the sentences of hanging to life imprisonment for several Japanese who had been condemned for crimes they could not possibly have committed.

As each such case was debated, General Tomkins left the five men in no doubt as to his contempt for their views. 'Goddam Nip sympathisers,' he often suggested, and not always under his breath. As the General still held sway over the twelve-man tribunal, the Colonel's successes turned out to be few in number.

When the time came to determine the fate of those who had been in command of the PoW camp at Tonchan the General demanded mass hanging for every Japanese officer involved without even the pretence of a proper trial. He showed no surprise when the usual five tribunal members raised their voices in protest. Colonel Moore spoke eloquently of having been a prisoner at Tonchan and petitioned in the defence of Major Sakata, Sergeant Akida and Corporal Sushi. He attempted to explain why hanging them would in its own way be as barbaric as any atrocity carried out by the Japanese. He insisted their sentence should be commuted to life imprisonment. The General yawned throughout the Colonel's remarks and, once Moore had completed his case, made no attempt to justify his position but simply called for a vote. To the General's surprise, the result was six-all; an American lawyer who previously had sided with the General raised his hand to join the Colonel's five. Without hesitation the General threw his casting vote in favour of the gallows. Tomkins leered down the table at Moore and said, 'Time for lunch, I think, gentlemen. I don't know about you but I'm famished. And no one can say that this time we didn't give the little yellow bastards a fair hearing.'

Colonel Moore rose from his place and without offering an opinion left the room.

He ran down the steps of the courthouse and instructed his driver to take him to British HQ in the centre of the city as quickly as possible. The short journey took them some time because of the mêlée of people that were always thronging the streets night and day. Once the Colonel arrived at his office he asked his secretary to place a call through to England. While she was carrying out his order Moore went to his green cabinet and thumbed through several files until he reached the one marked 'Personal'. He opened it and fished out the letter. He wanted to be certain that he had remembered the sentence accurately . . .

'If for any reason you should require my help in your deliberations, do not hesitate to contact me personally.'

'He's coming to the phone, sir,' the secretary said nervously. The Colonel walked over to the phone and waited. He found himself standing to attention when he heard the gentle, cultivated voice ask, 'Is that you, Colonel?' It took Richard Moore less than ten minutes to explain the problem he faced and obtain the authority he needed.

Immediately he had completed his conversation he

returned to the tribunal headquarters. He marched straight back into the conference room just as General Tomkins was settling down in his chair to start the afternoon proceedings.

The Colonel was the first to rise from his place when the General declared the tribunal to be in session. 'I wonder if I might be allowed to open with a statement?' he requested.

'Be my guest,' said Tomkins. 'But make it brief. We've got a lot more of these Japs to get through yet.'

Colonel Moore looked around the table at the other eleven men.

'Gentlemen,' he began. 'I hereby resign my position as the British representative on this commission.'

General Tomkins was unable to stifle a smile.

'I do it,' the Colonel continued, 'reluctantly, but with the backing of my Prime Minister, to whom I spoke only a few moments ago.' At this piece of information Tomkins's smile was replaced by a frown. 'I shall be returning to England in order to make a full report to Mr Attlee and the British Cabinet on the manner in which this tribunal is being conducted.'

'Now look here, sonny,' began the General. 'You can't—'

'I can, sir, and I will. Unlike you, I am unwilling to have the blood of innocent soldiers on my hands for the rest of my life.'

'Now look here, sonny,' the General repeated. 'Let's at least talk this through before you do anything you might regret.'

There was no break for the rest of that day, and by late afternoon Major Sakata, Sergeant Akida and Corporal Sushi had had their sentences commuted to life imprisonment.

Within a month, General Tomkins had been recalled by

the Pentagon to be replaced by a distinguished American marine who had been decorated in combat during the First World War.

In the weeks that followed the new appointment the death sentences of two hundred and twenty-nine Japanese prisoners of war were commuted.

Colonel Moore returned to Lincolnshire on November 11th, 1948, having had enough of the realities of war and the hypocrisies of peace.

Just under two years later Richard Moore took holy orders and became a parish priest in the sleepy hamlet of Weddlebeach, in Suffolk. He enjoyed his calling and although he rarely mentioned his wartime experiences to his parishioners he often thought of his days in Japan.

'Blessed are the peacemakers for they shall . . .' the vicar began his sermon from the pulpit one Palm Sunday morning in the early 1960s, but he failed to complete the sentence.

His parishioners looked up anxiously only to see that a broad smile had spread across the vicar's face as he gazed down at someone seated in the third row.

The man he was staring at bowed his head in embarrassment and the vicar quickly continued with his sermon.

When the service was over Richard Moore waited by the east door to be sure his eyes had not deceived him. When they met face to face for the first time in fifteen years both men bowed and then shook hands.

The priest was delighted to learn over lunch that day back at the vicarage that Chopsticks Sakata had been released from prison after only five years, following the Allies' agreement with the newly installed Japanese government to release all prisoners who had not committed capital crimes. When the Colonel enquired after 'Sweet and Sour Pork' the Major admitted that he had lost touch with Sergeant Akida (Sweet) but that Corporal Sushi (Sour) and he were working for the same electronics company. 'And whenever we meet,' he assured the priest, 'we talk of the honourable man who saved our lives, "the British Bullfrog".'

Over the years, the priest and his Japanese friend progressed in their chosen professions and regularly corresponded with each other. In 1971 Ari Sakata was put in charge of a large electronics factory in Osaka while eighteen months later Richard Moore became the Very Revd Richard Moore, Dean of Lincoln Cathedral.

'I read in the London *Times* that your cathedral is appealing for a new roof,' wrote Sakata from his homeland in 1975.

'Nothing unusual about that,' the Dean explained in his letter of reply. 'There isn't a cathedral in England that doesn't suffer from dry rot or bomb damage. The former I fear is terminal; the latter at least has the chance of a cure.'

A few weeks later the Dean received a cheque for ten thousand pounds from a not-unknown Japanese electronics company.

When in 1979 the Very Revd Richard Moore was appointed to the bishopric of Taunton, the new managing director of the largest electronics company in Japan flew over to attend his enthronement.

'I see you have another roof problem,' commented Ari Sakata as he gazed up at the scaffolding surrounding the pulpit. 'How much will it cost this time?'

'At least twenty-five thousand pounds a year,' replied the Bishop without thought. 'Just to make sure the roof doesn't fall in on the congregation during my sterner sermons.' He sighed as he passed the evidence of reconstruction all around him. 'As soon as I've settled into my new job I intend to launch a proper appeal to ensure my successor doesn't have to worry about the roof ever again.'

The managing director nodded his understanding. A week later a cheque for twenty-five thousand pounds arrived on the churchman's desk.

The Bishop tried hard to express his grateful thanks. He knew he must never allow Chopsticks to feel that by his generosity he might have done the wrong thing as this would only insult his friend and undoubtedly end their relationship. Rewrite after rewrite was drafted to ensure that the final version of the long hand-written letter would have passed muster with the Foreign Office mandarin in charge of the Japanese desk. Finally the letter was posted.

As the years passed Richard Moore became fearful of writing to his old friend more than once a year as each letter elicited an even larger cheque. And, when towards the end of 1986 he did write, he made no reference to the Dean and Chapter's decision to designate 1988 as the cathedral's appeal year. Nor did he mention his own failing health, lest the old Japanese gentleman should feel in some way responsible, as his doctor had warned him that he could never expect to recover fully from those experiences at Tonchan.

The Bishop set about forming his appeal committee in January 1987. The Prince of Wales became the patron and the Lord Lieutenant of the county its chairman. In his opening address to the members of the appeal committee the Bishop instructed them that it was their duty to raise not less than three million pounds during 1988. Some apprehensive looks appeared on the faces around the table.

On August 11th, 1987, the Bishop of Taunton was umpiring a village cricket match when he suddenly collapsed from a heart attack. 'See that the appeal brochures are printed in time for the next meeting,' were his final words to the captain of the local team.

Bishop Moore's memorial service was held in Taunton Cathedral and conducted by the Archbishop of Canterbury. Not a seat could be found in the cathedral that day, and so many crowded into every pew that the west door was left open. Those who arrived late had to listen to the Archbishop's address relayed over loudspeakers placed around the market square.

Casual onlookers must have been puzzled by the presence of several elderly Japanese gentlemen dotted around the congregation.

When the service came to an end the Archbishop held a private meeting in the vestry of the cathedral with the chairman of the largest electronics company in the world.

'You must be Mr Sakata,' said the Archbishop, warmly shaking the hand of a man who stepped forward from the small cluster of Japanese who were in attendance. 'Thank you for taking the trouble to write and let me know that you would be coming. I am delighted to meet you at last. The Bishop always spoke of you with great affection and as a close friend – "Chopsticks", if I remember.'

Mr Sakata bowed low.

'And I also know that he always considered himself in your personal debt for such generosity over so many years.'

'No, no, not me,' replied the former Major. 'I, like my dear friend the late Bishop, am representative of higher authority.'

The Archbishop looked puzzled.

'You see, sir,' continued Mr Sakata, 'I am only the chairman of the company. May I have the honour of introducing my President?'

Mr Sakata took a pace backwards to allow an even smaller figure, whom the Archbishop had originally assumed to be part of Mr Sakata's entourage, to step forward.

The President bowed low and, still without speaking, passed an envelope to the Archbishop.

'May I be allowed to open it?' the church leader asked, unaware of the Japanese custom of waiting until the giver has departed.

The little man bowed again.

The Archbishop slit open the envelope and removed a cheque for three million pounds.

'The late Bishop must have been a very close friend,' was all he could think of saying.

'No, sir,' the President replied. 'I did not have that privilege.'

'Then he must have done something incredible to be deserving of such a munificent gesture.'

'He performed an act of honour over forty years ago and now I try inadequately to repay it.'

'Then he would surely have remembered you,' said the Archbishop.

'Is possible he would remember me but if so only as the sour half of "Sweet and Sour Pork".'

There is one cathedral in England that has never found it necessary to launch a national appeal.

Jason Gathorne-Hardy

freedom series

Jason Gathorne-Hardy was born in 1968 in Malaysia and brought up in Britain on the Suffolk coast. He studied Zoology at Oxford University and now works as a cartoon illustrator and painter, with a bit of woodcarving on the side. Recent publications to which he has contributed include: *The Rainforest Database* (Living Earth Foundation, 1991); *A Guide to the Colleges of Oxford* (Constable & Co, 1991); *Reaching Out* (Living Earth Foundation, 1992); *Myth or Reality? Is Population Growth a Problem or an Asset?* (Population Concern, 1994/5); *SimIsle* (Intelligent Games, 1994).

In 1994 he exhibited cartoon drawings at the Chelsea Old Town Hall and received a bursary from the Delfina Studio Trust to paint in Spain.

'I paint mostly with mud, using bits of plants and stones as brushes and tools. The paintings in this book, forming the Freedom Series, were done in August 1994 on the north shore of Lake Attersee in Austria. I used mud and crushed tiles from the lake bottom, soil from a nearby field, Indian ink and pencils. While they were still wet, I washed the paintings in the lake and then left them to dry in the sunshine.'

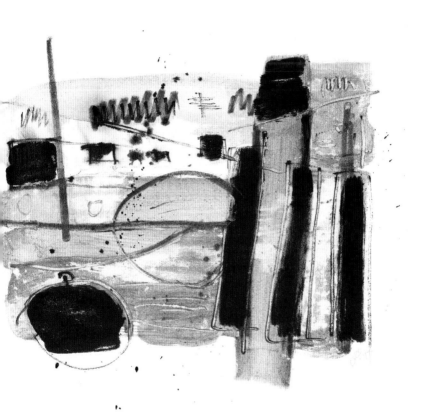

P.D. James

freedom and the creative writer

P.D. James was born in 1920 and educated at the Cambridge High School for Girls. She is the widow of a doctor and has two children and five grandchildren. For thirty years she was engaged in public service, first as an administrator in the National Health Service and then in the Home Office, from which she retired in 1979. She has written thirteen crime novels, nine of them featuring the poet-detective, Commander Adam Dalgliesh.

P.D. James was a Governor of the BBC from 1988–93. She is a Fellow of the Royal Society of Literature and of the Royal Society of Arts, and an Associate Fellow of Downing College, Cambridge. From 1988–93 she was on the Board of the British Council and is a member of its Literature Committee, and from 1988–92 on the Board of the Arts Council and Chairman of its Literature Advisory Panel. In 1987 she was Chairman of the Booker Prize panel of judges. She is ex-chairman of the Society of Authors and has served as a Justice of the Peace in Inner London and Middlesex. She was awarded an Honorary Degree of Doctor of Letters from the University of Buckingham in 1992, and Honorary Degrees of Doctor of Literature from the University of London in 1993 and from the University of Hertfordshire in 1994.

She was awarded an OBE in 1983 and a life peerage as Baroness James of Holland Park in 1991.

Freedom is a strong and emotive word. All down the ages men have died with it on their lips and there are probably as many definitions of what the word has meant to mankind as there have been martyrs in its cause. For some, like the Pilgrim Fathers, it has meant above all the freedom of worship and of religious belief, a fundamental right for which human beings have always been prepared to risk life and liberty and to travel over dangerous seas. For prisoners of conscience physically incarcerated, the word 'freedom' has a more immediate and practical meaning: the striking off of fetters and the opening of prison doors. For others, freedom means to live where and how they please, to retain what they earn and spend it as they wish, to walk down city streets without fear of assault, to exercise their democratic rights without fear of the secret police and the knock on the door in the night. For many victims of war and famine, those the Red Cross exists to succour and support, it can mean the freedom to life itself, the right to live in peace untroubled by invading tribes or civil unrest and the elemental freedom to enjoy the basic human needs of food, water and shelter without which, of course, all other freedoms are meaningless.

J.S. Mill, in his book *On Liberty*, wrote, 'Neither one person, nor any number of persons, is warranted in saying to another human creature of ripe years, that he shall not do with his life for his own benefit what he chooses to do with it'. This is an attractive definition of freedom but it certainly does not operate in our modern world. We cannot today build a house just where we like, drive at any speed we wish through our cities, refuse to have our children educated, or open a restaurant without conforming to a multitude of regulations designed to protect customers and staff alike. Many personal freedoms are constrained by considerations of the greater human good. But the human imagination is subject to no such constraints; it ranges freely through time and space. The freedom of the creative writer to be true to his or her vision, and to write that truth without fear, is linked to all those fundamental freedoms – of worship, of conscience, of free speech – which are fundamental to mankind's liberty.

For all writers, important as are these other freedoms, there is a professional freedom without which life would be emotionally if not physically deprived. For the journalist freedom means the right to tell the truth as he sees it, free of censorship and without threat to his life, liberty and livelihood. For the creative writer the meaning is little different except that his truth is the truth of the creative imagination. And this freedom, both for the journalist and for the creative writer, has frequently been under threat.

The invention of printing was seen by many powerful forces in the state and in religion as a threat to orthodox opinions. It was realised that sedition and heresy as well as truth could be spread by the written word. All down the ages men and women have been persecuted, imprisoned and sometimes even killed because of the books they have written or translated. But today in all civilised states there is a very great degree of creative freedom; indeed it is the mark of a democratic society that it can tolerate dissent whether written or spoken. And because the novelist deals in the world of imagination, no writer, certainly in Britain and I believe throughout the western world, enjoys greater artistic freedom both in the choice of subject and treatment. A novel may have a shelf-life of only a few brief months before the surplus copies are cast into oblivion, or have an enduring influence for generations. It may change ways of thinking, influence lives or be a spur to action. A book can provide inspiration, entertainment, solace, comfort and joy. It can also kill. Many creative writers acknowledge that the freedom we enjoy also carries with it responsibilities. And like all freedoms, its preservation requires vigilance.

A civilised country will jealously preserve the right to free speech and free writing, even when the result is uncomfortable, unwelcome or unorthodox. And it can be threatened by more than overt censorship. The growth of political correctness in ideas and language can easily intimidate, and the concentration of publishing, whether of books or newspapers, in a few powerful hands can have its potential dangers. Books that librarians regard as undesirable may be denied a place on their shelves. The price of freedom for the writer is, indeed, eternal vigilance.

Censorship, of course, is not always enshrined in law. The social mores of the society in which a novelist writes also has an influence. In Victorian England, for example, a novelist could not deal frankly with sex. Nancy in Dickens' *Oliver Twist* was obviously a prostitute; Dickens could not say so openly. Charlotte Brontë's *Jane Eyre* was criticised by some journalists of the time as scandalous and indecent, a criticism which caused her considerable pain, yet it is surely one of the most moral of classical novels. In George Eliot's great novel *Middlemarch*, she makes it subtly plain that the marriage between Casaubon and Dorothea was never consummated Today the novelist would have taken us into the bedroom and described that failure in detail. Anthony Trollope leaves the perceptive reader in no doubt about the physical love between some of his heroes and heroines but this sexual attraction is not made explicit and indeed, like most Victorian novelists, he expressed a high moral purpose which must have been highly acceptable to the socially aspiring and respectable middle-class customers of Mudie's Circulating Library. 'I do believe that no girl has risen from the reading of my pages less modest than she was before, and that some may have learnt from them that modesty is a charm worth preserving. I think that no youth has been taught that in falseness and flashness is to be found the road to manliness; but some may perhaps have learnt from me that it is to be found in truth and a high but gentle spirit.' It is difficult to imagine a modern novelist describing the purpose of his work in such a way, and of all the freedoms which the modern writer enjoys, freedom of expression in matters of sex is the most liberal.

But does the freedom which today's novelist enjoys – freedom to choose any subject, freedom of language, freedom to explore aspects of the human condition free from the constraints of Victorian prudery – impose its own obligations?

Has the novelist a moral responsibility to society and his readers? Do we agree with George Eliot in her *Leaves from a
Notebook* that 'the man or woman who publishes writings
inevitably assumes the office of teacher or influencer of the
public mind', and that the writer who says 'I will make the
most of my talent while the public likes my wares, as long as
the market is open and I am able to supply it at a money
profit' is on a level with 'a manufacturer who gets rich by
colouring his wares with arsenic green'? Or do we agree with
an eighteenth-century, less well-known writer, Richard
Cumberland, whose view was 'all that I am bound to do as a
story-maker is to make a story'? This is a decision which every
novelist has to face and answer for him or herself. If I write a
book, for example, which is grossly offensive to Christians I
can reasonably expect it to be strongly criticised and in some
countries it may even be banned. What I would not expect is
for it to be burnt in public or for the Pope or the Archbishop
of Canterbury to issue an edict of murder against me. The
case of Salman Rushdie shows us that, even today and in certain societies, there is no absolute freedom of subject if a
writer is to live in safety.

One ethical question which is often of greater interest to
readers of novels than to writers, although no writer can
ignore it, arises from the main business of fiction. How far
does a particular novelist draw his characters from life and
how far is this justified? Am I free to draw so closely from real
people that a name can be given to almost every leading character? Have I not a moral duty to the distress which this may
cause? If I see a friend in the extremity of grief or distress, I

cannot help noticing how that distress manifests itself even as I put my arms around her and seek to comfort. The experience is, as it were, filed away in the subconscious and when the time comes to use it, then it will be used. This is what it means to be a writer and perhaps this is what Graham Greene meant when he spoke of the splinter of ice in a writer's heart. But how far have I a responsibility to make enough changes so that my friend doesn't feel, 'This is exactly my story. This is my distress. All that I suffered and confided has been exploited to make a better book'? Should I censor myself in order to prevent possible pain, even at the expense of the work to which I am committed?

Joseph Conrad described 'words, groups of words and words standing alone' as the very symbols of life. In handling these symbols the modern writer enjoys a freedom of expression which would seem unbelievable to a Victorian novelist, mainly of course in the use of what is commonly called strong language and in the description of human sexuality. This freedom goes beyond that available to the broadcaster or film-maker and is circumscribed only by the rarely-invoked obscenity law. Most writers welcome this freedom from one particular form of censorship, and yet we may wonder whether it is always used responsibly. Much writing today is so explicit and so anatomically salacious that it is neither honest in intention nor truly erotic. What pervades much modern writing about sex is not enjoyment but disgust. It sometimes seems that novelists, in their anxiety to understand and accurately describe human sexuality, have lost the ability to understand and describe human love.

Most writers would say that the only proper censorship of literature is self-censorship. The degree of self-censorship which an individual writer may impose on himself or herself will depend on that writer's view of his art. He may believe, as did Tolstoy, that art has a moral purpose and that it should affect the daily lives of men and women and the moral health, justice and good order of society. He may see the novel as an agent for social reform, as were the novels of Charles Dickens. Or he may feel that his only duty is to do the best he can with the idea which has come to him and that the giving of pleasure, excitement, solace and joy, particularly in dangerous times, is a good end in itself. Whatever his belief, what is important is that his writing should be free. In the words of Sir William Golding in his Nobel Lecture of 7th December 1983: 'Put simply, the novel stands between us and the hardening concept of statistical man. It performs no less an act than the rescue and preservation of the individuality and dignity of the single being, be it man, woman or child.' This is a high claim to make for an art commonly regarded as basically designed for entertainment and relaxation, and even if it is only partially true, then every writer has a moral responsibility, not least to the truth and the sincerity of his own imagination.

Herbert Lomas

goshawk

Herbert Lomas is a freelance poet, translator and regular critic for *London Magazine* and other journals. *Trouble* (Sinclair-Stevenson, 1992) is the only one of his seven books of poems still in print, and his *Selected Poems* appears in autumn 1995. His *Letters in the Dark* was an *Observer* book of the year, and he has received Guinness, Arvon and Cholmondely awards. The most recent of his translations of Finnish poetry and prose is Paasilinna's bestselling novel *The Year of the Hare* (Peter Owen, January 1995), and his *Contemporary Finnish Poetry* (Bloodaxe, 1991) won the Poetry Society's biennial translation award. In 1991 he was made Knight First class, Order of the White Rose of Finland. A former lecturer at the universities of Helsinki and London, he is married with two children and lives in Aldeburgh, Suffolk.

A fledgeling is out of the down
not sure if he can trust
feathers and a programme to fly.

Fluttering on a chimney pot
not daring to take the air
he finally has no choice.

The lark struggles from grass
carols above the clouds
and cannot stop singing.

Quartering the wood-edges a goshawk
with a wide white stripe above his eye
will never be liberated from killing.

A man in a net of history
watches a bird fluttering on a chimney
and cannot choose a future.

New choices of himself
are cringing and fluttering
in the claws of the goshawk.

Tim Heald

past cell
by date

Tim Heald is the author of between twenty and thirty books of fiction and non-fiction as well as a number of short stories. His 'Simon Bognor' crime novels were televised by Thames TV and his non-fiction books include an analysis of the 'Old Boy Network' and a definitive portrait of the Duke of Edinburgh. From 1986 to 1989 he was the Co-ordinator of P.E.N's Writers-in-Prison Committee. His most recent books are biographies of the romantic novelist Barbara Cartland and the cricketer Denis Compton. He is presently working on the authorised biography of the late Brian Johnston, a study of Hong Kong in the last days of British rule and a novel set in the world of contemporary journalism.

It was an uncommonly difficult letter to write. Simon had little experience of this sort of thing and the group's guidelines were only helpful up to a point. Information on Dr Mbanefo was sketchy. Simon had his address in Block 4 of the Queen Victoria Prison, Fort Garnet, and a grainy black and white mug shot which could have been anyone. Beyond that he knew only that the President had locked him up because he didn't care for a slim volume of poems that Mbanefo had published in samizdat form a few months earlier. As these were written in the language of the country and were untranslated into English they didn't leave Simon much the wiser.

Simon sighed and tried again.

'Dear Dr Mbanefo,' he wrote, 'I have recently joined my local branch of The Right to Write Union and you have been assigned to me as my prisoner. This letter is to introduce myself and to send you my greetings. My colleagues and I will do everything we can to secure your release and in the meantime to try to ensure that you are kept in civilised and acceptable conditions.'

Simon paused and pondered. He had little idea what he meant by 'civilised and acceptable'. He himself lived in a small basement flat in South London, paying the rent from a respectable but not over generous salary as an English teacher in a nearby comprehensive. His girlfriend came round every so often and helped him eat a take-out curry. Occasionally they went up to the West End for a play or a concert. One day, perhaps, he might marry but he was only twenty-five and for the time being content in a mildly dissatisfied way, sensing that there might be greener grass on the other side of the fence but also that he was lucky to have regular employment, a roof over his head and someone to make love with.

He sighed. 'Civilised and acceptable' was a horribly vague, bureaucratic phrase but until he knew more about Dr Mbanefo and his prison it would just have to do. It could be that the doctor was being kept in some spanking new Scandinavian-style gaol with air-conditioning and three meals a day. Simon rather doubted it. From what little he knew, prisons in the People's Republic of Bandi would be primitive. He could imagine the Queen Victoria Prison only too well. It would have a grand Imperial façade and a grim Dickensian interior. It would be overcrowded and essentially untouched since the British left in the mid-1950s.

'Although my job is in teaching,' he continued, 'I would like to be a poet one day myself. I have written a number of poems already and have been lucky enough to have one or two published in small magazines.'

This was true. The magazines were very small indeed. Even though he was still quite young Simon already had a sinking realisation that he would continue writing poetry all his life but would never quite make the grade. He would be a schoolmaster who wrote verse in his spare time, never a poet who did a little teaching on the side. The thought of forty years trying to convince uninterested teenagers of the wonders of Eng.Lit. was depressing and he tried not to think about it.

His conscience had always pricked. Since he himself had been at school his politics had tended towards the Green and he had an admittedly woolly sympathy for underdogs in whatever shape or form. He bought the *Big Issue*, gave coins to beggars, took part in the occasional demo. You couldn't exactly call him an activist but he was, in his gentle way, 'concerned'. Hence his joining 'Right to Write'. He wanted to *do* something. And here he was, in however tiny a way, actually doing something concrete and tangible for poor Dr Mbanefo.

It was difficult knowing how much he should tell his prisoner about himself. On the whole, thought Simon, self-revelation had perhaps better come later when their pen-friendship was more soundly established. To bang on about himself at this stage could well seem patronising.

'My colleagues,' he continued, 'have told me that very often letters to writers in prison do not reach the people for whom they are intended. I understand also that it may not be easy for you to reply to me. However I shall continue to write. Even if you do not read my letters someone will.'

He rather liked this concept. Naturally he hoped that Dr Mbanefo would read the letters himself and be encouraged and cheered. But if they were opened and read by the censors or the prison governor they would still have some effect. The powers-that-be in Bandi would know that someone out there, beyond their shores, in the democratic west, actually cared about Dr Mbanefo and was campaigning on his behalf.

In some way, Simon felt, this must make a difference.

'Apart from writing to you,' he wrote, 'I shall be sending a letter to the President of the Republic explaining that you have been adopted by me and my friends and asking him at least to ensure that you have a proper trial. I shall also be writing to our own Foreign Office in the hope that we can get them to exert pressure on your behalf through the British High Commission in Fort Garnet.

'Meanwhile if there is anything I can do for you please let me know. Our organisation does not have a great deal of money but we can sometimes send books to prisoners. Also medical supplies. If there is anything we can do for your family please let me know. I shall think of you and pray for you and will write again soon. Good luck, from your friend and colleague, Simon Lewis.'

Simon brooded over the business about prayers. He was lapsed Church of England and not usually of a prayerful disposition but in the circumstances he thought it might be an appropriate sentiment. He also thought twice about the word 'colleague' and eventually dropped it. 'Friend' sounded more sincere and 'colleague' was pushing his luck. Dr Mbanefo was not only a published poet, he had been sent to prison for his art. Simon knew that he was unlikely ever to be such a martyr to his muse.

His letters to the President of the Republic and to the Foreign Office were, as the Union always suggested, short, courteous and to the point. He sent them all off marked 'URGENT' and buckled down to his teaching duties. Over the next few days he thought about them from time to time but without a lot of hope. In a sense, he told himself, it didn't altogether matter what result they had. He had done his bit.

The President of the People's Republic of Bandi was universally supposed to be suffering from a form of paranoia precipitated by something sexual picked up in student days. Like others of his ilk he was heavily into uniforms, concubines, malt whisky and Rolls-Royces. Extraordinary how unimaginative and conformist the average dictator can be.

Reading his post was not a habitual activity but occasionally he took a random sample out of little more than curiosity.

It just so happened that Simon's letter was one of those that came under presidential scrutiny in this way.

The President read it twice then crumpled it up and threw it in his bin. Although he was smiling he did not look very amused. He sat, seemingly lost in thought for some minutes, then walked over to the bin and picked out the crumpled letter, unfolded it and read it once more. Then he shook his head and smiled again. This time he seemed to see a joke though it was not one he looked as if he was going to share. And given his record in the matter of humour it was doubtful whether many other people would see the funny side of it.

Edward Harrington, a middle rank Foreign Office chap on a two year secondment to the Central Africa desk (though his principal area of expertise was South America) scanned Simon's letter to the Secretary of State for Foreign Affairs with a pursed lip.

'These bloody do-gooders', he muttered, and then to his

secretary, 'Standard aware and concern job, Lois'. He handed it across the desk.

That afternoon he signed the note. It said, 'Dear Mr Lewis, Thank you for drawing my attention to the case of Dr Arthur Mbanefo at present imprisoned in Fort Garnet, Bandi. Her Majesty's Government is aware of Dr Mbanefo's case and our High Commissioner in Fort Garnet continues to monitor its progress. We are naturally concerned at any violation of human rights wherever they may occur and Her Majesty's Government has voiced this concern to the Government of Bandi. I am sure, however, that you will understand that Her Majesty's Government is unable to interfere in the internal affairs of another sovereign state. Thank you for your interest.'

Harrington signed in crisp business-like blue ink and allowed himself another little shake of the head and another disparaging mutter about the perils of uninformed do-goodery.

Arthur Mbanefo was surprised that the letter had got through. At least he would have been surprised if he had still retained the capacity for surprise. After all it was only six months ago that he had been the respected Professor of Literature at the University of Bandi with a goodish salary, a viable faculty and apparently sound prospects. He supposed that he had been over-confident in publishing his verse though in all truth the poem about the sheep and the grasshoppers which was apparently the one that had so angered the President was not a specific allegory about the Bandi dictatorship, hateful though that might be, but more of a general diatribe about the evils of despotism. It was, essentially, a literary piece, but of course the President had not viewed it like this.

Dr Mbanefo suspected that Ntosi, the Minister of Culture, was behind his imprisonment. They were old rivals, ever since schooldays together here in the old English Grammar School in Fort Garnet with its crusty English expat teachers, its dog-eared textbooks and its Latin school song. The school was much as it had been thirty years before when he and Leonard Ntosi had vied for the Virginia Woolf Memorial Essay Prize and Ntosi had won with a piece of shameless plagiarism which, inexplicably, none of the staff had managed to spot.

Dr Mbanefo read the letter again, squinting in the gloom. He had been allowed to retain his spectacles but his sight was poor. He suspected he needed a cataract operation but knew he was unlikely to get it under present circumstances.

Apart from the spectacles all he had in his little cell was a blanket, a pair of underpants and a bucket. Every so often he was given a meal. Sometimes this was beans; sometimes bread; sometimes a thin liquid described as soup. There was enough water to drink though it was stiflingly hot. For half an hour a day he was allowed out for exercise though the chains on his ankles meant he could do little more than shuffle. The chains were the only thing approaching physical violence that had been offered him. Otherwise it was simply a catalogue of deprivation. He had no visitors, nothing to read, nothing with which to write, no dignity, no freedom except that which existed inside his head. And luckily his head was well stocked for he had a magic memory and could recite massive folkloric tales of his native land as well as almost the whole of *Macbeth* and Milton's *Areopagitica.*

On waking he always recited, like a mantra, Milton's famous passage about killing books, for it seemed horribly apposite: 'As good almost kill a man as kill a good book: who kills a man kills a reasonable creature, God's image; but he who destroys a good book, kills reason itself, kills the image of God, as it were in the eye.'

These were bleak words but Dr Mbanefo found comfort in them.

It was very strange. Not only had he been allowed this letter from the school-teacher in London but he had been given a paper and pencil with which to reply. They had only given him a single sheet of rough, squared graph paper, so he would have to write small. He was touched by the naïve sentiments of the young would-be poet all those thousands of miles away and aware too of the difficulty the man had had in knowing what to say and how to express it. But touched he definitely was. He had assumed himself forgotten even by friends and colleagues and family and yet here for the first time in weeks there was evidence that his plight was known. A stranger had written him a letter. The least he could do was to compose a polite reply, so despite his failing sight and the dusky light and the constant pain in his stomach, which never went away now, Dr Mbanefo squatted on the floor and began to compose a small hymn of praise and gratitude which attempted to explain the solace of knowing that one was not after all alone.

He must have dozed off because suddenly it was dawn. A timid luminous pink shaft of light penetrated the small barred window high in the wall and there was the sound of someone unbolting the door of his cell. It must be time to slop out. Stretching out, he suddenly remembered the letter which lay on the floor alongside him. It was almost finished and he wanted to give it to the guard in the hope that he would post it for him. It seemed extraordinary but otherwise why should they give him pencil and paper? They must wish him to reply.

So he signed the letter, 'With thanks and love from your friend, Arthur Mbanefo' and he gave it to the guard who took the pencil too and escorted him to where he was allowed to empty his bucket and then took him back and locked him up once more.

He was allowed to keep the letter however and all day the Doctor mused on it, speculating about the young man who had written it, about the organisation to which he belonged, about their motivation and their ideals and their circum-stances – what they ate and drank, how they lived and what they thought. He had been to England many years ago when he was writing his postgraduate thesis on the non-conformist Literature of the Protectorate, so visualising Simon and his life did not require too much imagination even though it was so obviously and so painfully far removed from his own.

It never occurred to him that anything the London teacher and his friends could do would make the slightest difference. He had known the President all his life and witnessed his deterioration. Who knew what determined the man's think-ing? He was so wilful and capricious that it seemed improbable he knew himself what he was going to do from one moment to the next. He appeared to lack the capacity for logical thought or for forward planning of any kind. As to how he would react to outside pressure from the former colonial power, official or unofficial . . . again there was simply no way of knowing.

Dr Mbanefo was thinking along these lines, treating it, as was his wont, as if it were an academic conundrum rather than something which affected his whole future, when again there was the familiar sound of the door being unbolted. This was odd for he was not expecting a visit.

When the door opened a guard was standing there together with a smartly dressed figure in military uniform. The man in the uniform carried a swagger stick under one arm and stood like a Guardsman. Dr Mbanefo knew that he was the Governor because he had met him on the day of his internment. The guard was holding clothing – a pair of trousers, a jacket, shoes.

'Comrade Mbanefo.' The Governor's voice was carefully neutral, machine-like.

'Yes,' answered the Doctor, knowing that he too should be neutral and respectful.

'Comrade Mbanefo, you are a lucky man. His Excellency our President has graciously decreed that you are to be released. You are free to go. Here are clothes. In a little while when you are prepared to face the world, we will return and open the gates so that you may walk free. Your punishment is ended. Although you have done a very bad thing our great President has forgiven you out of the goodness of his heart.'

And they turned and were gone.

In South London, thousands of miles from the Queen

Victoria Prison in Fort Garnet, Simon Lewis slept badly and dreamed a dream. He seldom dreamt and was surprised. The night was hot and he slept badly. Whenever he woke he knew that he had been dreaming but he could not remember the dream. It was not a good dream for he woke calling out. His girlfriend, who was sleeping with him that night, asked if he was ill because he kept crying out 'Doctor! Doctor!'

Yet what was so peculiar was that instead of seeking help from a doctor he seemed to be offering it. The girl told him that he called out 'Doctor! Doctor! Take care! Take care!'

It was a bad dream, a nightmare really, but Simon didn't believe in dreams and turned over to try to sleep again, failing, and waking perversely with the same refrain.

He was as good as his word, the Governor of the Queen Victoria Prison.

He escorted Dr Mbanefo along the echoing corridors and through the clanking gates and doors. From some of the cells there could be heard the sound of sobbing and this affected Dr Mbanefo, who felt that he was deserting friends and colleagues though this was ridiculous since he had been in solitary confinement throughout his visit and had never once met a fellow prisoner. He told himself this as they walked towards his freedom but he was not convinced.

Finally they reached the great gate, modelled apparently on the main gate of Dartmoor prison itself, and the Governor opened a little door set into the wood.

'Goodbye, comrade,' he said, gently pushing his charge into the night outside. It would take the Doctor more than an hour to walk to his home. He supposed that that was where he would go. He felt very disorientated, and oddly light-legged without the chains at his ankles, almost as if he were walking on air.

'I hope we shall not meet again,' said the Governor. And he closed the door behind the Doctor, retreating into his prison, as much a prisoner of it as the prisoners themselves. Though he would never have admitted this, not even to himself.

For a second the Doctor stood there under the shadow of the hideous nineteenth-century building, just breathing in and out, savouring the moment and staring at the stars and murmuring the passage of Milton's *Areopagitica* which had so comforted him in these last lonely weeks. He thought too of the school-teacher in London and his colleagues and wondered if this was in any way their doing.

Then he started to walk steadily home.

The white Land Rover of the Central Police Intelligence Unit was parked down a side street about a hundred yards from the gaol. Dr Mbanefo heard its engine start up as he approached the intersection but thought nothing of it as he walked on air softly singing a Bandi song of his childhood and thinking of his wife and family and friends.

He hardly saw the vehicle as it headed straight for him. He hardly heard it either. Nor felt the impact as it smashed into him and over him and then stopped briefly and reversed to make sure the job was properly done, then left him lying, a bundle of bone and blood and rags, crushed in the gutter under the star-filled African sky.

*

A couple of days later Edward Harrington, in Whitehall, sipped a mug of instant coffee and read idly through a dispatch from the High Commission in Fort Garnet.

'Lois,' he said, passing into the outer office, 'Dr Mbanefo from Bandi rings some sort of bell. Didn't we have a note about him from some do-gooder? If you can find the man's address I might just drop him a line. Seems the Doctor's snuffed it. Some sort of hit and run. Suspicious circumstances. "Trying to escape" is the official Bandi line. I do wish these people would leave this sort of stuff to the experts.'

There were three letters in Simon's post the following morning. One was in a stiff beautifully typed envelope from the Foreign and Commonwealth Office. The other two bore flamboyant stamps depicting the Life President of Bandi. These had taken surprisingly little time to arrive from the Republic, a fact which might have made a less suspicious man than Simon Lewis give pause for thought.

He opened the Foreign Office letter first. It made him cry.

He opened the one from Dr Mbanefo next and that made him cry too.

Then he opened the third.

It was headed 'From the Office of the President of Bandi' and it was unsigned. There was only one line. It said, 'Thank you for your letter regarding Dr Arthur Mbanefo, the contents of which have been noted.'

This letter made Simon cry most of all.

Pauline Cutting

children of
the siege

In 1985 I was recruited, together with a handful of other Europeans, by a British charity (Medical Aid for Palestinians) to work as a surgeon in a Palestinian refugee camp in Beirut, Lebanon. I knew there was a civil war going on in Lebanon, but beyond that I knew precious little about the Middle East. The hospital in which I worked was a tiny bomb-damaged field hospital in the middle of the ramshackle shanty town of the camp. In 1986, in another phase in the fifteen-year-old civil war, the camp (and several others) was attacked with tanks, bombs and guns by a Lebanese militia. Our hospital soon filled up with wounded men, women and children. The militia besieged the camp and the fighting dragged on for months. Food stocks were depleted and supplies in the hospital ran out. I was hungry, tired, homesick, dirty and louse-ridden. I longed to go home to freedom from war and deprivation. But so did everyone else in the camp, and what kept me going during those dark times was the kindness, bravery and generosity of the people around us. Even when food in the camp was almost finished, people braved the bombs to bring us plates of food from their homes. They made sure I had a safe place in the hospital when it was repeatedly bombarded, and they accepted their lot in the miserable refugee camp with a stoical equanimity. I could not abandon them and stronger than my longing to go home was a driving urge to tell the truth about what was happening to these people.

Haifa Hospital had become a symbol of resistance in the camp and we were determined not to stop working, but everyone knew we were still desperately short of fuel, medicines and gauze. Some women tried to bring in medical supplies under their dresses and in their underwear, but if they were discovered they risked a beating and the vital supplies were confiscated.

The wife of Salah, the head nurse, was questioned one morning about the hospital by a group of Amal militiamen. 'Yes, it is still working very well,' she told them defiantly.

They did not seem at all happy at the news. 'And who is working in there?' they demanded to know.

Salah's wife mentioned a few names and a 'foreign doctor'.

They scowled. 'Yes, we know about her,' they said angrily. 'We are going to cut her into pieces.'

For a few days, no one told me of this, but when I was talking to Dr Rede one morning, I said, 'If I ever get out of here I want to go to Saida for a holiday.' He replied, 'I don't think that will be possible,' and told me what had been said.

I have to confess that I was frightened. I had known that speaking out exposed us as named individuals, but I was not prepared to remain silent and even this direct threat changed nothing. 'The truth cannot be cut to pieces,' I thought. 'I will not be silenced.'

That night I thought again about writing a letter to my family, to be opened 'in the event of my death'. 'I'll do it tomorrow,' I wrote in my diary, but in the event I didn't.

A few days after I had learned of the threats against my life, a stranger appeared in the hospital during our morning ward round. It was the very same journalist who had come in with the Hezbollah and the Iranians. He arrived alone, totally unannounced, and seemed nervous and uneasy. He wanted photos of the doctors, but especially he wanted to take a photograph of me. Indeed he did not seem very interested in anything else. After he had taken a couple of pictures he asked permission to fix up his flash. I became more suspicious. 'Why a photo of me,' I thought, 'and how did he get into the camp on his own? All the entrances are controlled by Amal.' In a moment of paranoia I thought, 'He has been sent by them to take my picture so they will know what I look like when they come to kill me.'

I was not the only one who was suspicious about him. 'Do you trust him?' I whispered to Dr Rede.

'No, not entirely,' he replied.

Salah also advised, 'Don't let him take your photo. We don't know who he is.'

I became more and more uneasy and eventually I told him, 'If you take my photo after I have asked you not to, I will tell them to take your film away.'

After that he left, but he returned, undaunted, with a video camera. This time he had gone first to the camp committee, one of whom knew him and verified his credentials as a bona fide journalist. I was very apologetic; he had braved the dangers of getting into the camp and paid a lot of money to a Lebanese soldier to help him – and I had refused to co-operate. So this time Susie and I consented to a lengthy videotaped interview, which he said was for ITN in England.

A few days later, at dusk, one of the hospital porters came running to find me. He shouted in garbled Arabic, 'There is a man here. Come, come, foreign, foreign, English, English!' I followed him to the administrator's office and stared with disbelief at Brent Sadler, an ITV journalist I recognised from having seen him on the television in England. He was sitting with the same Lebanese journalist who had made the video. I was terribly excited. I had so much to tell him, and I plied him with questions about what was happening outside and at home in England. I took him to meet Hannes, then down to the clinic to see Ben and Susie. We talked into the night.

'You seem so cheerful,' he commented at one point.

'We are so happy to see you,' we told him.

That same day four girls between the ages of seven and thirteen had come to see Dr Rede in the hospital. 'We think we can get out and back into the camp over the sand-hills,' said the eldest. 'We will go to Mar Elias and collect medicines.' They left at once, reached Mar Elias safely and stayed there overnight.

The following morning they reappeared, triumphant. They had succeeded in sneaking in from the airport road over the sand-hills with four carrier-bags full of medicines, bandages and gauze.

Brent Sadler asked them to carry the bags to the front of

the hospital so they could be filmed. 'What will happen if they are caught?' he asked me.

'Until now they have not been seen,' I told him, 'and as they are only children I don't think they would be harmed.'

His question was prophetic. The girls went out again that same night and, returning the following morning, were spotted by Brent Sadler as he was filming in the cemetery. He turned his camera on the girls as they crossed the distant sandhills. At that moment they were seen and a fusillade of bullets raised puffs of sand around them. They dived to the ground, then pelted down into the cemetery, into the arms of the waiting men. They were frightened but miraculously unharmed.

Brent Sadler and the Lebanese journalist stayed for two days, making a film about Bourj al Barajneh. They interviewed both Susie and me. On the morning of the day they were due to leave, someone brought a video machine and a television to the hospital so that we could watch the videotapes while the generator was on for an operation. People crowded into the room next to the operating-theatre and the four girls were given seats at the front. When they saw themselves on television they jumped to their feet in excitement.

Brent brought Susie, Ben and me a cassette tape and a small recorder so that we could tape messages for our families. We tried hard to sound cheerful, sending our love and saying that we were healthy and happy.

As darkness fell, Brent and the Lebanese journalist crept out of the camp again.

The daily shooting of the women, if and when they were

allowed out, continued, so the women staged a demonstration. They wanted permission to go out from the airport road exit, which was safer as it was guarded by soldiers of the official Lebanese Army. Three hundred or so women gathered near the airport road but were sent back to the camp. The next day, even more collected in the same place, but this time, after refusing an order from Amal to use the other exit, they were scattered by a sudden heavy bombardment of the camp. They ran for cover in all directions and some were wounded.

Dr Dergham had never quite returned to normal after his crisis over Ali, the boy who developed gas gangrene. Morose and gloomy, he moved out of the doctors' room down to a small deserted area in the basement. He went to bed in the early evening, then got up and sat with the night nurses before doing his allocated work at six or seven in the morning. This was eccentric enough, but one day the nurses told me that he had woken a patient at 5 a.m. in order to change his dressing.

I spoke with Sol-Britt and Øyvind on the walkie-talkie, and they told me they were trying to bring in relief medical staff, both foreign and Palestinian. But when they visited the office of Nabih Berri he told them that there was no need for a medical team in Bourj al Barajneh. He also informed them that 'supermarkets' were open in the camp. I was incensed. There were no supermarkets, and the only items left for sale in the shops were large numbers of electric light-bulbs as, without electricity, they were less than useless.

For two days we were miserable. Sporadic bombing began again and the news from Chatila was grim. They had an outbreak of typhoid – three cases at least. Without a clean water-supply, they were scooping rainwater out of the bomb craters. Their food stocks were finished and they too were now facing starvation. Dr Rede was pessimistic. 'They may prolong this war to try to take Chatila,' he said. 'They are hitting them hard, which is why it has become quieter here.'

Then our spirits were raised again by the arrival of two more journalists, Marie Colvin and Tom Stoddart from the *Sunday Times*. It seemed that if one had the resources it was becoming quite easy to bribe one's way into the camp.

We took them on a tour of Bourj al Barajneh and looked after them as best we could. We gathered some food from friends near the clinic – reheated rice and tinned fish from the day before, and some tomatoes and cheese – but Tom, the photographer, could only eat a couple of mouthfuls. I think his lack of appetite can be ascribed partly to fear, partly to guilt at eating our food – Tom said he was 'well-padded' – and partly to the fact that to an outsider it must have seemed extremely unappetising. We had long ceased to care, eating everything put before us.

Marie, an attractive woman in her late twenties with a mass of curly brown hair, was an object of enormous interest for some of the young men, but eventually she and Susie extricated themselves from the throng of admirers and went to sleep with a family nearby. I took Tom up to the hospital.

Just as we were saying goodnight to Marie we saw a bright red flash and felt the shock-wave of a deafening explosion. We all jumped, Tom's cameras clanking round his neck. 'That was TNT,' said one of the young men casually.

In the hospital awaited a worse nightmare for Tom. A huge

rat was scampering around the corridors. 'Not rats,' Tom moaned as I chased it down the stairs. 'They're the one thing I'm really frightened of.'

I left him to sleep in a cubicle next to Hannes, and went off to bed. I don't think he slept a wink, lying awake all night watching for rats under his bed.

The following day Marie and Tom were confronted with the true horror of life in Bourj al Barajneh. They saw a young woman shot through the head and abdomen just outside the camp. For half an hour she lay there as the bullets of the snipers kept people away. They made frantic efforts to haul her in with a rope. Eventually two girls dashed out and dragged her in.

In the hospital, Tom took photos as we tried vainly to resuscitate the injured woman. We did not have enough fuel for the necessary operation, so in the end a group of women carried her out to the airport road and to a hospital in the city.

Marie interviewed some of the patients in the hospital. The woman who had crawled in with the broken thigh spoke to her vehemently, gesturing with her arms. 'What's the matter with her?' asked Marie.

'She wants you to tell the world her story,' I translated. And a few days later Marie did just that.

When the time came for Tom and Marie to leave they looked a picture of misery as they sat waiting for the moment to cross the wasteland. 'I feel like Butch Cassidy and the Sundance Kid before they had to jump off that cliff,' said Tom.

*

One quiet evening after dark Adham took Ben and me to his front-line position. 'Walk on this side,' he instructed, 'the other is exposed.' He switched off his torch and led us down into a small courtyard surrounded by white houses with overhanging balconies. In the centre of the courtyard a small tree rustled in the breeze. The scene was eerily beautiful in the moonlight.

Adham took my arm and pointed to a building across the wasteland. 'See that,' he whispered. 'Sometimes they shoot women from there.'

As we made our way back to the hospital Adham told us that his dream was to go to Cambridge University to read engineering. He had been studying at the Arab University, but did not think he could go back. 'As a Palestinian I would not be safe in West Beirut,' he said with a shrug. He had missed nearly six months' lectures and tutorials. I promised to find out what qualifications he would need for Cambridge, but in my heart I knew it would remain a dream. The fees alone were prohibitive.

Adham said something else that night – something I shall never forget. Describing how imprisoned he felt within the confines of the camp, he quoted Byron: 'I had no thought, no feeling, none – among the stones I stood a stone.'

At the beginning of April it at last began to get warm. The situation improved too. Fewer women than before were being shot at and many were allowed easier passage. Amal still engaged in petty harassment, though. They now insisted that the women buy the Amal magazine every Friday; one woman who refused was shot.

There were the usual rumours that the Syrians and the International Red Cross were on their way, but I had long ceased to believe them. 'I'll believe it when I see them' I said.

But this time the rumours were true. On 7 April the Syrians deployed around Chatila. The next day they arrived at Bourj al Barajneh. The shooting stopped at once. For the first day in five and half months, the hospital register showed the admission of no new wounded.

The Syrians were greeted with mixed feelings – relief at the end of the fighting, and resentment that they had waited six weeks before coming. During those six weeks eighteen women had been killed and more than fifty wounded. Some people still felt that the Syrians bore the responsibility for the Camp Wars.

The next day the International Red Cross arrived with twelve cars. We had no critical patients now, but the hospital was so badly damaged, our stocks were all gone, and the staff were so exhausted, that we decided to send out as many patients as we could.

The scene was chaos. Hordes of journalists had come in with the Red Cross, including Julie Flint of the *Guardian*, who had interviewed me once after the first fighting. People were shouting, crowding round their relatives. Some patients who were almost fully recovered wanted to go out just to escape; others, who did need further treatment, refused to go, preferring to stay in Haifa than risk the open road. The woman, who had been shot in the legs while collecting grass to feed her family, had been in traction for nearly two months. As they came to carry her out she burst into tears and clasped me in her arms. I cried too.

As the convoy of cars departed, a crowd surged behind it to the border of the camp, some of them still hopeful of getting out. But the Syrian soldiers barred their way.

An hour or so later Øyvind arrived, bringing relief medical staff for the hospital — a British surgeon called Dr Alberto Gregori, Françoise, a French nurse, and a young Palestinian doctor.

After 163 days the siege was over, but Bourj al Barajneh still had its surprises. A friend of Ben's told us about an old woman who had lived in a building in the most dangerous part of the front line throughout the entire war. I couldn't believe it.

'Come,' he said. 'We can go and see her. It's quite safe now.'

Ben, Alberto and I followed him through the maze of alleyways to the north-east corner of the camp. There we crossed a narrow road to a five-storey building standing on its own. 'We had to dig a trench to get across here safely,' said Ben's friend.

The destruction of the buildings around the edge of the camp was unbelievable. Many of the houses I had known had been completely levelled, all of them were severely damaged. The building next to the one we were entering had completely collapsed, its five floors folding in on themselves like a fallen house of cards.

The young man led us up to the second floor of the apartment block next door. There, in a room, barricaded on all sides by mattresses, wardrobes and chairs so that there was only a tiny space in the middle, sat an enormously fat old woman wearing a scarf and a long nightdress.

'She is Lebanese,' explained the young man. 'She is so fat she cannot walk, and so she could not leave. She used to live on the fourth floor, but one night we heard her screaming and found that the floor above her was on fire.' It was Imad, Ben's friend who had later lost both legs, who had run into the building and helped her crawl down the stairs to her present room. Then he put out the fire.

'We bring her food and water every day and empty her bedpan,' said the young man.

'Yes,' said the woman, 'these boys have been very good. They looked after me all the time.'

With the lifting of the siege the first shop opened up in the camp. The woman who ran it had managed to bring in a few sackloads of goods. The news spread rapidly and, by the time I arrived, hoping to buy some eggs, there were fifty people crowded around the door, shouting and shoving. I was just deciding whether or not to join the fray when I was rescued by Adham. 'Come through here,' he beckoned, and led me into the parlour.

The shopkeeper was sitting on the floor holding a sort of auction. She was selling various items of food and cigarettes, and had a large wad of money stuffed inside her blouse. I had treated her once when she was very ill, so – much to my embarrassment – she decided to serve me first. I ordered some cheese and she asked for a knife to cut some from the big block in front of her.

Omar, a big man who was always a bit wild and had become noticeably crazier during the fighting, leapt to his feet. 'I've got a knife!' he bellowed, flourishing a large flick-knife and making sweeping cuts in the air.

Someone calmed him down, cut the cheese, and I crept out just as Ben arrived to buy some tobacco. We walked back to the clinic laughing

Rachel Billington

thomas leaves home

Rachel Billington is the author of twelve novels, the latest of which is *Bodily Harm*. Her most recent non-fiction work is *The Great Umbilical, Mother Daughter Mother, The Unbreakable Bond?* She has also written five children's books.

The train moved out of the station very very slowly. A mockery, torture, as far as Thomas was concerned, for it allowed his mother to walk beside the carriage, peering close because the glass was darkened, screwing up her eyes all the better to see him with, mouthing last minute advice which, because of her over-excited contorted face, gave the appearance of witch-like imprecations. How Thomas hated his mother's gusto. What a fool she made of herself, of him. He tried moving back a little but the carriage was completely full so he found himself nudging a cross woman on his right. Women everywhere. Besides, as he swayed back it drew his mother closer still till her face was nearly touching the window. And she was *walking*. For Christ's sake she was walking beside the train making all these faces. Why didn't someone tell her to Stand Clear? Surely it wasn't allowed. And why was it still moving so slowly? Thomas felt tears of frustration and rage start in his eyes. Yet all the time his mouth smiled, a rictus expressing nothing but pain but it would keep her happy, make her feel he was all right. That was essential, that she thought him all right or she'd follow him to the ends of the earth if needs be. Why was the train going so slowly? This time of escape, these last moments stretching out to an eternity of separation, an agony of parting. No trains left stations as slowly as this, slowly enough for her to leave her breath on the window. And it was a short country station. That was it. She knew the station manager. He had married her gardener's daughter. She had instructed him to instruct the driver to leave the station at the walking pace of a devoted mother, although at last, he noticed, she was breaking into an ungainly trot to keep up. She was a fixer, a finger-in-the-pie person, a protective, caring loving . . . Thomas's smile broadened for, centimetre by centimetre, she was losing ground, slipping away from him, losing her grip. Perhaps – oh wicked thought! – she really would slip, disappear under the wheels like Anna Karenina, except that she was not like Anna Karenina. If she wanted to go under a train, and she only did what she wanted, she would have done it years ago when Hugo died. Banish that thought. Besides, on a more light-hearted and realistic note, she would probably be fished out by her friend, the station manager and his cohorts and whisked off to the local hospital where she sat on the Board, of course, and he would have to sit at her bedside while she ran her affairs with decisive energy despite several 'major ops'. No, it was better she continued wearing herself out in desperation at losing her last beloved surviving son – why couldn't she count her daughter? Or even her husband? – and the train would, must, eventually reach the lights, the level crossing and the end of the platform. Even she couldn't have had the platform extended. And look, her face was purple, her mouth gasping, her eye-balls popping. What an old fool! Why couldn't she care about him with *moderation*?

Thomas's mother gave one last wave and stood still, her whole body trembling, like a horse at the end of a race. Well. She'd done it. Seen him off to the very last second. No one could say she hadn't given him her all, her life-blood. No one could reproach her for not loving, not taking care. She had taken every care, every day when he was at home and even when he was at school – it was he who had begged to go to boarding school – she had written twice a week and thought of him every day. She had done everything a mother could do for what seemed like years and years. It *was* years and years. Sixteen years since Hugo had died which made Thomas eighteen. That was the way he had always remembered his age, how many years since Hugo died. Thomas's mother had stopped trembling, for the English winter morning was cold and bracing, and strolled slowly, head a little up, sniffing a nice bonfire smell, from the station. She had thought the train would never go, that she was doomed forever to see her son's strained face, his pallor, his fear, his utter dependency. But the train had gone, he had gone and now she felt, well, different. No disloyalty, she wasn't going to accuse herself of that, but the sense of a job well done, very well done. Thomas done, eighteen years old now, schooling finished, university place secured, back-pack packed, aeroplane booked, money arranged, Cynthia to greet him in New York, job secured there. Yes. She had done well by him. Thomas's mother began to walk faster, swinging her arms a little, greeted the friendly porter and the handsome station manager, agreed what a surprisingly bright day it was turning into for the time of year and decided she would have a coffee at that place newly opened in town before going back home and sorting her desk, perhaps just putting her feet up. Thomas was on his way, on his journey to adulthood, a natural progression – yes, that was what it was. Now, after sixteen years, she could think of Hugo.

The train had stopped at three stations before Thomas's breathing had regained its normal pattern. He couldn't read yet, that was too much to ask, his mother was still there, expecting, protecting, clawing, but at least he could breathe. He stirred from the rigid hunch he had taken up to sustain the maternal barrage and at last gave the woman on his right the chance to add her comment. 'I expect you're her only son?'

'Yes,' replied Thomas curtly, refusing to look at her. Was the whole world filled with concerned women? He lifted his eyes to the bony old man opposite him who was staring with an empty expression out of the window. How much better men were, with their dignity, reticence and lack of curiosity. Thomas thought of his father and an image accompanied his thoughts, as it often did, of a smooth granite wall, beautiful, cool, clear, impermeable in a way that demanded no serving, no effort, in fact, one might almost say, repelled effort. Thomas took a quiet, deep breath and allowed himself the luxury of believing he was going to New York for six months *on his own*.

The snow came out of a clear blue sky, sharp-edged, close relation to the ice-cubes that were Thomas's principal impression of New York, that and the skyscrapers, of course. But he had known about those. Thomas looked out of his tenth-floor window of the publishing house where he had been given too little work to do and saw ice-cubes raining down on the Twin Towers and the Empire State and the Chrysler Building, and what he was putting off thinking about – but was there all the time on his mind – was the fridge at home in the square kitchen with the round wooden table, because there was his mother taking out the one little ice-box, running it under the hot tap with the accompanying noises – she had a range of accompanying noises, a whole hideous symphony of hummings and grunts and gulps and tuts and slurps and hisses and wee truncated growls. All unconscious, of course. She had accompanying movements as well; her hands did the most amazing things, thumbs jutted at just the same angle as she arranged her saucepan handles along the shelf, little fingers chuntered and stretched as if searching for a piano, wrists twisted the arm outwards. These movements were unconscious too, he was sure, the dips at the knees, the taps of the left foot, always the left foot . . .

'Why don't you call it a day, Tom. We'll have more for you to do tomorrow.'

Thomas walked thirty-four blocks to his apartment block and only thought of his mother once when a large man of a racial mix Thomas had never encountered before groaned words of threat into his ear. Then Thomas thought of his mother for a moment, the terror she would have felt on his behalf, the flush of maternal spunk which would have clothed her cheeks and seeped even into her neck. The man who, in the event, had disappeared finally into whatever drug-haunt he inhabited, would have turned, under her anxious attention, into a monster of gargantuan proportions. That was how all his fears, threats, problems had grown into puffed-up genii under her caring attention. He had learnt not to tell her about them, eventually, to preserve them secretly and deal with them unaided. Which policy had worked well enough, although now and again he had tried the alternative of throwing them at the granite wall of his father. They bounced back at him then, hardened a little by contact with the wall, but not inflated. His mother was the mistress of making the difficult unbearable.

'Welcome,' said Cynthia, wearing bright lipstick and opening the door the moment he rang the bell. 'Your mother's on the line.'

He knew at once they'd been talking about him, his worrying silence, his lankiness, his sweet nature. He did not have a 'sweet' nature.

'Hi, Mum.'

'Hi, darling. It seems ages since you left. Cynthia tells me you're fine. The journey was fine. How was your day?'

'Fine,' said Thomas and was surprised to find Cynthia was inserting a glass with what appeared to be a gin and tonic in his hand. 'Thanks.'

'What, darling?'

'Nothing.'

She was checking up, that was all. Thomas stared beyond the telephone and saw his mother's friend, Cynthia, crossing her legs on the sofa.

Thomas's mother put down the telephone and sighed. Was she happy? She let her great hairy dog jump on the sofa and then she went to find an expensive packet of chocolate biscuits.

'This is my favourite bar in the world,' said Cynthia. 'Far better than any husband.'

Thomas wanted to ask why she had never married but he was finding it very difficult to bring words whole into the open, let alone sentences. He realised this had something to do with the two gin and tonics he had drunk and did not want to appear ridiculous.

'You are very handsome,' Cynthia said, 'just like your mother when I first knew her.'

'Hand some?' pronounced Thomas with a long break between syllables.

'Handsome and wild. But don't let's talk about her.'

'Lesshnot,' agreed Thomas.

'You'd better eat something,' said Cynthia and she ordered a tuna fish sandwich.

Thomas watched her, the barman, their fellow drinkers, with a splitting smile, splitting his face open, curling back at the edges. He had never ever felt so good, so benevolent, so relaxed, so happy, so loving. He tried to tell Cynthia something of this but the words turned into slush long before they reached his smiling mouth. She did, however, seem to catch his drift.

'That's freedom for you,' she said.

Thomas left for work the next morning without seeing Cynthia. Cynthia did not care. He was just a young son of her old friend's whom she'd given room space in her apartment and passed time with in a hotel bar. She was not going to make sure he got up, had breakfast, arrived at the publisher's at the proper time.

Thomas walked along the streets as cold as the inside of a fridge except where gushes of steam erupted from a volcanic source.

'I'm fine,' he told himself when he looked up to the blue sky as glassy and uncaring as Cynthia's eyeballs. 'I'm fine,' he told his editor when he asked how he was before dumping a manuscript on the subject of ethnic cleansing with the suggestion 'Just track through it, Tom, and then give me a verbal.'

'Fine,' he repeated for he was covering his tracks as he thought, thought, thought again, whom did Cynthia remind him of and at last he tossed the manuscript aside as unreadable, incomprehensible, irrelevant and came up with the answer. Cynthia reminds me of my father because she too is made of repellent, even propellant, rather than absorbent, touch-here-and-you'll-sink-without-trace, (sucked and squeezed and pummelled) stuff which is, which is my mother. Amen.

Thomas had lunch on his own in a diner where every inch of food was so hygienically wrapped that he'd only managed to get through half of it before he had to be back in his office where a new manuscript, very small, was waiting. It was entitled, 'The Corruption of Drains' but Thomas hardly minded because he was still thinking. By the time he'd tossed away this manuscript, which was even more unreadable, incomprehensible and irrelevant than the last, he had decided to drop in on a bar called P.J. O'Batty, noticed on his way back the evening before and have a drink *all on his own.*

'Tuborg, Pilsner or Holstein?' inquired the bartender, looking up at the ceiling which was painted with four-leaved shamrocks.

'As it comes,' suggested Thomas, blowing on his fingers. It had been very cold outside.

'It doesn't come,' said the bartender, eyeing Thomas from a face as well plucked and tended as a suburban housewife's, hair as coiffed and dyed, mouth as ready for fun. 'It doesn't come,' repeated the bartender, caressing the top of the beer, 'unless I *pull* it.'

'I see.' Indeed his meaning was clear. Thomas had not been to a public school for nothing. He looked along his fellow drinkers who gazed at him one behind the other, caressing female expressions on male faces. 'Oh, dear.' Thomas looked at his watch intently. 'I'm late.' Laughter followed his exit.

Thomas walked another ten blocks picturing those smothering female-male smiles with a sense of revulsion. However, soon he remembered the joys of last night's splitting, gob-smiked, joyful smirk, the only smile in which his mother had no place, no part, no knowledge, not even in her bones and he chose, with more care, a bar called 'Texan Blue'. It was very very dark inside Texan Blue, which made it easier for Thomas to drink two whiskey sours before noticing the leering, peering going on among his neighbours. Not at him, he was relieved to see, but towards a couple of tall women dressed in cowboy hats and boleros and little skirts and high ornamental boots. Thomas smiled to see their skin bulging between the two because the whiskey was already having its delicious, delightful effect.

'Hey, what's the joke?' One of the women came close to Thomas where he giggled and swayed on his stool and his voice was deeper than a Welsh baritone's so it didn't even take Thomas's level of education to realise he was a man. A large, threatening man.

'Sorry,' apologised Thomas, shimmying off his stool and heading for the door. He could not speak and he had to laugh so once in the icy air he sent jackal cackles reverberating up and down the sky-scraper canyon. What his mother would have thought of Texan Blue!

Thomas's mother sat at her pretty little rosewood desk that she had been given by her godmother for her twenty-first birthday, and felt guilty. She must write to her son, her son so far away, gone for a week and no more contact than a single telephone call. Thomas's mother went and lay on the sofa with a novel, where one hundred and five pages later, her husband found her.

'You seem very, er, quiet,' he said.

'I feel guilty because I haven't written to Thomas.'

'Do people write these days?' asked her husband, going to make them both drinks. 'Anyway, I've just heard I need to go to New York in a week or two or three so I can take any messages.'

'It isn't a question of messages.'

'Never mind.' Thomas's father concentrated on the newspaper.

After a week or more Thomas became bored of after-work

drinks on his own and since he was too shy to effect a pick-up with a stranger, he took the secretary nearest to him in the office, although she was called an editorial assistant. She showed him bars where everybody was heterosexual and in couples. She seemed surprised when he bought the drinks twice running and told him that she had hated London on her one visit. Thomas had told her he didn't live in London at which she had shown hardly suppressed disappointment. This he thought illogical but they drank together happily enough. One evening Thomas had to leave early. 'Cynthia has a friend for me,' he explained.

'Oh,' said Melanie, 'who is Cynthia?'

'My mother's friend.'

'Your mother?'

Thomas peered more closely at his drinking companion. Her face appeared to express horror, disgust, terror.

'You're living with your mother's friend?'

'She has a spare room.'

'But your mother's friend?' Her small pale face screwed up until it looked like a golf ball.

'Don't you like your mother?' asked Thomas warily.

'Let me tell you, "vampire, succubus, sponge" – those are the words that spring to mind.'

'Ah, well,' Thomas smiled, laughed and looked at his watch. 'We should be off, I guess.'

Thomas's father took Cynthia and his son out to dinner. He was jet-lagged and irritable but pleased that Thomas seemed to stride out more, hail cabs, order drinks, that sort of thing.

After three gin and tonics, which his father thought was straight tonic, followed by wine, Thomas realised he had overdone it. He went to the gents to be sick.

'I hope Thomas isn't a nuisance.' Thomas's father wanted to go to his hotel.

'A most independent boy,' said Cynthia. 'Out to work early, back late. No trouble.'

'Good. Good. Independent, you say. That will surprise his mother.

Thomas's mother had not written to her son. Instead she wrote her innermost thoughts about him to Cynthia. These included words like 'clinging', 'leech', 'blood-sucking'. She knew she shouldn't have posted it but she did. Afterwards she lay on her bed and pictured Hugo. Sixteen years after his death, the images had a formulaic, much-repeated quality about them, like the well-thumbed photographs. She saw a sturdy, sunburnt boy of four going off to school in blue shorts and a grey Aertex shirt. That was it. The last time she had seen him. All that hot summer's day she had spent with Thomas and at three o'clock she had had the call. Hugo had died of an unidentifiable virus at his desk while she and Thomas played water games in the garden.

Thomas's mother took two sleeping pills but still didn't sleep. She thought of her daughter travelling in India, of her son who tore at her heart strings till they sagged, of her husband whom she loved but who was as impermeable as a wall, both in New York with Cynthia, her oldest friend, although they really had nothing in common, and she thought that she was staring into a long, lonely future.

Thomas was reading a manuscript that shone, vibrated, screamed with life and energy. He advanced on the editor, waving it, crying out, 'So good! So good! So absolutely good!' After all, in six weeks this was the first manuscript that he'd been able to finish.

'Yeah. Yeah,' said the editor. 'We bought it.'

'You bought it – already?'

The editor nodded. 'So you're on the right line, Tom. Here, try this.' He pushed over his desk a manuscript two feet tall, then seeing Tom's expression, divided it into two as you might cut a pack of cards and put the top part aside. 'The second half should tell you enough.' He looked at his watch. 'Hey. Closing shop time. Come for a drink.'

Thomas and his editor drank in an Art Deco hotel bar and quite soon Thomas could not tell the black suns on the walls from the black tables on the floor.

'Do you always put away the whiskey sours?' asked his editor, not unkindly.

'Issh to forget my mossher,' explained Thomas, too far gone to care.

'Could be worse reasons,' agreed the editor, looking at his watch. 'But I'd go easy.'

'Eashy come, eashy go,' agreed Thomas fervently.

Thomas's mother thought she should find a proper job – with her husband at work all day, no daughter and no son, although she had at last written him a loving note. There was a problem.

'I think of Hugo all the time,' she told her husband one sleepless night.

He patted and stroked her but was wary too. 'It's such a very very long time ago.'

'Oh, yes, sixteen years.'

Thomas's mother, who had been so happy in her freedom, could not find a job and began to fall into a decline which meant she produced dull meals and read novels set in the 1930s and after a few weeks found herself crying two or three times a day.

'You're missing Thomas,' suggested Thomas's father.

'Don't be silly. I'm not missing Thomas at all. I'm missing Hugo now I've got time.'

Cynthia had a new boyfriend. He was younger than her but nevertheless loved her body in the kind of way that took them all over the apartment. This made Thomas *de trop* so she found a place for him with a friend who had two sons not much older than Thomas. This made him sociable and so busy that he had less time for steady drinking and very little time for thinking of his mother. Summer came. No more chunks of ice-cubes dropped from the sky and he decided to extend his visit beyond six months so that he could share a weekend house on Fire Island where the sea crept up over the sand like blue paint and the wooden boardwalks made creaking music under his toes. One night, under the stars, a girl ran her fingers all over his body and he felt a smile splitting his face just as he had when the second or third whiskey sour reached his stomach.

'Now you touch me,' she invited him. So he ran his fingers over her, wriggling and coolly golden.

Cynthia was not surprised when her boyfriend left her but she had to sit down after Thomas's father's telephone call. Where, if it came to that, could she find Thomas? He didn't even have the same job as far as she knew.

Several hours later, Thomas, tracked down in the coolly golden girl's father's office – a PR firm who liked his English quiet – heard Cynthia's voice with reluctance. She, of course, reminded him of his mother. He was, nevertheless, polite.

'How can I help you?'

'It's not me. Look, I think you should come round here.'

Reluctantly, but he could hear the emergency in her voice, Thomas came.

'It's your mother. She's taken an overdose.'

A huge black pit opened in front of Thomas.

'Your father rang. You must fly back at once.'

'Dead?'

'Dead?' Cynthia blinking, making her glassy blue eyes glisten. 'Dead, you cruel boy?'

'But how am I to know?'

'She's calling for you. That is, she can't speak with all the tubes but your father is.'

Thomas looked at his feet but only saw the ever-deepening black pit. 'She's only done it to get me back.'

'What? What? What?' Cynthia looked at the bleak cold

creature, bent down looking at his feet, mumbling, stumbling. 'She's your mother! She nearly died.'

'I nearly died.'

'You nearly died?'

'She nearly killed me with her love. Her love squeezed me, crushed me, angled me out of existence. After Hugo died she wanted me to be everything. I hate her.'

Cynthia felt ill and trembly. It was all so dreadfully muddled but could she, in low energy, put it right? Then she remembered Thomas's mother's letter written all those months ago.

'I have something for you to read,' she said and went to find it.

It seemed a good idea after she had handed over the letter for them both to have large gin and tonics, like old times.

Thomas's hands shook so that the letter frilled in front of his face like a fan. He became confused. Were not these his own words that he was reading? Yet there was his mother's too well-known writing. He looked up at Cynthia imploringly.

'How could she write all this? I don't understand.' He put down the letter.

'Well, I expect you do love each other,' said Cynthia, making a stab at helping. 'After all, you only have one mother, although I must say mine was a thoroughly selfish human being. But no one could say that about yours. She's lived her life for her family. And then your brother died.'

Thomas sat beside his mother's bed, tubes no longer affixed. When she opened her eyes for the first time and saw this sturdy golden boy she smiled and said 'Hugo'.

'No,' said Thomas, who'd had hours to think, on the aeroplane, beside the still unconscious woman. 'I'm Thomas, not Hugo, Thomas who is strong and healthy and will never be Hugo. And all the clinging and clawing and caring will never bring Hugo back and all it will do is make sure you want to get rid of me and stop you loving me because I'm not Hugo and because you're working so hard at keeping me alive that it's worn you out when actually it was all quite unnecessary, because even without your help I'm perfectly fine, indeed much finer, but on the other hand, now I've come back to you, Mum, I have to say one thing, which is no threat to either of us, nor to Hugo, I'd like to say, but now I see you so low, so helpless, ill, defeated, just another middle-aged, depressed woman facing the future, I want to say, Mum my mother who tried to squash me out of existence with so much concentrated caring, that I love you. I love you, Mum, and, as I said at the beginning, I'll be with you and help you get well and hold your hand like this – just see how big and strong and brown mine is now – and when you want to talk about the day Hugo died I won't shut you up but give you a bit of my strength and I'll tell you about my coolly golden girlfriend and, although I can't make your life what you want, I shall not be a weight or a drag, but Thomas, your son.'

It was not clear whether Thomas's mother heard all of this, not only because of her pill-induced wooziness but because Thomas mouthed and muttered as much as he spoke out. Nevertheless her hand, her capable fingers, fingers in every pie once she was up and round and about again, gripped Thomas with a gentle steadiness, no grasping necessary.

Deborah Moggach

a pedicure
in florence

Deborah Moggach was born in 1948, one of four girls in a family of writers. She has written ten novels, including *Porky* and *The Stand-In*, and has adapted several for television. She has also written screenplays and a book of short stories. She lives in London with her two children.

Be honest. Look into your heart. Do you prefer to get a post-card saying 'Having a wonderful time' or one saying 'Holiday a total disaster, wish we could come home'?

Helen, shamefully, felt a small rush of pleasure from other people's misfortunes. Perhaps she wasn't very nice at all; perhaps that was why Alan had divorced her. But then holidays with Alan had always been a strain; to compare them with other's non-successes was some small consolation, she supposed. Events conspired to irritate him – her map-reading, the children's bleary refusal to get up early and seize the day, the presence of other British people in some remote and inaccessible location where he thought himself and his family alone and speaking the language like natives. She always remembered his bellow of pain when, staying the night in a chai house in the middle of the Hindu Kush, he had opened the visitor's book and found the names of Denise and Donald Waterman, the couple who lived opposite them in Ealing.

Such a strain, keeping him happy, silently urging the children to ask inquiring questions about Romanesque architecture rather than moaning that their Walkman batteries had run out. But all that was over now; she was a single woman again. After twenty-two years she and Alan had parted. Mysteriously, marriage itself seemed to have been the coup de grâce. They had met in that long-lost golden age when everyone was hanging loose, hanging out, whatever they all did then. After seventeen years of living together and bringing up a family their increasingly mutinous children had rebelled. 'We keep on having to explain to people!' they moaned. Finally, they delivered their own coup de grâce. 'It's so *seventies*, not being married.'

That had done it. Stung, she and Alan had gone to a register office and got married. Things had started disintegrating and within four years they were divorced.

Alan-less, the summer holidays approached. Welling up beneath her sense of panic and failure she was aware of an exhilarating new feeling – freedom. The children were almost grown up; she was forty-four. She could go anywhere; do anything. She would do what she had always wanted to do: rent a house in Italy and not do anything cultural. She would swim and sunbathe and drink litres of red wine. She wouldn't visit any museums and churches at all – not unless she felt like it. Alan, laden with guide-books, had always insisted they did these things thoroughly; he could even pronounce 'Ghirlandaio'.

She went with her friend Xandra, a cheerful, accommodating woman who was also man-less, though a veteran of two marriages and a recent disastrous liaison with a young motorbike messenger who worked at her courier firm. Helen was fond of Xandra, but the real basis of their bond was their two daughters, who were best friends at school and the only ones of their various children who had condescended to come on holiday with them.

'Four women in Italy!' chortled Xandra, snorting smoke through her nostrils. 'Two young, two old – three thin and one—' prodding herself '—fat. We're going to have a ball! They won't know what's hit them.' She laughed her laugh that sounded like dried beans rattling in a glass jar.

It started off all right. 'How romantic!' Helen cried as they drove up a gravel track. It climbed miles up a hillside above Perugia. The undercarriage scraped over a rock; they laughed. How grateful she was that Alan wasn't here to wince at the scraping noise, to hear the girls' complaints that it was miles from anywhere, to have heard Xandra's ribald and explicit assessment of the local talent lounging outside the village shop – or, as she put it, resting on their zimmer-frames.

The house stood at the top of the hill – a handsome stone building complete with pool and a wonderful view. 'Look at the wonderful view!' cried Helen. The German couple who owned it lived in an apartment on the ground floor. The man, Hans, a bronzed, overweight bull in tiny trunks, was fiddling with the filter in the swimming pool.

'They *live* here?' hissed Annie, Helen's daughter. 'How am I going to take my top off?'

'Look at the swallows!' cried Helen. 'Look at the flowers! Oh look – a darling little lizard!'

They had forgotten to buy bread so Helen drove back down the gravel track to the village. It took twenty minutes and just as she arrived she saw the shutter crash down on the shop. She banged on it and after a moment an old woman with a flourishing moustache appeared and jabbered rapidly in Italian.

'*Aperto? Aperto?*' asked Helen. An old retainer sitting outside the bar held up four fingers. Watched by the row of geriatrics, she climbed back into the car. Half of her thought: I'm glad Alan's not here; *we* don't mind! We'll eat biscuits! The other half thought: if only he were here, he would have remembered that the whole country closes down from one to four.

When she returned she heard girlish laughter and splashes. Her spirits rose until she saw that it was not their two daughters jumping into the pool but a small, coffee-coloured girl wearing water-wings. Annie and Abigail sat fully clothed on the terrace, looking mutinous and scratching their mosquito bites. Charcoal smudges on the concrete floor betrayed where they had been stubbing out their Marlboros.

'There's somebody else staying with the Germans!' they hissed. 'An Australian woman called Biddie!' They pointed to the little girl. 'That's her daughter!'

Biddie turned out to be a talkative, pear-shaped woman who was blithely unaware of their territorial rights to the pool. Like many single parents of a single child she devoted herself to her daughter's development, informing her at some length about her every move. Her daughter was called Mena and over the next couple of days they learnt to stiffen as Biddie approached the pool. 'Now Mena, Mummy's going to take you for a swim and then you can have an ice-lolly and then we'll lie in the sun with these nice people . . .' Presuming anyone who was reading had to be bored she would look at their books. 'Oh, *The Age of Grief,* Helen, is that a sad book?'

'She's always *here!*' hissed the girls. 'She's always talking! She's so boring!'

Xandra gazed at the little girl, splashing in the pool. 'Looks like the only interesting thing she's ever done is sleep with a black guy.'

It seemed churlish to object to a small child playing in their pool – after all, like them, Biddie was a single mother. Helen's irritation sprang partly from her own suspicion that she herself was being petty. So she smiled sweetly – so sweetly that Biddie stopped asking if she could use the pool and ensconced herself on the best lounger, the only one with a mattress.

The other problem – no, not problem, they did *live* there – was the German couple. Hans was always at the poolside, fishing out insects with his net or fiddling with a complicated tangle of filters and hoses. The girls tried to find a secluded place to sunbathe but then his wife came out there to hang up her washing and ask them what they felt about the Royal Family. The girls retreated to the house.

'Look, we're still white! We've got to get brown, to show our friends! They're sitting on our terrace. They're using our barbecue!'

'They did ask,' said Helen. 'They've got friends coming round tonight.'

'Why didn't you say no?'

'I couldn't.'

Trapped by their own cowardice, they cowered indoors. Helen thought: if Alan were here – if any man were here – he would have made our territorial rights politely clear at the beginning. Women are so feeble. We are trapped by our eagerness to be liked. That evening, to avoid their hosts, they forsook the terrace with its swallows and its wonderful views over the Umbrian hills and drove down to the village where they sat in the small, concrete bar. Lit by a strip of fly-bespattered neon it was a quiet place, its clientele the geriatric men who spent the rest of the day sitting outside the shop. One of them cleared his throat and spat into a handkerchief. The girls gazed at the pensioners and stubbed out the cigarettes their mothers no longer had the strength to stop them smoking.

'When I was your age,' said Helen, 'I went on holiday with my parents to Malta and the first night I went out with a waiter and got love bites all over my neck. For the next whole week I had to wear a scarf. My parents kept saying *aren't you hot? Why don't you take it off?*'

Annie snorted. 'Huh. The only things biting us are effing mosquitoes.'

Abigail looked around. 'None of this lot have got any teeth anyway.'

Xandra, chuckling, leafed through her phrase book. '*C'è defetto. Me lo potrebbe cambiare!*' She looked up. '*This is faulty. Can I have a replacement!*'

It took them a week to admit, openly, that their holiday was a disaster. Abigail had constipation, then diarrhoea, and spent a great deal of time in the lavatory, which abutted the kitchen. To spare her embarrassment they kept away, getting hungrier and hungrier. Annie wrote long letters to her friends bemoaning the lack of men and wishing she were home. Xandra's period was late and, terrified that she had been impregnated by her toyboy motorbike messenger, drove down to the village to phone him up but couldn't get through. Her daughter, who had overheard this from the lavatory, emerged and snorted: 'You're not pregnant. You're getting the menopause.' At this Xandra burst into tears and drank a bottle of Chianti.

Helen, to escape, tried to go for a walk but unlike Xandra the countryside proved impregnable. Walking down one gravel path she arrived at a rubbish dump and walking down the other she was stopped by a gate saying *STRADA PRIVATA*. Walking back to the house she reflected upon the illusions of liberty. Now she was here, how free seemed her life in London! In Ealing she could walk anywhere. Unchained from the domestic grind she could shop anytime, rather then be in thrall to the siesta. Best of all, she had the personal liberty of her own privacy and didn't have to wait, behind a window, for the moment to dart out to the pool, and spend the rest of her time trying to find a saucepan lid or gazing at someone else's hideous furniture. Outside the German invasion was gathering pace and several more house-guests had arrived; they lay around the pool, grilling themselves. Xandra said, 'I feel like pricking them with a fork.'

Trapped in the house, Xandra and the two girls began to get on Helen's nerves. They still had a week to go. So when the girls, desperate at the lack of local talent, said they were going to take a day trip to Florence she felt secretly relieved.

'You're only seventeen!' Xandra said to them.

Abigail snorted: 'At seventeen you got pregnant with Ben.'

'Exactly,' said her mother. 'That's what I'm worried about.'

But after a short tussle the teenagers won and at an unearthly hour – unearthly for the girls – they were dispatched on to the train for Florence.

Can you sense these things? As a mother, can you sense them? At seven o'clock Helen began to feel uneasy. Xandra was trying to get her out to the terrace for a drink before the Germans emerged from the house. 'If we're sitting there already, maybe they won't talk to us,' she whispered – they had taken to whispering. After a week the Germans, encouraged by the women's feebleness, had presumed their company was always welcome and engaged them in long conversations about the British parliamentary system when they were trying to read their books. They carried out their wine, willing Biddie not to join them with the latest instalment of the saga of Mena's mosquito bites. They drank, unmolested. The girls were due back at ten-ish; they were going to take a taxi from Perugia station.

'What'll I do?' wailed Xandra. 'I can't have another baby! I'm forty-three!'

Helen, gazing at the sinking sun, thought of the hot bonds of motherhood, how one was never free of it, not until one died. How when even a grown child was absent a terrible scenario played over and over in one's head; increasingly lurid, it ceased only with the child's return. How could one start again with all that?

At ten o'clock she said: 'Do you think they're all right?'

At a quarter past eleven Hans appeared. 'Phone for you!' he bellowed.

It was Annie. They had been robbed. 'We were sitting on these steps outside the whatsit, the Duomo,' she sobbed faintly, 'and these boys came up to us and we thought they were so nice . . .' Her voice broke. 'We've only got this phone card and it's running out . . .'

Helen, her bowels churning, shouted: 'Check into a hotel, one that takes Visa cards! Wait for us there!' The line went dead.

The next morning Helen and Xandra drove to Florence. The girls had phoned with the name of their hotel and by noon they had found it – a leprous-looking *pensione* up a side street near the railway station. At the reception desk a man jerked his head, indicating upstairs. A fan lifted and lowered his newspaper.

In Room 26 the curtains were closed. It was a narrow cell, smelling of last night's cigarettes. The girls, who had only just woken, lay in bed watching an Italian game-show on TV. Around them lay scattered the empty contents of their mini-bar. 'We've lived off it,' said Annie, as Helen hugged her. 'There isn't room service and we missed breakfast.'

With some pride, Abigail pointed out the empties to her mother. 'Coke, Kronenbourg, Sanpellegrino Aranciata, J & B, Campari soda, a bag of peanuts and that funny liqueur even *you* don't drink.'

Xandra's face froze. She looked at them all and then darted into the bathroom. Behind the closed door they heard a yelp.

'It's started!' she called. 'The Saints be praised, my period's started!'

Helen pulled open the curtains; the sun blazed in. Suddenly they all burst out laughing. Strange, wasn't it? Imprisoned in their cell, they were filled with joy. Why? Because they had found their girls? Because they were alone, at last? Because when they were supposed to be enjoying their holiday they weren't, and now they weren't, they were? Helen felt an airy, shuddering sense of liberation. Freedom is a Visa card, she thought. Freedom is not being pregnant. Freedom is not being married, for it seemed suddenly very simple to be four females alone in this squalid room. Nobody to blame them, nobody to know. To celebrate, they shared the last bottle – Asti Spumante, which the girls hadn't touched because they thought it was champagne and too expensive.

Later they sat on the rim of a fountain and ate pieces of pizza in smeary paper napkins. Junk food for tourists, according to Alan, but Alan wasn't here. And after lunch Helen didn't visit the Uffizi or the Pitti Palace or the Santa Maria Novella. She stopped somebody and, using the phrase book, asked: '*Dove il piu vicino . . .* er, *istituto di bellezza?*'

Never in her life had she done this before. Never in her life had she had a pedicure. She went into a scruffy little beauty parlour and sat in an airless cubicle whilst a chain-smoking beautician clipped her toenails and pushed back her cuticles. The only culture she saw was a view of Venice on the heaped ashtray, and a scorched reproduction of Botticelli's *Birth of Venus* printed on the lampshade.

She gazed at her toe-nails, freshly painted crimson. She

smiled at the woman. '*Bene!*' she said. She thought: freedom is doing exactly what I've always wanted to do. For the first time since her divorce – no, since way back in her marriage – she felt truly grown up.

And later that day she wrote postcards. 'Having a terrible time,' she wrote, 'robberies, stomach upsets, boring Germans.' She wrote that because happiness made her generous.

Rachel Cusk

typist

Rachel Cusk was born in 1967, grew up in Los Angeles and East Anglia, and was educated at New College, Oxford. Her first novel, *Saving Agnes*, won the Whitbread First Novel Award 1993. She lives in London.

At around 8.58 a.m. Stephanie Sparks emerges from the tube station, advancing briskly towards the exit. She walks in step with a dense body of commuters like one of the feet of a monstrous, elegant multipede, heels clacking against the tiled floor with the menacing din of gyrating mandibles. She waits while the flow backs up into a disorderly pool around the ticket barriers, tapping her toe at double speed with an impatience begotten not by any desire to reach her destination, but rather with a sense of time congealing unpleasantly around her like something viscous.

She shuffles forward as the crowd is fed between the jaws of the ticket machines and then spat out into the rainy vista beyond, where they scatter mercurially among buses and taxis and foggy coffee shops. A man with a leather briefcase is standing just in front of her to the right. He turns and looks at her legs, which she has been informed are shapely. Then he looks at her breasts. When finally he catches her eye he stands back, allowing her to pass before him through the barriers with a nod of the head and an ushering hand. She smiles at him charmingly. He murmurs inaudibly. She feeds her ticket into the slot and proceeds elegantly forward, giving him ample opportunity to view her assets from behind. The barrier gates snap closed in front of her and then open again.

Stephanie Sparks recoils instinctively, as if she has been punched. She hurries through the gates and out of the station, her cheeks aflame. She doesn't look back.

At 9.05 she reaches the offices of Lancing & Louche Investments Limited, a subsidiary of Lancing & Lancing Inc., where the lift awaits which will bear her aloft to the office of Mr Lance Lancing himself. The lift is full of people, the open doors give them the vulnerable and exposed aspect of canned goods whose lid has been removed. A man standing by the controls sees Stephanie approach across the foyer and slams his hand bravely over the red button which directs the doors to remain open. He keeps it there forcefully until she has entered. She smiles at him charmingly and he releases the button, but his body remains alert and ready for action.

An apartheid seems to have been established within the confines of the lift. Those who dictate stand to the right, their bodies a silent, striated sea of pinstripe. Those who take dictation stand to the left in a scented grove of mingled perfumes, their curled and coloured heads a murmuring canopy of fronds.

The lift reaches the fifth floor and Stephanie hurries away, her shoes whispering along the beige-carpeted corridor as if it were made of soft summer grass.

At 9.10 she reaches her desk, one of a fleet which lies anchored in the expanse of Mr Lancing's headquarters. She takes her position before the blinking screen and keyboard. She is lucky to have a place so close to the window. From it she can see the giant heads of other office buildings, behind whose glass eyes small figures are discernible. Sometimes she watches them. Once, wondering if they could see her, she waved excitedly.

The sun comes out and for a moment she is a pilot, her fingers at the controls, the blazing blue sky all around, the battalion to hand, the day full with the promise of hope and glory, eminently conquerable.

At 9.15 Stephanie leaves her desk and goes to the ladies'. At 9.17 she returns. The day lies before her like a vast empty house which she must furnish with activity. Mr Lancing is out having his hair cut. Stephanie made the appointment on Friday by telephone. The barber's shop sounded cheerful, with a radio playing and bursts of male laughter in the background. She imagines Mr Lancing there now, high in a chair, laughing. He has left her a letter on tape, which she must transcribe through a pair of earphones on to her computer screen. She puts on the earphones and switches on the tape. He has evidently recorded it from the back seat of a cab, his mouth pressed close to the microphone. Stephanie can hear the thunder of the car engine, the blare of horns. Mr Lancing breathes heavily in her ear like an obscene caller. Her fingers move automatically, responding to messages sent from her brain, where Mr Lancing has set up a makeshift centre of operations.

At 9.45 Stephanie makes coffee for the team. 'Team' is Mr Lance Lancing's word. A verbal virus, it has spread. Mr

Lancing has spent time in America and has brought contagion back with him to the patrician portals of Lancing & Louche. 'Input', 'player' and 'way off the mark' are some of the strains currently resisting inoculation. She takes coffee to Mr Lesley Louche, whose desk stands on a podium at the far end of the office. Mr Louche is young and dynamic. He has a framed photograph on his desk of Kim Basinger, signed 'With love and kisses, Kim'. He signed it himself, using a photograph cleverly cut from a magazine.

At 10.00 Mr Lancing enters the office. His hair has been cut and one or two of the secretaries compliment him on its shortness. Mr Lancing tells Mr Louche that his cab was held up in severe traffic. He does this not in the manner of one requiring absolution, but rather seeking to apportion blame. Mr Louche explains that a bomb went off in the City early that morning. Mr Lancing grins boyishly, excited by the idea of an explosive device.

'Did anyone die?' he says. He turns suddenly and looks out of the window, giving an impersonation of someone witnessing the passage of an object travelling at high velocity through his field of vision. 'Look, *there go the casualties!*' he cries hilariously, pointing out of the window to the sky.

Mr Louche emits a loud, uncomprehending guffaw. An uncertain wave of laughter ripples the surface of the secretarial pool. Stephanie looks at her watch. It is 10.10 a.m. She gets up and goes to the ladies'.

At 11.00 Mr Louche goes out to get a haircut. Stephanie

makes coffee for Mr Lancing and returns to her desk. He is reading a report and occasionally shouts 'What the hell is this?', but his remarks do not appear to be addressed to her. She stares at her computer screen, on which Mr Lancing's letter trails off like an interrupted suicide note. Presently, Mr Lancing gets up from his desk and comes over.

'How's it going?' he says vaguely, his fingers sifting distractedly through the papers on her desktop like small rodents working as a team.

'Fine,' says Stephanie. She smiles. He has forgotten her name, she knows. 'Did you have a good weekend?'

'What?'

He looks up and seems to have trouble focusing on her. Finally, for a moment, their eyes meet and Stephanie experiences a feeling of unfamiliarity. She can think of nothing whatsoever to say which will ameliorate her foray into the personal. The silence frames her ill-judged remark, exhibiting its flaws.

'Give 'em hell,' Mr Lancing eventually advises, accompanying his comment with a successful lopsided grin and a sporty punch in the air.

'OK,' she agrees, nodding foolishly behind him as he ambles away. She taps feverishly at her keyboard, face aglow, and a jumble of upper-register symbols appears on the screen like an expletive.

At 12.05 Mr Lesley Louche returns to the office. His hair is now shorter than Mr Lancing's and his scalp looks bare and ashamed, as if it has been punished.

'Any chance of seeing that report before lunch?' he demands, pausing at Stephanie's desk as if on the way to somewhere more urgent than his own. His tone is assertive, but his face looks appalled, bereft at the amputation of hair.

'I'm doing a letter for Mr Lancing at the moment,' says Stephanie, wielding Mr Lancing's superiority. She enjoys handling their power, fingering it like an unaffordable gem in a jeweller's shop. Mr Louche comprehends the blow, but his haircut has made him vulnerable and he is unable to resist it.

'Perhaps if you stopped filing your nails or whatever it is you girls do over here,' he snaps, 'then you could get more than one piece of work done in an entire morning.'

The other secretaries look up, suddenly alert, like dozing fishermen who have just felt a tug on the line. Mr Louche walks unapologetically back to his desk, leaving them to reel in a large and libellous lunch topic. Stephanie gets up defiantly to make coffee for herself, but spooning sugar into her cup is driven by compunction to make it for the whole team. When she places his cup beside him, Mr Louche does not look up.

At 12.58 Mr Lancing and Mr Louche stroll from the office in the friendly and conspiratorial manner of enemy politicians.

'Bye girls,' says Mr Louche from the door. His voice is meaningful.

A wave of conversation surges in their wake, rises, breaks, and ripples out across the office. Above the talk emerges a loud percussion of rustling bags, popping cans and tearing foil. Stephanie eats a tuna fish sandwich made that morning in her kitchenette in Barnes. She didn't add enough mayonnaise and the fish is dry and flaky in her mouth. She eats quickly and leaves the office without speaking to anyone.

Outside, the street is grey and noisy, with buses moving slowly along it like dinosaurs. The demarcation of the lunch hour has imposed panic on the pavements, and people rush heedlessly across the road to shout their orders in heaving sandwich shops. One or two women lumber through the crowd with bags of shopping from the supermarket. In Stephanie's office they have thoughtfully installed a fridge, in which women may deposit their shopping until it is time to return home, although once, Stephanie remembers, one of the secretaries had a package of frozen meat in hers which thawed and dripped watery blood over the shelves below.

She walks purposefully but without direction. Finally, she reaches a street which contains shops and she slows her pace, pausing in front of plate glass behind which everything appears suddenly personal and unreachable, like possessions glimpsed through the windows of a house. She gazes at her own reflection. After a while she cannot remember who or where she is, or how much time has passed. She goes quickly back to the office.

At 2.45 Mr Lancing and Mr Louche return from lunch. Mr Louche stops at Stephanie's desk. His face is flushed and con-ciliatory. He has grown accustomed to his haircut, and his acceptance of it seems somehow to have rendered it accept-able. Stephanie tries to remember how he looked before and can't. She hands him the report, which she typed blindly, frantically, when she returned to the office.

'Good girl,' he says, winking.

At 2.55 Stephanie Sparks looks at the office clock. In two hours' time she can go home. The apparent brevity of the interlude gives her the mistaken impression that it will not have to be endured. She moves things cheerfully around her desk, safe in the certainty of the day's passing, its inevitable termination. Time ceases to weigh on her now that there is so much less of it. A gentle, pleasing vacancy grows in her thoughts. As it expands she forgets herself altogether, and after a while, realising this, she congratulates herself by looking again at the clock. Inexplicably, it is still 2.55.

At 3.05 Stephanie puts on her earphones and continues with Mr Lancing's letter. He has left the cab and is walking, his words coming in grunts. At one point he growls for several seconds, as if he is in pain. She rewinds the tape two or three times in an attempt to rescue sentences from the noise which floods through her ears. They elude her, drowned in crashing breaths, and she is forced to leave blank spaces in their memory. Towards the end the tape becomes clearer and she types efficiently. As Mr Lancing says 'Yours sincerely,' she can hear the compressed sigh of doors closing as he enters a lift. Stephanie moves her hand to switch off the tape.

'Typist!' he barks suddenly in the ensuing lull of ascent, his voice all at once urgent with the threat of disconnection, as if she were about to replace the receiver at the end of a call. His summons causes Stephanie to start, and a strange fear pools in her stomach. 'Typist, this is to be marked "urgent" and circulated to the usual people no later than the end of the day. Do you understand?'

Stephanie rewinds the tape.

'Typist!' says Mr Lancing.

She stops the tape and removes her earphones. Then she gets up and goes to the ladies'.

At 3.30 Stephanie Sparks has not returned from the ladies'.

At 3.45 Stephanie Sparks is still absent. One of the secretaries gets up and goes to the ladies'. She comes back seconds later and runs to Mr Louche's podium. Her face is white and in it her eyes jump like animals caught in a trap. Mr Louche stands, placing an authoritative and comforting hand on her back. They leave the office quickly, together.

At 4.00 Mr Louche returns to the office alone. He approaches Mr Lancing's desk. They converse for several minutes while the rest of the office observes a respectful silence.

'Which one was she?' says Mr Lancing loudly. 'Was she fat?'

At 4.10 the office buzzes, a hive of speculation. It caws and shrieks like an aviary. It chatters like a chimpanzee cage. Mr Louche sits at his desk, a finger in one ear, making a telephone call.

At 4.40 the office is quiet. People speak in low murmurs,

consulting over sheaves of paper. Computers hum, printers whirr. A new girl sits at Stephanie Sparks' old desk.

At 4.45 she gets up to make coffee for herself and is rapidly apprehended by one of the older secretaries. The girl nods, her face aflame. She makes coffee for the team.

Anthony Thwaite

freedom

Anthony Thwaite has published eleven books of poems, the most recent *The Dust of the World*, which came out in 1994. He was born in 1930 and has taught in universities in Japan and Libya, as well as at the University of East Anglia. He has worked for the BBC, been literary editor of both *The Listener* and the *New Statesman* and was co-editor of *Encounter* from 1973 to 1985. He has won the Richard Hillary Memorial Prize, a Cholmondeley Award and the O.B.E. for services to poetry. He edited the *Collected Poems* and *Selected Letters* of Philip Larkin and was given an honorary doctorate by the University of Hull. He is married to the biographer Ann Thwaite and lives in Norfolk.

Through the vast crowded wards, thousands came round,
Limbs twitched; mouths opened, uttering strange old cries;
Wild smiles and tears, and snarls at what went on
Through decades of paralysis.

                Bodies are found
Strewn in the corridors. A doctor lies
Battered in blood. The warders have all gone,
Savaged by patients who woke up to see
The doors were open. Healers are unmasked
As torturers; nurses crucified
When drugs, withdrawn, reveal them all to be
Captors and guards.

              And those who this way died
Are faceless as their patients.

                And some asked
How the great hospital would care for those
Who lie there still, free, in a deep repose.